The Complete Works

of

Clara Dillingham Pierson

Among the Farmyard People
Among the Forest People
Among the Meadow People
Among the Night People
Among the Pond People

Contents

Among the Farmyard People

The Story That The Swallow Didn't Tell

"Listen!" said the Nigh Ox, "don't you hear some friends coming?"

The Off Ox raised his head from the grass and stopped to brush away a Fly, for you never could hurry either of the brothers. "I don't hear any footfalls," said he.

"You should listen for wings, not feet," said the Nigh Ox, "and for voices, too."

Even as he spoke there floated down from the clear air overhead a soft "tittle-ittle-ittle-ee," as though some bird were laughing for happiness. There was not a cloud in the sky, and the meadow was covered with thousands and thousands of green grass blades, each so small and tender, and yet together making a most beautiful carpet for the feet of the farmyard people, and offering them sweet and juicy food after their winter fare of hay and grain. Truly it was a day to make one laugh aloud for joy. The alder tassels fluttered and danced in the spring breeze, while the smallest and shyest of the willow pussies crept from their little brown houses on the branches to grow in the sunshine.

"Tittle-ittle-ittle-ee! Tittle-ittle-ittle-ee!" And this time it was louder and clearer than before.

"The Swallows!" cried the Oxen to each other. Then they straightened their strong necks and bellowed to the Horses, who were drawing the plow in the field beyond, "The Swallows are coming!"

As soon as the Horses reached the end of the furrow and could rest a minute, they tossed their heads and whinnied with delight. Then they looked around at the farmer, and wished that he knew enough of the farmyard language to understand what they wanted to tell him. They knew he would be glad to hear of their friends' return, for had they not seen him pick up a young Swallow one day and put him in a safer place?

"Tittle-ittle-ittle-ee!" and there was a sudden darkening of the sky above their heads, a whirr of many wings, a chattering and laughing of soft voices, and the Swallows had come. Perched on the ridge-pole of the big barn, they rested and visited and heard all the news.

The Doves were there, walking up and down the sloping sides of the roof and cooing to each other about the simple things of every-day life. You know the Doves stay at home all winter, and so it makes a great change when their neighbors, the Swallows, return. They are firm friends in spite of their very different ways of living. There was never a Dove who would be a Swallow if he could, yet the plump, quiet, gray and white Doves dearly love the dashing Swallows, and happy is the Squab who can get a Swallow to tell him stories of the great world.

"Isn't it good to be home, home, home!" sang one Swallow. "I never set my claws on another ridge-pole as comfortable as this."

"I'm going to look at my old nest," said a young Swallow, as she suddenly flew down to the eaves.

"I think I'll go, too," said another young Swallow, springing away from his perch. He was a handsome fellow, with a glistening dark blue head and back, a long forked tail which showed a white stripe on the under side, a rich buff vest, and a deep blue collar, all of the finest feathers. He loved the young Swallow whom he was following, and he wanted to tell her so.

"There is the nest where I was hatched," she said. "Would you think I was ever crowded in there with five brothers and sisters? It was a comfortable nest, too, before the winter winds and snow wore it away. I wonder how it would seem to be a fledgling again?" She snuggled down in the old nest until he could see only her forked tail and her dainty head over the edge. Her vest was quite hidden, and the only light feathers that showed were the reddish-buff ones on throat and face; these were not so bright as his, but still she was beautiful to him. He loved every feather on her body.

"I don't want you to be a fledgling again," he cried. "I want you to help me make a home under the eaves, a lovely little nest of mud and straw, where you can rest as you are now doing, while I bring food to you. Will you?"

"Yes," she cried. "Tittle-ittle-ittle-ee! Oh, tittle-ittle-ittle-ee!" And she flew far up into the blue sky, while he followed her, twittering and singing.

"Where are those young people going?" said an older Swallow. "I should think they had flown far enough for to-day without circling around for the fun of it."

"Don't you remember the days when you were young?" said the Swallow next to him.

"When I was young?" he answered. "My dear, I am young now. I shall always be young in the springtime. I shall never be old except when I am moulting."

Just then a family of Doves came pattering over the roof, swaying their heads at every step. "We are so glad to see you back," said the father. "We had a long, cold winter, and we thought often of you."

"A very cold winter," cooed his plump little wife.

"Tell me a story," said a young Dove, their son.

"Hush, hush," said the Father Dove. "This is our son," he added, "and this is his sister. We think them quite a pair. Our last brood, you know."

"Tell us a story," said the young Dove again.

"Hush, dear. You mustn't tease the Swallow," said his mother. "They are so fond of stories," she cooed, "and they have heard that your family are great travellers."

"But I want him to tell us a story," said the young Dove. "I think he might."

This made the Swallow feel very uncomfortable, for he could see that the children had been badly brought up, and he did not want to tell a story just then.

"Perhaps you would like to hear about our journey south," said he. "Last fall, when the maples began to show red and yellow leaves among the green, we felt like flying away. It was quite warm weather, and the forest birds were still here, but when we feel like flying south we always begin to get ready."

"I never feel like flying south," said the young Dove. "I don't see why you should."

"That is because I am a Swallow and you are a farmyard Dove. We talked about it to each other, and one day we were ready to start. We all had on our new feathers and felt strong and well. We started out together, but the young birds and their mothers could not keep up with the rest, so we went on ahead."

"Ahead of whom?" said the young Dove, who had been preening his feathers when he should have been listening.

"Ahead of the mothers and their fledglings. We flew over farms where there were Doves like you; over rivers where the Wild Ducks were feeding by the shore; and over towns where crowds of boys and girls were going into large buildings, while on top of these buildings were large bells singing, 'Ding dong, ding dong, ding dong.'"

"I don't think that was a very pretty song," said the young Dove.

"Hush," said his mother, "you mustn't interrupt the Swallow."

"And at last we came to a great lake," said the Swallow. "It was so great that when we had flown over it for a little while we could not see land at all, and our eyes would not tell us which way to go. We just went on as birds must in such places, flying as we felt we ought, and not stopping to ask why or to wonder if we were right. Of course we Swallows never stop to eat, for we catch our food as we fly, but we did sometimes stop to rest. Just after we had crossed this great lake we alighted. It was then that a very queer thing happened, and this is really the story that I started to tell."

"Oh!" said the young Dove and his sister. "How very exciting. But wait just a minute while we peep over the edge of the roof and see what the farmer is doing." And before anybody could say a word they had pattered away to look.

The birds who were there say that the Swallow seemed quite disgusted, and surely nobody could blame him if he did.

"You must excuse them," cooed their mother. "They are really hardly more than Squabs yet, and I can't bear to speak severely to them. I'm sure they didn't mean to be rude."

"Certainly, certainly," said the Swallow. "I will excuse them and you must excuse me. I wish to see a few of my old friends before the sun goes down. Good afternoon!" And he darted away.

The young Doves came pattering back, swaying their heads as they walked. "Why, where is the Swallow?" they cried. "What made him go away? Right at the best part of the story, too. We don't see why folks are so disagreeable. People never are as nice to us as they are to the other young Doves."

"Hush," said their mother. "You mustn't talk in that way. Fly off for something to eat, and never mind about the rest of the story."

When they were gone, she said to her husband, "I wonder if they did hurt the Swallow's feelings? But then, they are so young, hardly more than Squabs."

She forgot that even Squabs should be thoughtful of others, and that no Dove ever amounts to anything unless he begins in the right way as a Squab.

The Lamb With The Longest Tail

The Sheep are a simple and kind-hearted family, and of all the people on the farm there are none who are more loved than they. All summer they wander in the fields, nibbling the fresh, sweet grass, and resting at noon in the shadow of the trees, but when the cold weather comes they are brought up to the farmyard and make their home in the long low Sheep-shed.

That is always a happy time. The Horses breathe deeply and toss their heads for joy, the Cows say to each other, "Glad to have the Sheep come up," and even the Oxen shift their cuds and look long over their shoulders at the woolly newcomers. And this is not because the Sheep can do anything for their neighbors to make them warm or to feed them. It is only because they are a gentle folk and pleasant in all they say; and you know when people are always kind, it makes others happy just to see them and have them near.

Then, when the cold March winds are blowing, the good farmer brings more yellow straw into the Sheep-shed, and sees that it is warm and snug. If there are any boards broken and letting the wind in, he mends them and shuts out the cold. At this time, too, the Horses and Cattle stop often in their eating to listen. Even the Pigs, who do not think much about their neighbors, root in the corners nearest the Sheep-shed and prick up their ears.

Some bleak morning they hear a faint bleating and know that the first Lamb is there. And then from day to day they hear more of the soft voices as the new Lambs come to live with the flock. Such queer little creatures as the Lambs are when they first come—so weak and awkward! They can hardly stand alone, and stagger and wobble around the little rooms or pens where they are with their mothers. You can just imagine how hard it must be to learn to manage four legs all at once!

There is one thing which they do learn very quickly, and that is, to eat. They are hungry little people, and well they may be, for they have much growing to do, and all of the food that is to be made into good stout bodies and fine long wool has to go into their mouths and down their throats to their stomachs. It is very wonderful to think that a Cow eats grass and it is turned into hair to keep her warm, a Goose eats grass and grows feathers, and a Sheep eats grass and grows wool. Still, it is so, and nobody in the world can tell why. It is just one of the things that are, and if you should ask "Why?" nobody could tell you the reason. There are many such things which we cannot understand, but there are many more which we can, so it would be very foolish for us to mind when there is no answer to our "Why?"

Yes, Sheep eat grass, and because they have such tiny mouths they have to take small mouthfuls. The Lambs have different food for a while,—warm milk from their mothers' bodies. When a mother has a Lamb to feed, she eats a great deal, hay, grass, and chopped turnips, and then part of the food that goes into her stomach is turned into milk and stored in two warm bags for the Lamb to take when he is hungry. And how the Lambs do like this milk! It tastes so good that they can hardly stand still while they drink it down, and they give funny little jerks and wave their woolly tails in the air.

There was one Lamb who had a longer tail than any of the rest, and, sad to say, it made him rather vain. When he first came, he was too busy drinking milk and learning to walk, to think about tails, but as he grew older and stronger he began to know that he had the longest one. Because he was a very young Lamb he was so foolish as to tease the others and call out, "Baa! your tails are snippy ones!"

Then the others would call back, "Baa! Don't care if they are!"

After a while, his mother, who was a sensible Sheep and had seen much of life, said to him: "You must not brag about your tail. It is very rude of you, and very silly too, for you have exactly such a tail as was given to you, and the other Lambs have exactly such tails as were given to them, and when you are older you will know that it did not matter in the least what kind of tail you wore when you were little." She might have told him something else, but she didn't.

The Lamb didn't dare to boast of his tail after this, but when he passed the others, he would look at his mother, and if he thought she wouldn't see, he would wiggle it at them. Of course that was just as bad as talking about it, and the other Lambs knew perfectly well what he meant; still, they pretended not to understand.

One morning, when his mother's back was turned, he was surprised to see that she had only a short and stumpy tail. He had been thinking so much of his own that he had not noticed hers. "Mother," he cried, "why didn't you have a long tail too?"

"I did have once," she answered with a sheepish smile.

"Did it get broken?" he asked in a faint little voice. He was thinking how dreadful it would be if he should break his.

"Not exactly," said his mother. "I will tell you all about it. All little Lambs have long tails——"

"Not so long as mine, though," said he, interrupting.

"No, not so long as yours," she replied, "but so long that if they were left that way always they would make a great deal of trouble. As the wool grows on them, they would catch burrs and sharp, prickly things, which would pull the wool and sting the skin. The farmer knows this, so when the little Lambs are about as old as you are now, he and his men make their tails shorter."

"Oh!" cried the Lamb, curling his tail in as far between his legs as he could, "do you mean that they will shorten my tail, my beautiful long tail?"

"That is just what I mean," said his mother, "and you should be very glad of it. When that is done, you will be ready to go out into the field with me. A lot of trouble we should have if the men did not look after such things for us; but that is what men are for, they say,—to look after us Sheep."

"But won't they laugh at me when my tail is shorter?" asked her son.

"They would laugh at you if you wore it long. No Lamb who pretends to be anybody would be seen in the pasture with a dangling tail. Only wild Sheep wear them long, poor things!"

Now the little Lamb wished that he had not boasted so much. Now, when the others passed him, he did not put on airs. Now he wondered why they couldn't have short tails in the beginning. He asked his uncle, an old Wether Sheep, why this was and his uncle laughed. "Why, what would you have done all these days if things happened in that way? What would you have had to think about? What could you have talked about?" The little Lamb hung his head and asked no more questions.

"What do you think?" he called to a group of Lambs near by. "I'm going to have one of the men shorten my tail. It is such a bother unless one does have it done, and mine is so very long!"

The Wonderful Shiny Egg

"CUT-CUT-CA-DAH-CUT! Cut-cut-cut-ca-dah-cut!" called the Dorking Hen, as she strutted around the poultry-yard. She held her head very high, and paused every few minutes to look around in her jerky way and see whether the other fowls were listening. Once she even stood on her left foot right in the pathway of the Shanghai Cock, and cackled into his very ears.

Everybody pretended not to hear her. The people in the poultry-yard did not like the Dorking Hen very well. They said that she put on airs. Perhaps she did. She certainly talked a great deal of the place from which she and the Dorking Cock came. They had come in a small cage from a large poultry farm, and the Dorking Hen never tired of telling about the wonderful, noisy ride that they took in a dark car drawn by a great, black, snorting creature. She said that this creature's feet grew on to his sides and whirled around as he ran, and that he breathed out of the top of his head. When the fowls first heard of this, they were much interested, but after a while they used to walk away from her, or make believe that they saw Grasshoppers whom they wanted to chase.

When she found that people were not listening to her, she cackled louder than ever, "Cut-cut-ca-dah-cut! Look at the egg—the egg—the egg—the egg that I have laid."

"Is there any particular reason why we should look at the egg—the egg—the egg—the egg that you have laid?" asked the Shanghai Cock, who was the grumpiest fowl in the yard.

Now, usually if the Dorking Hen had been spoken to in this way, she would have ruffled up her head feathers and walked away, but this time she had news to tell and so she kept her temper. "Reason?" she cackled. "Yes indeed! It is the finest egg that was ever laid in this poultry-yard."

"Hear her talk!" said a Bantam Hen. "I think it is in very poor taste to lay such large eggs as most of the Hens do here. Small ones are much more genteel."

"She must forget an egg that I laid a while ago with two yolks," said a Shanghai Hen. "That was the largest egg ever laid here, and I have always wished that I had hatched it. A pair of twin chickens would have been so interesting."

"Well," said the Dorking Hen, who could not keep still any longer, "small eggs may be genteel and large ones may be interesting, but my last one is bee-autiful."

"Perhaps you'd just as soon tell us about it as to brag without telling?" grumbled the Shanghai Cock. "I suppose it is grass color, or sky color, or hay color, or speckled, like a sparrow's egg."

"No," answered the Dorking Hen, "it is white, but it is shiny."

"Shiny!" they exclaimed. "Who ever heard of a shiny egg?"

"Nobody," she replied, "and that is why it is so wonderful."

"Don't believe it," said the Shanghai Cock, as he turned away and began scratching the ground.

Now the Dorking Hen did get angry. "Come to see it, if you don't believe me," she said, as she led the others into the Hen-house.

She flew up to the row of boxes where the Hens had their nests, and picked her way along daintily until she reached the farthest one. "Now look," said she.

One by one the fowls peeped into the box, and sure enough, there it lay, a fine, shiny, white egg. The little Bantam, who was really a jolly, kind-hearted creature, said, "Well, it is a beauty. I should be proud of it myself."

"It is whiter than I fancy," said the Shanghai Cock, "but it certainly does shine."

"I shall hatch it," said the Dorking Hen, very decidedly. "I shall hatch it and have a beautiful Chicken with shining feathers. I shall not hatch all the eggs in the nest, but roll this one away and sit on it."

"Perhaps," said one of her friends, "somebody else may have laid it after all, and not noticed. You know it is not the only one in the nest."

"Pooh!" said the Dorking Hen. "I guess I know! I am sure it was not there when I went to the nest and it was there when I left. I must have laid it."

The fowls went away, and she tried to roll the shiny one away from the other eggs, but it was slippery and very light and would not stay where she put it. Then she got out of patience and rolled all the others out of the nest. Two of them fell to the floor and broke, but she did not care. "They are nothing but common ones, anyway," she said.

When the farmer's wife came to gather the eggs she pecked at her and was very cross. Every day she did this, and at last the woman let her alone. Every-day she told the other fowls what a wonderful Chicken she expected to have. "Of course he will be of my color," said she, "but his feathers will shine brightly. He will be a great flyer, too. I am sure that is what it means when the egg is light." She came off the nest each day just long enough to stroll around and chat with her friends, telling them what wonderful things she expected, and never letting them forget that it was she who had laid the shiny egg. She pecked airily at the food, and seemed to think that a Hen who was hatching such a wonderful Chicken should have the best of everything. Each day she told some new beauty that was to belong to her child, until the Shanghai Cock fairly flapped his wings with impatience.

Day after day passed, and the garden beyond the barn showed rows of sturdy green plants, where before there had been only straight ridges of fine brown earth. The Swallows who were building under the eaves of the great barn, twittered and chattered of the wild flowers in the forest, and four other Hens came off their nests with fine broods of downy Chickens. And still the Dorking Hen sat on her shiny egg and told what a wonderful Chicken she expected to hatch. This was not the only egg in the nest now, but it was the only one of which she spoke.

At last a downy Chicken peeped out of one of the common eggs, and wriggled and twisted to free himself from the shell. His mother did not hurry him or help him. She knew that he must not slip out of it until all the blood from the shell-lining had run into his tender little body. If she had pushed the shell off before he had all of this fine red blood, he would not have been a strong Chicken, and she wanted her children to be strong.

The Dorking Cock walked into the Hen-house and stood around on one foot. He came to see if the shiny egg had hatched, but he wouldn't ask. He thought himself too dignified to show any interest in newly hatched Chickens before a Hen. Still, he saw no harm in standing around on one foot and letting the Dorking Hen talk to him if she wanted to. When she told him it was one of the common eggs that had hatched, he was quite disgusted, and stalked out of doors without a word.

The truth was that he had been rather bragging to the other Cocks, and only a few minutes later he spoke with pride of the time when "our" shiny egg should hatch. "For," he said, "Mrs. Dorking and I have been quite alone here as far as our own people are concerned. It is not strange that we should feel a great pride in the wonderful egg and the Chicken to be hatched from it. A Dorking is a Dorking after all, my friends." And he flapped his wings, stretched his neck, and crowed as loudly as he could.

"Yes," said the Black Spanish Cock afterward, "a Dorking certainly is a Dorking, although I never could see the sense of making such a fuss about it. They are fat and they have an extra toe on each foot. Why should a fowl want extra toes? I have four on each foot, and I can scratch up all the food I want with them."

"Well," said the grumpy old Shanghai Cock, "I am sick and tired of this fuss. Common eggs are good enough for Shanghais and Black Spanish and Bantams, and I should think——"

Just at this minute they heard a loud fluttering and squawking in the Hen-house and the Dorking Hen crying, "Weasel! Weasel!" The Cocks ran to drive the Weasel away, and the Hens followed to see it done. All was noise and hurry, and they saw nothing of the Weasel except the tip of his bushy tail as he drew his slender body through an opening in the fence.

The Dorking Hen was on one of the long perches where the fowls roost at night, the newly hatched Chicken lay shivering in the nest, and on the floor were the pieces of the wonderful shiny egg. The Dorking Hen had knocked it from the nest in her flight.

The Dorking Cock looked very cross. He was not afraid of a Weasel, and he did not see why she should be. "Just like a Hen!" he said.

The Black Spanish Hen turned to him before he could say another word. "Just like a Cock!" she exclaimed. "I never raise Chickens myself. It is not the custom among the Black Spanish Hens. We lay the eggs and somebody else hatches them. But if I had been on the nest as long as Mrs. Dorking has, do you suppose I'd let any fowl speak to me as you spoke to her? I'd—I'd——" and she was so angry that she couldn't say another word, but just strutted up and down and cackled.

A motherly old Shanghai Hen flew up beside Mrs. Dorking. "We are very sorry for you," she said. "I know how I should have felt if I had broken my two-yolked egg just as it was ready to hatch."

The Bantam Hen picked her way to the nest. "What a dear little Chicken!" she cried, in her most comforting tone. "He is so plump and so bright for his age. But, my dear, he is chilly, and I think you should cuddle him under your wings until his down is dry."

The Dorking Hen flew down. "He is a dear," she said, "and yet when he was hatched I didn't care much for him, because I had thought so long about the shiny egg. It serves me right to lose that one, because I have been so foolish. Still, I do not know how I could stand it if it were not for my good neighbors."

While Mrs. Dorking was talking with the Bantam by her nest, the Black Spanish Hen scratched a hole in the earth under the perches, poked the pieces of the shiny egg into it, and covered them up. "I never raise Chickens myself," she said, "but if I did——"

The Shanghai Cock walked away with the Dorking Cock. "I'm sorry for you," he said, "and I am more sorry for Mrs. Dorking. She is too fine a Hen to be spoken to as you spoke to her this morning, and I don't want to hear any more of your fault-finding. Do you understand?" And he ruffled his neck feathers and stuck his face close to that of the Dorking Cock. They stared into each other's eyes for a minute; then the Dorking Cock, who was not so big and strong as the Shanghai, shook his head and answered sweetly, "It was rude of me. I won't do it again."

From that day to this, nobody in the poultry yard has ever spoken of the shiny egg, and the Dorkings are much liked by the other fowls. Yet if it had not been for her trouble, Mrs. Dorking and her neighbors would never have become such good friends. The little Dorkings are fine, fat-breasted Chicks, with the extra toe on each foot of which all that family are so proud.

The Duckling Who Didn't Know What To Do

"Quack! Quack!" called the Duck who had been sitting on her nest so long. "My first egg is cracked, and I can see the broad yellow bill of my eldest child. Ah! Now I can see his downy white head." The Drake heard her and quacked the news to every one around, and flapped his wings, and preened his feathers, for was not this the first Duckling ever hatched on the farm?

The Drake had not been there long himself. It was only a few days before the Duck began sitting that she and her five sisters had come with him to this place. It had not taken them long to become acquainted with the other farmyard people, and all had been kind to them. The Geese had rather put on airs, at first, because they were bigger and had longer legs, but the Ducks and Drake were too wise to notice this in any way, and before long the Geese were as friendly as possible. They would have shown the Ducks the way to the water if it had been necessary, but it was not, for Ducks always know without being told just where to find it. They know, and they do not know why they know. It is one of the things that are.

Now that the first Duckling had chipped the shell, everybody wanted to see him, and there was soon a crowd of fowls around the nest watching him free himself from it. The Drake stood by, as proud as a Peacock. "I think he looks much like his mother," said he.

"Yes, yes," cackled all the Hens. "The same broad yellow bill, the same short yellow legs, and the same webbed feet."

The mother Duck smiled. "He looks more like me now than he will by and by," she said, "for when his feathers grow and cover the down, he will have a stiff little one curled up on his back like the Drake's. And really, except for the curled feather, his father and I look very much alike."

"That is so," said the Black Spanish Cock. "You do look alike; the same white feathers, the same broad breast, the same strong wings, the same pointed tail, the same long neck, the same sweet expression around the bill!" That was just like the Black Spanish Cock. He always said something pleasant about people when he could, and it was much better than saying unpleasant things. Indeed, he was the most polite fowl in the poultry-yard, and the Black Spanish Hen thought his manners quite perfect.

Then the Duckling's five aunts pushed their way through the crowd to the nest under the edge of the strawstack. "Have you noticed what fine large feet he has?" said one of them. "That is like his mother's people. See what a strong web is between the three long toes on each foot! He will be a good swimmer. The one toe that points backward is small, to be sure, but he does not need that in swimming. That is only to make waddling easier."

"Yes, yes," "A fine web," and "Very large feet," cried the fowls around the nest, but most of them didn't care so much about the size of his feet as the Ducks did. Large feet are always useful, you know, yet nobody needs them so badly as Geese and Ducks. The Geese were off swimming, and so could not see the Duckling when first he came out of the shell.

"Tap-tap, tap-tap," sounded inside another shell, and they knew that there would soon be a second damp little Duckling beside the first. The visitors could not stay to see this one come out, and they went away for a time. The eldest Duckling had supposed that this was life, to have people around saying, "How bright he is!" "What fine legs!" or "He has a beautiful bill!" And now that they all walked away and his mother was looking after the Duckling who was just breaking her shell, he didn't like it—he didn't like it at all.

Still, it was much better so. If he had had no brothers and sisters, he would have been a lonely little fellow; besides, he would have had his own way nearly all the time, and that is likely to make any Duckling selfish. Then, too, if all the other fowls had petted him and given him the best of everything, he would have become vain. Truly, it was a good thing for him not to be the only child, and he soon learned to think so.

After there were two Ducklings, a third one came, and a fourth, and a fifth, and so on until, when the broken shells were cleared away and the mother had counted bills, she could call to the Drake and her sisters, "Nine Ducklings hatched, and there were only nine eggs in the nest."

"Then come to the brook," said the Drake, "and let the children have a bath. I have been swimming a great many times to-day, and they have not even set foot in water yet. Why, our eldest son was out of his shell before the Horses were harnessed this morning, and here it is nearly time for their supper."

"I couldn't help it," said the mother Duck. "I couldn't leave the nest to take him swimming until the rest were ready to go. I am doing the best I can."

"I didn't mean to find fault," said the Drake, "and I suppose you couldn't get away, but we know that Ducklings should be taught to bathe often, and there is nothing like beginning in time."

"I might have taken some of them to the brook," said one of the aunts. The mother straightened her neck and held her head very high, while she answered, "You? You are very kind, but what do you know about bringing up Ducklings?"

Now the aunt might have said, "I know just as much as you do," for it was the young mother's first brood, yet she kept still. She thought, "I may hatch Ducklings of my own some day, and then I suppose I shall want to care for them myself."

"Wait," said the Drake, as they reached the brook. "Let us wait and see what the children will do." The words were hardly out of his bill when—flutter—splash—splash!—there were nine yellow-white Ducklings floating on the brook and murmuring happily to each other as though they had never done anything else.

The Dorking Cock stood on the bank. "Who taught them to swim?" said he.

"Nobody," answered their mother proudly. "They knew without being told. That is the way a Duck takes to water." And she gave a dainty lurch and was among her brood.

"Well!" exclaimed the Dorking Cock. "I thought the little Dorkings were as bright as children could be, but they didn't know as much as that. I must tell them." He stalked off, talking under his breath.

"They know more than that," said the Drake. "Did you see how they ran ahead of us when we stopped to talk? They knew where to find water as soon as they were out of the shell. Still, the Cock might not have believed that if I had told him."

They had a good swim, and then all stood on the bank and dried themselves. This they did by squeezing the water out of their down with their bills. The Drake, the mother Duck, the five aunts, and the nine Ducklings all stood as tall and straight as they could, and turned and twisted their long necks, and flapped their wings, and squeezed their down, and murmured to each other. And their father didn't tell the little ones how, and their mother didn't tell them how, and their five aunts didn't tell them how, but they knew without being told.

The Ducklings grew fast, and made friends of all the farmyard people. Early every morning they went to the brook. They learned to follow the brook to the river, and here were wonderful things to be seen. There was plenty to eat, too, in the soft mud under the water, and it was easy enough to dive to it, or to reach down their long necks while only their pointed tails and part of their body could be seen above the water. Not that they ate the mud. They kept only the food that they found in it, and then let the mud slip out between the rough edges of their bills. They swam and ate all day, and slept all night, and were dutiful Ducklings who minded their mother, so it was not strange that they were plump and happy.

At last there came a morning when the eldest Duckling could not go to the brook with the others. A Weasel had bitten him in the night, and if it had not been for his mother and the Drake, would have carried him away. The rest had to go in swimming, and his lame leg would not let him waddle as far as the brook, or swim after he got there.

"I don't know what to do," he said to his mother. "I can't swim and I can't waddle far, and I've eaten so much already that I can't eat anything more for a long, long time."

"You might play with the little Shanghais," said his mother.

"They run around too much," he replied. "I can't keep up with them."

"Then why not lie near the corn crib and visit with the Mice?"

"Oh, they don't like the things that I like, and it isn't any fun."

"How would it suit you to watch the Peacock for a while?"

"I'm tired of watching the Peacock."

"Then," said the mother, "you must help somebody else. You are old enough to think of such things now, and you must remember this wise saying: 'When you don't know what to do, help somebody.'"

"Whom can I help?" said the lame Duckling. "People can all do things for themselves."

"There is the Blind Horse," answered his mother. "He is alone to-day, and I'm sure he would like somebody to visit him."

"Quack!" said the Duckling. "I will go to see him." He waddled slowly away, stopping now and then to rest, and shaking his little pointed tail from side to side as Ducks do. The Blind Horse was grazing in the pasture alone.

"I've come to see you, sir," said the Duckling. "Shall I be in your way?"

The Blind Horse looked much pleased. "I think from your voice that you must be one of the young Ducks," said he. "I shall be very glad to have you visit me, only you must be careful to keep away from my feet, for I can't see, and I might step on you."

"I'll be careful," said the Duckling. "I can't waddle much anyway this morning, because my leg hurts me so."

"Why, I'm sorry you are lame," said the Horse. "What is the matter?"

"A Weasel bit me in the night, sir. But it doesn't hurt so much as it did before I came to see you. Perhaps the pasture is a better place for lame legs than the farmyard." He didn't know that it was because he was trying to make somebody else happy that he felt so much better, yet that was the reason.

The Blind Horse and the Duckling became very fond of each other and had a fine time. The Horse told stories of his Colthood, and of the things he had seen in his travels before he became blind. And the Duckling told him what the other farmyard people were doing, and about the soft, fleecy clouds that drifted across the blue sky. When the mother Duck came to look for him, the little fellow was much surprised. "Didn't you go to the brook?" he asked.

"Yes," said his mother, with a smile. "We have been there all the morning. Don't you see how high the sun is?"

"Why-ee!" said the Duckling. "I didn't think I had been here long at all. We've been having the nicest time. And I'm coming again, am I not?" He asked this question of the Blind Horse.

"I wish you would come often," answered the Blind Horse. "You have given me a very pleasant morning. Good-bye!"

The mother Duck and her son waddled off together. "How is your leg?" said she.

"I forgot all about it until I began to walk," answered the Duckling. "Isn't that queer?"

"Not at all," said his mother. "It was because you were making somebody else happy. 'When you don't know what to do, help somebody.'"

The Fussy Queen Bee

In a sheltered corner of the farmyard, where the hedge kept off the cold winds and the trees shaded from hot summer sunshine, there were many hives of Bees. One could not say much for the Drones, but the others were the busiest of all the farmyard people, and they had so much to do that they did not often stop to visit with their neighbors.

In each hive, or home, there were many thousand Bees, and each had his own work. First of all, there was the Queen. You might think that being a Queen meant playing all the time, but that is not so, for to be a really good Queen, even in a Beehive, one must know a great deal and keep at work all the time. The Queen Bee is the mother of all the Bee Babies, and she spends her days in laying eggs. She is so very precious and important a person that the first duty of the rest is to take care of her.

The Drones are the stoutest and finest-looking of all the Bees, but they are lazy, very, very lazy. There are never many of them in a hive, and like most lazy people, they spend much of their time in telling the others how to work. They do not make wax or store honey, and as the Worker Bees do not wish them to eat what has been put away for winter, they do not live very long.

Most of the Bees are Workers. They are smaller than either the Queen Mother or the Drones, and they gather all the honey, make all the wax, build the comb, and feed the babies. They keep the hive clean, and when the weather is very warm, some of them fan the air with their wings to cool it. They guard the doorway of the hive, too, and turn away the robbers who sometimes come to steal their honey.

In these busy homes, nobody can live long just for himself. Everybody helps somebody else, and that makes life pleasant. The Queen Mother often lays as many as two thousand eggs in a day. Most of these are Worker eggs, and are laid in the small cells of the brood comb, which is the nursery of the hive. A few are Drone eggs and are laid in large cells. She never lays any Queen eggs, for she does not want more Queens growing up. It is a law among the Bees that there can be only one grown Queen living in each home.

The Workers, however, know that something might happen to their old Queen Mother, so, after she has gone away, they sometimes go into a cell where she has laid a Worker egg, and take down the waxen walls between it and the ones on either side to make a very large royal cell. They bite away the wax with their strong jaws and press the rough edges into shape with their feet. When this egg hatches, they do not feed the baby, or Larva, with tasteless bread made of flower-dust, honey, and water, as they would if they intended it to grow up a Worker or a Drone. Instead, they make what is called royal jelly, which is quite sour, and tuck this all around the Larva, who now looks like a little white worm.

The royal jelly makes her grow fast, and in five days she is so large as to nearly fill the cell. Then she stops eating, spins a cocoon, and lies in it for about two and a half days more. When she comes out of this, she is called a Pupa. Sixteen days after the laying of the egg, the young Queen is ready to come out of her cell. It takes twenty-one days for a Worker to become fully grown and twenty-five for a Drone.

In the hive by the cedar tree, the Queen Mother was growing restless and fussy. She knew that the Workers were raising some young Queens, and she tried to get to the royal cells. She knew that if she could only do that, the young Queens would never live to come out. The Workers knew this, too, and whenever she came near there, they made her go away.

The Queen Larvæ and Pupæ were of different ages, and one of them was now ready to leave her cell. They could hear her crying to be let out, but they knew that if she and the Queen Mother should meet now, one of them would die. So instead of letting her out, they built a thick wall of wax over the door and left only an opening through which they could feed her. When she was hungry she ran her tongue out and they put honey on it.

She wondered why the Workers did not let her out, when she wanted so much to be free. She did not yet know that Queen Mothers do not get along well with young Queens.

The Workers talked it over by themselves. One of them was very tender-hearted. "It does seem too bad," said she, "to keep the poor young Queen shut up in her cell. I don't see how you can stand it to hear her piping so pitifully all the time. I am sure she must be beautiful. I never saw a finer tongue than the one she runs out for honey."

"Humph!" said a sensible old Worker, who had seen many Queens hatched and many swarms fly away, "you'd be a good deal more sorry if we did let her out now. It would not do at all."

The tender-hearted Worker did not answer this, but she talked it over with the Drones. "I declare," said she, wiping her eyes with her forefeet, "I can hardly gather a mouthful of honey for thinking of her."

"Suppose you hang yourself up and make wax then," said one Drone. "It is a rather sunshiny day, but you ought to be doing something, and if you cannot gather honey you might do that." This was just like a Drone. He never gathered honey or made wax, yet he could not bear to see a Worker lose any time.

The Worker did not hang herself up and make wax, however. She never did that except on cloudy days, and she was one of those Bees who seem to think that nothing will come out right unless they stop working to see about it. There was plenty waiting to be done, but she was too sad and anxious to do it. She might have known that since her friends were only minding the law, it was right to keep the new Queen in her cell.

The Queen Mother was restless and fussy. She could not think of her work, and half the time she did not know whether she was laying a Drone egg or a Worker egg. In spite of that, she did not make any mistake, or put one into the wrong kind of cell. "I cannot stay here with a young Queen," said she. "I will not stay here. I will take my friends with me and fly away."

Whenever she met a Worker, she struck her feelers on those of her friend, and then this friend knew exactly how she felt about it. In this way the news was passed around, and soon many of the Workers were as restless as their Queen Mother. They were so excited over it at times that the air of the hive grew very hot. After a while they would become quiet and gather honey once more. They whispered often to each other. "Do you know where we are going?" one said.

"Sh!" was the answer. "The guides are looking for a good place now."

"I wish the Queen Mother knew where we are going," said the first.

"How could she?" replied the second. "You know very well that she has not left the hive since she began to lay eggs. Here she comes now."

"Oh dear!" exclaimed the Queen Mother. "I can never stand this. I certainly cannot. To think I am not allowed to rule in my own hive! The Workers who are guarding the royal cells drive me away whenever I go near them. I will not stay any longer."

"Then," said a Drone, as though he had thought of it for the first time, "why don't you go away?"

"I shall," said she. "Will you go with me?"

"No," said the Drone. "I hate moving and furnishing a new house. Besides, somebody must stay here to take care of the Workers and the young Queen."

The Queen Mother walked away. "When we were both young," she said to herself, "he would have gone anywhere with me."

And the Drone said to himself, "Now, isn't that just like a Queen Mother! She has known all the time that there would be young Queens coming on, and that she would have to leave, yet here she is, making the biggest kind of fuss about it. She ought to remember that it is the law."

Indeed she should have remembered that it was the law, for everything is done by law in the hive, and no one person should find fault. The law looks after them all, and will not let any one have more than his rightful share.

That same afternoon there was a sudden quiet in their home. The Workers who had been outside returned and visited with the rest. While they were waiting, a few who were to be their guides came to the door of the hive, struck their wings together, and gave the signal for starting. Then all who were going with the Queen Mother hurried out of the door and flew with her in circles overhead. "Good-bye!" they called. "Raise all the young Queens you wish. We shall never come back. We are going far, far away, and we shall not tell you where. It is a lovely place, a very lovely place."

"Let them go," said the Drones who stayed behind. "Now, isn't it time to let out the young Queen?"

"Not yet," answered a Worker, who stood near the door. "Not one feeler shall she put outside her cell until that swarm is out of sight."

The tender-hearted Worker came up wiping her eyes. "Oh, that poor Queen Mother!" said she. "I am so sorry for her. I positively cannot gather honey to-day, I feel so badly about her going."

"Better keep on working," said her friend. "It's the best thing in the world for that sad feeling. Besides, you should try to keep strong."

"Oh, I will try to eat something from the comb," was the answer, "but I don't feel like working."

"Zzzt!" said the other Worker. "I think if you can eat, you can hunt your food outside, and not take honey we have laid up for winter or food that will be needed for the children."

The Drones chuckled. It was all right for them to be lazy, they thought, but they never could bear to see a Worker waste time. "Ah," cried one of them suddenly, "what is the new swarm doing now?"

The words were hardly out of his mouth when the Queen Mother crawled into the hive again. "Such dreadful luck!" said she. "A cloud passed over the sun just as we were alighting on a tree to rest."

"I wouldn't have come back for that," said a Drone.

"No," said she, in her airiest way, "I dare say you wouldn't, but I would. I dare not go to a new home after a cloud has passed over the sun. I think it is a sign of bad luck. I should never expect a single egg to hatch if I went on. We shall try it again to-morrow."

All the others came back with her, and the hive was once more crowded and hot. "Oh dear!" said the tender-hearted Worker, "isn't it too bad to think they couldn't go?"

The next morning they started again and were quite as excited over it as before. The Queen Mother had fussed and fidgeted all the time, although she had laid nine hundred and seventy-three eggs while waiting, and that in spite of interruptions. "Being busy keeps me from thinking," said she, "and I must do something." This time the Queen Mother lighted on an apple-tree branch, and the others clung to her until all who had left the hive were in a great mass on the branch,—a mass as large as a small cabbage. They meant to rest a little while and then fly away to the new home chosen by their guides.

While they were hanging here, the farmer came under the tree, carrying a long pole with a wire basket fastened to the upper end. He shook the clustered Bees gently into it, and then changed them into an empty hive that stood beside their old home.

"Now," said the Workers who had stayed in the old hive, "we will let out the new Queen, for the Queen Mother will never return."

It did not take long to bite away the waxen wall and let her out. Then they gathered around and caressed her, and touched their feelers to her and waited upon her, and explained why they could not let her out sooner. She was still a soft gray color, like all young Bees when they first come from the cell, but this soon changed to the black worn by her people.

The Workers flew in and out, and brought news from the hive next door. They could not go there, for the law does not allow a Bee who lives in one home to visit in another, but they met their old friends in the air or when they were sipping honey. They found that the Queen Mother had quite given up the idea of living elsewhere and was as busy as ever. The farmer had put a piece of comb into the new hive so that she could begin housekeeping at once.

The new Queen was petted and kept at home until she was strong and used to moving about. That was not long. Then she said she wanted to see the world outside. "We will go with you," said the Drones, who were always glad of an excuse for flying away in pleasant weather. They said there was so much noise and hurrying around in the hive that they could never get any real rest there during the daytime.

So the young Queen flew far away and saw the beautiful world for the first time. Such a blue sky! Such green grass! Such fine trees covered with sweet-smelling blossoms! She loved it all as soon as she saw it. "Ah," she cried, "what a wonderful thing it is to live and see all this! I am so glad that I was hatched. But now I must hurry home, for there is so much to be done."

She was a fine young Queen, and the Bees were all proud of her. They let her do anything she wished as long as she kept away from the royal cells. She soon began to work as the old Queen Mother had done, and was very happy in her own way. She would have liked to open the royal cells and prevent more Queens from hatching, and when they told her it was the law which made them keep her away, she still wanted to bite into them.

"That poor young Queen Mother!" sighed the tender-hearted Worker. "I am so sorry for her when she is kept away from the royal cells. This is a sad, sad world!" But this isn't a sad world by any means. It is a beautiful, sunshiny, happy world, and neither Queen Bees nor anybody else should think it hard if they cannot do every single thing they wish. The law looks after great and small, and there is no use in pouting because we cannot do one certain thing, when there is any amount of delightful work and play awaiting us. And the young Queen Mother knew this.

The Bay Colt Learns To Mind

The span of Bays were talking together in their stalls, and the other Horses were listening. That was one trouble with living in the barn, you could not say anything to your next-door neighbor without somebody else hearing. The farmer had solid walls between the stalls, with openings so far back that no Horse could get his head to them without breaking his halter. This had been done to keep them from biting each other, and as nobody but the Dappled Gray ever thought of doing such a thing, it was rather hard on the rest. It made it difficult for the mothers to bring up their children properly, for after a Colt was old enough to have a stall to himself, his mother had to call out her advice and warnings so loudly that everybody could hear, and you know it is not well to reprove a child before company if it can be helped. Indeed, it was this very question that was troubling the span of Bays now. Each of them had a two-year-old Colt, and they knew that it was nearly time for the farmer to put these Colts to work. The span of Bays were sisters, so of course their children were cousins, and they were all very fond of each other and of the Blind Horse, who was the uncle of the Bays and the great-uncle of the Bay Colt and the Gray Colt.

"I am worried about the Bay Colt," said his mother. "Since he was brought into the barn last fall and had a stall away from me, he has gotten into bad ways. I have told him again and again that he must not nibble the edge of the manger, yet the first thing I heard this morning was the grating of his teeth on the wood."

"Well," said his aunt, "you know he is teething, and that may be the reason."

"That is no excuse," said his mother sternly. "He has been teething ever since he was five days old, and he will not cut his last tooth for three years yet. I don't call it goodness to keep from cribbing when you don't want to crib, and the time to stop is now. Besides, if he waits until he has all his teeth, he won't be able to break himself of the habit when he does try."

"That is so," said his aunt, "and he will ruin his teeth, too."

"Pooh!" exclaimed the Bay Colt, who had heard what they were saying. "I can stop whenever I want to, and they're my own teeth, anyway. It isn't anybody else's business if I do ruin them."

"There!" said his mother to his aunt, "you see what I mean. That is just the way he talks all the time. Now what would you do?"

"Let him alone," snorted the Dappled Gray. "Let him alone, and he will get some Horse sense after he has been broken. He'll have a hard time of it, but he'll come out all right."

The Bay Colt kicked against the side of the stall, he was so vexed. "I'll thank you to let me alone," said he. "I don't see why everybody tells me what I ought to do. Guess I know a thing or two."

"I'll tell you why," said the Dappled Gray, in a voice that sounded as though he were trying very hard not to lose his temper. "It is because you are young and we like you, and we can save you trouble if you mind what we tell you. I had lost the black pits in my front teeth before you were born, and when a Horse has lived long enough to lose the black pits from his front teeth, he knows a good deal. You don't know a curb-bit from a snaffle now, but you will learn many things when you are broken—a very great many things."

The Bay Colt tossed his head and did not answer. When he was led out to drink, the Dappled Gray spoke quickly to his friends. "We will let him alone," said he, "as he wishes. We will not advise him until he asks us to do so." They were all whinnying "Yes" when the Bay Colt came back. Then it became so still that you could have heard a stem of hay drop.

For a few days after this, the Bay Colt had a very good time. Nobody gave him any advice, and even when he gnawed at the edge of the manger, his mother did not seem to notice it. After he found that she didn't say anything, he didn't gnaw, or crib, so much. He was such a foolish and contrary young fellow that when people told him not to do a thing, he always wanted to do that thing worse than anything else in the world. His cousin, the Gray Colt, was not at all like him. She was a gentle little two-year-old whom everybody loved. She was full of fun and was the gayest possible companion in the meadow, yet when the older Horses gave her advice, she always listened and obeyed.

The Bay Colt was very fond of his cousin, but he did like to tease her, and once in the fall, before they came to stay in the barn, he called her a "goody-goody" because she wouldn't jump the fence and run away with him. He said she wouldn't do such things because she didn't know what fun was. Then she did show that she had a temper, for her brown eyes snapped and her soft lips were raised until she showed all her biting teeth. "I'm not a 'goody-goody,'" she cried, stamping the ground with her pretty little hoofs, "and I just ache to go. I feel as though there were ropes that I couldn't see, pulling me toward that fence every time I think of it, but I won't go! I won't go! My mother says that she jumped a fence and ran away when she was a Colt, and that she felt as mean as could be afterward."

"I don't care," said her cousin, "I'm going anyway, and you can stay at home if you want to. Good-bye!" He ran and leaped over the fence, and trotted down the road with his head well up and his tail in the air. And then how the Gray Colt did want to follow! "I won't!" she said again. "I won't do it. I'll look the other way and try to forget it, but I wish he knew how hard it is to be good sometimes."

The next morning the Bay Colt was in the pasture again. The farmer and his man had found him far away and led him back. "I had a fine time," he said to his cousin, "and I don't feel a bit mean. I'm going again to-day, but don't you tell." When his mother scolded him as he deserved, he just switched his tail and thought about something else until she stopped talking. Then he ran away again.

The next morning when the Gray Colt saw him, he had a queer wooden thing around his neck, and fastened to this was a pole that stuck out ahead of him. It tired his neck and bothered him when he wanted to run. If he had tried to jump the fence, it would have thrown him down. When the Gray Colt came toward him, he pretended not to see her. He might just as well have looked squarely at her as soon as she came, because, you know, he had to look at her sometime, but he had a mean, slinking, afraid feeling, such as people always have when they have done something wrong and have had time to think about it. Besides, he had changed his mind since the wooden poke had been put on him, and somehow his running away seemed very foolish now. He wondered how he could ever have thought it any fun, and he was so disgusted that he couldn't keep his ears still, but moved them restlessly when he remembered his own silliness.

The Gray Colt was too polite to say anything about his wearing the poke, and she talked about the grass, the sky, the trees, and everything else she could think of. Once she was about to speak of the fence, and then she remembered and stopped short. The Bay Colt noticed this. "You might just as well go on," said he. "You are very kind, but I know how foolish I have been, and there's no use in keeping still. You were right, and it doesn't pay to jump fences for a few minutes of what you think will be fun. I feel sick all over when I think about it."

"It's too bad," whinnied the Gray Colt. "I'm very sorry for you."

"And what do you think?" said the Bay Colt. "I heard the Dappled Gray say this morning that I was like a Pig! Imagine a Colt being like a Pig! He said that it didn't make any difference on which side of a fence Pigs were, they always wanted to be on the other side, and that I was just as stupid."

This was all in the fall, before the cold weather had sent them to live in the barn, and while the Bay Colt was wearing the poke he could not well forget the lesson he had learned about jumping and running away. His mother grew quite proud of him, and the Dappled Gray had been heard to say that he might amount to something yet. That was a great deal for the Dappled Gray to say, for although he had a very kind heart, he did not often praise people, and hardly ever said such things about two-year-olds. That made it all the harder for him when the Bay Colt became cross over being told to stop cribbing.

You know there are some Colts who learn obedience easily, and there are others who have one hard struggle to stop jumping, and another to stop cribbing, and another to stop kicking, and so on, all through their Colthood. The older Horses are sorry for them and try to help them, for they know that neither Colt nor Horse can really enjoy life until he is trying to do right. To be sure, people sometimes do wrong even then, but if they will take advice and keep on trying they are certain to turn out well.

And now, when the Bay Colt seemed to have forgotten the lesson he had in the fall, and after he had told the other Horses to let him alone, very strange things began to happen. The farmer took him from his stall and made him open his mouth. Then a piece of iron was slipped into it, which lay on top of his tongue and fitted into the place on each side of his jaw where there were no teeth. Long lines were fastened to this iron on either side, and when he tossed his head and sidled around, these lines were gently pulled by the farmer and the iron bit pressed down his tongue.

The farmer was very kind, but the Bay Colt did not want the bit in his mouth, so he acted as ugly as he knew how, and kicked, and snapped with his jaws open, and tried to run. The farmer did not grow angry or cross, yet whenever the Bay Colt showed his temper, the bit would press down his tongue and stretch the corners of his mouth until he had to stop. Once in a while the farmer would try to pat him and show him that it was all right, but the Bay Colt would not have this, and he was a very cross and sweaty two-year-old when he was taken back to his stall.

He missed the Gray Colt from her usual place, but soon she came in with one of the farmer's men. She had been driven for the first time also.

"Hallo!" said he. "Have you had a bit in your mouth too? Wasn't it dreadful? I am so angry that my hoofs fairly tingle to hit that farmer."

"It was hard," said the Gray Colt, "but the man who drove me was very kind and let me rest often. He patted me, too, and that helped me to be brave. My mother says we won't mind the bit at all after we are used to it."

"Well," said the Bay Colt, "I'm never going to be used to it. I won't stand it, and that's all there is about it." He stamped his hoofs and looked very important. Two-year-olds often look quite as important as ten-year-olds, and they feel much more so. The Bay Colt was rather proud of his feet, and thought it much nicer to have solid hoofs than to have them split, like those of the Cows, the Hogs, and the Sheep.

When he said that he would not stand it to be driven, a queer little sound ran through the stalls. It was like the wind passing over a wheatfield, and was caused by the older Horses taking a long breath and whispering to themselves. The Bay Colt's mother was saying, "Poor child! What hard work he does make of life!"

The next day both Colts were driven again, and the next day, and the next, and the next. By this time the Gray Colt was quite used to it. She said she rather enjoyed knowing what the man was thinking, and that she could tell his thoughts by the feeling of the lines, much as she used to understand her mother by rubbing noses when she was a tiny Colt. Her cousin had a sore mouth from jerking on the lines, and he could not enjoy eating at all. That made it even harder for him, because he got very hungry, and it is not so easy to be sensible when one is hungry.

When the Gray Colt learned to walk steadily and turn as her driver wished, she was allowed to draw a light log through the furrows of a field. This tired her, but it made her very proud, and she arched her neck and took the daintiest of steps. It was not necessary that the log should be drawn over the field; still, she did not know this, and thought it was real work, when it was done only to teach her to pull. The man who was driving her patted her neck and held her nose in his hand. When he stopped to eat an apple, he gave her the core, and she thought she had never tasted anything so good. As she went back to her stall, she called to the Horses near, "I have been working. I have drawn a log all around a field."

The Blind Horse spoke softly to her. "You will have a happy life, my dear, because you are a willing worker."

Although the Bay Colt didn't say anything, he thought a great deal, and about many things. While he was thinking he began to crib, but the noise of his biting teeth on the wood startled him, and he shook his head and whispered to himself, "I will never crib again." When he ate his supper, his sore mouth hurt him, but he didn't whimper. "You deserve it," he said to himself. "It wouldn't have been sore if you had been steady like your cousin." The Bay Colt was growing sensible very fast.

The Dappled Gray had noticed how suddenly he stopped cribbing, and so watched him for a few days. He saw that the Bay Colt was in earnest, that he drew the log up and down without making any fuss, and was soon hitched with his mother to a plow. The Dappled Gray and the Blind Horse were also plowing that day, and they called across from their field. "Fine day for plowing," they said.

"Perfect," answered the Bay Colt. "Did you notice the last furrow we turned? Can you do any better than that? If I had jumped, it would have been crooked instead of straight; and if I had stopped, it would not be done yet."

"Good furrow! Wonderful furrow!" answered the Dappled Gray. "Always knew you'd be a good worker when you got down to it. You are one of us now, one of the working Horses. Glad of it. Good-bye!" And he turned away to start his plow across the field again.

"Do you like being grown up?" said the Bay Colt's mother to him.

"Like it?" he answered with a laugh. "I'm so proud that I don't know what to do. I wouldn't go back to the old life of all play for anything in the world. And my little cousin made me see my mistakes. Was there ever another Colt as foolish as I?"

"A great many of them," said his mother. "More than you would guess. They kick and bite and try to run because they cannot always have their own way; and then, when they have tried the farmer's way, and begin to pay for his care of them, they find it very much better than the life of all play. Colts will be Colts."

The Twin Lambs

There was a Lamb, a bright, frisky young fellow, who had a twin sister. Their mother loved them both and was as kind to one as to the other, but the brother wanted to have the best of everything, and sometimes he even bunted his sister with his hard little forehead. His mother had to speak to him many times about this, for he was one of those trying children who will not mind when first spoken to.

He did not really mean to be naughty—he was only strong and frisky and thoughtless. Sometimes he was even rude to his mother. She felt very sad when this was so, yet she loved him dearly and found many excuses for him in her own heart.

There were three other pairs of twins in the flock that year, and as their mothers were not strong enough to care for two Lambs apiece, the farmer had taken one twin from each pair to a little pen near the house. Here they stayed, playing happily together, and drinking milk from a bottle which the farmer's wife brought to them. They were hungry very often, like all young children, and when their stomachs began to feel empty, or even to feel as if they might feel empty, they crowded against the side of the pen, pushed their pinkish-white noses through the openings between the boards, and bleated and bleated and bleated to the farmer's wife.

Soon she would come from the kitchen door and in her hand would bring the big bottle full of milk for them. There was a soft rubber top to this bottle, through which the Lambs could draw the milk into their mouths. Of course they all wanted to drink at once, though there was only a chance for one, and the others always became impatient while they were waiting. The farmer's wife was patient, even when the Lambs, in their hurry to get the milk, took her fingers into their mouths and bit them instead of the top of the bottle.

Our twin Lamb wanted to have his sister taken into the pen with the other three, and he spoke about it to his mother. "I know how you can manage," said he. "Whenever she comes near you, just walk away from her, and then the farmer will take her up to the pen."

"You selfish fellow!" answered his mother. "Do you want your dear little twin sister to leave us?"

He hung his head for a minute, but replied, "She'd have just as good a time. They have all they can eat up there, and they have lots of fun."

"If you think it is so pleasant in the pen," said his mother, "suppose I begin to walk away from you, and let the farmer take you away. I think your sister would rather stay with me."

"Oh, no!" cried her son. "I don't want to leave my own dear woolly mother! I want to cuddle up to you every night and have you tell me stories about the stars."

"Do you think you love me very much?" said she. "You don't know how to really love yet, for you are selfish, and there is not room in a selfish heart for the best kind of love."

That made the Lamb feel very badly. "I do love her dearly," he cried, as he stood alone. "I believe I love her ever so much more than my sister does."

That was where the little fellow was mistaken, for although his sister did not talk so much about it, she showed her love in many other ways. If she had been taken from her mother for even a few days, they could never again have had such sweet and happy days together. Sheep look much alike, and they cannot remember each other's faces very long. If a Lamb is taken away from his mother for even a short time, they do not know each other when they meet afterward. Perhaps this is one reason why they keep together so much, for it would be sad indeed not to know one's mother or one's child.

His sister never knew that he had wanted her taken away. She thought he acted queerly sometimes, but she was so loving and unselfish herself that she did not dream of his selfishness. Instead of putting the idea out of his woolly little head, as he could have done by thinking more of other things, the brother let himself think of it more and more. That made him impatient with even his mother, and he often answered her quite crossly. Sometimes, when she spoke to him, he did not answer at all, and that was just as bad.

His mother would sigh and say to herself, "My child is not a comfort to me after all, yet when I looked for the first time into his dear little face, I thought that as long as I had him beside me I should always be happy."

One night, when the weather was fair and warm, the farmer drove all the Sheep and Lambs into the Sheep-shed. They had been lying out under the beautiful blue sky at night, and they did not like this nearly so well. They did not understand it either, so they were frightened and bewildered, and bleated often to each other, "What is this for? What is this for?"

The Lambs did not mind it so much, for they were not warmly dressed, but the Sheep, whose wool had been growing for a year and was long and heavy, found it very close and uncomfortable. They did not know that the farmer had a reason for keeping them dry that night while the heavy dew was falling outside. The same thing was done every year, but they could not remember so long as that, and having a poor memory is always hard.

"Stay close to me, children," said the mother of the twins. "I may forget how you look if you are away long."

"It seems to me," said the brother, "that we always have to stay close to you. I never have a bit of fun!"

When they had cuddled down for the night, the twin Lambs slept soundly. Their mother lay awake for a long, long time in the dark, and she was not happy. A few careless words from a selfish little Lamb had made her heart ache. They were not true words either, for during the daytime her children ran with their playmates and had fine frolics. Still, we know that when people are out of patience they often say things that are not really so.

In the morning, men came into the barn, which opened off the Sheep-shed. They had on coarse, old clothing, and carried queer-looking shears in their hands. The Sheep could see them now and then when the door was open. Once the farmer stood in the doorway and seemed to be counting them. This made them huddle together more closely than ever. They could see the men carrying clean yellow straw into the barn and spreading it on the floor. On top of this was stretched a great sheet of clean cloth.

Then the men began to come into the shed and catch the Sheep and carry them into the barn. They were frightened and bleated a good deal, but when one was caught and carried away, although he might struggle hard to free himself, he did not open his mouth. The old Wether Sheep was the first to be taken, and then the young ones who had been Lambs the year before. For a long time not one of the mothers was chosen. Still, nobody knew what would happen next, and so, the fewer Sheep there were left, the more closely they huddled together.

At last, when the young Sheep had all been taken, one of the men caught the mother of the twins and carried her away. She turned her face toward her children, but the door swung shut after her, and they were left with the other Lambs and their mothers. From the barn came the sound of snip-snip-snipping and the murmur of men's voices. Once the twins thought they saw their mother lying on the floor and a man kneeling beside her, holding her head and forelegs under his arm, yet they were not sure of this.

The brother ran to the corner of the shed and put his head against the boards. He suddenly felt very young and helpless. "My dear woolly mother!" he said to himself, over and over, and he wondered if he would ever see her again. He remembered what he had said to her the night before. It seemed to him that he could even now hear his own voice saying crossly, "Seems to me we always have to stay close to you. I never have a bit of fun!" He wished he had not said it. He knew she was a dear mother, and he would have given anything in the world for a chance to stay close to her again.

His sister felt as lonely and frightened as he, but she did not act in the same way. She stood close to a younger Lamb whose mother had just been taken away, and tried to comfort her. One by one the mothers were taken until only the Lambs remained. They were very hungry now, and bleated pitifully. Still the twin brother stood with his head in the corner. He had closed his eyes, but now he opened them, and through a crack in the wall of the shed, he saw some very slender and white-looking Sheep turned into the meadow. At first they acted dizzy, and staggered instead of walking straight; then they stopped staggering and began to frisk. "Can it be?" said he. "It surely is!" For, although he had never in his short life seen a newly shorn Sheep, he began to understand what had happened.

He knew that the men had only been clipping the long wool from the Sheep, and that they were now ready for warm weather. No wonder they frisked when their heavy burdens of wool were carefully taken off.

Now the farmer opened the door into the barn again, and let the Lambs walk through it to the gate of the meadow. They had never before been inside this barn, and the twin brother looked quickly around as he scampered across the floor. He saw some great ragged bundles of wool, and a man was just rolling up the last fleece. He wondered if that had been taken from his mother and was the very one against which he had cuddled when he was cold or frightened.

When they first reached the pasture, the Lambs could not tell which were their mothers. Shearing off their long and dingy fleeces had made such a difference in their looks! The twin brother knew his mother by her way of walking and by her voice, but he could see that his sister did not know her at all. He saw his mother wandering around as though she did not know where to find her children, and a naughty plan came into his head. If he could keep his sister from finding their mother for even a short time, he knew that the farmer would take her up to the pen. He thought he knew just how to do it, and he started to run to her. Then he stopped and remembered how sad and lonely he had been without his mother only a little while before, and he began to pity the Lambs in the pen.

Now his selfishness and his goodness were fighting hard in him. One said, "Send your sister away," and the other, "Take her to your mother." At last he ran as fast as he could toward his sister. "I am good now," he said to himself, "but it may not last long. I will tell her before I am naughty again."

"Oh sister!" cried he. "Come with me to our mother. She doesn't know where to find us."

He saw a happy look on his sister's sad little face, and he was glad that he had done the right thing. They skipped away together, kicking up their heels as they went, and it seemed to the brother that he had never been so happy in his life. He was soon to be happier, though, for when they reached his "new, white mother," as he called her, and his sister told her how he had shown her the way, his mother said, "Now you are a comfort to me. You will be a happier Lamb, too, for you know that a mother's heart is large enough for all her children, and that the more one loves, the better he loves."

"Why, of course," said the twin sister. "What do you mean?"

But the mother never told her, and the brother never told her, and it is hoped that you will keep the secret.

The Very Short Story Of The Foolish Little Mouse

The Mice who lived in the barn and around the granaries had many cousins living on the farm who were pleasant people to know. Any one could tell by looking at them that they were related, yet there were differences in size, in the coloring of their fur, in their voices, and most of all in their ways of living. Some of these cousins would come to visit at the barn in winter, when there was little to eat in the fields. The Meadow Mice never did this. They were friendly with the people who came from the farmyard to graze in the meadow, yet when they were asked to return the call, they said, "No, thank you. We are an out-of-door family, and we never enter houses. We do not often go to the farmyard, but we are always glad to see you here. Come again."

When the Cows are in the meadow, they watch for these tiny people, and stop short if they hear their voices from the grass near by. Of course the Horses are careful, for Horses will never step on any person, large or small, if they can help it. They are very particular about this.

All through the meadow you can see, if you look sharply, shallow winding paths among the grasses, and these paths are worn by the running to and fro of the Meadow Mice. Their homes are in stumps of trees or in the higher ground near the ditches. In these homes the baby Meadow Mice stay until they are large enough to go out into the great world and eat roots, grasses, and seeds with their fathers and mothers. Sometimes they do go out a little way with their mother before this, and they go in a very funny fashion. Of course, when they are babies, they drink warm milk from her body as the children of most four-legged people do. Sometimes a young Meadow Mouse does not want to stop drinking his milk when it is time for his mother to leave the nest, so he just hangs on to her with his tiny, toothless mouth, and when she goes she drags him along on the ground beside her. The ground is rather rough for such soft little babies, and they do not go far in this way, but are glad enough to snuggle down again with their brothers and sisters.

There is no danger of their being lonely, even when their mother is away, for the Meadow Mice have large families, and where there are ten babies of the same age, or even only six, which is thought a small family among their people, it is not possible for one to feel alone.

There were two fine Meadow Mice who built their nest in the bank of a ditch and were much liked by all their relatives. They had raised many children to full-grown Mousehood, and were kind and wise parents. When their children were married and had homes of their own, they still liked to come back to visit. The father and mother were gentle and kindly, as all Mice are, and were almost as handsome as when they first began to gnaw. Nobody could say that he ever saw a bit of dust on either of them.

The brown fur of the upper part of their bodies and the grayish-white fur underneath always lay sleek and tidy, and from their long whiskers to the tips of their hairless tails, they were as dainty as possible. That was one reason why they were so fine-looking, for you know it makes no difference how beautiful one may be in the first place, if he does not try to keep clean he is not pleasant to look at, while many quite plain people are charming because they look well and happy and clean.

Now this pair of Mice had eight Mouse babies in their nest. The babies were no larger than Bumble Bees at first and very pink. This was not because their fur was pink, but only because it was so very short that through it and their thin skin one saw the glow of the red blood in their veins.

"Did you ever see such beautiful babies?" said their mother proudly to her neighbors. "They are certainly the finest I ever had." Her friends smiled, for she always said the same thing whenever she had little ones. Yet they understood, for they had children of their own, and knew that although mothers love all alike, there is always a time when the youngest seems the most promising. That is before they are old enough to be naughty.

The days passed, and the eight baby Meadow Mice ate and slept and pushed each other around, and talked in their sweet, squeaky little voices. They were less pink every day and more the color of their father and mother. They grew, too, so fast that the nest was hardly large enough for them, and the teeth were showing in their tiny pink mouths. Their mother saw that they would soon be ready to go out into the world, and she began to teach them the things they needed to know. She took them outside the nest each pleasant day and gave them lessons in running and gnawing, and showed them how to crouch down on the brown earth and lie still until danger was past. After she had told them many things, she would ask them short questions to make sure that they remembered.

"How many great dangers are there?" she said.

"Five," answered the little Mice.

"What are they?"

"Hawks, Owls, Weasels, Cats, and men."

"Tell me about Hawks."

"Hawks are big birds who seem to float in the air. They have very sharp eyes, and when they see a Mouse they drop suddenly down and catch him. They fly in the daytime."

"Tell me about Owls."

"They are big birds who fly by night without making any noise. They can see from far away, and they catch Mice."

"Tell me about Weasels."

"They are slender little animals, nearly twice as long as a Mouse. They have small heads, four short legs, and sharp claws; have brown fur on their backs and white underneath, and sometimes, when the weather is very cold, they turn white all over."

"Tell me about Cats."

"Cats are very much bigger than Weasels, and are of many colors. They have long tails and whiskers, and dreadful great eyes. They walk on four legs, but make no noise because they have cushions on their feet."

"Tell me about men."

"Men are very big, two-legged people, and when they are fully grown are taller than Cows. They make noise in walking, and they can neither smell nor see us from afar."

"And what are you to do when you see these dangers coming?"

"We are to run away as fast as we can from Hawks, Weasels, Owls, and Cats. If a man comes near us, we are to lie perfectly still and watch him, and are not to move unless we are sure that he sees us or is likely to step on us. Men do not know so much about Mice as the other dangers do."

"And what if you are not sure that some creature is a Hawk, an Owl, a Weasel, or a Cat?"

"If we even think it may be, we are to run."

"When are you to run?"

"At once."

"Say that again."

"We are to run at once."

"Very good. That is all for to-day."

You can see how well the Meadow Mouse mother brought up her children, and how carefully she taught them about life. If they had been wise and always minded her, they would have saved themselves much trouble.

Seven of them were dutiful and obedient, but the largest of the eight, and the finest-looking, liked to decide things for himself, and often laughed at his brothers and sisters for being afraid. Because he was so big and handsome, and spoke in such a dashing way, they sometimes wondered if he didn't know as much as their mother.

One sunshiny day, when all the eight children were playing and feeding together in the short grass, one of them saw a great black bird in the air. "Oh, look!" she cried. "That may be a Hawk. We'd better run."

"Pooh!" said the biggest little Meadow Mouse. "Who's afraid?"

"Mother said to run," they squeaked, and seven long bare tails whisked out of sight under a stump.

"Ho-ho!" said the biggest little Meadow Mouse. "Before I'd be so scared! I dare you to come back! I dare you to——"

Just then the Hawk swooped down. And that is the end of the story, for after that, there was no foolish little Meadow Mouse to tell about.

The Lonely Little Pig

One day the Brown Hog called to her twelve young Pigs and their ten older brothers and sisters, "Look! look! What is in that cage?"

The twenty-two stubby snouts that were thrust through the opening of the rail-fence were quivering with eagerness and impatience. Their owners wished to know all that was happening, and the old mother's eyes were not so sharp as they had once been, so if the Pigs wanted to know the news, they must stop their rooting to find it out. Bits of the soft brown earth clung to their snouts and trembled as they breathed.

"It looks like a Pig," they said, "only it is white."

"It is a Pig then," grunted their mother, as she lay in the shade of an oak tree. "There are white Pigs, although I never fancied the color. It looks too cold and clean. Brown is more to my taste, brown or black. Your poor father was brown and black, and a finer looking Hog I never saw. Ugh! Ugh!" And she buried her eyes in the loose earth. The Pigs looked at her and then at each other. They did not often speak of their father. Indeed the younger ones did not remember him at all. One of the Cows said he had such a bad temper that the farmer sent him away, and it is certain that none of them had seen him since the day he was driven down the lane.

While they were thinking of this and feeling rather sad, the wagon turned into their lane and they could plainly see the Pig inside. She was white and quite beautiful in her piggish way. Her ears stood up stiffly, her snout was as stubby as though it had been broken off, her eyes were very small, and her tail had the right curl. When she squealed they could see her sharp teeth, and when she put her feet up on the wooden bars of her rough cage, they noticed the fine hoofs on the two big toes of each foot and the two little toes high on the back of her legs, each with its tiny hoof. She was riding in great style, and it is no wonder that the twenty-two Brown Pigs with black spots and black feet opened their eyes very wide. They did not know that the farmer brought her in this way because he was in a hurry, and Pigs will not make haste when farmers want them to. The Hogs are a queer family, and the Off Ox spoke truly when he said that the only way to make one hurry ahead is to tie a rope to his leg and pull back, they are so sure to be contrary.

"She's coming here!" the Brown Pigs cried. "Oh, Mother, she's coming here! We're going to see the men take her out of her cage."

The old Hog grunted and staggered to her feet to go with them, but she was fat and slow of motion, so that by the time she was fairly standing, they were far down the field and running helter-skelter by the side of the fence. As she stared dully after them she could see the twenty-two curly tails bobbing along, and she heard the soft patter of eighty-eight sharp little double hoofs on the earth.

"Ugh!" she grunted. "Ugh! Ugh! I am too late to go. Never mind! They will tell me all about it, and I can take a nap. I haven't slept half the time to-day, and I need rest."

Just as the Mother Hog lay down again, the men lifted the White Pig from the wagon, cage and all, so she began to squeal, and she squealed and squealed and squealed and squealed until she was set free in the field with the Brown Pigs.

Nobody had touched her and nobody had hurt her, but it was all so strange and new that she thought it would make her feel better to squeal. When she was out of her cage and in the field, she planted her hoofs firmly in the ground, looked squarely at the Brown Pigs, and grunted a pleasant, good-natured grunt. The Brown Pigs planted their hoofs in the ground and grunted and stared. They didn't ask her to go rooting with them, and not one of the ten big Pigs or the twelve little Pigs said, "We are glad to see you."

There is no telling how long they would have stood there if the Horses had not turned the wagon just then. The minute the wheels began to grate on the side of the box, every Brown Pig whirled around and ran off.

The poor little White Pig did not know what to make of it. She knew that she had not done anything wrong. She wondered if they didn't mean to speak to her.

At first she thought she would run after them and ask to root with them, but then she remembered something her mother had told her when she was so young that she was pink. It was this: "When you don't know what to do, go to sleep." So she lay down and took a nap.

The Brown Pigs did not awaken their mother, and when they stopped in the fence-corner one of them said to their big sister, "What made you run?"

"Oh, nothing," said she.

"And why did you run?" the little Pigs asked their big brother.

"Because," he answered.

After a while somebody said, "Let's go back to where the White Pig is."

"Oh, no," said somebody else, "don't let's! She can come over here if she wants to, and it isn't nearly so nice there."

You see, they were very rude Pigs and not at all well brought up. Their mother should have taught them to think of others and be kind, which is really all there is to politeness. But then, she had very little time left from sleeping, and it took her all of that for eating, so her children had no manners at all.

At last the White Pig opened her round eyes and saw all the Brown Pigs at the farther end of the field. "Ugh!" said she to herself, "Ugh! I must decide what to do before they see that I am awake." She lay there and tried to think what her mother, who came of a very fine family, had told her before she left. "If you have nobody to play with," her mother had said, "don't stop to think about it, and don't act as though you cared. Have a good time by yourself and you will soon have company. If you cannot enjoy yourself, you must not expect others to enjoy you."

"That is what I will do," exclaimed the White Pig. "My mother always gives her children good advice when they go out into the world, and she is right when she says that Pigs of fine family should have fine manners. I will never forget that I am a Yorkshire. I'm glad I didn't say anything mean."

So the White Pig rooted in the sunshine and wallowed in the warm brown earth that she had stirred up with her pink snout. Once in a while she would run to the fence to watch somebody in the lane, and before she knew it she was grunting contentedly to herself. "Really," she said, "I am almost having a good time. I will keep on making believe that I would rather do this than anything else."

The big sister of the Brown Pigs looked over to the White Pig and said, "She's having lots of fun all by herself, it seems to me."

Big brother raised his head. "Let's call her over here," he answered.

"Oh, do!" cried the twelve little Pigs, wriggling their tails. "She looks so full of fun."

"Call her yourself," said the big sister to the big brother.

"Ugh!" called he. "Ugh! Ugh! Don't you want to come over with us, White Pig?"

You can imagine how the White Pig felt when she heard this; how her small eyes twinkled and the corners of her mouth turned up more than ever. She was just about to scamper over and root with them, when she remembered something else that her mother had told her: "Never run after other Pigs. Let them run after you. Then they will think more of you."

She called back, "I'm having too good a time here to leave my rooting-ground. Won't you come over here?"

"Come on," cried all the little Pigs to each other. "Beat you there!"

They ate and talked and slept together all afternoon, and when the Brown Hog called her children home, they and the White Pig were the best of friends. "Just think," they said to their mother, "the White Pig let us visit her, and she is just as nice as she can be."

The White Pig in her corner of the pen heard this and smiled to herself. "My mother was right," she said; "'Have a good time alone, and everybody will want to come.'"

The Kitten Who Lost Herself

"I think," said the Blind Horse, "that something is the matter with my ears." He and the Dappled Gray had been doing field-work all the morning, and were now eating a hearty dinner in their stalls. They were the only people on the first floor of the barn. Even the stray Doves who had wandered in the open door were out in the sunshine once more. Once in a while the whirr of wings told that some Swallow darted through the window into the loft above and flew to her nest under the roof. There was a deep and restful quiet in the sun-warmed air, and yet the Blind Horse had seemed to be listening to something which the other did not hear.

The Dappled Gray stopped eating at once. "Your ears?" said he. "What is wrong with them? I thought your hearing was very good."

"It always has been," was the answer, "and finer than ever since I lost my sight. You know it is always so with us blind people. We learn to hear better than we could before losing our sight. But ever since we came in from the field I have had a queer sound in my ears, and I think there is something the matter with them."

The Dappled Gray stopped eating and stood perfectly still to listen. He did not even switch his tail, although at that minute there were three Flies on his left side and one on his neck. He was trying as hard as he could to hear the queer sound also, for if he did, it would prove that the noise was real and that the Blind Horse's hearing was all right.

He could not hear a thing. "What is it like?" he asked.

"Like the loud purring of a Cat," was the answer, "but everybody knows that the Cat is not purring anywhere around here."

"She might be," said the Dappled Gray. "Where does the sound seem to be?"

"Above my head," said the Blind Horse; "and she certainly would not be purring up there at this time. She would either be sound asleep, or off hunting, or else out in the sunshine, where she loves to sit."

The Dappled Gray felt that this was so, and he could not say a word. He was very sorry for his friend. He thought how dreadful it would seem to be both blind and deaf, and he choked on the oats he was swallowing.

"Now don't worry," said the Blind Horse; "if I should be deaf, I could still feel the soft touch of the breeze on my skin, and could taste my good food, and rub noses with my friends. I wouldn't have spoken of it, only I hoped that you could hear the noise also, and then I would know that it was real." That was just like him. He was always patient and sweet-tempered. In all the years he had been blind, he had never once complained of it, and many times when the other Horses were about to say or do some ill-natured thing, they thought of him and stopped. They were ashamed to be impatient when they were so much better off than he.

The Horses kept on eating their oats and resting from their hard work. In the hay-loft above their heads, the Cat lay and purred and purred and purred, never dreaming that her doing so made trouble for her friends downstairs.

She had been hunting all the night before, creeping softly through the barn and hiding behind bags and boxes to watch for careless Mice and young Rats. They were night-runners as well as she, and many things happened in the barn and farmyard while the larger four-legged people were sound asleep and the fowls were dreaming with their heads tucked under their wings. Sometimes there were not so many Mice in the morning as there had been the evening before, and when this was so, the Cat would walk slowly through the barn and look for a comfortable resting-place. When she found it, she would turn around three times, as her great-great-great-great-great-great-grandmother used to do to trample a bed in the jungle, and then lie down for a long nap. She said she always slept better when her stomach was full, and that was the habit of all Cats.

Sometimes she hunted in the fields, and many a morning at sunrise the Cows had seen her walking toward the barn on the top of the fences. She did not like to wet her feet on the dewy grass when it could be helped; so, as soon as she was through hunting, she jumped on to the nearest fence and went home in that way.

Yes, last night she had been hunting, yet she was not thinking of it now. Neither was she asleep. A Rat gnawed at the boards near her, and she hardly turned her head. A Mouse ran across the floor in plain sight, and she watched him without moving. What did she care about them now? Her first Kittens lay on the hay beside her, and she would not leave them on this first day of their lives unless she really had to.

Of course she had seen little Kittens before—Kittens that belonged to other Cats—but she was certain that none of them had looked at all like her three charming babies. She could not decide which one of them was the most beautiful. She was a Tortoise-shell Cat herself, and her fur was spotted with white, black, and yellow. The babies had the same colors on their soft coats, but not in just the same way as hers.

At first she thought her largest daughter was the beauty of the family; she was such a clear yellow, with not a hair of any other color on her. "I always did like yellow Cats," said the young mother, "and they are said to be very strong."

Then she looked at her smaller daughter, who was white with tiny yellow and black spots on neck and head. "Such a clean-looking baby," she exclaimed, "and I am sure that when her eyes are open I shall find them blue like my own."

Just at this moment, the warm, dark little bunch of fur between her forepaws moved, and she looked lovingly down upon him, her only son. "He is certainly a very remarkable one," she said. "I never before saw such a fine mixture of yellow and black, first a hair of one and then a hair of the other, so that, unless one is very close to him it looks like a rich brown. And then his feet!" She gave him a loving little poke with one forefoot and turned him onto his back. This made him wave his tiny paws in the air. The thick cushions of skin on each were as black as black could be, and that is very uncommon. They are usually pink, like those of his sisters.

The little fellow lay there, wriggling very feebly, until his mother gave him another poke that turned him over. Then he stretched and crawled toward her, reaching his head first one way and then another. He was so weak that he could not raise his body from the hay, but dragged it along by taking short and uncertain steps with his four shaking legs. It was only a short time since he found that he had legs, and he hadn't any idea how to use them. He just moved whichever one seemed most in his way.

He didn't know where he was going, or what he was going for, but his little stomach was empty and he was cold. Something, he didn't know what, made him drag himself toward the big, warm creature near by. When his black nose touched the fur of her body, he stopped pushing ahead and began to feel from side to side. He did not know now for what he was feeling, yet when he found something his tiny mouth closed around it and a stream of sweet warm milk began to flow down his throat and into his empty stomach. He did not know that it was milk. He did not know anything except that it was good, and then he fell asleep. His sisters did in the same way, and soon the happy mother could look down and see her three babies in a row beside her, all sound asleep. Their pointed little tails lay straight out behind them, and their soft ears were bent forward close to their heads.

"I wonder," said she, "if I was ever as small as they are, and if my mother loved me as I love them." She stretched out one of her forepaws and looked at it. It was so much larger, so very much larger, than the paws of the Kittens. Such a soft and dainty paw as it was, and so perfectly clean. She stretched it even more, and saw five long, curved, sharp claws slide out of their sheaths or cases. She quickly slid them back into their sheaths, for fear that in some way they might happen to touch and hurt her babies.

A Swallow flew down from his nest and passed over her head, then out of the open window. "Kittens!" said he. "Kittens!" He flew over the fields and saw two Horses standing by the fence while the farmer was oiling his machine. "We have new neighbors in the barn," said he, "and the Cat is purring louder than ever."

"Who are the neighbors?" asked the Dappled Gray.

"Kittens!" sang the Swallow. "Oh, tittle-ittle-ittle-ee."

The Blind Horse drew a long breath. "Then I did hear her purr," said he; "I am so glad." He never made a fuss about his troubles, for he was brave and unselfish, yet the Dappled Gray knew without being told how much lighter his heart was since he heard that the Cat had really been purring above his head.

The days passed by, and the Kittens grew finely. They got their eyes open, first in narrow cracks, and then wider and wider, until they were round and staring. The White Kitten had blue ones, the others brown. In the daytime, they had long, narrow black spots in the middle of their eyes, and as the bright light faded, these black spots spread out sideways until they were quite round. When it was very dark, these spots glowed like great Fireflies in the night. Then the Mice, who often scampered through the loft when the Cat was away, would see three pairs of eyes glowing in the hay, and they would squeak to each other: "See! The Kittens are watching us."

And the Kittens, who were not yet old enough to go hunting, and who were afraid of everything that stirred, would crowd up against each other, arch their little backs, raise their pointed tails, stand their fur on end, and say, "Pst! Ha-a-ah!"

Sometimes they did this when there was not a person in sight and what frightened them was nothing but a wisp of hay, blown down by the wind. Afterward, when anything moved, they sprang at it, held it down with their sharp little claws, and chewed on it with their pointed white teeth. When they were tired of this game, they played hide-and-seek, and when they were tired of that they chased their tails. It was so nice always to have playthings with them. Sometimes, too, they chased each other's tails, and caught them and bit them hard, until the Kitten who owned the tail cried, "Mieow!" and tumbled the biter over.

They were allowed to play all through the loft except over the mangers. Their mother was afraid that if they went there they would fall through the holes which had been left in the floor. During the winter, the farmer used to throw hay down through these to the hungry Horses. When the Cat saw her children going toward these places, she called them back and scolded them. Sometimes she struck them lightly on the ears with her forepaw. "I don't like to," said she, "but they must learn to keep away. It is not safe for them to go there."

One morning when she was away, they were playing hide-and-seek, and the White Kitten was hunting for a good hiding-place. "I'll hide near one of these holes," she said, "and they won't dare come there to look. Then, after they have hunted a long, long time, I'll get another place and let them find me." She did hide there, and after a long, long time, when her brother and sister were in the farther end of the loft, she tried to run over to another dark corner. Instead of that, the hay began to slip and slide under her and she went down, down, down, through a long dark box, and hit with a hard thud at the bottom.

She was so scared that she couldn't have told how many toes she had on her forefeet. Of course, she had five on each, like all Kittens, and four on each hind-foot, but if anybody had asked her then, she would have been quite likely to say "three."

She was sore, too, and when she felt a warm breath on her and opened her eyes, she saw that some great creature had thrust his nose through a hole in the side of the dark box. "It must be a Horse," she thought, "and my mother says that they are kind to Cats. I think I'd better tell him who I am. I don't want him to take me for a Pig, because he may not like Pigs." You see, she forgot that Horses had been living in the great world and could tell to what family a person belonged the very first time they saw him. The only people she had ever seen were Swallows and Mice.

"If—if you please, sir," she said, "I am the White Kitten, and I just tumbled down from the hay-loft, but I didn't mean to."

"I am the Blind Horse," answered a strong and gentle voice outside, "and I hope you are not hurt."

"Not very much," answered the Kitten. "I just feel ache-y in my back and scared all over."

"Come out into the manger, White Kitten," said the Blind Horse, "and perhaps you won't be so scared. I won't touch you, although I should like to. You know I am blind, and so, unless I can touch people I don't know how they look."

The White Kitten crawled out and saw him, and then she wasn't afraid at all. She was so sorry for him that she couldn't be afraid. She remembered the time before her eyes opened when she had to feel for everything she wanted. It was not so hard then, because she did not know anything different, but now she could not bear to think of not being able to see all that was around her. "If you will put your nose down in the other end of the manger," she said, "I will rub up against it, and you will know more how I look."

The Blind Horse did this, and who can tell how happy it made him when her warm and furry back rubbed up against his nose? "Thank you," he whinnied; "you are very good."

"Would you know I was a Kitten if I hadn't told you?" she said.

"Indeed I would," he answered.

"And you wouldn't have thought me a Pig?" she asked.

"Never!" said he; "I wouldn't even have believed you if you had told me that you were one."

The Blind Horse and the White Kitten became firm friends, and when she tried to wash off the dirt that got into her fur she sat in the very middle of the manger and told him all about it.

"My mother always has washed me," she said, "but my tongue is getting big enough to wash with now. It is getting rougher, too, and that is a good thing. My mother says that the reason why all the prickles on Cats' tongues point backward is because then we can lick all the meat off from bones with them. I'm 'most old enough to eat meat now. I can't wash the top of my head though. You have to wet your paw and scrub it with that. Can you wash the top of your head?"

Then the Blind Horse told her how the men kept him clean; and while he was telling this the Cat came into his stall, crying and looking for her child.

"Oh, mother," cried the White Kitten, "I tumbled down, but I didn't mean to, and I'm sorry I didn't mind you, and the Blind Horse can't wash the top of his head, and he knew that I wasn't a Pig."

The Cat was so glad to find the White Kitten that she didn't scold at all, but jumped into the manger and washed her clean, and then caught the loose skin of the Kitten's neck between her teeth and carried her through the stalls, across the barn-floor, and up the stairs to their home. That made the Kitten much ashamed, for she thought that she was old enough to go alone.

For two whole days after this the White Kitten was so lame from her fall that she could only lie still on the hay, and she could see that her mother did not treat her as before. "I won't ever go near those places again," she said. "I never will."

"You promised me before that you would stay away," said her mother, "and you broke your promise." She did not punish the White Kitten, but she felt very sad and she could not help showing it. There was a dreadful ache in her child's little Kitten-heart that was a great deal worse than the lameness in her back or in her neck or in her legs.

At last there came a day when the whole family walked downstairs, and the Cat showed her three children to the farmyard people and spoke a few words about each. "The yellow Kitten, my big daughter," said she, "promises to be the best hunter: she is a wonderful jumper, and her claws are already nearly as long as mine. My son, the brown one, has a remarkable voice. And this White Kitten, my little daughter, is the most obedient of all. She has never disobeyed me since the day she fell into the manger, and I can trust her perfectly."

Then the White Kitten knew that she was quite forgiven, and she was the happiest person on the farm.

The Chicken Who Wouldn't Eat Gravel

It was some time after the Dorking Hen had come off the nest with her little brood, that the mother of the Shanghai Chickens began to have so much trouble. She had twelve as fine Chickens as you could find anywhere: tall, wide-awake youngsters with long and shapely legs and thick down and feathers. She was very proud of them, as any Hen mother might well be, and often said to the Shanghai Cock, "Did you ever see so fine a family? Look at those twenty-four legs, all so long and straight, and not a feather on one of them." His eyes would shine and he would stretch his neck with pride, but all he ever said to her was, "They will do very well if they only behave as well as they look." He did not believe in praising children to their faces, and he thought their mother spoiled them.

Perhaps he was right, for the little Shanghais soon found out that they were good-looking, and they wanted everybody in the poultry-yard to notice their legs. It was very foolish, of course, to be proud of such things, but when the other fowls said, "We should think you would be cold without feathers on your legs," they answered, "Oh, we are Shanghais, and our family never wear feathers there!" And that was true, just as it is true that the Dorkings have extra toes, and that the Black Spanish fowls have white ears.

The Shanghai mother was now roaming the fields with her brood, and there was rich picking in the wheat-stubble. All the fowls were out of the yard now, and would not be shut up until cold weather. Early in the morning they would start out in parties of from six to a dozen, with a Cock at the head of each. He chose the way in which they should go; he watched the sky for Hawks, and if he saw one, gave a warning cry that made the Hens hurry to him. The Cocks are the lords of the poultry-yard and say how things shall be there; but when you see them leading the way in the fields,—ah, then you know why all the fowls obey them.

The farmyard people still tell of the day when a Hawk swooped down on one of the young Dorkings and would have carried him off if the Black Spanish Cock had not jumped out, and pecked him and struck at him with his spurs, and fought, until the Hawk was glad to hurry away. The Cocks are not only brave—they are polite, too, and when they find food they will not eat it until they have called the Hens to come and share with them.

You can imagine what good times the Chickens had in the stubble-fields. They were so old now that their down was all covered with feathers, and some of them wondered if they couldn't feel their spurs growing. Still, that was all nonsense, as a Bantam told them, because spurs do not start until the fowl is a year old. They had long been too large to cuddle under their mother's feathers at night, and had taken their first lessons in roosting before they went to the stubble-fields. They had learned to break up their own food, too, and that was a great help to their mother. Fowls, you know, have no teeth, and no matter how big a mouthful one takes he has to swallow it whole. The only way they can help themselves is to break the pieces apart with their feet or peck them apart with their bills before eating them.

The yellow grains of wheat that lay everywhere in the field were fine food, and should have made the little Shanghais as fat as the Grouse who sometimes stole out from the edge of the forest. Eleven of the brood were quite plump, but one Chicken was still thin and lank. His mother was very much worried about him and could not think what was the matter. She spoke of it to the Black Spanish Hen one day, but the Black Spanish Hen had never raised a brood, and said she really didn't know any more about the care of Chickens than if she were a Dove. Then the anxious mother went to the Shanghai Cock about it. He listened to all she said and looked very knowing.

"I don't think there is anything the matter," said he. "The Chick is growing fast, that is all. I remember how it was with me before I got my long tail-feathers. I was very thin, yet see what a fine-looking fellow I am now." He was really a sight worth seeing as he towered above the other fowls, flapping his strong wings in the sunshine and crowing. His feathers were beautiful, and the bright red of his comb and wattles showed that he was well. "Ah," thought the Shanghai Hen, "if my Chicken could only become such a fine-looking Cock!" And she didn't worry any more all day.

That night she and her brood roosted in the old apple-tree in the corner of the orchard nearest the poultry-yard. She flew up with the older fowls and fluttered and lurched and squawked and pushed on first one branch and then another, while the Chickens were walking up a slanting board that the farmer had placed against one of the lower branches. It always takes fowls a long time to settle themselves for the night. They change places and push each other, and sometimes one sleepy Hen leans over too far and falls to the ground, and then has to begin all over again.

At first the Chickens had feared that they would tumble off as soon as they were asleep, but they soon learned that their feet and the feet of all other birds are made in such a way that they hang on tightly even during sleep. The weight of the bird's body above hooks the toes around the branch, and there they stay until the bird wishes to unhook them.

After a long time, all the fowls were asleep with their heads under their wings. The Sheep, Pigs, and Cows were dreaming, and even the Horses were quiet in their stalls. There was not a light to be seen in the big white farmhouse, when the Dorking Cock crowed in his sleep. That awakened him and all the other fowls as well. Then the other Cocks crowed because he did and he crowed again because they did, and they crowed again because he had crowed again, and the Chickens asked if it were not almost morning, and their mothers told them not to talk but to go to sleep at once and make morning come more quickly.

All of this took quite a while, and the Shanghai mother could not sleep again. She could see her brood quite plainly in the moonlight, and one of them was not plump like the rest. She roosted there and worried about him until suddenly (she could never tell how it happened) she seemed to know just what was the matter.

She flew down beside him and poked him under his wing. "Wake up," she said. "I want to ask you something. Do you eat gravel?"

"No," he answered sleepily, "I don't like gravel."

"Didn't I bring you up to eat it?" she asked sternly.

"Yes, but I don't like it, and now that I am old enough to roost in a tree I don't mean to eat any more. So!"

Just imagine a Chicken talking to his mother in that way! His mother, who had laid the egg from which he was hatched; who had sat upon the nest through all the weary days and nights while he was growing inside his shell; who had cuddled him under her soft feathers; who had taught him all he knew, and would have fought any hawk to save him! She had begun to love him before he even knew that he was, and had lived for him and his brother and sisters ever since.

The mother said nothing more to him then. She spent the rest of the night watching the stars and the moon and the first rosy flush of the eastern sky which told that morning was near. Then she said to her naughty Chicken, as he began to stir and cheep, "I shall never try to make you eat gravel if you think you are too big to mind your mother. I shall just tell you this, that you will never be strong unless you do. I have not told you why, because you never asked, and I supposed you would do as you ought without knowing the reason. You have no teeth, and you cannot chew the grain you eat before it is swallowed. You have a strong stomach, and if you eat gravel this stomach or gizzard will rub and press the tiny stones against the grain until it is well broken up and ready to make into fat and strength for your body."

"But it doesn't taste good," he replied, "and I'd rather eat other things. I don't believe it matters, and I won't eat it anyway."

The Shanghai Hen flew down from the tree and clucked to her Chickens. She would not waste time talking to him. Whenever he came near her that day, he ate everything but gravel. He had his own way and yet he was not happy. For some reason, nothing seemed to be any fun. Even lying under the bushes on the sunshiny side was not comfortable, and when he wallowed in the dust with his brothers and sisters he didn't enjoy that.

Things went on this way for a good many days, and at last he saw that his shadow was only a small black spot on the ground, while his brothers and sisters had big fat shadows. He heard the Black Spanish Cock call him a Bantam, and the Shanghai Cock say that he wouldn't live until his spurs grew. One of the Dorking Chickens was talking to her sister, and he heard her say, "Imagine him at the head of a flock!" Then she laughed, a mean, cackling little laugh.

That night, when the rest were asleep in the apple-tree, he walked softly down the slanting board and ate gravel. The next morning he felt better than he had in a long time, so when there was nobody around he ate some more. He didn't want anyone else to know that he had found out his mistake. Every morning he looked at his shadow, and it grew fatter and fatter. Still he was not happy, and he knew it was because he had not told his patient old mother. He wanted to tell her, too. One day he heard her telling his brother to eat more gravel, and the brother said he didn't like the taste of it. That made him speak at last.

"Suppose you don't like it, you can eat it. Queer world it would be if we didn't have to do unpleasant things. I've just made up my mind that the people who won't do hard things, when they ought to, have the hardest times in the end. Wish I'd minded my mother and eaten gravel when she told me to, and I'm not going to let you be as foolish as I was."

Just then he heard somebody say of him, "What a fine-looking fellow he is growing to be! I like him ever so much now."

It was the Dorking Chicken who had laughed at him. He ran after a Grasshopper, and she ran after the same Grasshopper, and they ran against each other and the Grasshopper got away, so of course they had to wander off together to find something to eat, and after that they became great friends.

The Shanghai Hen looked lovingly after him and raised one foot in the air. "Now," she said, "I am perfectly happy."

The Goose Who Wanted Her Own Way

It would be hard to tell which family is the most important among the farmyard people. There is no one animal so wise as Collie, the farmer's dog, and all the rest love him and mind him when he is sent to bring them up from the pasture or to drive them to the water. Still, he does not spend his days in barn or field and only comes with his master or for a visit now and then.

You may remember how the Garter Snake and the old Tree Frog were the leaders in the meadow, and how in the forest all looked up to the Ground Hog. These people were patient and old, and partly because they were old and had had many years in which to think about life, they were very wise. In the farmyard the Oxen were the most patient and the oldest, and it was to them that all the animals went when they were in trouble.

There were also the Horses, fine strong creatures, always helping somebody else and working all day during most of the year. They drew the reaper through the tall grain, and where in the morning had been a field of waving golden wheat, at sunset were bundles or sheaves of gathered grain, and the stubble was ready for the fowls. They were busy people; and sometimes during the winter they liked to remind their neighbors how much they had done.

Then again, there were the Cows, who are the sisters of the Oxen. They are large and there are many of them, yet they are not so wise, and that is easily understood. All that they have to do on the farm is to give milk for the butter-and cheese-making, and for the farmer's children to drink. No farmer could get along without his Cows, but they do not work like their brothers. They have so easy a time that they do not learn much. You know, when people work, they have to think, and when people think enough useful thoughts it makes them wise. That is one of the many reasons why it is so foolish to be lazy.

Truly, it would be hard to say which farmyard family is the most important, but there is no trouble at all in telling which family think themselves the most so. If you ask any Goose, she will tell you that one of their flock is worth five Horses or a dozen Cows. Nobody else would tell you this, and if you should speak of it to the span of Bays, or the Dappled Gray, or even the youngest Colt in the stable, they would answer you only with a hearty Horse laugh. The Cows would smile and reply, "What a Goose she was to say that!"

There has always been a flock of Geese on the farm, and their neighbors are so used to their queer ways that they only smile when the Geese put on airs, and it is a good-natured smile, too. They even feel rather sorry for them when they lose their feathers, although the Nigh Ox once said that if it were not for being plucked once in a while, the Geese would really be too airy to live with.

Perhaps the Nigh Ox was right in what he said, for certainly after they have worn their feathers all winter, they hold their heads higher than ever, and tell what they think and what they would do, and it is well they should be reminded that they work for a living like all their neighbors. The farmer's wife never plucks the Geese until warm weather comes. Then she takes all the soft, short feathers that they have worn through the winter, and this leaves them looking very ragged indeed. There was a time, years ago, when Geese had to give up their long tail-and wing-feathers to be whittled into pens, but these Geese didn't know about that, and there was nobody in the farmyard old enough to remember it and tell them, so they thought they had a pretty hard time in even giving up their breast feathers.

"Sssss!" the Gander used to say, "if the farmer's boys must have feather pillows on which to lay their heads, why do they not grow their own feathers?"

"Humph!" said the Nigh Ox once; "If you must have oats to eat, why don't you grow the oats?" But the Gander was already waddling away and pretended not to hear him.

It is in the winter that the Geese put on the most airs. Then, when the Horses are being harnessed, they say to each other, "Dear me! Wouldn't it be dreadful to work in that way for a living?" And sometimes, when the team is hitched to a post by the farmhouse, they waddle past in a single line with the Gander at the head, and say to the Horses: "Hear you have to take a load of wood to town. It's too bad. Hope you won't get very tired. We are going to the river for a nice cold swim. Good-bye." Then they march off with their heads held high, and as soon as their backs are turned, the Horses look at each other and laugh softly. They know that there is nothing in the world better than good, honest, hard work, no matter of what kind it is.

Every winter the Geese forget about having to be plucked, and every spring they are surprised to lose their feathers. They are plucked four times before fall comes, and these four times come so near together that even they can remember from one to another. You would think that then they would not be so airy, but instead of saying, "Of course we work for our living—why shouldn't we?" they say, "Why, yes, we do let the farmer's wife have some of our feathers when she wants them. We suppose you might call it work to grow feathers for her, still it does not take much of our time, and it is quite different from drawing loads and getting tired as the Horses and Oxen do. Growing feathers is genteel."

They do not remember anything long, and so, when they have made a mistake once, they are likely to make the same mistake over and over again. Then, too, they cannot tell big things from little things, and they are not happy unless they can have their own way all the time. And you know that nobody can be sure of that. It all comes of their not being willing to think hard, and sometimes it makes them a great deal of trouble, as it did on the day when the Gray Goose would not go through the farmyard gate.

This was soon after the Gander and his wife had hatched their brood of seven Goslings, and they were taking them at once to the brook. It was a happy day for all the flock. The Gander and the Mother Goose were glad because their children were safely out of the shell, and because they would no longer have to sit with cramped legs on the nest. Ganders are good fathers, for they cover the eggs half of the time, while the Mother Goose is resting. The other Geese were not only proud of the Goslings, but they were glad to have the Gander and the Mother Goose free to go around with them again. They had missed them very much.

The gate from the farmyard into the meadow stood wide open, and all the Geese except the Gray one followed the Gander through. The Gray Goose tried to go through a small hole in the fence very near the gate. She squeezed her head into it and stretched her neck on the meadow side of the fence, but she could not get any farther, although she pushed until she was dizzy.

"Wait for me," she cried. "Wait for me-ee!"

"Hurry, then," said the Gander.

"I am hurrying," she cried, and she pushed with all her strength, but since the hole in the fence was so small, she did not get any farther than before.

"Go through the gateway," said the Nigh Ox, who was grazing near by.

"Sssss!" said the Gray Goose stiffly. "I would rather go through here. I have chosen to go this way."

"Oh!" said the Nigh Ox, "excuse me! Do go through there by all means!"

"We are going on," called the Gander; "we would wait, but the Goslings are in a hurry to take their first bath. Come as soon as you can."

The Gray Goose tried harder than ever to go the way that she had chosen, but it only made her so out of breath that she had to lie down and rest. Once she thought she heard somebody laugh, yet when she looked at the Nigh Ox, who was the only person around, he was lying with closed eyes and solemnly chewing his cud, so she decided that she must have been mistaken.

Down by the brook the rest of the flock were cackling merrily, and she could see the seven Goslings swimming with the Geese and the Gander. "Oh," she cried, "how I wish I were with them! I don't see what is the matter with this hole in the fence. The farmer ought to make it bigger."

She pushed and scolded and fussed until her neck was sore and she was too tired to swim if she had a chance, so she sat down to rest. She did remember what the Nigh Ox had said; still, if she couldn't go as she had planned, she wouldn't go at all. She walked into the barn to find a cool and shady place, lowering her head as she stepped over the threshold of the high front door.

"What did you do that for?" twittered a Swallow.

"Because I don't want to hit my head on the top of the doorway;" she replied. "I always do so. All of our flock do so."

"Tittle-ittle-little-ee," laughed the Swallow, as she darted away and alighted on the fence by the Nigh Ox. "Why isn't the Gray Goose in swimming with the rest?" asked she.

"Because she can't push her fat body through that hole in the fence," said the Nigh Ox, switching his tail toward it as he spoke.

"Why doesn't she go through the gateway, then?" asked the Swallow.

"Because she says she would rather go the other way, and that if she can't go that way, she won't go at all."

"And she is missing all that fun?" said the Swallow.

"All of it," answered the Nigh Ox, "but then, you know, she is such a Goose!"

Why The Sheep Ran Away

It was during the hottest summer weather that the wind-storm came. The farmyard people always spoke of it as "the" wind-storm, because not even the Blind Horse, who had lived on the farm longer than any of his neighbors, could remember anything like it. "I recall one time," he said, "when a sweet-apple tree was blown down in the fall. The Hogs found it and ate all the fruit before the farmer knew that it was down. You should have heard them grunt over it. They were afraid the farmer would drive them away before they had eaten it all. Eh, well! They ate all they wanted, but one of the Pigs told me afterward that it made them sick, and that he never wanted to see another sweet apple as long as he lived. That was a hard storm, but not like this, not like this."

It had come in the night when the farmyard people were asleep, and there was much scampering to shelter. The fowls, who were roosting in the old apple-tree, did not have time to oil their feathers and make them water-proof. They just flew off their perches as fast as they could and ran for the open door of the Hen-house. When they were once inside, they ruffled up their feathers and shook themselves to get rid of the rain-drops. Fowls do not like wet weather, and it vexes them very much to be in the rain. Their neighbors know this so well that it has become their custom to say of an angry person that he is "as mad as a wet Hen."

The Cows were in their part of the barn with their necks between the stanchions, so there was nothing for them to do but to keep still and think of those who were out of doors. The Horses were in their comfortable stalls. They had been working hard all day and the farmer had gotten a good supper of oats ready for them in their mangers, so that they could eat quickly and go to sleep, instead of staying awake and walking around to get their own suppers in the pasture.

Out in the meadow the Sheep huddled close together under a low-branching tree, and stood still until the storm passed. They had been so warm that the cool rain made them comfortable, but the wind pushed them and swayed the branches of the trees. The loud thunder made the Lambs jump. They liked the lightning and made a game out of it, each one telling what he had seen by the last flash. The clouds, too, were beautiful, and flew across the sky like great dark birds with downy breasts, dropping now and then shining worms from their beaks.

At last the air became cool and clear, and the clouds flew far away toward the east. Next, the stars peeped out, first one, then two, then six, then twenty, and then so many that you could not have counted them,—more than the leaves on a maple-tree, more than the grass-blades of the meadow. The Sheep ran around a little to shake off the rain-drops and warm themselves, then they huddled down again to sleep.

When the sun arose in the eastern sky, his warm beams fell upon the Sheep and awakened them. "How cool and beautiful a day," they said. "What a morning for a run!"

"I can beat you to the tall grass!" called one little Lamb to the rest, and they all scampered around the field, throwing up their heels for joy. They had been away from their mothers for awhile, and had learned to eat grass instead of milk. They were quite proud of the way in which they broke it off, with quick upward jerks of their heads, and their teeth were growing finely. They did not expect any upper front teeth, for in place of them the Sheep have only a hard pad of flesh.

Soon they came running back to the flock. "There is a Dog over there," they cried, "a strange Dog. He doesn't look like Collie. He is coming this way, and we are afraid."

Their uncle, the Bell-Wether, looked over to where the strange Dog was, then turned quickly and began to run. The bell around his neck clinked at every step. When the other Sheep heard the bell they raised their heads and ran after him, and the Lambs ran after them. The strange Dog did not follow or even bark at them, yet on they went, shaking the shining rain-drops from the grass as they trod upon it. Not one of them was thinking for himself what he really ought to do. The Bell-Wether thought, "I feel like running away from the Dog, and so I will run."

The other Sheep said to themselves, "The Bell-Wether is running and so we will run."

And the Lambs said, "If they are all running we will run."

Along the fence they went, the bell clinking, their hoofs pattering, and not one of them thinking for himself, until they reached a place where the fence was blown over. It was not blown 'way down, but leaned so that it could be jumped. If a single one of the flock, even the youngest Lamb, had said, "Don't jump!" they would have stayed in the pasture; but nobody said it. The Bell-Wether felt like jumping over, so he jumped. Then the Sheep did as the Bell-Wether had done, and the Lambs did as the Sheep had done.

Now they were in the road and the Bell-Wether turned away from the farmhouse and ran on, with the Sheep and the Lambs following. Even now, if anybody had said, "Stop!" they would have stopped, for they knew that they were doing wrong; but nobody said it.

After a while a heavy wagon came rumbling down the road behind them, and the Bell-Wether jumped over a ditch and ran into a hilly field with woodland beyond. Because he went the Sheep did, and because the Sheep went the Lambs did, and nobody said "Stop!" You see, by this time they were very badly frightened, and no wonder. When they saw the strange Dog they were a little scared, for they thought he might chase them. If they had made themselves stay there and act brave they would soon have felt brave. Even if the Dog had been a cruel one, they could have kept him from hurting them, for Sheep have been given very strong, hard foreheads with which to strike, and the Bell-Wether had also long, curled horns with three ridges on the side of each. But it is with Sheep as it is with other people,—if they let themselves be frightened they grow more and more fearful, even when there is no real danger and now all of their trouble came from their not stopping to think what they ought to do.

They hurried up to the highest ground in the field, and when they were there and could go no farther, they stopped and looked at each other. One Lamb said to his mother, "Why did we come here? It isn't nearly so nice as our own meadow."

"Why, I came because the Bell-Wether did," she answered. Then she turned to the Bell-Wether and said, "Why did you bring us here?"

"I didn't bring you here," he replied. "I felt like coming, and I came. I didn't make you follow."

"N-no," answered the Sheep; "but you might have known that if you came the Sheep would come."

"Well," said the Bell-Wether, "you might have known that if you Sheep came the Lambs would, so you'd better not say anything."

"Baa!" cried the Lambs. "We are hot and thirsty and there isn't any water here to drink. We want to go back."

Everybody was out of patience with somebody else, and nobody was comfortable. They did not dare try to go home again, for fear they would have more trouble, so they huddled together on the top of the hill and were very miserable and unhappy. They hadn't any good reason for coming, and they could not even have told why they ran to the hilltop instead of staying in the pleasant hollow below.

There was a reason for their running up, however, although they didn't know it. It was because their great-great-great-great-great-great-grandfather and-grandmother were wild Sheep in the mountains, and when frightened ran up among the rocks where there was nobody to hurt them. They got into the habit of running up-hill when scared, and their children did the same, and their children's children did the same, and now even the farmyard Sheep do so, although they long ago forgot the reason why.

"Bow-wow-wow!" rang out on the still morning air.

"There's Collie!" cried the Lambs joyfully. "He's coming to take us home. Let's bleat to help him find us more quickly." All the Lambs said, "Baa! Baaa!" in their high, soft voices, and their mothers said "Baa! Baaa!" more loudly; and the Bell-Wether added his "Baa! Baaa!" which was so deep and strong that it sounded like a little, very little, clap of thunder.

Collie came frisking along with his tail waving and his eyes gleaming. He started the flock home, and scolded them and made fun of them all the way, but they were now so happy that they didn't care what he said. When they were safely in the home meadow again and the farmer had mended the fence, Collie left them. As he turned to go, he called back one last piece of advice.

"I'm a Shepherd Dog," he said, "and it's my work to take care of Sheep when they can't take care of themselves, but I'd just like to be a Bell-Wether for a little while. You wouldn't catch me doing every foolish thing I felt like doing and getting all the flock into trouble by following me! Nobody can do anything without somebody else doing it too, and I wouldn't lead people into trouble and then say I didn't think. Bow-wow-wow-wow!"

The Bell-Wether grumbled to himself, "Well, the rest needn't tag along unless they want to. Pity if I can't jump a fence without everybody following." But down in his heart he felt mean, for he knew that one who leads should do right things.

The Fine Young Rat And The Trap

The Mice were having a great frolic in the corn-crib. The farmer's man had carelessly left a board leaning up against it in such a way that they could walk right up and through one of the big cracks in the side. It was the first time that some of them had ever been here. When the farmer built the crib, he had put a tin pan, open side down, on top of each of the wooden posts, and had then nailed the floor beams of the crib through these pans. That had kept the hungry Mice from getting into the corn.

This was a great day for them, and their gnawing-teeth would certainly be worn down enough without giving them any extra wear. That, you know, is one thing about which all Rats and Mice have to be very careful, for their front teeth are growing all the time, and they have to gnaw hard things every day to keep them from becoming too long.

There was only one thing that ever really troubled these Mice, and that was the Cat. They did not feel afraid of Hawks and Owls because they lived indoors. Weasels did not often come up to the barn, and men made so much noise when they were around that any wide-awake Mouse could easily keep out of their way. With the Cat it was different. She was always prowling around in the night-time, just when they had their finest parties; and many a young Mouse had been scared away from a midnight supper by seeing her eyes glowing like balls of fire in the darkness. By daylight it was not so bad, for they could see her coming, and besides, she slept much of the time then.

They were talking about her when in the corn-crib. "Have any of you seen the Cat to-day?" asked the Oldest Mouse.

Nobody answered. Then one young fellow, who was always worrying, said: "Supposing she should come out of the barn now! Supposing she should come right toward this corn-crib! Supposing she should stand right under the floor! Supposing she should catch us as we jumped down! Supposing——"

But here the other young Mice all squeaked to him to stop, and one of them declared that it made her fur stand on end to think of it. The Oldest Mouse spoke quite sharply. "Supposing," said he to the first young Mouse, "you should eat more and talk less. There are enough pleasant things to speak about without scaring all your friends in this way."

The young Mouse who said that her fur stood on end couldn't eat anything more, she was so frightened. "What could we do," she said, "if the Cat should come?"

"Stay right where we are," answered her mother. "She couldn't reach us with the door closed. Now go on with your eating and don't be foolish."

A Rat ran up the board. "Good-morning," said he. "Have you heard the news?"

"No, no!" cried the Mice, hurrying to that side of the corn-crib, and peeping through the crack.

"The Yellow Kitten has been hunting with her mother, and they say that her brother is going to-night."

"Well," said a mother Mouse, "I knew we would have to expect it, but I did hope they would wait a while. Now, children," she added, "do be careful! I know that when you are looking for food you have to go into dangerous places, but don't stop there to talk or to clean your fur. Find safe corners for that, or I shall worry about you all the time."

"We will," squeaked all the little Mice together. "We will be very, very careful."

"Thank you for the news," said the Oldest Mouse to the Rat. "We will try to send you word of new dangers when we hear of them."

The Rat, who was a fine young fellow, ran down the board and away. They could not ask him in to lunch, because he was too large and stout to squeeze through the cracks, but he understood how it was, and knew that he could find food elsewhere. Now he ran to the Pig-pen to snatch a share of the breakfast which the farmer had just left there. He often did this as soon as the farmer went away, and the Pigs never troubled him. Perhaps that was because they knew that if they drove him away when he came alone, he would bring all his sisters and his cousins and his aunts, and his brothers and his uncles too, the next time, and would eat every bit of food they had.

After he had taken a hearty breakfast, he ran under the edge of the barn to clean himself. He was always very particular about this. His mother had taught him when very small that he must keep his fur well brushed and his face washed, and he did it just as a Cat would, by wetting his paws and scrubbing his face and the top of his head. He brushed his fur coat with his paws also.

While he was here, one of his cousins came from the barn above. She ran down the inside of the wall, head foremost, and her hind feet were turned around until they pointed backward. That let her hold on with her long, sharp claws, quite as a Squirrel does, and kept her from tumbling. She was much out of breath when she reached the ground, but it was not from running.

"What do you think that farmer has done now?" she cried. "It was bad enough for him to nail tin over the holes we gnawed into his grain-bins, but this is worse still. It needn't make us so much trouble, but it hurts my feelings."

"What is it?" asked her cousin.

"A trap!" said she. "A horrible, shining trap. The Rat from the other farm told me about it. It lies open and flat on the floor of a grain-bin,—the very one you and I gnawed into last night,—and there is a lovely piece of cheese in the middle of it. The Rat who told me about it says that as soon as one touches the cheese, the trap springs shut on him."

"Bah!" exclaimed the young Rat who had just eaten breakfast in the Pig-pen. "Let it stay there! We don't have to touch it, although I do mean to look at it some time. I believe in knowing about things."

"I wish you wouldn't look at it," said his cousin, who was very fond of him.

"The Rat from the other farm says it is very dangerous to even look at traps, especially if your stomach is empty."

"Then the Rat from the other farm might better keep away," said this young fellow, as he put one paw up to see that his whiskers were all right. "I don't think very much of him anyway. He thinks he knows everything because he has travelled.

I wish you would have nothing to do with him. I dare say you were in the grain-bin with him when you saw the trap."

"Yes," said she, "I was."

"Well," said he, "you both got away safely, and I shall too. I may not be very clever, but I think I do know enough to keep out of a trap." Then he turned into his hole and went to sleep. He had been running around all night, and was very tired. He was cross, too. This was the second time that his cousin had told him what the Rat from the other farm had said, and he thought she liked him altogether too well.

When he awakened, it was night again and he was aroused by the stamping of the Dappled Gray on the floor above his head. For a minute he could hardly think where he was. Then it all came to him. He was in his own cozy little hole under the barn, and it was night. He remembered something about the Yellow Kitten. What was it? Oh yes, she had begun hunting. Well, he was not afraid of her yet. But there was something else—the trap! He wondered if his cousin were in that bin again. As like as not her friend, the Rat from the other farm, was showing her the trap now. He would go up there himself, and at once, too.

He ran up the wall, through an opening, and across the barn floor to the grain-bin. It was a moonlight night and the barn was not very dark. The cover of the bin was raised. Perhaps the farmer's man had forgotten to close it. Perhaps there was so little grain left in it that the man didn't care to. At any rate, he could now see the trap quite plainly. There was nobody else in the bin, and he went close to it.

"I would not touch it for anything," said he, as he entered the bin, "but it will not hurt me to look at it."

When he went nearer, he was very careful to see that his tail did not even brush against the chain which held the trap down. "So that is the terrible, dangerous trap?" said he. "It doesn't look particularly dreadful. That is fine-smelling cheese though." He sniffed two or three times. "I have tasted cheese only once in my whole life," said he, "and I am almost starved now. I wouldn't mind a nibble at that." He looked at it and thought about it until it seemed to him he could not go away and leave that cheese there.

Then he thought, "If I am very careful to step over these shining steel things and rest my feet only on the floor, it cannot spring the trap. Then I will snatch the cheese and jump.... I am pretty sure I can do it.... Why, yes, I know I can." So the Rat who had come just to look at the trap, began to lift first one foot and then another over the shining curved bars, and got all ready to catch up the cheese and run.

"Now!" he cried. "One, two, three!" He did snatch it and jump, but the trap jumped, too, in its own trappy way, and the Rat who got the cheese left the three tip rings of his tail to pay for it. "Ouch!" he cried. "My tail! My tail! My beautiful, long, bony tail, all covered with scales and short hair!" He did not care at all for the cheese now. He did not want to see it, for he would rather have had the point on his tail again than to eat a whole binful of cheese.

"How it will look!" said he. "So stumpy and blunt. And it has been so very useful always. I could wind it around a stick to hold myself up when my paws were full, and many a time I have rolled eggs across the floor by curling it around them." Then he heard Rat voices and scampered out and down to his own hole.

His cousin and the Rat from the other farm came into the bin. "Don't look at the trap," he was saying, "but just eat your grain from the farther corner."

"I won't," she answered, and she half closed her eyes to keep from seeing it. He was beside her and they stumbled over the cheese, which now lay on the floor away from the trap. "How does this happen?" said he. "We will eat it first and then find out." By this advice he showed that he was a Rat of excellent sense.

When they had eaten it, they began to look toward the trap. As there was no longer any cheese in it to tempt them, they felt perfectly safe in doing so. They found that it had been sprung, and there lay the last three rings of some Rat's tail.

"How dreadful!" she exclaimed. "I hope that was not lost by any of our friends."

"Hum-hum!" said the Rat from the other farm. "Now, whom have I seen wearing that? I have certainly seen that tail before—it was your cousin!"

"Poor fellow!" said she. "I must go to see him."

"Oh, don't go now," cried the Rat from the other farm. "I think he might want to be alone for a while. Besides," he added coaxingly, "you haven't tasted of the grain yet, and it is very good."

"W-well," answered she, "perhaps my cousin would just as soon not have me come now." So she waited, and the Rat from the other farm told her wonderful stories of his travels, and they had a very fine supper.

When her cousin began to run around again, he was a much sadder and wiser Rat. Sometimes the younger Rats would ask him how he lost the tip of his tail. "By not turning it toward a tempting danger," he would answer, very solemnly. Then, after he had told them the story, he always added, "The time to turn your tail toward a tempting danger is the minute you see it, for if you wait and look and long for something you ought not to take, there is sure to be trouble, and many a Rat has lost more than the tip of his tail in just that way."

The Quick-Tempered Turkey Gobbler

There was only one Gobbler on the farm, and he was so used to having his own way that he never tried to make the best of it when he couldn't, and sometimes he became exceedingly cross. He was bigger than the Cocks, the Hens, the Geese, and the Ducks, so when they were in his way and he gobbled a gruff "Move along," they murmured "Oh, certainly," and scampered away as fast as their legs would carry them. The Peacock was larger than the Turkey Gobbler, it is true, but as long as he could sit on a fence in the sunshine and have somebody admiring his train, he did not care anything about the Gobbler, and they did not get in each other's way.

There were seven Hen Turkeys, timid, sweet-tempered people, who were fond of walking. They had never been known to answer back when the Gobbler scolded them, although at times he was very unreasonable. This was polite of them, but it made the Gobbler more careless than ever of the way in which he spoke. The Black Spanish Hen said it made her wattles tingle to hear him find fault with them. She wouldn't have stood it—no, indeed!

When the Black Spanish Cock heard her say so, he shook his feathers and smiled a queer little smile, and said, "I certainly know that she would not." The other fowls looked at each other, and the Shanghai Cock winked his round little eyes at the Dorking Hen, and she had to oil a feather on the under side of her wing just then, so, of course, nobody saw her laugh—if she did laugh.

The Black Spanish fowls were kind-hearted and honest, and had fine manners, but they would not stand it to be spoken to hastily by any one who was not very much bigger than they, and it was said that the Cock had once—only once—but then, perhaps it would be just as well not to tell what the other fowls had heard about their family quarrel, for, after all, it did not come very straight, the Pigs having told the Geese, and the Geese telling the Ducks, and the Ducks just mentioning it to the Peacock, and the Peacock having spoken of it to the Dorking Hen.

It was now late in the fall, and all the Turkeys went walking together again. One would think that, after being separated from the rest all summer and part of the spring, the Gobbler would have been very polite when he joined them, but no; he was more quick-tempered than ever. He was not fond of young Turkeys, and their constant chattering annoyed him. "Can't you find some way to keep those children quiet?" he would say, and made such a fuss that the Hen Turkeys called them aside and tried to amuse them for a while.

Hen Turkeys are most loving mothers, and in the early spring first one and then another had stolen away to lay and hatch her eggs. If a Hen Turkey wanted a chance to lay an egg at this season, she watched the Gobbler and left the flock when his back was turned. As she came near her nest, she would stop and look around to make sure he did not see where it was. She knew that the Gobbler did not like to have her raise young Turkeys, and that if he could find the nest, he would break every egg in it. After she had laid her egg, she would wander back in a careless way, quite as though she had only been to the watering-trough for a drink.

Once the Hen Turkeys had talked about this when the Gobbler could not hear. "It doesn't seem right not to tell him," the youngest had said.

"Well, my dear," said another, "it is the only way we can do, if we want to save our eggs and raise our children. Gobblers always act in that way."

"Are you sure?" said the young Hen Turkey.

"Sure!" was the answer. "You wouldn't be here to-day if your mother hadn't done as we do."

So the youngest Hen Turkey had changed her mind and hidden her eggs like the rest, for, in spite of aching legs and all that is hard in hatching eggs, Hen Turkeys always want to raise broods in the springtime. When one of them had laid as many eggs as she wanted to hatch, she began sitting on them, and would not walk with the flock at all. One by one the Hen Turkeys had done this until the Gobbler was left quite alone. He did not like it at all, and wanted more than ever to find and break the eggs. When the Turkey Chicks were hatched, their mothers kept them out of the Gobbler's way, because, you know, he did not like small children and it was better that they should not meet.

The Hen Turkeys were very sorry for him, and often wished that he might watch with them the growth of their piping darlings, to see the tiny feathers push their way through the down and broaden and lengthen until there was no down to be seen—only feathers. It was too bad; yet that was the way in all Turkey families, and the Gobblers couldn't help disliking the children any more than the Hen Turkeys could help wanting to sit in the springtime.

By another year the Gobbler would love the young Turkeys dearly. Even now he did not try to strike them, as he might have done a while before. They were afraid of him, yet down in their hearts the brothers all thought that when they were grown up they wanted to be just like him and strut around with their wings trailing, their tails spread, their necks drawn back, and their feathers ruffled. Then, they thought, when other people came near them, they would puff and gobble and cry, "Get out of my way!" They tried it once in a while to see how it would seem, but they were still slender and their voices were not yet deep enough. The sisters laughed at them when they did this, and that made them feel very uncomfortable. The long, limp red wattles that grew out between their eyes became redder and redder as they swung to and fro under their short, thick bills.

"Just wait," said one young fellow to another. "Just you wait until I am really grown up and strut before your sister next spring. I don't think she will laugh at me then." And he comforted himself by eating fully twice as much grain as he should have done.

The farmer's little girl came into the farmyard, and all the fowls stopped eating to look at her. She was so young that she had never before been out there alone. Her father had brought her in his arms, and she had laughed with delight and clapped her little hands when the farmyard people passed by her. Now she had slipped out of the house and stood in the sunshine smiling at every one. She came without a cap, and the wind blew her soft yellow curls around her rosy face. It fluttered her red dress, too, and the Gobbler saw it and became exceedingly angry.

"Red-red-red!" he cried. "Why in the world did she wear red? I hate it!" He stalked toward her in his most disagreeable way, and you could tell by the stiff brushing of his wing-tips on the ground that he was very angry. "Get away from here!" he cried. "This is my home and little girls can't wear red dresses when they visit me. Pffff! Get away!"

The little girl turned to run as the big Gobbler came puffing toward her. In her fright she stumbled and fell, and he hurried forward to strike her. The Black Spanish Cock began to ruffle his neck feathers and stretch his head forward. He did not mean to have their visitor treated so. He ran between the Gobbler's feet and they tumbled over together. The little girl picked herself up and hurried into the house.

If the Gobbler was angry before, he was much more so after his fall. "What do you mean, sir," he said, "by tripping me?"

"And what do you mean," said the Black Spanish Cock, "by knocking me over?"

"Pffff! You were under my feet."

"Erruuuu! You were over my head."

Now nobody had dared to disagree with the Gobbler in so long that he did not know what to make of it, and when the Shanghai Cock strolled over to help his friend, the Gobbler was fairly sputtering with rage. "Ah, Gobbler," said the Shanghai, "wonder what has become of the little girl? It was nice of her to come out here, and I wish she had stayed longer."

"I told her to get away," was the answer. "She had on a red dress. I chased her. I always have chased anybody who wore red, and I always shall. It's my way."

"Is it your way, too, to be cross whenever you feel like it?"

"Of course. I wouldn't be cross when I didn't feel like it," answered the Gobbler.

"Some of us are not cross when we do feel like it," said the Dorking Cock. "I am always happier for keeping my temper when I can."

"Pffff!" said the Gobbler. "That is not my way. I say right out what I think, and then I am all right again and forget all about it."

"Humph!" said the Bantam Hen. "I wonder if the other people forget as soon? It would do him more good to remember it and feel sorry. He needs a lesson." Then she stalked up to him, looking as brave as you please, although she was really quite frightened. "I never noticed it before," she cackled, "but the tuft of hairy feathers on your breast is dreadfully ragged. And what very ugly looking feet you have! If I were going to have any webs between my toes I should want good big ones like those of the Ducks and Geese, not snippy little halfway webs like yours. I hope you don't mind my speaking of it. I always say what I think. It's just my way, and I never remember it afterward." She gave a graceful flutter and a queer little squawk, and was off before the Gobbler got over his surprise.

Fowls do enjoy a joke, and now the Dorking Cock took his turn. "I've always wanted to know how you spread your tail in that fashion. It's a good time to see." He walked up beside the Gobbler and pecked and pulled until three feathers lay on the ground. "Ah," said the Dorking Cock, "I see I loosened some of your tail feathers. I hope you don't mind. It is just my way, when I want to know about anything, to find out as soon as I can."

And so one fowl after another teased and troubled the Gobbler, and explained afterward that "it was just their way." Then they laughed at him and ran off.

It would be nice if one could say that the Gobbler never again lost his temper, but he did, a great many times, for he should have begun to master it when he was a

Chick. But one can tell truly that he never again excused his crossness by saying that "it was only his way." The youngest Duckling in the poultry-yard had always known that this was no excuse at all, and that if people have disagreeable habits which make others unhappy, it is something of which they should be much ashamed.

The Bragging Peacock

The farmyard people will never forget the coming of the Peacock; or rather they will never forget the first day that he spent with them. He came in the evening after all the fowls had gone to roost, and their four-legged friends were dozing comfortably in meadow and pasture corners, so nobody saw him until the next morning.

You can imagine how surprised they were when a beautiful great fowl of greenish-blue strutted across the yard, holding his head well in the air and dragging his splendid train behind him. The fowls were just starting out for their daily walks, and they stopped and held one foot in the air, and stared and stared and stared. They did not mean to be rude, but they were so very much surprised that they did not think what they were doing. Most of them thought they were asleep and dreaming, and the dream was such a beautiful one that they did not want to move and break it off. They had never seen a Peacock and did not even know that there was such a fowl.

A Lamb by the pasture fence called to his mother. "Ba-baa!" cried he. "One of the cloud-birds is walking in the farmyard." He was thinking of the night of the storm, when all the Sheep and Lambs huddled together in the meadow and watched the clouds, and thought that they were birds and dropped shining worms from their beaks.

Then the Peacock, who understood the Sheep language perfectly, said, "Paon! I am no cloud-bird. I am a Peacock." He said this in a very haughty way, as though to be a Peacock were the grandest thing in the world, far better than having one's home in the sky and bringing showers to refresh the thirsty earth-people.

The Turkey Gobbler never could stand it to have others speak in that way when he was around, so he thought he would show the newcomer how important he was. He drew up his neck and puffed out his chest; he pulled his skin muscles by thinking about them, and that made his feathers stand on end; next he dropped his wings until their tips touched the ground; then he slowly spread his tail. "Pffff!" said he. "I am no Peacock. I am a Turkey Gobbler."

The Hen Turkeys looked at each other with much pride. They were a little afraid of him themselves, but they liked to have him show the newcomer that Turkeys are important people. Their children looked at each other and murmured, "Isn't the Gobbler fine though? Guess the Peacock will wish now that he hadn't put on airs."

But the Peacock did not seem to feel at all sorry. He stood and looked at them all without saying a word, and they all wondered what he was thinking. Then a Duckling who stood near him exclaimed, "Look at his train! Oh, look at his train!" Everybody looked and saw all those beautiful long feathers rising into the air. Up and up they went, and spreading as they rose, until there was a wonderful great circle of them back of his body and reaching far above his head. The Gobbler's spread tail looked as small beside this as a Dove's egg would beside that of a Goose.

"Paon!" said the Peacock. "I am no Turkey Gobbler. I am a Peacock."

"Pffff!" said the Gobbler. Then he turned to the Hen Turkeys. "My dears," he said, "I think it is time that we walked along. The children should not be allowed to see and speak with any stray fowl that comes along. We cannot be too particular about that." Then he stalked off, with the meek Hen Turkeys following and the children lagging behind. They did so want to stay and see the Peacock, and they thought the Ducklings and Goslings were much luckier than they.

The Geese were delighted with the newcomer, and hoped he would be quite friendly with them. They wished he were a swimmer, but of course they could tell with one look that he was not. He did not have the trim, boat-shaped body that swimmers have, and then, his feet were not webbed. The Gander noticed that they were remarkably homely feet. He thought he would remember this and speak of it to the Geese some time when they were praising the Peacock's train.

The Drake was the first to speak politely to the Peacock. "We are glad to meet you, sir," he said. "Will you be with us long?"

"Thank you," answered the Peacock. "I have come to stay."

"We hope you will like it here. I'm sorry to see you do not swim. We should be very glad of your company if you did. You will excuse us if we go on to the brook. We are late already." He and all of his family waddled away to the water. "A fine-looking fellow," said he heartily. "Even my cousins, the Mallard Ducks, have not such a beautiful sheen on their neck feathers." The Drake was a kind, warm-hearted fellow, and it never troubled him to know that other people were handsomer than he.

The Geese were eager to reach the water, too, but they could not leave without asking one question. First they told the Gander to ask it, but he replied that if they wanted to know, they should ask it for themselves. Then they hung back and said to each other, "You ask him. I can't." At last the Gray Goose stepped forward, saying, "Excuse us, sir. You said that you were to stay with us, and we wish to know if you work for your living."

"I work!" cried he. "Paon! Never. The farmer invited me here to be beautiful, that is all."

"We are so glad," cackled the Geese, and the Gander joined with them. "So many of the people here work. They are very good, but not at all genteel, you understand."

"And don't you do anything?" asked the Peacock. "I thought Geese grew feathers for beds and pillows. It seems to me you look rather ragged. Haven't you been plucked?"

This was very embarrassing to the Geese. "Why, yes," they said, "we do let the farmer's wife have some feathers once in a while, when the weather is warm, but that is very different from really working, you know."

"Perhaps," said the Peacock. "If they want any of my feathers, they can wait until I moult. Then you will see how much they think of me, for whenever they find one of my train feathers (not tail, if you please; every bird has a tail, but I have a train) they carry it carefully into the house to be made into a duster for the parlor. I never give away any but my cast-off plumage. I am so very, very beautiful that I do not have to work."

This impressed the Geese very much. "We are glad to know you. Quite honored, we assure you!"

The Peacock bowed his crested head, and they bowed their uncrested and very silly ones, and then they went to the river. The Peacock thought them most agreeable, because they admired him, and they thought him the best sort of acquaintance, because he didn't work. It was all very foolish, but there are always foolish people in the world, you know, and it is much better to be amused by it and a little sorry for them, than for us to lose our tempers and become cross about it. That was the way the Shanghais, Black Spanish, Dorking, and Bantam fowls felt. They were polite enough to the newcomer, but they did not run after him. The Chickens used to laugh when the Peacock uttered his cry of "Paon! Paon!" His voice was harsh and disagreeable, and it did seem so funny to hear such dreadful sounds coming from such a lovely throat.

The Black Spanish Cock reproved the Chickens sharply for this. "It is very rude," said he, "to laugh at people for things they cannot help. How would you like to have a Lamb follow you around and bleat, 'Look at that Chicken! He has only two legs! Hello, little two-legs; how can you walk?' It is just as bad for you to laugh at his harsh voice, because he cannot help it. If he should say foolish and silly things, you might laugh, because he could help that if he tried. Don't ever again let me hear you laughing when he is just saying 'Paon.'"

The Chickens minded the Black Spanish Cock, for they knew he was right and that he did not do rude things himself. They remembered everything he said, too.

One day the Peacock was standing on the fence alone. He did this most of the time. He usually stood with his back to the farmyard, so that people who passed could see his train but not his feet. A party of young fowls of all families came along. Their mothers had let them go off by themselves, and they stopped to look at the Peacock.

"I do think you have the most beautiful tail, sir," said a Duckling, giving her own little pointed one a sideways shake as she spoke.

"Please call it my train," said the Peacock. "It is beautiful and I am very proud of it. Not every fowl can grow such a train as that."

"Oh, dear, no!" giggled a jolly little Bantam Chicken. "I'd grow one in a minute if I could."

This made all the other young fowls laugh, for they thought how funny the little brown Bantam would look dragging around a great mass of feathers like that.

The Peacock did not even smile. He never understood a joke anyway. He was always so busy thinking about himself that he couldn't see the point. Now he cleared his throat and spoke to the Bantam Chicken.

"I hope you don't think that I grew my train in a minute," said he. "It took me a long, long time, although I kept all the feathers going at once."

"Look at his crest!" exclaimed one young Turkey in his piping voice.

The Peacock turned his head so that they could see it more plainly. "That is a crest to be proud of," he said. "I have never seen a finer one myself. Have you noticed the beauty of my neck?"

"Charming!" "Wonderful!" "Beautiful!" exclaimed the young fowls. Just then one of the spoiled Dove children flew down from the barn roof and sat beside the Peacock.

"What homely feet you have!" this Squab exclaimed. "Are you not dreadfully ashamed of them?"

The young fowls thought this rude. Not one of them would have said it. The Peacock became very angry. "I know my feet are not so handsome as they might be," he said, "but that is no reason why I should be ashamed of them. I couldn't help having that kind of feet. They run in my family. I don't feel ashamed of things I can't help."

The young fowls felt so uncomfortable after this that they walked away, and the Squab flew back to the Dove-cote. For a time nobody spoke. Then a Gosling, who had heard her mother talk about the Peacock, said, "I should think he would be proud of his train, and his crest, and his neck, and—and everything!"

"Everything except his feet," giggled the Bantam Chicken, "and you know he couldn't help having them."

"I wonder if he could help having his train, and his crest, and his neck, and—and everything?" said a young Turkey.

They all stopped where they were. "We never thought of that!" they cried. "We never thought of that!"

"Let's go and ask the Blind Horse," said a Duckling. "He is a good friend of mine, and he knows almost everything."

They stalked and waddled over to the Blind Horse, and the Duckling told him what was puzzling them. The Blind Horse laughed very heartily. "So the Peacock is proud of having grown such a fine train and crest, but he isn't ashamed of his homely feet, because he couldn't help having those! There is no reason for either pride or shame with the Peacock. He has just such a body as was given him, and he couldn't make one feather grow differently if he tried."

"I don't see what anybody can be proud of, then," said a Gosling sadly; for, you see, she wanted to be proud of something.

"Be proud of what you have done yourself," said the Blind Horse gently. "Be proud of keeping clean, or of telling the truth, or of speaking pleasantly when things go wrong. There are plenty of chances to be proud in a good way, if one must be proud."

The Discontented Guinea Hen

"Well," said the Gobbler, "I should like to know what next! Last spring it was the White Pig, when we had never had any but black and brown ones on the place. Next it was Ducks, because one of the farmer's boys wanted them. Then it was the Peacock, to please the farmer's wife. Now it is Guinea Fowls for the farmer's other son. Society isn't what it used to be here, and while some of the new people may be very pleasant, I must say that I preferred the good old quiet days."

"I think it is lovely," cackled the cheerful little Bantam Hen. "One hears so much of the world outside, and for people like myself, who stay at home, that is a good thing. Everybody loved the White Pig before she had been here two days, and my children are very fond of the Ducklings. I like to have them together, too, for after I had told them positively that my Chickens could not go in swimming, they stopped teasing and became most delightful playmates."

"What would you say about the Peacock?" asked the Shanghai Cock, who had never been friendly with him, although, to tell the truth, the Shanghai Cock was not so grumpy as he used to be.

"Er—er—well," said the Bantam Hen, who tried not to say unpleasant things about people unless she really had to, "he—he is certainly beautiful, although I can't say that I am fond of hearing him sing."

This made all the fowls laugh, even the Gobbler looking a little smiling around the beak on the side where his hanging wattle did not hide his face. When the Hen Turkeys on the smiling side saw that he was pleased, they began to smile too; and then the Hen Turkeys on the other side, who hadn't been sure that it was safe for them to do so, smiled also. And it did them all a great deal of good.

"I didn't see the Guinea Fowls," said one of the Geese. "We were swimming when they came. How do they look? Are they handsomely dressed? We shall not call upon them unless they are our kind of people." It was some time since their last plucking for the season, and the Geese were growing more airy every day now.

"They are really very peculiar," said the Black Spanish Hen, "and not at all common-looking. I should call them decidedly genteel." Here the Geese looked at each other and nodded. They were always talking about being genteel, although if you had asked them, they might not have been able to tell what they meant by the word. "They are shaped quite like small Hen Turkeys," added the Black Spanish Hen "and their feathers are a dark bluish-gray with round white spots all over them. They do not wear any feathers on top of their heads. When I saw the first one, I thought she must have lost hers in an accident, but after the others came up, I knew it must be the custom in their family."

"And they are shaped like us?" asked the Hen Turkeys all together. They were thinking that perhaps the Black Spanish Hen would call them genteel-looking also, but she didn't.

"Very much like you," she replied. "In fact, I think they said something about being related to your family, although I am not sure. Do you remember, dear?" she said, turning to the Black Spanish Cock.

"Certainly," he answered. "The Guinea Hen with the orange-colored legs said that their family was related to both the Turkeys and the Peacocks, and that they were pleased to see members of those families here."

"Gobble-gobble-gobble," called the Gobbler to the Hen Turkeys. "You must call upon our relatives as soon as you can. I will go later. I always wait to find out more about strangers before calling. It is my way." He didn't stop to think that if everybody waited as long as he did, the strangers would be very lonely.

After this, they scattered to feed, and the Hen Turkeys and their children looked for the Guinea Fowls. "Listen," said one, "and we may hear them talking to each other." They stood still, with their heads well up and turned a little to one side. They heard a harsh voice saying, "Ca-mac! Ca-mac!" and as none of their old friends ever said "Ca-mac!" they knew at once that it was one of the newcomers. They walked around the corner of the Sheep-shed, and there found them, a Guinea Cock and two Guinea Hens. One of the Guinea Hens had orange-colored legs, while the others had dark grayish-brown ones.

"Good-morning," said the Hen Turkeys. "Are you the Guinea Fowls?"

"We are," said the one with the bright-colored legs, "and you are the Turkeys, are you not?"

"We are the Hen Turkeys," said they, "and these are our children. The Gobbler didn't feel that he could come with us this morning, but he will come later. He got very tired in Grasshopper season and is hardly over it yet."

"That is too bad," said the Guinea Cock politely. "We hope he will soon be better. It is a hard time for all Turkeys—so much running to and fro, besides the stretching of the neck whenever a Grasshopper comes near."

"Perhaps he overate somewhat," said one of the Hen Turkeys. "We were quite worried about him for a time. He slept so poorly and dreamed that he was being chased. He always has a good appetite, and you know how it is when there is so much food around. One cannot let it alone."

So they chatted on about one thing and another, and walked as they visited. The Guinea Fowls were more fussy and restless than the Turkeys, and even when they were speaking would run after some dainty bit of food that had just caught their eyes. Of course the Hen Turkeys said how glad they were to have the Guinea Fowls come there to live, and hoped that they would enjoy their new home. All of the farmyard people thought it a most delightful place.

"Oh, yes," cried the Guinea Hen with the bright-colored legs, "it is very pleasant, of course, but I wish you could see the farm we left."

"Why! Was it better than this?" asked the Turkey Chicks, crowding around her. They were so surprised that they forgot their mothers' telling them that if they came they must be very quiet, and making them all repeat together, "Little Turkeys should be seen and not heard."

"Better? My dears, it was not to be spoken of in the same breath. I understand that when one has always lived here, this may seem very nice, but when one has known better things, it is hard to be contented."

"Still, we shall be very happy here, I am sure," said the other Guinea Hen, the one with the brown legs. "People all seem so bright and pleasant. I like it very much indeed."

"We are glad of that," said the Turkeys all together. "We really must be going. We fear we have stayed too long already. The Gobbler will wonder if we are never coming back. Good-morning."

As they walked off to look for him, one Hen Turkey said to another, "It must be hard to come here after living on that farm."

"Yes," was the answer, "I suppose that we don't really know what comfort is here."

When the Gobbler asked them about the Guinea Fowls, and how they were enjoying their new home, the Hen Turkeys sighed and answered, "Oh, as well as they can enjoy this farm, we suppose." The Gobbler was a little surprised by this reply, but he said nothing, and as he pecked at the corn which had just been spilled from the load the Oxen were drawing, he thought, "I wish we could have better corn to eat. This does not taste quite as it should."

When the Geese met the Guinea Fowls, they began to speak of the pleasure of living on such a fine farm. "Ah," said the Guinea Hen with the bright-colored legs, "how I wish you might see the one we left when we came here. It was so different."

The other Guinea Fowls looked uncomfortable when she spoke in this way, and stood first on one foot and then on the other. Then the Cock said something about the sunshiny fall weather, and the good neighbors, and—and——

The Gander spoke again of the farm. "It is not all that we could wish," said he; "still there are some good things about it. There are several swimming places which are fine and cold in winter."

"If it were only better cared for," said the Gray Goose. "I had a dreadful time a while ago, when I tried to get through a hole in the fence. I don't remember what was the matter with the hole, and perhaps I never knew, but the farmer should have such things fixed. My neck was lame for days afterward, and he was wholly to blame."

After this, the Geese found fault with almost everything, and when there was no one thing to grumble about, they sighed because, "It was so different from what it might be." It was not long before even the spring Chickens, the Goslings, and the Ducklings were speaking in the same way, and the poultry-yard was a most doleful place. The Bantam Hen was the only really cheerful fowl there, and she got so tired of hearing the rest sigh and grumble, that she often slipped between the pickets of the fence and went to have a comfortable chat with the Oxen.

One day she fluttered toward them in a most excited manner. "Do I look nearly crazy?" said she. "I feel so. Ever since our last storm, the Guinea Fowls have been shut in with us, and I would give half of my tail-feathers if they had never come here. That one with the orange-colored legs can't see good in anything, and all of our steady, sensible fowls have heard it until they begin to believe that this farm is a wretched place."

"What do they do?" asked the Nigh Ox, who always enjoyed hearing the Bantam Hen talk.

"Do?" said she, shaking her dainty little head. "They don't do much of anything. That is what is the matter, and the young fowls are the worst of all. You know how it used to be at feeding time? We all fluttered and squabbled for the first chance at the food. Some Hen got the biggest piece, and then the rest would chase her from one corner to another, and not give her a chance to break and swallow any of it until she would share with them. It was great fun, and we never left a scrap uneaten. Now, what do you think?"

"Can't imagine," exclaimed the Oxen in one breath.

"Well, they all stand around on one foot for a while, and I am the only one eating. Then somebody says, 'I wonder if this is any better than the last we had.' Another will groan, 'Oh, is it time to eat again?' or, 'Suppose I must eat something to keep up my strength.' Then I hear the bright-legged Guinea Hen say, 'Ca-mac! Ca-mac! This is all so different, so very different from what I have been used to.' The Cock and the other Hen of that family are nice enough if you only get them away from her."

"What nonsense!" exclaimed the Oxen together, and they spoke quite sharply for them.

"I wish," said the Bantam Hen very slowly, and as though she meant every word—"I wish the bright-legged one were back where it was 'so different.' Perhaps then my friends would begin to act like themselves."

"Where did she come from?" asked the Off Ox. "It seems to me that I saw a bright-legged Guinea Hen somewhere not long ago." He thought very hard, so hard that he swallowed his cud without knowing he did so.

"Wasn't it at the place where we took that load of stone the other day?" asked the Nigh Ox, trying to help his brother. He knew how disagreeable it is not to be able to recall anything of that sort.

"It was," cried the Off Ox; "and a very poor farm it is. It was the same Hen too. Talk about its being different! I should say it was different from this place, but there are a good many ways of being different. Um-hum! I think I will talk with the discontented Guinea Hen before long, and I want you to see that the other fowls are listening when I do."

Although he would say nothing more, the Bantam Hen saw from the look in his eyes that he meant to stop the Guinea Hen's complaining, so she went away feeling happier. Then the Off Ox unswallowed his cud and began to chew it as though nothing had happened. His brother heard him chuckle once in a while, and say, "Different!" under his breath.

When the Off Ox awakened from time to time during that night and heard the Guinea Hens talking in the dark, he chuckled again to himself. The Guinea Cock was a sound sleeper, but the Hens always talked a great deal between sunset and sunrise, and especially if it were about to rain. Other people thought that they might talk more in the daytime and then keep quiet when their neighbors wanted to sleep. They declared that they always remembered so many things to say as soon as they went to roost, and that if they waited until morning they might forget more than half.

The very next day, the Off Ox had the chance he wanted. He and his brother were yoked to the stone-boat and left standing by the poultry-yard. "Good-afternoon," said he. "Is the bright-legged Guinea Hen here?"

"I am," she answered, coming close to the pickets.

"We are just going over to your old home," said he, "with this load of stone. Have you any messages to send to your friends?"

The Guinea Hen looked rather uncomfortable, and stood first on one foot and then the other. "Tell them I am well," said she.

"I will," said the Off Ox, in his hearty way. "I will try to tell them all. I think I can, too, for there did not seem to be many people in that farmyard. I didn't see Ducks or Geese at all. Are there any living there?"

"No," said the Guinea Hen. She did not seem to think of anything else to say, although nobody spoke for a long time.

"Of course not!" exclaimed the Off Ox. "How stupid of me to ask. There is no brook or river on that farm."

Still the Guinea Hen said nothing.

"We are dragging stone for their new barn," said the Off Ox. "Or perhaps I should say for their barn. One could hardly say that they have any yet, although I suppose they use those loosely built sheds for barns. I wonder people can spend a winter where there are such drafts; still, home is always home, and people love it for that reason. We are glad to have your family with us, not only to keep away the Crows (which was part of the Guinea Fowls' work), but because you will be more comfortable. I've never yet in all my travels seen so good a farm as this, and the one you left was so different! Good-bye."

There was not much talking in the poultry-yard the rest of the afternoon, although most of the fowls looked happier than they had for many days. When supper-time came, the Dorking Hen snatched the biggest pieces of food, and the others chased her from corner to corner in quite the old way. Every scrap was eaten, and nobody laughed when the Shanghai Cock said that the fine weather had given him a better appetite. It was really a dark and chilly day, but they had stopped thinking how much better off they would be if they only lived somewhere else. As soon as they stopped thinking that, they could see how well they were cared for at home. And so, although nobody had really looked at the sky or thought about the weather, everybody had a feeling that the sun must have been shining.

Perhaps the Guinea Cock and the other Guinea Hen were the happiest of all, for they had not known what to do or say when the bright-legged one talked about her old home. It all seemed like a joke now, yet she never liked the Off Ox after that day. The other fowls were as nice to her as ever, for they knew it was a sad thing to be so discontented, and they knew, also, that if they had not been foolish enough to let her, she could never have made them unhappy.

The Oxen Talk With The Calves

It was a clear, cold winter morning, and the Cattle stood in the barnyard where the great yellow straw-stacks were. They had nibbled away at the lower part of these stacks until there was a sheltered place underneath. The Calves liked to stand on the sunshiny side with an over-hanging ledge of straw above their heads. The wind did not strike them here, and they could reach up and pull out wisps to eat when they had nothing else to do. Not that they were so fond of eating straw, but it was fun to pull it out. There was, however, usually something else to be done, for there was always their cud to chew.

Among all the farmyard people, there were none more particular about their food. They might eat in a hurry when time was short, or when the grass was fresh and green, but after they had swallowed it and filled the first of their four stomachs with partly chewed food, they would find some quiet and comfortable place where they could stand or lie easily and finish their eating. To do this, they had to bring the partly chewed food from the first stomach to the mouth again. They called this "unswallowing it," although they should have said "regurgitating."

After the food was back in their mouths again, it was spoken of as their cud, and the stout muscles in the sides of their faces pulled their lower jaws up and down and sideways, and the food was caught over and over again between the blunt grinding teeth in the back part of their mouths, and was crushed, squeezed, and turned until it was fine, soft, and ready to swallow into the second stomach.

Then the Cattle do not have to think of it again, but while they are doing something quite different, and perhaps forgetting all about it, there are many nerves and muscles and fine red blood-drops as busy as can be, passing it into the third and fourth stomachs, and changing the strength of the food into the strength of the Cattle. The Cows and the Oxen do not know this. They never heard of muscles and nerves, and perhaps you never did before, yet these are wonderful little helpers and good friends if one is kind to them. All that Cattle know about eating is that they must have clean food, that they must eat because they are hungry and not just because it tastes good, and that they must chew it very carefully. And if they do these things as they should, they are quite sure to be well and comfortable.

The Oxen were standing by the barn door, and the Calves were talking about them. They liked their uncles, the Oxen, very much, but like many other Calves the world over, they thought them rather slow and old-fashioned. Now the Colts had been saying the same thing, and so these half-dozen shaggy youngsters, who hadn't a sign of a horn, were telling what they would do if they were Oxen. Sometimes they spoke more loudly than they meant to, and the Oxen heard them, but they did not know this.

"If I were an Ox," said one, "I wouldn't stand still and let the farmer put that heavy yoke on my neck. I'd edge away and kick."

"Tell you what I'd do," said another. "I'd stand right still when he tried to make me go, and I wouldn't stir until I got ready."

"I wouldn't do that," said a third. "I'd run away and upset the stone in a ditch. I don't think it's fair to always make them pull the heavy loads while the Horses have all the fun of taking the farmer to town and drawing the binder and all the other wonderful machines."

"Isn't it too bad that you are not Oxen?" said a deep voice behind them. The Calves jumped, and there was the Off Ox close to them. He was so near that you could not have set a Chicken coop between him and them, and he had heard every word. The Calves did not know where to look or what to say, for they had not been speaking very politely. The one who had just spoken wanted to act easy and as though he did not care, so he raised one hind hoof to scratch his ear, and gave his brushy tail a toss over one flank. "Oh, I don't know," said he.

"I used to talk in just that way when I was a Calf," said the Off Ox, with a twinkle in his large brown eyes. "All Calves think they'll do wonders when they're grown."

"I know I thought so," said the Nigh Ox, who had followed his brother.

"Well, if you wanted to," asked the Red Calf, "why don't you do those things now?" The others wondered how he dared to ask such a question.

"It doesn't pay," said the Nigh Ox. "Do all your frisking in playtime. I like fun as well as anybody, yet when our yoke is taken from its peg, I say business is business and the closer we stick to it the better. I knew a sitting Hen once who wanted to see everything that happened. She was always running out to see somebody or other, and sometimes she stayed longer than she meant to. I told her she'd better stick to her nest, and she said she didn't believe in working all the time."

"How soon did her Chickens hatch?" asked the Calves all together.

"Never did hatch, of course," chuckled the Nigh Ox. "She fooled herself into thinking she was working, and she made a great fuss about her legs aching and her giving up society, but she couldn't fool that nestful of eggs. They had gotten cold and they knew it, and not one of them would hatch."

"Wasn't she ashamed then?" asked the Calves.

"Didn't act so," snorted the Nigh Ox. "Went around talking about her great disappointment, and said she couldn't see why the other Hens had so much better luck."

The Off Ox chuckled. "He told her that he guessed it might have been something besides bad luck, and that the next time she'd better stay on her nest more. Then she asked him how many broods of Chickens he had hatched. Ho-ho-ho!"

Everybody laughed, and the Calves wondered how the Nigh Ox could think of it without being angry. "It wouldn't pay to be angry," he said. "What's the use of wasting a fine great Ox temper on a poor little Hen rudeness?"

This made them think. They remembered how cross and hot and uncomfortable they often became over very small things that bothered them, and they began to think that perhaps even Calf tempers were worth caring for.

At last the Black Calf, the prettiest one in the yard, said, "Do you like drawing that flat wagon which hasn't any wheels, and scrapes along in the dust?"

"The stone-boat?" asked the Off Ox. "We don't mind it. Never mind doing our kind of work. Wouldn't like to pull the binder with its shining knives and whirling arms, for whoever does that has to walk fast and make sudden turns and stops.

Wouldn't like being hitched to the carriage to carry the farmer's family to town. Wouldn't like to take care of the Sheep, like Collie, or to grow feathers like the Geese—but we can draw stone-boats and all sorts of heavy loads, if we do say it."

The Red Calf, who was always running and kicking up his heels, said, "Oh, it's such slow work! I should think you'd feel that you would never reach the end of your journey."

"We don't think about that," answered the Nigh Ox. "It doesn't pay. We used to, though. I remember the time when I wished myself a Swallow, flying a mile a minute, instead of step-step-stepping my way through life. My mother was a sensible Cow, and wore the bell in our herd. She cured me of that foolishness. She told me that Swallows had to fly one wing-beat at a time, and that dinners had to be eaten one mouthful at a time, and that nothing really worth while could be done in a minute. She said that if we were forever thinking how much work we had to do and how tiresome it was, we'd never enjoy life, and we wouldn't live long either. Lazy Oxen never do. That's another thing which doesn't pay."

The Red Calf and the White Calf spoke together: "We will always be sensible. We will never lose our tempers. We will never be afraid to work. We will be fine and long-lived cattle."

"Might you not better say you will *try* to be sensible?" asked the Nigh Ox. "You know it is not always easy to do those things, and one has to begin over and over again."

"Oh, no," they answered. "We know what we can do."

"You might be mistaken," said the Oxen gently.

"I am never mistaken," said the Red Calf.

"Neither am I," said the White Calf.

"Well, good-morning," called the Oxen, as they moved off. "We are going to talk with our sisters, the Cows."

After they had gone, the pretty Black Calf spoke in her pleasant way: "It seems to me I shall be an old Cow before I can learn to be good and sensible like them, but I am going to try."

"Pooh!" said the Red Calf. "It is easy enough to be sensible if you want to be—as easy as eating."

"Yes," said the White Calf. "I shall never lose my temper again, now that I am sure it is foolish to do so."

"Dear me!" said the pretty Black Calf. "How strong and good you must be. I can only keep on trying."

"Pooh!" said the Red Calf again. Then he lowered his voice and spoke to her. "Move along," said he, "and let me stand beside you in the cubby while I chew my cud."

"Don't you do it," cried the White Calf. "I want that place myself."

"I guess not!" exclaimed the Red Calf. "I'll bunt you first."

"Bunt away, then," said the White Calf, "but I'll have that place."

"Oh, please don't fight!" exclaimed the Black Calf. "I'll let one of you have my corner."

"Don't you move," cried each of them. "I want to stand by you." Then they lowered their heads and looked into each other's eyes. Next, they put their hard foreheads together, and pushed and pushed and pushed. Sometimes the Red Calf made the White Calf go backward, and sometimes it was the other way. Once in a while they stood still and rested. Then they began pushing again.

While they were quarrelling in this way, getting warmer and more angry all the time, and losing those very tempers which they had said they would always keep, a young Jersey had stepped into the cubby beside the Black Calf, and they were having a pleasant visit. "What are those fellows fighting about?" he asked.

The Black Calf smiled a funny little smile. "They are fighting," said she, "to see which one shall stand in the cubby with me and chew his cud."

The Jersey Calf was a shrewd young fellow of very good family. "Perhaps," said he, "I ought to stay and guard the place until it is decided who shall have it."

"I wish you would," said she.

And that was how it happened that the two Calves who lost their tempers had a cross, tiresome, and uncomfortable day, while another had the very corner which they wanted. When night came, they grumbled because the Jersey Calf had come out ahead of them, and they thought it very strange. But it was not strange, for the people who are quiet and good-natured always come out ahead in the end. And the people who are so very sure that it is easy to be good when they really want to, are just the very ones who sometimes do not want to when they should.

The Black Calf was right. The only way to be sensible and happy is to try and try and try, and it does pay.

Among the Forest People

Mr. Red Squirrel Comes To Live In The Forest

Life in the forest is very different from life in the meadow, and the forest people have many ways of doing which are not known in the world outside. They are a quiet people and do not often talk or sing when there are strangers near. You could never get acquainted with them until you had learned to be quiet also, and to walk through the underbrush without snapping twigs at every step. Then, if you were to live among them and speak their language, you would find that there are many things about which it is not polite to talk. And there is a reason for all this.

In the meadow, although they have their quarrels and their own troubles, they always make it up again and are friendly, but in the forest there are some people who can never get along well together, and who do not go to the same parties or call upon each other. It is not because they are cross, or selfish, or bad. It is just because of the way in which they have to live and hunt, and they cannot help it any more than you could help having eyes of a certain color.

These are things which are all understood in the forest, and the people there are careful what they say and do, so they get on very well indeed, and have many happy times in that quiet, dusky place. When people are born there, they learn these things without thinking about it, but when they come there from some other place it is very hard, for everybody thinks it stupid in strangers to ask about such simple matters.

When Mr. Red Squirrel first came to the forest, he knew nothing of the way in which they do, and he afterward said that learning forest manners was even harder than running away from his old home. You see, Mr. Red Squirrel was born in the forest, but was carried away from there when he was only a baby. From that time until he was grown, he had never set claw upon a tree, and all he could see of the world he had seen by peeping through the bars of a cage. His cousins in the forest learned to frisk along the fence-tops and to jump from one swaying branch to another, but when this poor little fellow longed for a scamper he could only run around and around in a wire wheel that hummed as it turned, and this made him very dizzy.

He used to wonder if there were nothing better in life, for he had been taken from his woodland home when he was too young to remember about it. One day he saw another Squirrel outside, a dainty little one who looked as though she had never a sad thought. That made him care more than ever to be free, and when he curled down in his cotton nest that night he dreamed about her, and that they were eating acorns together in a tall oak tree.

The next day Mr. Red Squirrel pretended to be sick. He would not run in the wheel or taste the food in his cage. When his master came to look at him, he moaned pitifully and would not move one leg. His master thought that the leg was broken, and took limp little Mr. Red Squirrel in his hand to the window to see what was the matter. The window was up, and when he saw his chance, Mr. Red Squirrel leaped into the open air and was away to the forest. His poor legs were weak from living in such a small cage, but how he ran! His heart thumped wildly under the soft fur of his chest, and his breath came in quick gasps, and still he ran, leaping, scrambling, and sometimes falling, but always nearer the great green trees of his birthplace.

At last he was safe and sat trembling on the lowest branch of a beech-tree. The forest was a new world to him and he asked many questions of a fat, old Gray Squirrel. The Gray Squirrel was one of those people who know a great deal and think that they know a great, great deal, and want others to think so too. He was so very knowing and important that, although he answered all of Mr. Red Squirrel's questions, he really did not tell him any of the things which he most wanted to know, and this is the way in which they talked:

"What is the name of this place?" asked Mr. Red Squirrel.

"This? Why this is the forest, of course," answered the Gray Squirrel. "We have no other name for it. It is possible that there are other forests in the world, but they cannot be so fine as this, so we call ours 'the forest.'"

"Are there pleasant neighbors here?" asked Mr. Red Squirrel.

"Very good, very good. My wife and I do not call on many of them, but still they are good enough people, I think."

"Then why don't you call?"

"Why? Why? Because they are not in our set. It would never do." And the Gray Squirrel sat up very straight indeed.

"Who is that gliding fellow on the ground below?" asked the newcomer. "Is he one of your friends?"

"That? That is the Rattlesnake. We never speak to each other. There has always been trouble between our families."

"Who lives in that hollow tree yonder?"

"Sh, sh! That is where the Great Horned Owl has his home. He is asleep now and must not be awakened, for Squirrels and Owls cannot be friendly."

"Why not?"

"Because. It has always been so."

"And who is that bird just laying an egg in her nest above us?"

"Speak softly, please. That is the Cowbird, and it is not her nest. You will get into trouble if you talk such things aloud. She can't help it. She has to lay her eggs in other birds' nests, but they don't like it."

Mr. Red Squirrel tried very hard to find out the reason for this, but there are always some things for which no reason can be given; and there are many questions which can never be answered, even if one were to ask, "Why? why? why?" all day long. So Mr. Red Squirrel, being a wise little fellow, stopped asking, and thought by using his eyes and ears he would in time learn all that he needed to know. He had good eyes and keen ears, and he learned very fast without making many mistakes. He had a very happy life among the forest people, and perhaps that was one reason. He learned not to say things which made his friends feel badly, and he did not ask needless questions. And after all, you know, it would have been very foolish to ask questions which nobody could answer, and worse than foolish to ask about matters which he could find out for himself.

It is in the forest as in the world outside. We can know that many things are, but we never know why they are.

Why Mr. Great Horned Owl Hatched The Eggs

If the Rattlesnake is the king of the forest in the daytime, the Great Horned Owl is the king at night. Indeed, he is much the more powerful of the two, for he is king of air and earth alike and can go wherever he wishes, while the snake can only rule over those who live near the ground or who are so careless as to come to him there.

There was but one pair of Great Horned Owls in the forest, and they lived in the deepest shade, having their great clumsy nest in the hollow of a tall tree. You might have walked past it a hundred times and never have guessed that any Owls lived there, if you did not notice the round pellets of bone and hair on the grass. They are such hungry fellows that they swallow their food with the bones in it. Then their tough little stomachs go to work, rolling all the pieces of bone and hair into balls and sending them back to be cast out of the Owls' mouths to the ground.

The Great Horned Owl was a very large bird. His whole body was covered with brown, dull yellow, and white feathers. Even his feet and legs were covered, and all that you could see besides were his black claws and his black hooked bill. Yes, at night you could see his eyes, too, and they were wonderful great eyes that could see in the dark, but they were shut in the daytime when he was resting. His wife, who was the queen of the forest at night, looked exactly like him, only she was larger than he. And that is the way among Owls,—the wife is always larger than her husband.

Every night when the sun had gone down, the Great Horned Owl and his wife would come out of their hollow tree and sit blinking on a branch near by, waiting until it got dark enough for them to see quite plainly. As the light faded, the little black spots in their eyes would grow bigger and bigger, and then off they would go on their great soft, noiseless wings, hunting in the grass and among the branches for the supper which they called breakfast.

Mrs. Owl could not be gone very long at a time, for there were two large round white eggs in the nest which must not get cold. Her husband was on the wing most of the night, and he often flew home with some tender morsel for her. He was really a kind-hearted fellow, although you could never have made the small birds think so. Sometimes his wife would sigh and tell how tired she was of sitting still, and how glad she would be when the eggs were hatched and she could go more with him. When she began to speak of that, the Great Horned Owl would get ready for another flight and go off saying: "It is *too* bad. I am *so* sorry for you. But then, one would never have young Owlets if one didn't stick to the nest." He was always proud of his children, and he thought himself a very good husband. Perhaps he was; still he had never taken his place on the nest while his wife went hunting.

One night, after they had both been flying through forest and over field, he came back to the hollow tree to rest. He expected to find Mrs. Owl, for she had started home before he did. She was not there and he grew quite impatient. "I should like to know what keeps her so long," he said, fretfully. After a while he looked into the nest and saw the two big white eggs. "It is a shame," he said. "Our beautiful eggs will be chilled, and it will be all her fault if we have no Owlets this summer."

You see, even then he did not seem to think that he could do anything to keep them warm. But the next time he looked in, he put one feathered foot on the round eggs and was surprised to find how cool they were.

It fairly made his head feathers stand on end to think of it, and he was so frightened that he forgot to be cross, and stepped right in and covered them with his own breast. What if they had already been left too long, and the Owlets within would never hatch? Would Mrs. Owl ever forgive him for being so stupid? He began to wonder if any of the other fellows would see him. He thought it so absurd for the king of the forest to be hatching out a couple of eggs, instead of swooping around in the dark and frightening the smaller birds.

The night seemed so long, too. It had always been short enough before, and he had often disliked to have daylight come, for then he had to go to bed. He was very much upset, and it is no wonder that when he heard a doleful wail from a neighboring tree, and knew that his cousin, the Screech Owl, was near, he raised his head and called loudly, "Hoo-hoo-oooo! Waugh-hoo!"

The Screech Owl heard him and flew at once to a branch beside the nest hollow. He was a jolly little fellow in spite of his doleful call, and before he could talk at all he had to bend his body, look behind him, nod his head, and shake himself, as Screech Owls always do when they alight. Then he looked into the tree and saw his big cousin, the Great Horned Owl, the night king of the forest, sitting on the eggs and looking very, very grumpy. How he did laugh! "What is the matter?" said he. "Didn't you like your wife's way of brooding over the eggs? Or did she get tired of staying at home and make you help tend the nest?"

"Matter enough," grumbled the Great Horned Owl. "We went hunting together at twilight and she hasn't come home yet. I didn't get into the nest until I had to, but it was growing very cold and I wouldn't miss having our eggs hatch for anything. Ugh-whoo! How my legs do ache!"

"Well," said his cousin, "you are having a hard time. Are you hungry?"

The Great Horned Owl said that he was, so the Screech Owl went hunting and brought him food. "I will look in every night," he said, "and bring you a lunch. I'm afraid something has happened to your wife and that she will not be back."

As he flew away he called out, "It is *too* bad. I am *very* sorry for you. But then, I suppose you would never have the Owlets if you didn't stick to the nest."

This last remark made the Great Horned Owl quite angry. "Much he knows about it," he said. "I guess if he had ever tried it he would be a little more sorry for me." And then he began to think, "Who have I heard say those very words before? Who? Who? Who?"

All at once the Great Horned Owl remembered how many times he had said just that to his patient wife, and he began to feel very uncomfortable. His ears tingled and he felt a queer hot feeling under his face feathers. Perhaps he hadn't been acting very well after all! He knew that even when he told her he was sorry, he had been thinking she made a great fuss. Well, if she would only come back now, that should all be changed, and he shifted his weight and wriggled around into a more comfortable position.

Now, if this were just a story, one could say that Mrs. Owl came back and that they were all happy together; but the truth is she never did come, and nobody ever knew what became of her. So her husband, the night king of the forest, had to keep the eggs warm and rear his own Owlets. You can imagine how glad he was on the night when he first heard them tapping on the inside of their shells, for then he knew that he would soon be free to hunt.

A finer pair of children were never hatched, and their father thought them far ahead of all his other broods. "If only Mrs. Owl were here to see them, how lovely it would be!" he said. Yet if she had been there he would never have had the pleasure of hearing their first faint cheeps, and of covering them with his soft breast feathers as he did each day. He forgot now all the weary time when he sat with aching legs, wishing that his cousin would happen along with something to eat. For that is always the way,—when we work for those we love, the weariness is soon forgotten and only happiness remains.

It is said that the Screech Owl was more thoughtful of his wife after his cousin had to hatch the eggs, and it is too bad that some of the other forest people could not have learned the same lesson; but the Great Horned Owl never told, and the Screech Owl kept his secret, and to this day there are many people in the forest who know nothing whatever about it.

The Swaggering Crow

When the Crows who have been away for the winter return to the forest, all their relatives gather on the tree-tops to welcome them and tell the news. Those who have been away have also much to say, and it sometimes seems as though they were all talking at once. They spend many days in visiting before they begin nest-building. Perhaps if they would take turns and not interrupt each other, they would get the news more quickly, for when people are interrupted they can never talk well. Sometimes, too, one hungry fellow will fly off for a few mouthfuls of grain, and get back just in time to hear the end of a story. Then he will want to hear the first part of it, and make such a fuss that they have to tell it all over again just for him.

At this time in the spring, you can hear their chatter and laughter, even when you are far away; and the song-birds of the forest look at each other and say, "Dear me! The Crows are back." They have very good reasons for disliking the Crows, as any Robin will tell you.

There was one great shining black Crow who had the loudest voice of all, and who was not at all afraid to use it. This spring he looked very lean and lank, for it had been a long, cold winter, and he had found but little to eat, acorns, the seeds of the wild plants, and once in a great while a frozen apple that hung from its branch in some lonely orchard.

He said that he felt as though he could reach around his body with one claw, and when a Crow says that he feels exceedingly thin. But now spring was here, and his sisters and his cousins and his aunts, yes, and his brothers and his uncles, too, had returned to the forest to live. He had found two good dinners already, all that he could eat and more too, and he began to feel happy and bold. The purple gloss on his feathers grew brighter every day, and he was glad to see this. He wanted to look so handsome that a certain Miss Crow, a sister of one of his friends, would like him better than she did any of the others.

That was all very well, if he had been at all polite about it. But one day he saw her visiting with another Crow, and he lost his temper, and flew at him, and pecked him about the head and shoulders, and tore the long fourth feather from one of his wings, besides rumpling the rest of his coat. Then he went away. He had beaten him by coming upon him from behind, like the sneak that he was, and he was afraid that if he waited he might yet get the drubbing he deserved. So he flew off to the top of a hemlock-tree where the other Crows were, and told them how he had fought and beaten. You should have seen him swagger around when he told it. Each time it was a bigger story, until at last he made them think that the other Crow hadn't a tail feather left.

The next day, a number of Crows went to a farm not far from the forest. Miss Crow was in the party. On their way they stopped in a field where there stood a figure of a man with a dreadful stick in his hand. Everybody was frightened except Mr. Crow. He wanted to show how much courage he had, so he flew right up to it. They all thought him very brave. They didn't know that down in his heart he was a great coward. He wasn't afraid of this figure because he knew all about it. He had seen it put up the day before, and he knew that there was no man under the big straw hat and the flapping coat. He knew that, instead of a thinking, breathing person, there was only a stick nailed to a pole. He knew that, instead of having two good legs with which to run, this figure had only the end of a pole stuck into the ground.

Of course, he might have told them all, and then they could have gathered corn from the broken ground around, but he didn't want to do that. Instead, he said, "Do you see that terrible great creature with a stick in his hand? He is here just to drive us away, but he dares not touch me. He knows I would beat him if he did." Then he flew down, and ate corn close beside the figure, while the other Crows stood back and cawed with wonder.

When he went back to them, he said to Miss Crow, "You see how brave I am. If I were taking care of anybody, nothing could ever harm her." And he looked tenderly at her with his little round eyes. But she pretended not to understand what he meant, for she did not wish to give up her pleasant life with the flock and begin nest-building just yet.

When they reached the barn-yard, there was rich picking, and Mr. Crow made such a clatter that you would have thought he owned it all and that the others were only his guests. He flew down on the fence beside a couple of harmless Hens, and he flapped his wings and swaggered around until they began to sidle away. Then he grew bolder (you know bullies always do if they find that people are scared), and edged up to them until they fluttered off, squawking with alarm.

Next he walked into the Hen-house, saying to the other Crows, "You might have a good time, too, if you were not such cowards." He had no more than gotten the words out of his bill, when the door of the Hen-house blew shut and caught there. It was a grated door and he scrambled wildly to get through the openings. While he was trying, he heard the hoarse voice of the Crow whom he had beaten the day before, saying, "Thank you, we are having a fairly good time as it is"; and he saw Miss Crow picking daintily at some corn which the speaker had scratched up for her.

At that minute the great Black Brahma Cock came up behind Mr. Crow. He had heard from the Hens how rude Mr. Crow had been, and he thought that as the head of the house he ought to see about it. Well! one cannot say very much about what happened next, but the Black Brahma Cock did see about it quite thoroughly, and when the Hen-house door swung open, it was a limp, ragged, and meek-looking Crow who came out, leaving many of his feathers inside.

The next morning Mr. Crow flew over the forest and far away. He did not want to go back there again. He heard voices as he passed a tall tree by the edge of the forest. Miss Crow was out with the Crow whom he had beaten, and they were looking for a good place in which to build. "I don't think they will know me if they see me," said Mr. Crow, "and I am sure that I don't want them to."

The Red-Headed Woodpecker Children

Mrs. Red-headed Woodpecker bent her handsome head down and listened. "Yes, it is! It certainly is!" she cried, as she heard for a second time the faint "tap-tap-tap" of a tiny beak rapping on the inside of an egg shell. She hopped to one side of her nest and stood looking at the four white eggs that lay there. Soon the rapping was heard again and she saw one of them move a bit on its bed of chips.

"So it is that one," she cried. "I thought it would be. I was certain that I laid that one first." And she arched her neck proudly, as the beak of her eldest child came through a crack in the shell. Now nobody else could have told one egg from another, but mothers have a way of remembering such things, and it may be because they love their children so that sometimes their sight is a little sharper, and their hearing a little keener than anybody else's.

However that may be, she stood watching while the tiny bird chipped away the shell and squeezed out of the opening he had made. She did not even touch a piece of the shell until he was well out of it, for she knew that it is always better for children to help themselves when they can. It makes them strong and fits them for life. When the little Red-headed Woodpecker had struggled free, she took the broken pieces in her beak and carried them far from the nest before dropping them to the ground. If she had done the easiest thing and let them fall by the foot of the hollow tree where she lived, any prowling Weasel or Blue Jay might have seen them and watched for a chance to reach her babies. And that would have been very sad for the babies.

The newly hatched bird was a tired little fellow, and the first thing he did was to take a nap. He was cold, too, although the weather was fine and sunshiny. His down was all wet from the moisture inside the egg, and you can imagine how he felt, after growing for so long inside a warm, snug shell, to suddenly be without it and know that he could never again have it around him. Even if it had been whole once more, he could not have been packed into it, for he had been stretching and growing every minute since he left it. It is for this reason that the barn-yard people have a wise saying: "A hatched chicken never returns to his shell."

When Mrs. Red-headed Woodpecker came back, she covered her shivering little one with her downy breast, and there he slept, while she watched for her husband's coming, and thought how pleased and proud he would be to see the baby. They were a young couple, and this was their first child.

But who can tell what the other three children, who had not cracked the shell, were thinking? Could they remember the time when they began to be? Could they dream of what would happen after they were hatched? Could they think at all? They were tiny, weak creatures, curled up within their shells, with food packed all around them. There had been a time when they were only streaks in the yellow liquid of the eggs. Now they were almost ready to leave this for a fuller, freer life, where they could open their bills and flutter their wings, and stretch their legs and necks. It had been a quiet, sheltered time in the shell; why should they leave it? Ah, but they must leave it, for they were healthy and growing, and when they had done so, they would forget all about it. By the time they could talk, and that would be very soon, they would have forgotten all that happened before they were hatched. That is why you can never get a bird to tell you what he thought about while in the egg.

After the young Woodpecker's three sisters reached the outside world, the father and mother were kept busy hunting food for them, and they were alone much of the time. It was not long before they knew their parents' voices, although, once in a while, before they got their eyes open, they mistook the call of the Tree Frog below for that of the Woodpeckers. And this was not strange, for each says, "Ker-r-ruck! Ker-r-ruck!" and when the Tree Frog was singing in his home at the foot of the tree, the four Woodpecker children, in their nest-hollow far above his head, would be opening their bills and stretching their necks, and wondering why no juicy and delicious morsel was dropped down their throats.

When they had their eyes open there was much to be seen. At least, they thought so. Was there not the hollow in their dear, dry old tree, a hollow four or five times as high as they could reach? Their mother had told them how their father and she had dug it out with their sharp, strong bills, making it roomy at the bottom, and leaving a doorway at the top just large enough for them to pass through. Part of the chips they had taken away, as the mother had taken the broken shells, and part had been left in the bottom of the hollow for the children to lie on. "I don't believe in grass, hair, and down, as a bed for children," their father had said. "Nice soft chips are far better."

And the Woodpecker children liked the chips, and played with them, and pretended that they were grubs to be caught with their long and bony tongues; only of course they never swallowed them.

It was an exciting time when their feathers began to grow. Until then they had been clothed in down; but now the tiny quills came pricking through their skin, and it was not so pleasant to snuggle up to each other as it had once been. Now, too, the eldest of the family began to show a great fault. He was very vain. You can imagine how sorry his parents were.

Every morning when he awakened he looked first of all at his feathers. Those on his breast were white, and he had a white band on his wings. His tail and back and nearly the whole of his wings were blue-black. His head, neck, and throat were crimson. To be sure, while the feathers were growing, the colors were not very bright, for the down was mixed with them, and the quills showed so plainly that the young birds looked rather streaked.

The sisters were getting their new suits at the same time, and there was just as much reason why they should be vain, but they were not. They were glad (as who would not be?) and they often said to each other: "How pretty you are growing!" They looked exactly like their brother, for it is not with the Woodpeckers as with many other birds,—the sons and daughters are dressed in precisely the same way.

As for the vain young Woodpecker, he had many troubles. He was not contented to let his feathers grow as the grass and the leaves grow, without watching. No indeed! He looked at each one every day and a great many times every day. Then, if he thought they were not growing as fast as they should, he worried about it. He wanted to hurry them along, and sometimes, when his sisters did not seem to be looking, he took hold of them with his bill and pulled. Of course this did not make them grow any faster and it did make his skin very sore, but how was he to know? He had not been out of the shell long enough to be wise.

It troubled him, too, because he could not see his red feathers. He twisted his head this way and that, and strained his eyes until they ached, trying to see his own head and neck. It was very annoying. He thought it would have been much nicer to have the brightest feathers in a fellow's tail, where he could see them, or at any rate on his breast; and he asked his mother why it couldn't be so.

"I once knew a young Woodpecker," she said, "who thought of very little but his own beauty. I am afraid that if he had been allowed to wear his red feathers in his tail, he would never have seen anything else in this wonderful great world, but just his own poor little tail." She looked out of the doorway as she spoke, but he knew that she meant him.

Things went on in this way until the children were ready to fly. Then there were daily lessons in flying, alighting, clinging to branches, and tapping for food on the bark of trees. They learned, too, how to support themselves with their stiff tails when they were walking up trees or stopping to eat with their claws hooked into the bark. Then Mrs. Red-headed Woodpecker taught them how to tell the ripest and sweetest fruit on the trees before they tasted it. That is something many people would like to know, but it is a forest secret, and no bird will tell anyone who cannot fly.

It was on his way back from an orchard one day, that the vain young Woodpecker stopped to talk with an old Gray Squirrel. It may be that the Gray Squirrel's sight was not good, and so he mistook the Woodpecker for quite another fellow. He was speaking of an old tree where he had spent the last winter. "I believe a family of Red-headed Woodpeckers live there now," he said. "I have met them once or twice. The father and mother are fine people, and they have charming daughters, but their son must be a great trial to them. He is one of these silly fellows who see the world through their own feathers."

As the young Red-headed Woodpecker flew away, he repeated this to himself: "A silly fellow, a silly fellow, who sees the world through his own feathers." And he said to his father, "Whose feathers must I look through?"

This puzzled his father. "Whose feathers should you look through?" said he. "What do you mean?"

"Well," answered the son, "somebody said that I saw the world through my own feathers, and I don't see how I can get anybody else's."

How his father did laugh! "I don't see why you should look through any feathers," said he. "What he meant was that you thought so much of your own plumage that you did not care for anything else; and it is so. If it were intended you should look at yourself all the time, your eyes would have been one under your chin and the other in the back of your head. No! They are placed right for you to look at other people, and are where they help you hunt for food."

"How often may I look at my own feathers?" asked the young Woodpecker. He was wondering at that minute how his tail looked, but he was determined not to turn his head.

The old Woodpecker's eyes twinkled. "I should think," he said, "that since you are young and have no family to look after, you might preen your feathers in the morning and in the afternoon and when you go to sleep. Then, of course, when it is stormy, you will have to take your waterproof out of the pocket under your tail, and put it on one feather at a time, as all birds do. That would be often enough unless something happened to rumple them."

"I will not look at them any oftener," said the young Red-headed Woodpecker, firmly. "I will *not* be called a silly fellow." And he was as good as his word.

His mother sighed when she heard of the change. "I am very glad," said she. "But isn't that always the way? His father and I have talked and talked, and it made no difference; but let somebody else say he is silly and vain, and behold!"

The Night Moth With A Crooked Feeler

The beautiful, brilliant Butterflies of the Meadow had many cousins living in the forest, most of whom were Night Moths. They also were very beautiful creatures, but they dressed in duller colors and did not have slender waists. Some of the Butterflies, you know, wear whole gowns of black and yellow, others have stripes of black and white, while some have clear yellow with only a bit of black trimming the edges of the wings.

The Moths usually wear brown and have it brightened with touches of buff or dull blue. If they do wear bright colors, it is only on the back pair of wings, and when the Moth alights, he slides his front pair of wings over these and covers all the brightness. They do not rest with their wings folded over their heads like the Butterflies, but leave them flat. All the day long, when the sun is shining, the Moths have to rest on trees and dead leaves. If they were dressed in yellow or red, any passing bird would see them, and there is no telling what might happen. As it is, their brown wings are so nearly the color of dead leaves or bark that you might often look right at them without seeing them.

Yet even among Moths there are some more brightly colored than others, and when you find part of the family quietly dressed you can know it is because they have to lay the eggs. Moths are safer in dull colors, and the egg-layers should always be the safest of all. If anything happened to them, you know, there would be no Caterpillar babies.

One day a fine-looking Cecropia Moth came out of her chrysalis and clung to the nearest twig while her wings grew and dried and flattened. At first they had looked like tiny brown leaves all drenched with rain and wrinkled by somebody's stepping on them. The fur on her fat body was matted and wet, and even her feelers were damp and stuck to her head. Her six beautiful legs were weak and trembling, and she moved her body restlessly while she tried again and again to raise her crumpled wings.

She had not been there so very long before she noticed another Cecropia Moth near her, clinging to the under side of a leaf. He was also just out of the chrysalis and was drying himself. "Good morning!" he cried. "I think I knew you when we were Caterpillars. Fine day to break the chrysalis, isn't it?"

"Lovely," she answered. "I remember you very well. You were the Caterpillar who showed me where to find food last summer when the hot weather had withered so many of the plants."

"I thought you would recall me," he said. "And when we were spinning our chrysalides we visited together. Do you remember that also?"

Miss Cecropia did. She had been thinking of that when she first spoke, but she hoped he had forgotten. To tell the truth, he had been rather fond of her the fall before, and she, thinking him the handsomest Caterpillar of her acquaintance, had smiled upon him and suggested that they spin their cocoons near together. During the long winter she had regretted this. "I was very foolish," she thought, "to encourage him. When I get my wings I may meet people who are better off than he.

Now I shall have to be polite to him for the sake of old friendship. I only hope that he will make other acquaintances and leave me free. I must get into the best society."

All this time her neighbor was thinking, "I am so glad to see her again, so glad, so glad! When my wings are dry I will fly over to her and we will go through the forest together." He was a kind, warm-hearted fellow, who cared more for friendship than for beauty or family.

Meanwhile their wings were growing fast, and drying, and flattening, so that by noon they could begin to raise them above their heads. They were very large Moths and their wings were of a soft dust color with little clear, transparent places in them and touches of the most beautiful blue, quite the shade worn by the Peacock, who lived on the farm. There was a brown and white border to their wings, and on their bodies and legs the fur was white and dark orange. When the Cecropias rest, they spread their wings out flat, and do not slide the front pair over the others as their cousins, the Sphinxes, do. The most wonderful of all, though, are their feelers.

The Butterflies have stiff feelers on their heads with little knobs on the ends, or sometimes with part of them thick like tiny clubs. The Night Moths have many kinds of feelers, most of them being curved, and those of the Cecropias look like reddish-brown feathers pointed at the end.

Miss Cecropia's feelers were perfect, and she waved them happily to and fro. Those of her friend, she was troubled to see, were not what they should have been. One of them was all right, the other was small and crooked. "Oh dear," she said to herself, "how that does look! I hope he will not try to be attentive to me." He did not mind it much. He thought about other things than looks.

As night came, a Polyphemus Moth fluttered past. "Good evening!" cried he. "Are you just out? There are a lot of Cecropias coming out to-day."

Miss Cecropia felt quite agitated when she heard this, and wondered if she looked all right. Her friend flew over to her just as she raised her wings for flight. "Let me go with you," he said.

While she was wondering how she could answer him, several other Cecropias came along. They were all more brightly colered than she. "Hullo!" cried one of them, as he alighted beside her. "First-rate night, isn't it?"

He was a handsome fellow, and his feelers were perfect; but Miss Cecropia did not like his ways, and she drew away from him just as her friend knocked him off the branch. While they were fighting, another of the strangers flew to her. "May I sit here?" he asked.

"Yes," she murmured, thinking her chance had come to get into society.

"I must say that it served the fellow right for his rudeness to you," said the stranger, in his sweetest way; "but who is the Moth who is punishing him—that queer-looking one with a crooked feeler?"

"Sir," said she, moving farther from him, "he is a friend of mine, and I do not think it matters to you if he is queer-looking."

"Oh!" said the stranger. "Oh! oh! oh! You have a bad temper, haven't you? But you are very good-looking in spite of that." There is no telling what he would have said next, for at this minute Miss Cecropia's friend heard the mean things he was saying, and flew against him.

It was not long before this stranger also was punished, and then the Moth with the crooked feeler turned to the others. "Do any of you want to try it?" he said. "You must understand that you cannot be rude before her." And he pointed his right fore leg at Miss Cecropia as she sat trembling on the branch.

"Her!" they cried mockingly, as they flew away. "There are prettier Moths than she. We don't care anything for her."

Miss Cecropia's friend would have gone after them to punish them for this impoliteness, but she clung to him and begged him not to. "You will be killed, I know you will," she sobbed. "And then what will become of me?"

"Would you miss me?" he asked, as he felt of one of his wings, now broken and bare.

"Yes," she cried. "You are the best friend I have. Please don't go."

"But I am such a homely fellow," he said. "I don't see how you can like me since I broke my wing."

"Well, I do like you," she said. "Your wing isn't much broken after all, and I *like* your crooked feeler. It is so different from anybody else's." Miss Cecropia looked very happy as she spoke, and she quite forgot how she once decided to go away from him. There are some people, you know, who can change their minds in such a sweet and easy way that we almost love them the better for it. One certainly could love Miss Cecropia for this, because it showed that she had learned to care more for a warm heart and courage than for whole wings and straight feelers.

Mr. Cecropia did not live long after this, unfortunately, but they were very, very happy together, and she often said to her friends, as she laid her eggs in the best places, "I only hope that when my Caterpillar babies are grown and have come out of their chrysalides, they may be as good and as brave as their father was."

The Bees And The Kingbird

There was in the forest a great hollow tree where for years a swarm of Bees had made their home. To look at it in winter, one would never guess what a store of honey was sealed up within, but in summer the Bees were always passing in and out, and it was indeed a busy place. Then the Workers had to gather honey and build the cells and look out for the Queen-Mother's many babies. The Queen-Mother had so much care of her eggs that she could really do nothing but attend to them. After they were ready in their cells, the Workers took care of them, and tucked in a lot of bread for the babies to eat when they were hatched. Then there was the bread-making to be done also, and all the Workers helped bring the pollen, or flower-dust, out of which it was made.

The Drones didn't do anything, not a thing, not a single thing, unless it were taking care of the Queen when she flew away from the tree. They had done that once, but it was long ago, before she had laid an egg and while she was still quite young. They were handsome great fellows, all black and gold, and if you didn't know about them, you might have thought them the pleasantest Bees in the tree. Of course you would not care for them after finding how lazy they were, for people are never liked just because they are fine-looking.

The Drones always found some excuse for being idle, and like many other lazy people they wanted the busy ones to stop and visit with them. "What is the hurry?" they would say. "There will be more honey that you can get to-morrow. Stop a while now."

But the Workers would shake their brown heads and buzz impatiently as they answered, "We can get to-morrow's honey when to-morrow comes, but to-day's honey must be gathered to-day."

Then the Drones would grumble and say that they didn't see the sense of storing up so much honey anyway. That also was like lazy people the world over, for however much they scold about getting the food, they are sure to eat just as much as anybody else. Sometimes lazy people eat even more than others, and pick for the best too.

On cloudy days, the Workers did stay at home in the tree, but not to play. They clung to the walls and to each other and made wax. It took much patience to make wax. When they were gathering honey there was so much that was interesting to be seen, and so many friends to meet, that it was really quite exciting; but when they made wax they had to hang for a long, long time, until the wax gathered in flakes over their bodies. Then it was ready to scrape off and shape into six-sided cells to hold honey or to be homes for the babies.

One sunshiny morning the Queen-Mother stopped laying her eggs and cried: "Listen! did you hear that?"

"What?" asked the Workers, crowding around her.

"Why, that noise," she said. "It sounded like a bird calling 'Kyrie! K-y-rie!' and I thought I heard a Worker buzzing outside a minute ago, but no one has come in. I am afraid—" and here she stopped.

"Of what are you afraid!" asked the Drones, who, having nothing to do but eat and sleep, were always ready to talk about anything and everything. The great trouble with them was that if you once began to talk they did not like to have you leave and go to work.

"Why," said the Queen-Mother, "I don't want to alarm you, but I thought it was a Kingbird."

"Well, what if it was?" said a big Drone. "There is only one of him and there are a great many of us."

"Yes," said the Queen-Mother, "but there may not be so many of us very long if he begins to watch the tree. I have lived much longer than you and I know how Kingbirds act."

This was true, for Queens live to be very old, and Drones never live long because they are so lazy.

"Well," said the big Drone, "we must find out about this. Just fly around and see if it is a Kingbird," he said to a Worker. "We must know about things before we act."

"Suppose you should go," she replied. "I have my leg-pockets full of pollen, and it ought to be made into bread at once. I never saw Larvæ so hungry as these last ones are."

"I only wish that I could go," said the big Drone, limping as he got out of her way; "but my fifth foot just stepped on my third foot, and I can hardly move."

When he said this, all the Workers smiled, and even the Queen-Mother had to turn away her head. The Drones looked as solemn as possible. It would not do for them to laugh at their brother. They did not want him to laugh at them when they made excuses for staying at home. They even pretended not to hear one of the Workers when she said that it was funny how some people couldn't use their wings if one of their feet hurt them.

"Yes," said another Worker, "and it is funny, too, how some people can get along very well on three legs when they have to, while others are too helpless to do anything unless they can use the whole six."

The Drones began to talk together. "I think that the whole swarm should fly at the Kingbird and sting him and drive him away," said one. "There is no sense in allowing him to perch outside our home and catch us as we pass in and out. *I* say that we should make war upon him!" He looked very fierce as he spoke, buzzing and twitching his feelers at every step.

"Exactly!" cried another Drone. "If I had a sting, I would lead the attack. As it is, I may be useful in guarding the comb. It is a great pity that Drones have no stings." You would have thought, to hear him speak, that if he had been given a sting like those of the Workers, not all the Bees in the tree could keep him from fighting.

While the Drones were talking about war, some of the Workers sent to their Queen for advice. "Tell us," they said, "how to drive away the Kingbird. Should we try to sting him? You know it kills a Bee to sting anybody, and we don't want to if we can help it, yet we will if you say so."

The Queen-Mother shook her head. "You must not bother me about such things," she said. "I have all that I can do to get the eggs ready, and you must look after the swarm. Nobody else can do my work, and I have no time to do yours." As she spoke, she finished the one hundred and seventeenth egg of that day's lot, and before night came she would probably have laid more than a thousand, so you can see she was quite right when she said she had no time for other things.

This left the Workers to plan for themselves, and they agreed that a number of them should fly out together and see where the Kingbird was. Then they could decide about attacking him later. When one gave the signal, they dashed out as nearly together as possible.

After the Workers returned with honey and pollen, the Drones crowded around them, asking questions. "Where is he? What does he look like? Did he try to catch you?" The Workers would not answer them, and said: "Go and find out for yourself. We all came back alive." Then they went about their work as usual.

"I don't see how they dared to go," said a very young Bee who was just out of her cocoon and was still too weak to fly.

"Pooh!" said the big Drone. "You wouldn't see me hanging around this tree if I were not lame."

"There is no use in stopping work even if you are scared," said one of the Workers. She smiled as she spoke, and whispered something to the Queen-Mother as she passed her. The Queen-Mother smiled also.

"Why don't you Drones go for honey?" she said. "You must be getting very hungry."

"We don't feel very well," they answered. "Perhaps it would be better for our health if we were to keep quiet for a while and save our strength. We will lunch off some of the honey in the comb if we need food."

"Not a bit of it!" exclaimed the Workers. "Stay in the tree if you want to for your health, but don't you dare touch the honey we have gathered for winter, when the day is clear and bright like this." And whenever a Drone tried to get food from the comb they drove him away.

The poor Drones had a hard day of it, and at night they were so hungry they could hardly sleep. The next morning they peeped out, and then rushed away to the flowers for their breakfast. They stayed out all day, and when they returned at night they rushed swiftly into the tree again.

"There!" they said; "we escaped the Kingbird."

"What Kingbird?" asked a Worker.

"The one who was there yesterday," answered the Drones. "Has he been back to-day?"

"There was no Kingbird near the tree yesterday," said the Worker.

"What!" cried the Drones.

"No," said the Queen-Mother, "I was mistaken when I thought I heard him. The Workers told me after they had been out for honey. Perhaps they forgot to tell you."

But her eyes twinkled as she spoke, and all the Workers smiled, and for some reason the Drones did not know what to say.

The Story Of The Cow Bird's Egg

On the edge of the forest next to the meadow, a pair of young Goldfinches were about to begin housekeeping. They were a handsome couple, and the birds who were already nesting near by were much pleased to see them tree-hunting there.

Mr. Goldfinch was a fine, cheerful little fellow, every feather of whose black and yellow coat was always well oiled and lying in its proper place. His wife was dressed in a dull, greenish brown with a touch of yellow on her breast. "Bright yellow and black does very well for Mr. Goldfinch," she would say, "but for one who has to sit on the nest as long as I shall have to, it would never do. People would see me among the leaves and know just where to find my eggs."

Mr. Goldfinch thought that there was never a bird who had a prettier, dearer, or harder-working little wife than he, and he would wonder how he was ever happy before he knew her. That is a way that people have of forgetting the days that are past; and the truth is that Mr. Goldfinch had made fun of the Robins and other birds all spring, because they had to build nests and hunt worms for their babies, while he had nothing to do but sing and sleep and feed himself. In those days the Robins used to call after him as he flew away, "Silly fellow! Silly fellow! Silly!" They knew that there is something sweeter in life than just taking good care of one's self.

One afternoon Mr. Goldfinch saw a tiny green-brown bird on a sweetbriar bush, and as he watched her he thought her the most beautiful creature he had ever seen. She had such a dainty way of picking out the seeds, and gave such graceful hops from one twig to another. Then Mr. Goldfinch fluffed up his feathers and swelled out his throat and sang her such songs as he had never sung before. He did not want her to speak to anybody else, and yet he could not help her doing so, for Goldfinches always go together in crowds until they have homes of their own, and at this time they were having concerts every morning. He showed her where the finest dandelion seeds could be found, and one bright and sunshiny day she became Mrs. Goldfinch, and they went together to find a place for their home.

They began one nest and had it nearly done, when Mr. Goldfinch said it was not in a good place, and tore it all to pieces. Mrs. Goldfinch felt very badly about this and talked it over with some of her Goldfinch neighbors. They told her not to mind it at all, that their husbands often did the same thing, and that sometimes they came to like the new place much better than the old. At any rate, there was no use in getting cross about it, because that was something she would have to expect.

Mr. Goldfinch was sure that they had built too near the ground, and he had chosen a crotch above. Toward this he was dragging the bits of grape-vine and cedar-bark which were woven into their first nest. He said they could also use some of the grasses and mosses which they had gotten together, and he even told his wife of some fine thistle-down which he could bring for the inside, where the eggs were to be laid. Mrs. Goldfinch watched him tugging with bill and both feet to loosen the bits of bark, and she said to herself: "Dear fellow! what a helper he is! I won't mind rebuilding if it makes him happy," and she went to work with a will.

When the sun went down in the west the next night the second nest was done, and it was the last thing at which the Goldfinches looked before tucking their heads under their wings and going to sleep. It was the first thing that they saw the next morning, too, and they hopped all around it and twittered with pride, and gave it little tweaks here and little pokes there before they flew away to get breakfast.

While they were gone, Mrs. Cowbird came walking over the grass and dry leaves to the foot of the tree. She wagged her head at every step, and put on as many airs as though she were showily dressed, instead of wearing, as she always does, a robe of dull brownish gray. She had seen the Goldfinches fly away, and she was looking for their home. She was a lazy creature in spite of her stirring ways, and she wished to find a nice little nest in which to lay an egg. You know Cowbirds never think of building nests. They want all of their time to take care of themselves, which is a very foolish way of living; but then, you could never make a Cowbird think so!

"That nest is exactly right," said Mrs. Cowbird. "I will lay my egg there at once, and when Mrs. Goldfinch has laid hers she will have to hatch them all together and take care of my baby for me. What an easy way this is to bring up one's family! It is really no work at all! And I am sure that my children will get along well, because I am always careful to choose the nests of small birds for them. Then they are larger and stronger than the other babies, and can get more than their share of food."

So she laid a big white egg with gray and brown spots on it in the Goldfinches' new home, and then she flew off to the Cowbird flock, as gay and careless as you please. When the Goldfinches came back, they saw the egg in their nest and called all their neighbors to talk it over. "What shall I ever do?" said Mrs. Goldfinch. "I wanted my nest for my own eggs, and I meant to lay them to-morrow. I suppose I shall have to sit on this one too, but it won't be at all comfortable."

"I wouldn't," said one of her neighbors, a Yellow Warbler. "I left my nest once when such a thing happened to me, and built a new one for my own eggs."

"Oh dear!" cried Mrs. Goldfinch, "we have built two already, and I cannot build another."

"Well, whatever you do," said a Vireo, "don't hatch the big egg out with your own. I did once, and such a time as I had! The young Cowbird pushed two of my little Vireos out onto the ground, and ate so much that I was quite worn out by the work of hunting for him."

"My dear," said Mr. Goldfinch, "I have an excellent plan. We will put another floor in our nest, right over this egg, and then by adding a bit all around the sides we can have plenty of room for our own children. It will be much less work than beginning all over again, and then the Cowbird's egg will be too cool to hatch."

Everybody called this a most clever plan, and Mr. Goldfinch was very proud to have thought of it. They went to work once more, and it was not so very long before the new floor was done and the new walls raised. Then, oh, wonder of wonders! there were soon four tiny, pearly eggs of their own lying on the thistle-down lining of the nest.

Mrs. Goldfinch had to stay very closely at home now, but her husband went off with his friends a great deal. He bathed and sang and preened his feathers and talked about his queer nest and his bright little wife, after the manner of Goldfinches everywhere.

His friends laughed at him for helping so much about the nest, for, you know, Goldfinches do not often help their wives about home. He cocked his handsome head on one side and answered: "My wife seemed to need me then. She is not so very strong. And I do not know what she would ever have done about the strange egg, if I had not been there to advise her."

When he got back to his home that night, Mrs. Goldfinch said: "I have been wondering why we did not roll the Cowbird's egg out on the ground, instead of going to all that trouble of building around it."

And Mr. Goldfinch declared that he believed she was the only bird who had ever thought of such a thing. "It could have been done just as well as not," he said. "I must tell that to the other birds in the morning. How lucky I am to have such a bright wife! It would be dreadful if such a clever fellow as I had a dull mate!"

Mrs. Mourning Dove's Housekeeping

Strange as it may seem, there had never been any Mourning Doves in the forest until this year, and when a pair came there to live, the people were much excited. They talked about the Doves' song, so sweet and sad, and about their soft coats of brown and gray, and they wondered very much what kind of home they would build. Would it be a swinging pocket of hairs, strings, and down, like that of the Orioles? Would it be stout and heavy like the nests of the Robins? Or would it be a ball of leaves and grasses on the ground, with a tiny doorway in one side, like that of the Ovenbird?

You can see that the forest people were really very much interested in the Mourning Doves, and so, perhaps, it is not strange that, when the new couple built their nest in the lower branches of a spruce tree, everybody watched it and talked about it.

"Really," said one of the Blackbirds, who had flown over from the swamp near by, "I never should think of calling that thing a nest! It is nothing but a few twigs and sticks laid together. It is just as flat as a maple-leaf, and what is to keep those poor little Doves from tumbling to the ground I can't see."

"I wouldn't worry about the little Doves yet," said a Warbler. "I don't think there will ever be any little Doves in that nest. The eggs will roll off of it long before they are ready to hatch, and the nest will blow to pieces in the first storm we have."

"Well," said the Blackbird, as she started for home, "I shall want to know how the Mourning Doves get on. If any of you are over my way, stop and tell me the news."

Some days after this, a Quail, passing under the Doves' home, happened to look up and see two white eggs in the nest. It was so very thin that she could see them quite plainly through the openings between the twigs. Later in the day, she spoke of this to a Grouse, saying, "I came by the Mourning Doves' nest and saw two white eggs through the bottom."

After she went away, the Grouse said to a wild Rabbit: "The Quail told me that the Mourning Dove's eggs went right through the bottom of her nest, and I don't wonder. It wasn't strong enough to hold anything."

At sunset, the Rabbit had a short visit with Mrs. Goldfinch, as she pulled a great thistle-head to pieces and made her supper from its seeds. He told her he had heard that the Mourning Dove's eggs had fallen through the bottom of the nest and broken on the ground, and Mrs. Goldfinch said: "Oh, that poor Mrs. Mourning Dove! I must go to see her in the morning." Then she fled home to her own four pearly treasures.

Now, of course the Rabbit was mistaken when he said anybody had told him that those two eggs were broken; just as much mistaken as the Grouse was when she said somebody had told her that the eggs had fallen. They both thought they were right, but they were careless listeners and careless talkers, and so each one had changed it a bit in the telling.

The next day it rained, and the next, and the next. Mrs. Goldfinch did not dare leave her nest to make calls, lest the cold raindrops should chill and hurt the four tiny birds that lay curled up in their shells. At last the weather was warm and sunshiny, and Mrs. Goldfinch and some of her bird neighbors went to call on Mrs. Mourning Dove. They found her just coming from a wheat-field, where she had been to get grain. "Oh, you poor creature!" they cried. "We have heard all about it. Your poor babies! How sorry we are for you!"

Mrs. Mourning Dove looked from one to another as though she did not know what to make of it. "What do you mean?" she cooed. "My babies are well and doing finely. Won't you come to see them?"

Then it was the turn of the other birds to be surprised. "Why," they chirped, "we heard that your eggs had fallen through your nest and had broken and killed the tiny Dove babies inside. Is it true?"

"Not a word of it," answered Mrs. Mourning Dove. "The nest is all right, and the eggs were not broken until my two little darlings broke them with their sharp beaks."

"Here they are," she added, fondly. "Did you ever see such pretty ones? See him open his bill, the dear! And did you ever see such a neck as she has? Mr. Mourning Dove thinks there never were such children."

"But do you feel perfectly safe to leave them in that nest?" asked the Oriole politely. "My babies are so restless that I should be afraid to trust them in it."

"That is what people always say," answered Mrs. Mourning Dove, with a happy coo, "and I fear that I am a rather poor housekeeper, but it runs in our family. Mr. Mourning Dove and I have raised many pairs of children, and they never rolled out, or tumbled through, or blew away, and I do not worry about these. I shall never be thrifty like you good builders, perhaps, but I'm sure you cannot love your little ones any more than I do mine. It was very kind of you to be so sorry for me when you heard I was in trouble. I think I have the best neighbors in the world."

When her callers went away, they could not say enough about Mrs. Mourning Dove's pleasant ways, and her gentle, well-behaved children. "It is too bad she is such a poor nest-maker," the Vireo said, "and I understand now what she meant when she told me that they sometimes used old Robins' nests for their young. She said they flattened them out and added a few twigs, and that they did finely. I thought it very queer in them to do so, but perhaps if I had not been a good builder I should have done the same thing."

"Perhaps we all would," the others agreed. "She certainly is a very pleasant bird, and she is bringing up her children well. Mr. Mourning Dove seems to think her perfect. We won't worry any more about her."

The Young Blue Jay Who Was Not Brave Enough To Be Afraid

Everybody who is acquainted with the Blue Jays knows that they are a very brave family. That is the best thing that you can say about them. To be sure, they dress very handsomely, and there is no prettier sight, on a fine winter morning, than a flock of Blue Jays flitting from branch to branch, dining off the acorns on the oak trees, and cocking their crested heads on one side as they look over the country. They are great talkers then, and are always telling each other just what to do; yet none of them ever do what they are told to, so they might just as well stop giving advice.

The other people of the forest do not like the Blue Jays at all, and if one of them gets into trouble they will not help him out. This always has been so, and it always will be so. If it could be winter all the time, the Blue Jays could be liked well enough, for in cold weather they eat seeds and nuts and do not quarrel so much with others. It is in the summer that they become bad neighbors. Then they live in the thickest part of the woods and raise families of tiny, fuzzy babies in their great coarse nests. It is then, too, that they change their beautiful coats, and while the old feathers are dropping off and the new ones are growing they are not at all pretty. Oh, then is the time to beware of the Blue Jays!

They do very little talking during the summer, and the forest people do not know when they are coming, unless they see a flutter of blue wings among the branches. The Blue Jays have a reason for keeping still then. They are doing sly things, and they do not want to be found out.

The wee babies grow fast and their mouths are always open for more food. Father and Mother Blue Jay spend all their time in marketing, and they are not content with seeds and berries. They visit the nests of their bird neighbors, and then something very sad happens. When the Blue Jays go to a nest there may be four eggs in it; but when they go away there will not be any left, nothing but pieces of broken egg-shell. It is very, very sad, but this is another of the things which will always be so, and all that the other birds can do is to watch and drive the Jays away.

There was once a young Blue Jay in the forest who was larger than his brothers and sisters, and kept crowding them toward the edge of the nest. When their father came with a bit of food for them, he would stretch his legs and flutter his wings and reach up for the first bite. And because he was the largest and the strongest, he usually got it. Sometimes, too, the first bite was so big that there was nothing left for anyone else to bite at. He was a very greedy fellow, and he had no right to take more than his share, just because he happened to be the first of the family to break open the shell, or because he grew fast.

This same young Blue Jay used to brag about what he would do when he got out of the nest, and his mother told him that he would get into trouble if he were not careful. She said that even Blue Jays had to look out for danger.

"Huh!" said the young Blue Jay; "who's afraid?"

"Now you talk like a bully," said Mother Blue Jay, "for people who are really brave are always willing to be careful."

But the young Blue Jay only crowded his brothers and sisters more than usual, and thought, inside his foolish little pin-feathery head, that when he got a chance, he'd show them what courage was.

After a while his chance came. All the small birds had learned to flutter from branch to branch, and to hop quite briskly over the ground. One afternoon they went to a part of the forest where the ground was damp and all was strange. The father and mother told their children to keep close together and they would take care of them; but the foolish young Blue Jay wanted a chance to go alone, so he hid behind a tree until the others were far ahead, and then he started off another way. It was great fun for a time, and when the feathered folk looked down at him he raised his crest higher than ever and thought how he would scare them when he was a little older.

The young Blue Jay was just thinking about this when he saw something long and shining lying in the pathway ahead. He remembered what his father had said about snakes, and about one kind that wore rattles on their tails. He wondered if this one had a rattle, and he made up his mind to see how it was fastened on. "I am a Blue Jay," he said to himself, "and I was never yet afraid of anything."

The Rattlesnake, for it was he, raised his head to look at the bird. The young Blue Jay saw that his eyes were very bright. He looked right into them, and could see little pictures of himself upon their shining surfaces. He stood still to look, and the Rattlesnake came nearer. Then the young Blue Jay tried to see his tail, but he couldn't look away from the Rattlesnake's eyes, though he tried ever so hard.

The Rattlesnake now coiled up his body, flattened out his head, and showed his teeth, while all the time his queer forked tongue ran in and out of his mouth. Then the young Blue Jay tried to move and found that he couldn't. All he could do was to stand there and watch those glowing eyes and listen to the song which the Rattlesnake began to sing:

"Through grass and fern,
With many a turn,
My shining body I draw.
In woodland shade
My home is made,
For this is the Forest Law.

"Whoever tries
To look in my eyes
Comes near to my poisoned jaw;
And birds o'erbold
I charm and hold,
For this is the Forest Law."

The Rattlesnake drew nearer and nearer, and the young Blue Jay was shaking with fright, when there was a rustle of wings, and his father and mother flew down and around the Rattlesnake, screaming loudly to all the other Jays, and making the Snake turn away from the helpless little bird he had been about to strike. It was a long time before the forest was quiet again, and when it was, the Blue Jay family were safely in their nest, and the Rattlesnake had gone home without his supper.

After the young Blue Jay got over his fright, he began to complain because he had not seen the Rattlesnake's tail. Then, indeed, his patient mother gave him such a scolding as he had never had in all his life, and his father said that he deserved a sound pecking for his foolishness.

When the young Blue Jay showed that he was sorry for all the trouble that he had made, his parents let him have some supper and go to bed; but not until he had learned two sayings which he was always to remember. And these were the sayings: "A really brave bird dares to be afraid of some things," and, "If you go near enough to see the tail of a danger, you may be struck by its head."

The Red Squirrels Begin Housekeeping

The first thing that Mr. Red Squirrel did after coming to the forest and meeting the Gray Squirrel was to look for something to eat. It was not a good season for a stranger who had no hidden store of nuts and seeds to draw upon. The apples and corn were not ripe, and last year's seeds and acorns were nearly gone. What few remained here and there had lost their sweet and wholesome taste. Poor Mr. Red Squirrel began to wish that he had eaten breakfast before he ran away. He even went to the edge of the forest and looked over toward the farmhouse, where his open cage hung in the sunshine. He knew that there were nuts and a fresh bit of fruit inside of it, and his mouth watered at the thought of them, but he was a sensible young fellow, and he knew that if he went back to eat, the cage door would be snapped shut, and he would never again be free to scamper in the beautiful trees.

"I will starve first!" he said to himself, and he was so much in earnest that he spoke quite loudly.

The words were hardly out of his mouth when "Pft!" a fat acorn came down at his feet. He caught it up with his forepaws before looking around. It was smooth and glossy, not at all as though it had passed a long winter on an oak branch. He took a good nibble at it and then looked up to see if there were more on the tree above him. You can think how surprised he was to find himself sitting beneath a maple, for in all the years since the world began no maple has ever borne acorns.

"There are no more to come," he said. "I must take small bites and make it last as long as I can." And he turned it around and around, clutching it tightly with his long, crooked claws, so that not the tiniest bit could be lost. At last it was all eaten, not a crumb was left, and then "Pft!" down came a walnut. This hit him squarely on the back, but he was too hungry to mind, and he ate it all, just stopping long enough to say: "If this maple bears such fruit as acorns and walnuts, I should like to live in a maple grove."

Next came a hazelnut, then a butternut, and last of all a fat kernel of yellow corn. He knew now that some friend was hidden in the branches above, so he tucked the corn in one of his cheek-pockets, and scampered up the maple trunk to find out who it was. He saw a whisking reddish-brown tail, and knew that some other Red Squirrel was there. But whoever it was did not mean to be caught, and such a chase as he had! Just as he thought he had overtaken his unknown friend, he could see nothing more of her, and he was almost vexed to think how careless he must have been to miss her. He ran up and down the tree on which he last saw her, and found a little hollow in one of its large branches. He looked in, and there she was, the same dainty creature whom he had so often watched from his cage. He could see that she was breathless from running so fast, yet she pretended to be surprised at seeing him. Perhaps she now thought that she had been too bold in giving him food, and so wanted him to think that it had been somebody else.

"Good morning!" said he. "Thank you very much for your kindness."

"What do you mean?" said she.

"As though you didn't know!" he answered. "I never heard of a maple tree that bore acorns, nuts, and corn, and that in the springtime."

"Oh, well," said she, tossing her pretty head, "you have lived in a cage and may not know what our forest trees can do."

That was a rather saucy thing to say, but Mr. Red Squirrel knew her kind heart and that she said it only in mischief. "How do you know I have lived in a cage?" he asked.

"I—I thought you looked like the Squirrel at the farmhouse," she said; and then forgetting herself, she added, "You did look so surprised when that walnut hit you."

"Where were you then?" he asked quickly.

"Oh! I was on a branch above you," she answered, seeing that he now knew all about it. "You looked so hungry, and I had plenty of food stored away. You may have some whenever you wish. It must have been dreadful in that cage."

Now Mr. Red Squirrel had loved his little friend ever since the first time he saw her on the rail fence, but he had never thought she would care for him—a tired, discouraged fellow, who had passed such a sorrowful life in prison. Yet when he heard her pitying words, and saw the light in her tender eyes, he wondered if he could win her for his wife.

"I shall never be able to do anything for you," said he. "You are young and beautiful and know the forest ways. I am a stranger and saddened by my hard life. I wish I could help you."

"The Blue Jays! The Blue Jays!" she cried, starting up. "They have found my hidden acorns and are eating them."

And sure enough, a pair of those handsome robbers were pulling acorn after acorn out of a tree-hollow near by, and eating them as fast as they could. You should have seen Mr. Red Squirrel then! He leaped from branch to branch until he reached the Blue Jays; then he stood by the hole where the acorns were stored, and scolded them. "Chickaree-chickaree-quilch-quilch-chickaree-chickaree!" he said; and that in the Red Squirrel language is a *very* severe scolding. He jumped about with his head down and his tail jerking, while his eyes gleamed like coals of fire. The Blue Jays made a great fuss and called "Jay! Jay!" at him, and made fun of him for being a stranger, but they left at last, and Mr. Red Squirrel turned to his friend.

"What would I have done without your help?" she said. "I was so dreadfully frightened. Don't you see how my paws are shaking still?" And she held out the prettiest little paws imaginable for him to see.

Then Mr. Red Squirrel's heart began to thump very fast and hard beneath the white fur of his chest, and he sighed softly. "I wish I might always help you and protect you," he said; "but I suppose there are better fellows than I who want to do that." And he sighed again.

"Yes, they might want to," she said, looking away from him and acting as though she saw another Blue Jay coming.

"You wouldn't be my little wife, would you?" he asked, coming nearer to her.

"Why—I—might!" she answered, with a saucy flirt of her tail, and she scampered away as fast as she could. Do you think Mr. Red Squirrel stopped then to eat his fat kernel of yellow corn? Or do you think he waited to see whether the Blue Jays were around? No, indeed! He followed as fast as his legs could carry him from tree to tree, from branch to branch, and it was not until he had reached the top of a tall beech that he overtook his little sweetheart. They were still there when the Gray Squirrel happened along in the afternoon.

"Ah!" said he, squinting at Mr. Red Squirrel, for his eyes were poor. "You are getting acquainted, are you? Pleasant society here. The Squirrel set is very select. You must meet some of our young people. Suppose you will begin housekeeping one of these days?"

"I have done so already, sir," answered Mr. Red Squirrel, although his wife was nudging him with one paw and motioning him to keep quiet. "Mrs. Red Squirrel and I will build our round home in the top fork of this tree. We shall be pleased to have you call when we are settled."

"Is that so?" exclaimed the Gray Squirrel. "I did not know that you were married. I thought you came alone to the forest."

"This is my wife, sir," said Mr. Red Squirrel, and the Gray Squirrel made his very best bow and looked at her as sharply as his poor eyes would let him.

"I think I must have seen you somewhere," he said; "your face is very familiar." And he scratched his poor old puzzled head with one claw.

"Why, Cousin Gray Squirrel, don't you know Bushy-tail?" she cried. "You lived the next tree to mine all winter."

"To be sure!" he exclaimed. "But isn't your marriage rather sudden?"

"No," she said, blushing under her fur. "We have always liked each other, although we never spoke until this morning. I used to scamper along the rail fence to see Mr. Red Squirrel in his cage."

"Did you truly come for that?" asked her husband, after their caller had gone.

"I truly did," she answered, "but I never expected anybody to know it. You poor fellow! I felt so sorry for you. I would have given every nut I had to set you free."

They were a very happy couple, and the next fall the Gray Squirrel watched them and their children gathering nuts for their winter stores. Mr. Red Squirrel, as the head of the family, planned the work, yet each did his share. The nuts were not yet ripe, and they gnawed off the stems, then came to the ground, filled their cheek-pockets with the fallen nuts, and scampered off to hide them in many places. They were stored in tree-hollows, under the rustling leaves which strewed the ground, in the cracks of old logs, beneath brush-heaps, and in holes in the ground.

"Don't stop to think how many you need," said the little mother to her children. "Get every nut you can. It may be a very long winter."

"And if you don't eat them all," said their hard-working father with a twinkle in his eyes, "you may want to drop a few down to some poor fellow who has none. That was your mother's way."

"When was it her way? What makes you smile when you say it? Mother, what does he mean?" cried the young Red Squirrels all in a breath.

"I gave some nuts to a hungry Squirrel once," she said, "and he was so grateful that he drove the Blue Jays away when they tried to rob me." But she looked so happy as she spoke that the children knew there was more to the story. They dared not tease her to tell, so they whispered among themselves and wondered what their father meant.

As they gathered nuts near the Gray Squirrel, he motioned them to come close. "S-sh!" said he. "Don't tell it from me, but I think the poor hungry fellow was your father, and it was a lucky thing for you that she had enough to give away."

"Do you suppose that was it?" the young Red Squirrels whispered to each other. "Do you really suppose so?"

The Biggest Little Rabbit Learns To See

Seven little Rabbits lay on their nest at the bottom of the burrow, and wriggled and squirmed and pushed their soft noses against each other all day long. Life was very easy for them, and they were contented. The first thing that they remembered was lying on their bed of fur, hay, and dried leaves, and feeling a great, warm, soft Something close beside them. After a while they learned that this Something was their Mamma Rabbit. It was she who had gotten the nest ready for them and lined it with fur that she tore from her own breast. She didn't care so much about looking beautiful as she did about making her babies comfortable.

It was their Mamma Rabbit, too, who fed them with warm milk from her own body until they should be old enough to go out of the burrow. Then they would nibble bark and tender young shoots from the roots of the trees, and all the fresh, green, growing things that Rabbits like. She used to tell them about this food, and they wondered and wondered how it would taste. They began to feel very big and strong now. The soft fur was growing on their naked little bodies and covering even the soles of their feet. It was growing inside their cheeks, too, and that made them feel important, for Papa Rabbit said that he did not know any other animals that had fur inside their cheeks. He said it was something to be very proud of, so they were very proud, although why one should want fur inside of one's cheeks it would be hard to say.

What tangles they did get into! Each little Rabbit had four legs, two short ones in front, and two long ones behind to help him take long jumps from one place to another. So, you see, there were twenty-eight legs there, pushing, catching in the hay, kicking, and sometimes just waving in the air when their tiny owners chanced to roll over on their backs and couldn't get right side up again. Then Mamma Rabbit would come and poke them this way and that, never hurting any of them, but getting the nest in order.

"It is a great deal of work to pick up after children," she would say with a tired little sigh, "but it will not be long before they have homes of their own and are doing the same thing."

Mamma Rabbit was quite right when she said that, for all of their people set up housekeeping when very young, and then the cares of life begin.

One fine morning when the children were alone in their burrow, the biggest little Rabbit had a queer feeling in his face, below and in front of his long ears, and above his eager little nose. It almost scared him at first, for he had never before felt anything at all like it. Then he guessed what it meant. There were two bunchy places on his face, that Mamma Rabbit had told him were eyes. "When you are older," she had said to him, "these eyes will open, and then you will see." For the Rabbit children are always blind when they are babies.

When his mother told him that, the biggest little Rabbit had said, "What do you mean when you say I shall 'see'? Is it anything like eating?"

And Mamma Rabbit said, "No, you cannot taste things until you touch them, but you can see them when they are far away."

"Then it is like smelling," said the biggest little Rabbit.

"No, it is not like smelling, either, for there are many things, like stones, which one cannot smell and yet can see."

"Then it surely is like hearing," said the biggest little Rabbit.

"Oh dear!" exclaimed his mother, who was tired of having questions asked which could not be answered. "It is not a bit like hearing. You could never hear a black cloud coming across the sky, but you could see it if you were outside your burrow. Nobody can make you understand what seeing is until your eyes are open, and then you will find out for yourself without asking."

This made the biggest little Rabbit lie still for a while, and then he said: "What is a black cloud, and why does it come across the sky? And what is the sky, and why does it let the cloud come? And what is—" But he did not get any answer, for his mother ran out of the burrow as fast as she could.

And now his eyes were surely opening and he should see! His tiny heart thumped hard with excitement, and he rubbed his face with his forepaws to make his eyes open faster. Ah! There it was; something round and bright at the other end of the burrow, and some queer, slender things were waving across it. He wondered if it were good to eat, but he dared not crawl toward it to see. He did not know that the round, bright thing was just a bit of sky which he saw through the end of the burrow, and that the slender, waving ones were the branches of a dead tree tossing in the wind. Then he looked at his brothers and sisters as they lay beside him. He would not have known what they were if he had not felt of them at the same time.

"I can see!" he cried. "I can see everything that there is to see! I'm ahead of you! Don't you wish that you could see, too?"

That was not a very kind thing to say, but in a minute more his brothers and sisters had reason to be glad that they couldn't see. Even while he was speaking and looking toward the light, he saw a brown head with two round eyes look in at him, and then a great creature that he thought must surely be a dog ran in toward him. How frightened he was then! He pushed his nose in among his blind brothers and sisters and tried to hide himself among them. He thought something dreadful was about to happen.

"I wish Mamma Rabbit would come," he squeaked, shutting his eyes as closely as he could. "I wish Mamma Rabbit would come."

"Why, here I am," she answered. "What are you afraid of?"

The biggest little Rabbit opened his eyes, and there was the creature who had frightened him so, and it was his own mother! You can imagine how glad she was to see that one of her children had his eyes open.

"I will call in some of my Rabbit friends," she said, "and let you see them, if you will promise not to be afraid."

The next day four of the other little Rabbits had their eyes open, and the day after that they all could see each other and the shining piece of sky at the end of the burrow. It was not so very long afterward that the Rabbit family went out to dine in the forest, and this was the first time that the children had seen their father. Often when their mother left them alone in the burrow she had pulled grass and leaves over the opening to hide it from him, for Rabbit fathers do not love their children until they are old enough to go out into the great world, and it would never do for them to know where their babies are kept. Then their father taught them how to gnaw tough bark to wear their teeth down, for Rabbits' teeth grow all the time, and if they were to eat only soft food, their teeth would get too long. He taught them, too, how to move their ears in the right way for keen hearing, and told them that when chased they must run for the burrow or the nearest thicket. "Then crouch down on some leaves that are the color of your fur," he said, "and you may not be seen at all."

"Why should we run?" said the biggest little Rabbit.

"Because you might be caught if you didn't."

"What might catch us?" asked the biggest little Rabbit.

"Oh, a Hawk, perhaps, or a Weasel."

"What does a Hawk look like?"

"Like a great bird floating in the sky," said Papa Rabbit. "Now, don't ask me a single question more."

"Does a Hawk look like that bird above us?" asked the biggest little Rabbit.

His father gave one look upward. "Yes!" he said. "Run!"

And just as the Hawk swooped down toward the ground, he saw nine white-tipped tails disappear into a burrow near by.

The Little Bat Who Wouldn't Go To Bed

"Come," said Mamma Bat, flying toward her home in the cave, "it is time that you children went to bed. The eastern sky is growing bright, and I can see the fleecy clouds blush rosy red as the sun looks at them."

The little Bats flitted along after her, and Papa Bat came behind them. They had been flying through the starlit forest all night, chasing the many small insects that come out after the sun has gone down, and passing in and out of the tangled branches without ever touching one. Indeed, Mamma Bat would have been ashamed if children of hers flew against anything in the dark. There might be some excuse for such a mistake in the daytime, for Bats' eyes do not see well then, but in the night-time! She would have scolded them well, and they would have deserved it, for Bats have the most wonderful way of feeling things before they touch them, and there are no other people in the forest who can do that. There are no other people who can tell by the feeling of the air when something is near, and the Bats made much fun of their friend, the Screech Owl, once, when he flew against a tree and fell to the ground.

And now the night was over and their mother had called them to go home. One of the little Bats hung back with a very cross look on his face, and twice his father had to tell him to fly faster. He was thinking how he would like to see the forest in the daytime. He had never seen the sun rise, and he wanted to do that. He had never seen any of the day-birds or the animals that awaken in the morning. He thought it was pretty mean to make poor little Bats go off to bed the minute the stars began to fade. He didn't believe what his father and mother said, that he wouldn't have a good time if he did stay up. He had coaxed and coaxed and teased and teased, but it hadn't made a bit of difference. Every morning he had to fold his wings and go to sleep in a dark crack in the rock of the cave, hanging, head downward, close to the rest of the family. Their father said that there never was a better place to sleep than in this same crack, and it certainly was easy to catch on with the hooks at the lower ends of their wings when they hung themselves up for the day. But now he just wouldn't go to bed, so there!

"It is your turn next," said Mamma Bat to him, when the rest of the children had hung themselves up.

"I'm not going to bed," the little Bat answered.

"Not going to bed!" said his father. "Are you crazy?"

"No," said the little Bat, "I'm *not*."

"I don't believe the child is well," said Mamma Bat. "He never acted like this before. I'm afraid he has overeaten." And she looked very anxious.

"I *am* well, and I *haven't* eaten too much," said the little Bat. "I think you might let a fellow have some fun once in a while. I've never seen the sun in my life, and there are whole lots of birds and animals in the forest that I've only heard about."

Papa and Mamma Bat looked at each other without speaking.

"I *won't* go to bed!" said the little Bat.

"Very well," said his father. "I shall not try to make you. Fly away at once and let us go to sleep."

After he had gone, Mamma Bat said, "I suppose you did right to let him go, but it seems too bad that children have to find out for themselves the trouble that comes from disobedience."

The little Bat flew away feeling very brave. He guessed he knew how to take care of himself, even in daylight. He felt sorry for his brothers who were in the cave, but he made up his mind that he would tell them all about it the next night.

The eastern sky grew brighter and brighter. It hurt his eyes to look at it, and he blinked and turned away. Then the song-birds awakened and began to sing. It was very interesting, but he thought they sang too loudly. The forest at night is a quiet place, and he didn't see the sense of shouting so, even if the sun were coming up. The night-birds never made such a fuss over the moon, and he guessed the moon was as good as the sun.

Somebody went scampering over the grass, kicking up his heels as he ran. "That must be a Rabbit," thought the little Bat. "The Screech Owl told me that Rabbits run in that way. I wish I could see him more plainly. I don't know what is the matter with my eyes."

Just then a sunbeam came slanting through the forest and fell on his furry coat as he clung to a branch. "Ow!" he cried. "Ow! How warm it is! I don't like that. The moonbeams do not feel so. I must fly to a shady corner." He started to fly. Just what was the matter, he never knew. It may have been because he couldn't see well, it may have been because he was getting very tired, or it may have been because the strangeness of it all was beginning to frighten him; but at all events, he went down, down, down until he found himself pitching and tumbling around in the grass.

A Crow had seen him fall, and cried loudly, "Come! Come! Come!" to his friends. The Rabbits, who were feeding near by, came scampering along, making great leaps in their haste to see what was the matter. The Goldfinches, the Robins, the Orioles, the Woodpeckers, and many other birds came fluttering up. Even a Blue Jay sat on a branch above the Bat and shrieked, "Jay! Jay! Jay!" to add to the excitement. And last of all, the Ground Hog appeared, coming slowly and with dignity, as a person who can remember his grandfather should do.

"What is the cause of all this commotion?" he asked. He might have said, "What is the matter?" and then they would have understood him at once, but he was too haughty for that. He thought he had to use big words once in a while to show that he could. If people didn't understand them, he was willing to explain what he meant.

"We've found such a queer bird, sir," said the biggest little Rabbit, without waiting to find out what a "commotion" was. "Just see him tumble around!"

"Bird? That is no bird," said a Woodpecker. "Look at his ears and his nose. He hasn't even a bill."

"Well, he flies," said the biggest little Rabbit, "because I saw him, so he must be a bird."

"Humph!" said a Chipmunk. "So does my cousin, the Flying Squirrel, in a way, yet he is no more bird than I am."

"And this fellow hasn't a feather to his skin!" cried an Oriole.

"I don't say that my son is right," said Papa Rabbit, "but this creature has wings." And he gave the Bat a poke that made him flutter wildly for a minute.

"Yes, but what kind of wings?" asked the Goldfinch. "A pair of skinny things that grow on to his legs and have hooks on both ends."

"He must be a very stupid fellow, at all events," said the Ground Hog. "He doesn't talk, or walk, or eat, or even fly well. He must come of a very common family. For my part, I am not interested in persons of that kind." And he walked away with his nose in the air.

Now the other forest people would have liked to watch the Bat longer, but after the Ground Hog had gone off in this way, they thought it would show too much curiosity if they stayed. So one after another went away, and the little Bat was left alone. He fluttered around until he reached the branch where the Blue Jay had been, and there he hung himself up to wait until night.

"Oh dear!" he said, "I wonder how long a day is. I am hot and blind and sleepy, and if any more of the forest people come and talk about me, I don't know what I shall do. They don't think me good-looking because my wings grow to my legs. I only wish I could see what they look like. I believe they are *just* as homely."

And then, because he was a very tired little Bat, and cross, as people always are when they have done wrong, he began to blame somebody else for all his trouble.

"If my father and mother had cared very much about me," he said, "they would never have let me stay up all day. Guess if I were a big Bat and had little Bats of my own, I'd take better care of them!" But that is always the way, and when, long afterward, he was a big Bat with little Bats of his own, he was a much wiser person.

A Swarm Leaves The Bee Tree

The old Bee tree was becoming very crowded and the Queen-Mother grew restless. There were many things to make her so. In the tree were thousands of cells made ready for her eggs, and she had been busy for days putting one in each. In the larger cells she laid eggs that would hatch out Drones, and in the smaller ones she laid Worker eggs. She never laid any Queen eggs. Perhaps she did not want any Queens among her children, for there can never be two Queens in one swarm, and when a new one is hatched, the Queen-Mother has to go away and find another home. That is a law among the Bees.

The Workers, however, knew that there must be young Queens growing up all the time. Supposing something should happen to the Queen-Mother, what would become of the swarm if there were nobody to lay eggs? So after she had laid several thousand Worker eggs, and it was time for the young ones to hatch, they decided to change some of the babies into young Queens. And this was easy enough. When they were out for honey, they filled the pockets on their hind legs with pollen, the yellow dust that is found in flowers. This was to be mixed with honey and water and made into bread for the babies, who were now awake, and looked like tiny white worms in the bottom of their cells. Then they made some that was almost like sour jelly, and put it in a few of the Worker cells for the tiny white worms, or Larvæ, to eat. The Larvæ that eat this jelly grow up to be Queens, and can lay eggs. Those that eat the common bread are either Drones or Workers, whichever their mother had planned them to be.

After the Larvæ were five or six days old, the Workers shut them up in their cells and stopped feeding them. That was because the Larvæ had other things to do than eat. They had to spin their cocoons, and lie in them until they were grown and ready to come out among the older Bees. When a Larva, or Bee baby, has finished its cocoon, and is lying inside, it is called a Pupa, and when a Pupa is full grown and has torn its way out of the cocoon and wax, it is called a Drone, or a Worker, or a Queen.

Now the Queen-Mother was restless. She could hear the young Queens piping in their cells, and she knew that they wanted to come out and drive her away. She wanted to get to them and stop their piping, but the Workers stood in her way and prevented her. They knew it would not be well for the Queen-Mother to meet her royal children, and when these children tried to come out the Workers covered the doors of their cells with another layer of wax, leaving little holes where they could put out their tongues and be fed.

This made the Queen-Mother more restless than ever. "If I cannot do as I wish to with my own children," she said, "I will leave the tree." And she began walking back and forth as fast as she could, and talked a great deal, and acted almost wild with impatience. The Workers saw how she felt, and part of them decided to go with her. When a Worker made up her mind to go with the Queen-Mother, she showed it by also acting wild and walking back and forth, and talking a great deal, sometimes fluttering her wings very fast. Then she would go for honey, because when Bees are about to swarm they fill their honey-pockets just as full as they can. At times the Queen-Mother would be quiet, and you might almost think that she had given up going. Then suddenly she would grow restless again, and all the Workers who were going with her would act as she did, and they would get so warm with excitement that the air in the tree became quite hot.

At last the Queen-Mother thought it time to start, and her followers came around her in the tree, and were very still for a minute. Several of the Workers had been flying in circles around the tree, and now they came to the doorway and called. Then all came out, and hovered in the air a few minutes before stopping to rest on a bush near by. When they rested, the first Bee held on to the bush, the next Bee held on to her, and that was the way they did until they were all clinging tightly together in a squirming, dark-brown mass.

Ah, then the Queen-Mother was happy! She felt that she was young again, and she thought, "How they love me, these dear Workers!" She stroked her body with her legs to make herself as fine as possible, and she noticed, with pleasure, how slender she was growing. "I had thought I should never fly again," she said, "yet this is delightful. I believe I will go off by myself for a little while."

So she flew off by herself and was talking rather airily to a Butterfly when two of the Workers came after her.

"You may return to the rest," she said in a queenly way, as she motioned to them with her feelers. "I will come by and by."

"No," said they, "you must come at once or we shall all go back to the Bee tree. You must stay with us. You must do your part as it should be done." And she had to go, for she knew in her heart that Queens have to obey the law as well as other people.

After she had hung with the Workers on the bush for some time, the ones who had gone ahead to find a new home for the swarm came back and gave the signal for the rest to follow. They went to an old log near the river-bank, and here they began the real work. Crawling through an opening at one end, they found a roomy place within, and commenced to clean house at once.

"If there is anything I do like," said a Worker, as she dropped a splinter of rotten wood outside the door, "it is house-cleaning."

"So do I," said her sister. "But what a fuss the Drones always make when we try to do anything of the sort! A pretty-looking home we'd have if they took care of it!"

"I'm glad none of them came with us to this place," said the first Worker. "I guess they knew they were not wanted."

"There, there!" said the Queen-Mother, coming up to where they were; "you must not talk in that way. It may be that you would rather do without Drones, and perhaps they would rather do without you; but I need you both and I will not have any quarreling." When she said this she walked away with her head in the air, and the Workers did not scold any more. They knew that she was right, and, after all, she was their Queen, even if she did have to obey the laws.

Next they got varnish from the buds of poplar trees and varnished over all the cracks and little holes in the walls of their home, leaving open only the place where they were to go in and out. They also covered with varnish a few heavy fragments of wood that lay on the floor of their home, and when this task was done it was all in order and ready for the furniture, that is, the comb.

You know how the comb looks, and you know how they get the wax from which to make it, but unless you are acquainted with the Bees, and have seen them at work, you have no idea what busy creatures they are. The Queen-Mother, as soon as the cells were ready and she could begin laying eggs again, was as contented and happy as ever.

One day, when she was walking around a corner of the comb, she ran against a sad and discouraged-looking Worker. "Why, what is the matter?" said she, kindly. "Are you sick?"

"No," answered the Worker. "I'm not sick and I'm not tired, only I want to get through."

"Through with what?" asked the Queen.

"With work! It is clean house, varnish the walls, make wax, build combs, get honey, make bread and jelly, and feed the babies. And when they get old enough they'll have to clean house, varnish the walls, make wax, build combs, get honey, make bread and jelly, and feed the babies. I want to know when it is going to stop, and Bees can spend their time in play."

"Never," said the Queen-Mother; and she spoke very gently, for she saw that the Worker was crazy. "It will never stop. If you had nothing to do but play all your life you would soon want to die, and you ought to, for there is no place in this world for idlers. You know that after a while the Drones die because they do nothing, and it is right they should."

"Don't you ever get tired of your eggs?" asked the Worker.

"No," answered the Queen-Mother, "I don't. You see, I have so much to think about, and happy thoughts make tasks light. And then, you know, it is not always the same kind of egg, and that makes a pleasant change for me. I will give you a motto to remember: 'As long as a Bee is well, work is pleasant when done faithfully.'"

"Perhaps that is the matter with me," said the Worker, raising her drooping head. "I have been careless lately when I thought nobody was looking. I will try your way."

When she had gone, the Queen-Mother smiled to herself and said: "Poor child! When work is no longer a pleasure, life is indeed sad. But any Larva should know better than to work carelessly when she is not watched."

The Haughty Ground Hog

Not far from the home of the Rabbits was another burrow where the Ground Hog lived, and there was a very kindly feeling between the neighbors. They liked the same food, and as there was plenty for all, they often nibbled together near the edge of the forest. The little Rabbits were fond of him and liked to listen to his stories. Once the biggest little Rabbit had run into the Ground Hog's burrow by mistake when he was frightened, and that was the beginning of a great friendship between them.

They were a queer-looking couple, for the Rabbit was small and quick and dainty, while the Ground Hog, with his stout body covered with thick, reddish fur, his broad, flat head, and his short legs, was a clumsy fellow. To be sure, he could get out of sight quickly if he had to, but he never scampered around and kicked up his heels for the fun of it, as the Rabbits did. He was too dignified to do that. He came of an old family and he could remember who his grandfather was. There were but few people in the forest who could do that; so, of course, he could not frisk like his neighbors.

Perhaps if the Ground Hog had not belonged to so old a family, he might have had a better time. Yet the thought that he could remember his grandfather was a great pleasure to him, and when he was talking he would often remark in the most careless way, "as my grandfather used to say"; or, "That reminds me of something my grandfather once did." Some people said that he did this to show off; but it may be that they were envious.

However that may have been, the Ground Hog was certainly a haughty fellow, and if he had not been so gentle and kind a neighbor people would not have liked him. Only once had he been known to get angry, and that was when a saucy young Chipmunk had spoken of him as a Woodchuck. "Woodchuck! Woodchuck!" he had grunted. "You young Bushy-tail, I am a Ground Hog, and the Ground Hog family lived in this forest long before you ever opened your eyes. People with good manners do not call us 'Woodchucks.' We do not like the name. My grandfather could not endure it."

It was not very long after this that he told the wondering young Rabbits about his grandfather. When talking, the Ground Hog rested by the edge of his burrow, sitting on his haunches, and waving his queer little forepaws whenever he told anything especially important. And this was the story:

"Perhaps you may have heard me speak of my grandfather. Ah, he was a Ground Hog worth seeing! He was large, and, although when I knew him the black fur on his back was streaked with gray, he was still handsome. He was clever, too. I have often heard my father say that he could dig the deepest and best burrow in the forest. And then he had such fine manners! There was not another Ground Hog in the country around who could eat as noisily as he, and it is said that when he was courting my grandmother she chose him because of the elegant way in which he sat up on his haunches. I have been told, children, that I am very much like him."

Just here, a Red-headed Woodpecker gave a loud "Rat-a-tat-tat" on the tree above the Ground Hog's head, and there was a look around her bill as though she wanted to laugh. The Ground Hog slowly turned his head to look at her as she flew away. "Quite a good-looking young person," he said, "but badly brought up. She should know better than to disturb those who are talking. What was I saying, children?"

"You were telling how well your grandfather sat up on his haunches," said the smallest little Rabbit.

"So I was! So I was! I must tell you how my grandfather came to know the world so well. When he was only a young fellow, he made his home for a time by a Hen house, and so heard the talk of the barn-yard people. Once he heard them tell how the farmer watched on a certain winter day to see my grandfather come out of his burrow. Of course, you children all know how we Ground Hogs do; in the fall we are very fat, and when the cold weather comes we go to sleep in our burrows to wait for spring. Sometimes we awaken and stretch, but we go to sleep again very soon. Then, when spring comes we are slender and have healthy appetites.

"The Hens treated my grandfather with great politeness, and the Black Brahma Cock showed plainly how honored they felt to have him there. They said that they were so glad my grandfather stayed out of his burrow awhile on this winter day when the farmer was watching, because they were in a hurry for warm weather. My grandfather did not know what they meant by that, but he was too wise to say so, and he found out by asking questions, that if a Ground Hog leaves his burrow on this certain day in winter, and sees his shadow, and goes back again, it will be cold for a long time after that. If he does not see his shadow, and stays out, it will soon be warm.

"You see now, children, how important our family is; and yet we are so modest that we had not even known that we made the weather until the Hens told my grandfather. But that is the way! Really great people often think the least of themselves."

"And do you make the weather?" asked the smallest little Rabbit.

"I suppose we do," said the Ground Hog, with a smile. "It is a great care. I often say to myself: 'Shall I have it warm, or shall I have it cold?' It worries me so that sometimes I can hardly eat."

"And how do you know when the day comes for you to make the weather?" said the smallest little rabbit.

"Ahem! Well-er! I am sorry to say that my grandfather did not find out exactly what day it is that they watch for us, so I have to guess at that. But to think that we Ground Hogs make the weather for all the other people! It is worth a great deal to belong to such a family. I suppose I might have been a Weasel, a Fox, an Owl, or an Oriole. And it is a great thing to have known one's grandfather."

The little Rabbits sat very still, wishing that they had known their grandfather, when suddenly the biggest one said: "If you should stay out of your burrow when that day comes, and another Ground Hog should go back into his burrow, how would the weather know what to do?"

"Children," said the old Ground Hog, "I think your mother is calling to you. You might better go to see. Good-by." And he waved his paw politely.

The seven little Rabbits scampered away, but their mother was not calling them. She wasn't even there, and when they went back they couldn't find the Ground Hog. They wondered how he happened to make such a mistake. The Red-headed Woodpecker who came along at about that time, twisted her head on one side and said: "Made-a-mistake! Rat-a-tat-tat! Not he!"

The Undecided Rattlesnake

It is not often that one of the Forest People has any trouble about making up his mind, but there was one large Rattlesnake who had great difficulty in doing so. She lived in the southern edge of the forest, where the sunshine was clear and warm, and there were delightful crevices among the rocks in which she and all her friends and relatives could hide.

It seemed very strange that so old a Snake should be so undecided as she was. It must be that she had a careless mother who did not bring her up in the right way. If that were so, one should indeed be sorry for her. Still even that would be no real excuse, for was she not old enough now to train herself? She had seven joints in the rattle on her tail and an eighth one growing, so you can see that she was no longer young, although, being healthy, she had grown her new joints and changed her skin oftener than some of her friends. In fact, she had grown children of her own, and if it had not been that they took after their father, they would have been a most helpless family. Fortunately for them, their father was a very decided Snake.

Yes, it was exceedingly lucky for them. It may not have been so good a thing for him. His wife was always glad to have things settled for her, and when he said, "We will do this," she answered, "Yes, dear." When he said, "We will not do that," she murmured, "No, dear." And when he said, "What shall we do?" she would reply, "Oh, I don't know. What do you think we might better do?" He did not very often ask her opinion, and there were people in the forest who said he would never have talked matters over with her if he had not known that she would leave the decision to him.

Now this is a bad way in which to have things go in any family, and it happened here as it would anywhere. He grew more and more selfish from having his own way all of the time, and his wife became less and less able to take care of herself. Most people thought him a very devoted husband. Perhaps he was. It is easy to be a devoted husband if you always have your own way.

One night Mr. Rattlesnake did not return to their home. Nobody ever knew what had become of him. The Red Squirrel said that Mrs. Goldfinch said that the biggest little Rabbit had told her that the Ground Hog had overheard Mr. Crow say that he thought he saw somebody that looked like Mr. Rattlesnake chasing a Field Mouse over toward the farm, but that he might have been mistaken. This was all so uncertain that Mrs. Rattlesnake knew no more than she had known before. It was very trying.

"If I only knew positively," she said to her friend, Mrs. Striped Snake, "I could do something, although I am sure I don't know what it would be."

Mrs. Striped Snake tried to help her. "Why not have one of your children come home to live with you?" she said pleasantly, for this year's children were now old enough to shift for themselves.

"I've thought of that," answered Mrs. Rattlesnake, "but I like a quiet life, and you know how it is. Young Snakes will be young Snakes. Besides, I don't think they would want to come back."

"Well, why not be alone, then?"

"Oh, it is so lonely," replied Mrs. Rattlesnake, with a sigh. "Everything reminds me so of my husband, and that makes me sad. If I lived somewhere else it would be different."

"Then why not move?" said Mrs. Striped Snake, briskly. "I would do that. Find a nice crack in the rock just big enough for one, or make a cosy little hole in the ground somewhere near here. Then if he comes back he can find you easily. I would do that. I certainly would."

She spoke so firmly that Mrs. Rattlesnake said she would, she would to-morrow. And her friend went home thinking it was all settled. That shows how little she really knew Mrs. Rattlesnake.

The more Mrs. Rattlesnake thought it over that night, the more she dreaded moving. "If he does not come back," she sighed, "I may marry again in the spring, and then I might have to move once more. I believe I will ask somebody else what I ought to do."

So in the morning she began to consult her friends. They all told her to move, and she decided to do it. Then she could not make up her mind whether to take a rock-crevice or make a hole in the ground. It took another day of visiting to settle that it should be a hole in the ground. A fourth day was spent in finding just the right place for her home, and on the fifth day she began work.

By the time the sun was over the tree-tops, she wished she had chosen some other place, and thought best to stop and talk to some of her friends about it. When she returned she found herself obliged to cast her skin, which had been growing tight and dry for some time. This was hard work, and she was too tired to go on with her home-making, so she lay in the sunshine and admired her beautiful, long, and shining body of reddish brown spotted with black. Her rattle had eight joints now, for when a Rattlesnake casts the old skin a new joint is always uncovered at the end of the tail. She waved it quickly to see how an eight-jointed rattle would sound. "Lovely!" she said. "Lovely! Like the seeds of the wild cucumber shaking around in their dry and prickly case."

One could not tell all the things that happened that fall, or how very, very, very tired her friends became of having her ask their advice. She changed her mind more times than there are seeds in a milkweed pod, and the only thing of which she was always sure was eating. When there was food in sight she did not stop for anybody's advice. She ate it as fast as she could, and if she had any doubts about the wisdom of doing so, she kept them to herself.

When winter came she had just got her new home ready, and after all she went when invited to spend the winter with a cave party of other Snakes. They coiled themselves together in a great mass and slept there until spring. As the weather grew warmer, they began to stir, wriggling and twisting themselves free.

Two bachelor Snakes asked her to marry. One was a fine old fellow with a twelve-jointed rattle. The other was just her own age.

"To be sure I will," she cried, and the pits between her nostrils and her ears looked more like dimples than ever. "Only you must wait until I can make up my mind which one to marry."

"Oh, no," they answered, "don't go to all that trouble. We will fight and decide it for you."

It was a long fight, and the older of the two Snakes had a couple of joints broken off from his rattle before it was over. Still he beat the other one and drove him away. When he came back for his bride he found her crying. "What is the matter?" said he, quite sternly.

"Oh, that p-poor other b-bachelor!" she sobbed. "I b-believe I will g-go after him. I think p-perhaps I l-love him the b-better."

"No, you don't, Mrs. Rattlesnake," said the fine old fellow who had just won the fight. "You will do no such thing. You will marry me and never speak to him again. When I have lost two joints of my rattle in fighting for you, I intend to have you myself, and *I* say that you love me very dearly. Do you hear?"

"Yes, darling," she answered, as she wiped her eyes on the grass, "very dearly." And they lived most happily together.

"He reminds me so much of the first Mr. Rattlesnake," she said to her friends. "So strong, so firm, so quick to decide!"

And the friends said to each other, "Well, let us be thankful he is. We have been bothered enough by her coming to us for advice which she never followed."

The Quarrelsome Mole

When the first hillock of fresh brown earth was thrown up in the edge of the Forest, the People who lived there said to each other. "Can it be that we have a new neighbor?"

Perhaps the Rabbits, the Ground Hogs, and the Snakes cared the most, for they also made their homes in the ground; yet even the Orioles wanted to know all about it. None of them had ever been acquainted with a Mole. They had seen the ridges in the meadows beneath which the Moles had their runways, and they knew that when the Moles were making these long streets under ground, they had to cut an opening through the grass once in a while and throw the loose earth out. This new mound in the forest looked exactly like those in the meadow, so they decided there must be a Mole in the neighborhood.

If that were so, somebody should call upon him and get acquainted; but how could they call? Mrs. Red Squirrel said: "Why can't some of you people who are so clever at digging, burrow down and find him?"

"Yes indeed," twittered the birds; "that is a good plan."

But Mr. Red Squirrel smiled at his wife and said: "I am afraid, Bushy-tail (that was his pet name for her) that none of our friends here could overtake the Mole. You know he is a very fast runner. If they were following they could never catch him."

"Let them burrow down ahead of the place where he is working, then," said she.

"And the Mole would turn and go another way, not knowing it was a friend looking for him."

"Well, why not make an opening into one of his runways and go into it, hunting until he is found?" said Mrs. Red Squirrel, who was like some other people in not wishing to give up her own ideas.

"Yes," cried a mischievous young Woodpecker; "let the Ground Hog go. You surely don't think him too fat?"

Now there was no denying that the Ground Hog was getting too stout to look well, and people thought he would be angry at this. Perhaps he was angry. The little Rabbits were sure of it. They said they knew by the expression of his tail. Still, you know, the Ground Hog came of a good family, and well-bred people do not say mean things even if they are annoyed. He combed the fur on his face with both paws, and answered with a polite bow: "If I had the slender and graceful form of my charming friend, Mrs. Red Squirrel, I should be delighted to do as she suggests."

That was really a very clever thing for Mr. Ground Hog to say. It was much more agreeable than if he had grunted out, "Much she knows about it! We burrowing people are all too large." And now Mrs. Red Squirrel was pleased and happy although her plan was not used.

That night Mrs. Ground Hog said to her husband: "I didn't know you admired Mrs. Red Squirrel so much." And he answered: "Pooh! Admire her? She is a very good-looking person for one of her family, and I want to be polite to her for her husband's sake. He and I have business together. But for my part I prefer more flesh. I could never have married a slender wife, and I am pleased to see, my dear, that you are stouter than you were." And this also shows how clever a fellow Mr. Ground Hog was.

The very next night, as luck would have it, the Mole came out of his runway for a scamper on the grass. Mr. Ground Hog saw him and made his acquaintance. "We are glad to have you come," said he. "You will find it a pleasant neighborhood. People are very friendly."

"Well, I'm glad of that," answered the Mole. "I don't see any sense in people being disagreeable, myself, but in the meadow which I have just left there were the worst neighbors in the world. I stood it just as long as I could, and then I moved."

"I am sorry to hear that," said the Ground Hog, gently. "I had always supposed it a pleasant place to live in." He began to wonder what kind of fellow the Mole was. He did not like to hear him say such unkind things before a new acquaintance. Sometimes unpleasant things have to be said, but it was not so now.

"Umph!" said the Mole. "You have to live with people to know them. Of course, we Moles had no friends among the insects. We are always glad to meet them in the ground, but they do not seem so glad to meet us. That is easily understood when you remember what hungry people Moles are. Friendship is all very well, but when a fellow's stomach is empty, he can't let that stand in the way of a good dinner. There was no such reason why the Tree Frog or the Garter Snake should dislike me."

"Are you sure they did dislike you?"

"Certain of it. I remember how one night I wanted to talk with the Garter Snake, and asked him to come out of his hole for a visit in the moonlight. He wouldn't come."

"What did he say?" asked the Ground Hog.

"Not a word! And that was the worst of it. Think how provoking it was for me to stand there and call and call and not get any reply."

"Perhaps he was not at home," suggested the Ground Hog.

"That's what he said when I spoke to him. Said he was spending the night down by the river. As though I'd be likely to believe that! I guess he saw that he couldn't fool me, though, for after I told him what I thought of him he wriggled away without saying a word."

"Still he is not so disagreeable as the Tree Frog," said the Mole, after a pause in which the Ground Hog had been trying not to laugh. The Ground Hog said afterward that it was the funniest sight imaginable to see the stout little Mole scampering back and forth in the moonlight, and stopping every few minutes to scold about the Meadow People. The twitching of his tiny tail and the jerky motions of his large, pink-palmed digging hands, showed how angry he grew in thinking of them, and his pink snout fairly quivered with rage.

"I will tell you about the Tree Frog," said the Mole. "He is one of these fellows who are always just so good-natured and polite. I can't endure them. I say it's putting on airs to act that way. I was telling him what I thought of the Garter Snake, and what should he do but draw himself up and say: 'Excuse me, but the Garter Snake is a particular friend of mine, and I do not care to hear him spoken of in that way.' I guess I taught him one good lesson, though. I told him he was just the kind of person I should expect the Garter Snake to like, and that I wished them much joy together, but that I didn't want anything to do with them.

"It was only a short time after this that I had such trouble about making my fort. Whenever I started to dig in a place I would find some other Mole there ahead of me."

"And then you would have to go somewhere else, of course?" said the Ground Hog.

"I'd like to know why!" said the Mole, with his glossy silver-brown fur on end. "No indeed! I had a perfect right to dig wherever I wished, and I would tell them so, and they would have to go elsewhere. One Mole was bad-tempered enough to say that he had as much right in the meadow as anybody, and I had to tussle with him and bite him many times before he saw his mistake.... They are disagreeable people over there,—but why are you going so soon? I thought we would have a good visit together."

"I promised to meet Mrs. Ground Hog," said her husband, "and must go. Good-night!" and he trotted away.

Not long afterward this highly respectable couple were feeding together in the moonlight. "What do you think of the Mole?" said she.

"Well,—er—ahem," answered her husband. "You know, my dear, that I do not like to talk against people, and I might better not tell you exactly what I think of him. He is a queer-looking fellow, and I always distrust anyone who will not look me in the eye. Perhaps that is not his fault, for the fur hides his eyes and he wears his ears inside of his head; but I must say that a fiercer or more disagreeable-looking snout I never saw. He has had trouble with all his old neighbors, and a fellow who cannot get along peaceably in one place will not in another. He is always talking about his rights and what he thinks——"

"You have told me enough," said Mrs. Ground Hog, interrupting him. "Nobody ever liked a person who insists on his 'rights' every time. And such a person never enjoys life. What a pity it is!" and she gave a sigh that shook her fat sides. "Now, I had it all planned that he should marry and set up housekeeping, and that I should have another pleasant neighbor soon."

"Ah! Mrs. Ground Hog," said her husband teasingly, "I knew you would be thinking of that. You are a born matchmaker. Now I think we could stand a few bachelors around here,—fine young fellows who have nothing to do but enjoy life." And his eyes twinkled as he said it.

"As though you did not enjoy life!" answered his wife. "Still, I could not wish any young Mole such a husband as this fellow. It is a great undertaking to marry a grumpy bachelor and teach him the happiness of living for others." And she looked very solemn.

"I suppose you found it so?" said Mr. Ground Hog, sidling up toward her.

"What a tease you are!" said his wife. "You know that I am happy." And really, of all the couples on whom the moon looked that night, there was not a happier one than this pair of Ground Hogs; and there was not a lonelier or more miserable person than the Mole, who guarded his own rights and told people what he thought of them. But it is always so.

The Wild Turkeys Come

The Wild Turkeys are a wandering people, and stay in one place only long enough to rear their young. One could hardly say that they lived in the Forest, but every year when the acorns and beechnuts were ripe, they came for a visit. It is always an exciting time when the Turkeys are seen gathering on the farther side of the river and making ready to fly over. Some of the Forest People have started for the warmer country in the South, and those who still remain are either talking over their plans for flight, or working hard, if they are to spend the winter in the North, to get their stores of food ready.

It was so this year. One morning a Red-headed Woodpecker brought the news that the Turkeys were gathering. The Ground Hog heard of it just as he was going to sleep after a night of feeding and rambling in the edge of the meadow. One of the young Rabbits told him, and coaxed him to stay up to see the newcomers.

"I've never seen Turkeys in my life," said the young Rabbit, "and they say it is great fun to watch them. Oh, please come with me to the river-bank and see the Turkeys cross over. Please do!"

"Ah-h-h," yawned the Ground Hog. "You might better ask somebody who has not been up all night. I am too sleepy."

"You won't be sleepy when you reach the river-bank," said the Rabbit. "Beside, I think there should be someone there to meet them."

At this, the Ground Hog raised his drooping head, opened his blinking eyes, and answered with great dignity: "There should indeed be someone. I will go at once."

When they reached the river-bank there was a sight well worth seeing. On the farther side of the water were a great many Turkeys. Old Gobblers were there, and the mother Turkeys with their broods of children, all looking as fine as you please, in their shining black coats. When they stood in the shadow, one might think that they wore no color but the brilliant red of their heads and necks, where there were no feathers to cover their wrinkled skin. When they walked out into the sunshine, however, their feathers showed gleams of beautiful purple and green, and the Rabbit thought them the most wonderful great creatures he had ever seen.

"Look at them now!" he cried. "Why do those largest ones walk up and down in front of the rest and scold them?"

"They are the Gobblers," answered the Ground Hog, "and they are doing that to show that they are not afraid to cross the river. They strut and gobble, and strut and gobble, and say: 'Who's-afraid? Who's-afraid?' until the rest are ready to fly over."

"Now the others are doing the same thing," said the Rabbit, as the mothers and young Turkeys began to strut back and forth.

"That shows that they are willing to cross," answered the Ground Hog. "Now they will fly up to the very tops of the trees on the hill and visit there for a time. It is always so. They start from the highest point they can find. It will be some time before they come over, and I will take a short nap. Be sure to awaken me when they start. I want to welcome them to the Forest." And the Ground Hog curled himself up beside a log and went to sleep.

The Rabbit wandered around and ate all the good things he could find. Then he fell to wondering how it would feel to be a bird. He thought it would be great fun to fly. To pass so swiftly through the air must be delightful, and then to sweep grandly down and alight softly on the ground without having people know that you were coming!

He had a good mind to try it. There was nobody to watch him, and he crept up the trunk of a fallen tree which leaned over against its neighbors. It was a foolish thing to do, and he knew it, but young Rabbits are too full of mischief to always be wise.

"I will hold my hind legs very still," he thought, "and flap my forelegs for wings." With that he jumped off and came crashing down upon the dry leaves. He felt weak and dizzy, and as he picked himself up and looked around he hoped that nobody had seen him. "It may be a great deal of fun to fly," he said, "but it is no fun alighting from your flight unless you have real feather wings. It is too bumpy when you fly with your legs."

At this minute he heard an old Gobbler call out, and saw the flock of Turkeys coming toward him. "Wake up! Wake up!" he cried to the Ground Hog. But the Ground Hog never moved.

Still the Turkeys came nearer. The Rabbit could see that the fat old ones were getting ahead of the others, and that here and there a young or weak Turkey had to drop into the river and swim, because his wings were tired. They got so near that he could see the queer little tufts of wiry feathers which the Gobblers wear hanging from their breast, and could see the swaying scarlet wattles under their beaks. He called again to the Ground Hog, and getting no answer, poked him three times with his head.

The Ground Hog turned over, stretched, yawned, moved his jaws a few times as though he dreamed of eating fresh spring grass, and then fell asleep once more. After that the Rabbit left him alone.

The first to alight were the Gobblers, and they began at once to strut and chatter. Next came the mother Turkeys and their young, and last of all came the weak ones who swam across. It was a fine sight to see them come in. The swimmers spread their tails, folded their wings tightly, stretched their necks, and struck out swiftly and strongly with their feet.

The young Rabbit could hear a group of mothers talking together. "The Gobblers are growing quite fond of the children," said one.

"Yes," said another; "my husband told me yesterday that he was very proud of our little ones."

"Well, it is the season for them to begin to walk together," said the first speaker; "but I never in my life had such a time as I had this spring. I thought my husband would break every egg I laid."

"I had a hard time too," said the other. "None of my eggs were broken, but after my chicks were hatched I had to hurry them out of their father's sight a dozen times a day."

"It is very trying," said a third mother Turkey with a sigh; "but that is always the way with the Gobblers. I suppose the dear fellows can't help it;" and she looked lovingly over at her husband as he strutted around with his friends. You would not have believed if you had seen her fond looks, and heard her husband's tender "Gobble," that they had hardly spoken to each other all summer. To be sure, it was not now as it had been in the springtime. Then he would have beaten any other Gobbler who came near her, he loved her so; still, the Rabbit could see as he watched them that when he found some very large and fine acorns, this Gobbler would not eat them all, but called his wife to come and share with him; and he knew that they were happy together in their own Turkey way of being happy.

At this minute the Ground Hog opened his eyes and staggered to his feet. The loud talking had awakened him. He did not look very dignified just now. His fur was rumpled, and he blinked often from sleepiness. There was a dry leaf caught on one of his ears, too, that made him look very odd. The Rabbit wanted to laugh, but he did not dare to do so. The Ground Hog walked toward the Gobblers, and raised himself on his haunches.

"Good-evening, good-evening," said he (it was really morning, you know). "We are very glad to welcome you to the forest. Make yourselves perfectly at home. The grass is not so tender as it was a while ago, yet I think that you will find good feeding," and he waved his paws politely.

"Thank-you,—thank-you!" answered the Gobblers, while the mothers and young Turkeys came crowding up to look at the Ground Hog. "We came for the acorns and nuts. We shall certainly enjoy ourselves."

"That is right," said the Ground Hog heartily. "We have a very fine forest here. You will pardon me for remarking it. The Pond People have a saying that is very true: 'It's a mighty poor Frog that won't croak for his own puddle.' And my grandfather used to say that if a Ground Hog didn't love his own home he was a very poor Hog indeed. Good-night, my friends, good-night." And he trotted happily away, followed by the Rabbit.

When he was gone, the Turkeys said: "How very kind of him!" and "What fine manners!" And the young Rabbit thought to himself: "It is queer. He was sleepy and his fur was rumpled, and that leaf bobbed around his ear when he talked. He said 'evening' instead of 'morning,' and spoke as though Turkeys came here to eat grass. And yet they all liked him, and were pleased by what he said."

You see the young Rabbit had not yet learned that the power of fine manners is more than that of looks; and that people could not think of the Ground Hog's mistakes in speaking because they knew his kindness of heart.

The Travellers Go South

One night a maple tree, the very one under which Mr. Red Squirrel sat when he first came to the forest, dreamed of her winter resting-time, and when she awakened early in the morning she found that her leaves were turning yellow. They were not all brightly colored, but on each was an edging, or a tip, or a splash of gold. You may be sure that the Forest People noticed it at once.

"I told you so," chirruped a Robin to her mate. "The Orioles went long ago, and the Bobolinks start to-day. We must think about our trip to the South." When she said this, she hopped restlessly from twig to twig with an air of being exceedingly busy.

Her husband did not answer, but began to arrange his new coat of feathers. Perhaps he was used to her fussy ways and thought it just as well to keep still. He knew that none of the Robins would start South until the weather became much colder, and he did not think it necessary to talk about it yet. Perhaps, too, Mr. Robin was a trifle contrary and was all the more slow and quiet because his wife was uneasy. In that case one could hardly blame her for talking over the family plans with the neighbors.

Later in the day, a Bobolink came up from the marsh to say good-by. He had on his travelling suit of striped brown, and you would never have known him for the same gay fellow who during the spring and early summer wore black and buff and sang so heartily and sweetly. Now he did not sing at all, and slipped silently from bush to bush, only speaking when he had to. He was a good fellow and everyone disliked to have him go.

Mrs. Cowbird came up while they were talking. Now that she did not care to lay any more eggs, the other birds were quite friendly with her. They began to talk over the summer that was past, and said how finely the young birds were coming on. "By the way," said she, in the most careless manner possible, "I ought to have a few children round here somewhere. Can anybody tell me where they are?"

Mrs. Goldfinch looked at her husband and he looked at the sky. The Warblers and the Vireos, who had known about the strange egg in the Goldfinches' nest, had already left for the winter, and there seemed to be no use in telling their secret now or quarrelling over what was past. Some of the other birds might have told Mrs. Cowbird a few things, but they also kept still.

"It is a shame," she said. "I never laid a finer lot of eggs in my life, and I was very careful where I put them. I wish I knew how many there were, but I forgot to count. I have been watching and watching for my little birds to join our flock; I was sure I should know them if I saw them. Mothers have such fine feelings, you know, in regard to their children." (As though she had any right to say that!)

The Mourning Doves were there with their young son and daughter, and you could see by looking at them that they were an affectionate family. "We shall be the last to go South," they cooed. "We always mean to come North in the very early spring and stay as late as possible. This year we came much later than usual, but it could not be helped." They had spoken so before, and rather sadly. It was said that they could tell a sorrowful story if they would; but they did not wish to sadden others by it, and bore their troubles together bravely and lovingly.

"How do the new feathers work?" asked a Crow, flying up at this minute and looking blacker than ever in his fall coat. Then all the birds began to talk about dress. As soon as their broods were raised, you know, their feathers had begun to drop out, and they had kept on moulting until all of the old ones were gone and the new ones on. When birds are moulting they never feel well, and when it is over they are both happy and proud.

"I changed later than usual this year," said the Crow, "and I feel that I have the very latest fashions." This was a joke which he must have picked up among the Barnyard People, and nobody knows where they got it. Fashions never change in the Forest.

"I think," remarked a Red-headed Woodpecker, "that I have the best wing feathers now that I ever had. They seem to be a little longer, and they hook together so well. I almost wish I were going South to try them on a long journey."

"Mr. Woodpecker's wing feathers are certainly excellent," said his wife, who was always glad to see him well dressed. "I am sure that the strongest wind will never part them. I don't see how the Owls can stand it to wear their feathers unhooked so that some of the air passes through their wings each time they flap them. It must make flying hard."

"Well, if you were an Owl you would understand," chuckled the Crow. "If their great wings were like ours, the noise of their flying would scare every creature within hearing, and there would not be much fun in hunting."

And so they chatted on, while from the meadow came the sound of the happy insects piping in the sunshine. It was chilly now at night and in the early morning, and they could give concerts only at noonday. The next day the Wild Turkeys came and there was great excitement in the forest. The Squirrels were busier than ever storing up all the acorns that they could before the newcomers reached the oak trees; and the Blue Jays were so jealous of the Turkeys that they overate every day for fear there would not be enough to go around. As though there were any danger!

The Ground Hog was getting so sleepy now that he would doze off while people were talking to him, and then he would suddenly straighten up and say: "Yes, yes, yes! Don't think that I was asleep, please. The colors of the trees are so bright that they tire my eyes and I sometimes close them." The dear old fellow really never knew how he had been nodding.

The Snakes, too, were growing dull and slow of motion, while the Bats talked freely of hanging themselves up for the winter. The Grouse and Quail made daily trips to the edges of the grain-fields, and found rich picking among the stubble. You could almost fancy that they came home each night fatter than when they went away in the morning.

Life went on in this way for many days, and the birds had all stopped singing. There were no more happy concerts at sunrise and no more carols at evening; only chirrupings and twitterings as the feathered people hopped restlessly from one perch to another. All could see that they were busily thinking and had no time for music. The truth was that each bird who was not to spend the winter in the Forest felt as though something were drawing—drawing—drawing him southward. It was something they could not see or hear, and yet it was drawing—drawing—drawing all day and all night. They spoke of it often to each other, and the older birds told the young ones how, before long, they would all start South, and fly over land and water until they reached their winter home.

"How do we know where to go?" asked the children.

"All that you have to do," the older ones said, "is to follow us."

"And how do you know?" they asked.

"Why, we have been there before," they answered; "and we can see the places over which we pass. But perhaps that is not the real reason, for sometimes we fly over such great stretches of water that we can see nothing else and it all looks alike. Then we cannot see which way to go, but still we feel that we are drawn South, and we only have to think about that and fly onward. The fathers and sons can fly the faster and will reach there first. The mothers and daughters come a few days later. We never make a mistake."

"It is wonderful, wonderful," thought a young Rabbit on the grass below. "I must watch them when they go."

The very next morning the Forest People awakened to find a silvery frost on the grass and feel the still air stirred by the soft dropping of damp red, brown, and yellow leaves from the trees. Over the river and all the lowland near it hung a heavy veil of white mist.

"It is time!" whispered the Robins to each other.

"It is time!" cooed the Mourning Doves.

"It is time!" cried the Cowbirds in their hoarse voices.

All through the forest there was restlessness and quiet haste. The Juncoes had already come from the cold northland and were resting from their long flight. The Ground Hogs, the Rabbits, and the Squirrels were out to say good-by. The Owls peeped from their hollow trees, shading their eyes from the strong light of the sun. And then the travellers went. The Robins started in family parties. The Mourning Doves slipped quietly away. The Cowbirds went in a dashing crowd. And the Crows, after much talking and disputing on the tree-tops, took a noisy farewell of the few members of the flock who were to remain behind, and, joining other flocks from the North, flew off in a great company which darkened the sky and caused a shadow to pass over the stubble-field almost like that of a summer cloud.

"They are gone!" sighed the Ground Hog and his wife. "We shall miss them sadly. Well, we can dream about them, and that will be a comfort."

"Jay! Jay!" shrieked a handsome-crested fellow from the tree above. "What if they are gone? They will be back in the spring, and we have plenty to eat. What is the use of feeling sad? Jay! Jay!"

But all people are not so heartless as the hungry Blue Jays, and the song-birds had many loving friends who missed them and longed for their return.

The Ruffed Grouse's Story

The Ruffed Grouse cocked his crested head on one side and looked up through the bare branches to the sky. It was a soft gray, and in the west were banks of bluish clouds. "I think it will snow very soon," said he. "Mrs. Grouse, are the children all ready for cold weather?"

"All ready," answered his cheerful little wife. "They have had their thickest feathers on for quite a while. The Rabbits were saying the other day that they had never seen a plumper or better clothed flock than ours." And her beautiful golden-brown eyes shone with pride as she spoke.

Indeed, the young Ruffed Grouse were a family of whom she might well be proud. Twelve healthy and obedient children do not fall to the lot of every Forest mother, and she wished with a sad little sigh that her other two eggs had hatched. She often thought of them with longing. How lovely it would have been to have fourteen children! But at that moment her brood came crowding around her in fright.

"Some cold white things," they said, "came tumbling down upon us and scared us. The white things didn't say a word, but they came so fast that we think they must be alive. Tell us what to do. Must we hide?"

"Why, that is snow!" exclaimed their mother. "It drops from the clouds up yonder quite as the leaves drop from the trees in the fall. It will not hurt you, but we must find shelter."

"What did I tell you, Mrs Grouse?" asked her husband. "I was certain that it would snow before night. I felt it in my quills." And Mr. Grouse strutted with importance. It always makes one feel so very knowing when he has told his wife exactly what will happen.

"How did you feel it in your quills?" asked one of his children. "Shall I feel it in my quills when I am as old as you are?"

"Perhaps," was the answer. "But until you do feel it you can never understand it, for it is not like any other feeling that there is."

Then they all started for a low clump of bushes to find shelter from the storm. Once they were frightened by seeing a great creature come tramping through the woods towards them. "A man!" said Mr. Grouse. "Hide!" said Mrs. Grouse, and each little Grouse hid under the leaves so quickly that nobody could see how it was done. One might almost think that a strong wind had blown them away. The mother pretended that she had a broken wing, and hopped away, making such pitiful sounds that the man followed to pick her up. When she had led him far from her children, she, too, made a quick run and hid herself; and although the man hunted everywhere, he could not find a single bird.

You know that is always the way in Grouse families, and even if the man's foot had stirred the leaves under which a little one was hiding, the Grouse would not have moved or made a sound. The children are brought up to mind without asking any questions. When their mother says, "Hide!" they do it, and never once ask "Why?" or answer, "As soon as I have swallowed this berry." It is no wonder that the older ones are proud of their children. Any mother would be made happy by having one child obey like that, and think of having twelve!

At last, the whole family reached the bushes where they were to stay, and then they began to feed near by. "Eat all you can," said Mr. Grouse, "before the snow gets deep. You may not have another such good chance for many days." So they ate until their little stomachs would not hold one more seed or evergreen bud.

All this time the snowflakes were falling, but the Grouse children were no longer afraid of them. Sometimes they even chased and snapped at them as they would at a fly in summer-time. It was then, too, that they learned to use snow-shoes. The oldest child had made a great fuss when he found a fringe of hard points growing around his toes in the fall, and had run peeping to his mother to ask her what was the matter. She had shown him her own feet, and had told him how all the Ruffed Grouse have snow-shoes of that kind grow on their feet every winter.

"We do not have to bother about them at all," she said. "They put themselves on when the weather gets cold in the fall, and they take themselves off when spring comes. We each have a new pair every year, and when they are grown we can walk easily over the soft snow. Without them we should sink through and flounder."

When night came they all huddled under the bushes, lying close together to keep each other warm. The next day they burrowed into a snow-drift and made a snug place there which was even better than the one they left; the soft white coverlet kept the wind out so well. It was hard for the little ones to keep quiet long, and to amuse them Mr. Grouse told how he first met their mother in the spring.

"It was a fine, sunshiny day," he said, "and everybody was happy. I had for some time been learning to drum, and now I felt that I was as good a drummer as there was in the forest. So I found a log (every Ruffed Grouse has to have his own place, you know) and I jumped up on it and strutted back and forth with my head high in the air. It was a dusky part of the forest and I could not see far, yet I knew that a beautiful young Grouse was somewhere near, and I hoped that if I drummed very well she might come to me."

"I know!" interrupted one of the little Grouse. "It was our mother."

"Well, it wasn't your mother then, my chick," said Mr. Grouse, "for that was long, long before you were hatched."

"She was our mother afterwards, anyway," cried the young Grouse. "I just know she was!"

Mr. Grouse's eyes twinkled, but he went gravely on. "At last I flapped my wing's hard and fast, and the soft drumming sound could be heard far and near. 'Thump-thump-thump-thump-thump; thump-thump-rup-rup-rup-rup-r-r-r-r-r-r-r-r.' I waited, but nobody came. Then I drummed again, and after that I was sure that I heard a rustling in the leaves. I drummed a third time, and then, children, there came the beautiful young Grouse, breaking her way through the thicket and trying to look as though she didn't know that I was there."

"Did she know?" cried the little Grouse.

"You must ask your mother that," he answered, "for it was she who came. Ah, what happy days we had together all spring! We wandered all through this great Forest and even made some journeys into the edge of the Meadow. Still, there was no place we loved as we did the dusky hollow by the old log where we first met. One day your mother told me that she must begin housekeeping and that I must keep out of the way while she was busy. So I had to go off with a crowd of other Ruffed Grouse while she fixed her nest, laid her eggs, and hatched out you youngsters. It was rather hard to be driven off in that way, but you know it is the custom among Grouse. We poor fellows had to amuse ourselves and each other until our wives called us home to help take care of the children. We've been at that work ever since."

"Oh!" said one of the young Grouse. "Oh, I am so glad that you drummed, and that she came when she heard you. Who would we have had to take care of us if it hadn't happened just so?"

That made them all feel very solemn and Mr. Grouse couldn't answer, and Mrs. Grouse couldn't answer, and none of the little Grouse could answer because, you see, it is one of the questions that hasn't any answer. Still, they were all there and happy, so they didn't bother their crested heads about it very long.

A Mild Day In Winter

It had been a cold and windy winter. Day after day the storm-clouds had piled up in the northwest and spread slowly over the sky, dropping great ragged flakes of snow down to the shivering earth. Then the forest trees were clothed in fleecy white garments, and the branches of the evergreens drooped under their heavy cloak.

Then there had been other days, when a strong wind stripped the trees of their covering, and brought with it thousands of small, hard flakes. These flakes were drier than the ragged ones had been, and did not cling so lovingly to everything they touched. They would rather frolic on the ground, rising again and again from their resting-places to dance around with the wind, and help make great drifts and overhanging ledges of snow in the edge of the Forest, where there was more open ground.

It is true that not all the winter had been cold and stormy. There were times when the drifts melted slowly into the earth, and the grass, which last summer had been so tender and green, showed brown and matted on the ground. Still the Great Horned Owl and his wife could not find enough to eat. "We do not mean to complain," said he with dignity, as he scratched one ear with his feathered right foot, "but neither of us has had a meal hearty enough for a healthy Robin, since the first heavy snow came."

This was when he was talking to his cousin, the Screech Owl. "Hearty enough for a Robin!" exclaimed Mrs. Great Horned Owl. "I should say we hadn't. I don't think I have had enough for a Goldfinch, and that is pretty hard for a bird of my size. I am so thin that my feathers feel loose."

"Have you been so hungry that you dreamed about food?" asked the Screech Owl.

"N-no, I can't say that I have," said the Great Horned Owl, while his wife shook her head solemnly.

"Ah, that is dreadful," said the Screech Owl. "I have done that several times. Only yesterday, while I lay in my nest-hollow, I dreamed that I was hunting. There was food everywhere, but just as I flew down to eat, it turned into pieces of ice. When I awakened I was almost starved and so cold that my beak chattered."

It was only a few days after the Screech Owl's call upon his cousins that he awakened one night to find the weather milder, and the ground covered with only a thin coating of soft snow. The beautiful round moon was shining down upon him, and in the western sky the clouds were still red from the rays of the setting sun.

Somewhere, far beyond the fields and forests of this part of the world, day-birds were beginning to stir, and thousands of downy heads were drawn from under sheltering wings, while in the barnyards the Cocks were calling their welcome to the sun. But the Screech Owl did not think of this. He aroused his wife and they went hunting. When they came back they did not dream about food. They had eaten all that they could, and the Great Horned Owl and his wife had made a meal hearty enough for a dozen Robins, and a whole flock of Goldfinches. It was a good thing

The Complete Works of Clara Dillinham Pierson

for the day-birds that this was so, for it is said that sometimes, when food is very scarce, Owls have been known to hunt by daylight.

When morning came and it was the moon's turn to sink out of sight in the west, the Owls went to bed in their hollow trees, and Crows, Blue Jays, Woodpeckers, Chickadees, Grouse, Quail, Squirrels, and Rabbits came out. The Goldfinches were there too, but you would never have known the husbands and fathers of the flock, unless you had seen them before in their winter clothing, which is like that worn by the wives and children. Here, too, were the winter visitors, the Snow Buntings and the Juncos, brimming over with happiness and news of their northern homes. This warm day made them think of the coming springtime, and they were already planning their flight.

"I wish you would stay with us all summer," said a friendly Goldfinch, as he dirted the snow off from a tall brown weed and began to pick out and eat the seeds.

"Stay all summer!" exclaimed a jolly little Snow Bunting. "Why should we want to stay? Perhaps if you would promise to keep the snow and ice we might."

"Why not ask the Goldfinches to come north with us?" suggested a Junco. "That would be much more sensible, for they can stand the cold weather as well as we, but we cannot stand warm days, such as I hear they have in this part of the country after the ice melts."

Then the older people of the group began to talk of the cares of life and many other things which did not interest their children, so the younger ones wandered away from them.

"I say," called a young Junco to a young Snow Bunting, "wouldn't you like to show some of these playmates of ours the countries where we were born?"

"Yes indeed," answered the Snow Bunting. "Wouldn't they open their eyes, though? I'd like to have them see the rocks up there."

"And the animals," said the Junco.

"Yes! Wouldn't they stare at the Bears, though!"

"Humph," said a Blue Jay. "I wouldn't care very much about seeing Bears, would you?" And he turned to a Crow near by.

"No," said the Crow. "I don't think very much of Bears anyway." He said this as though he had seen them all his life, but the Chickadees say that he never saw even a Cub.

"They haven't any big animals here," said the Junco to the Snow Bunting.

"Haven't we, though?" replied the Blue Jay. "Guess you wouldn't say that if you saw the Ground Hog. Would he say that?" he asked, turning to the young Grouse, Quail, Woodpeckers, Goldfinches, Chickadees, Squirrels, and Rabbits who stood around listening.

"No indeed!" they answered, for they wanted their visitors to understand that the Forest was a most wonderful place, and they really thought the Ground Hog very large.

"I don't believe he is as big as a Bear" said the Snow Bunting, with his bill in the air.

"How big is he?" asked the Junco.

Now the Blue Jay was afraid that the birds from the north were getting the better of him, and he felt very sure that they would leave before the Ground Hog had finished his winter sleep, so he did what no honest bird would have even thought of doing. He held his crested head very high and said, "He is bigger than that rock, *a great deal bigger*."

The Crow looked at the rock and gave a hoarse chuckle, for it was a hundred times larger than the Ground Hog. The Grouse, Quail, Woodpeckers, Goldfinches, Chickadees, Squirrels, and Rabbits looked at each other without saying a word. They knew how the Blue Jay had lied, and it made them ashamed. The Grouse pretended to fix their snow-shoes. They did not want to look at the birds from the north.

The Snow Buntings and Juncos felt that it would not do to talk about Bears to people who had such a great creature as the Ground Hog living among them. "He must be wonderful," they said. "Where does he sleep?"

"In the Bats' cave," answered the Blue Jay, who having told one lie, now had to tell another to cover it up. "He sleeps in the middle and there is just room left around the edges for the Bats."

Now at this very time the Ground Hog was awake in his burrow. He could feel that it was warmer and he wanted room to stretch. He thought it would seem good to have an early spring after such a cold winter, so he decided to take a walk and make the weather, as his grandfather had done. When he came out of his burrow he heard a great chattering and went to see what was the matter. That was how it happened that soon after the Blue Jay had told about the Bats' cave, one wide-awake young Junco saw a reddish-brown animal trotting over the grass toward them. "Who is that?" he cried.

The Grouse, Quail, Woodpeckers, Goldfinches, Chickadees, Squirrels, and Rabbits gave one look. "Oh, there is the Ground Hog!" they cried. Then they remembered and were ashamed again because of what the Blue Jay had said.

"Oh!" said the Snow Buntings and the Juncos. "So that is the Ground Hog! Big as that rock, is he? And you don't think much of Bears?"

The Crow pointed one claw at the Blue Jay. "I never said he was as big as that rock. *He* is the fellow that said it."

"I don't care," said the Blue Jay; "I was only fooling. I meant to tell you after a while. It's a good joke on you." But he had a sneaky look around the bill as he spoke, and nobody believed him. Before long, he and the Crow were glad enough to get away from the rest and go away together. Yet even then they were not happy, for each began to blame the other, and they had a most dreadful fight.

When the Ground Hog was told about it he said, "What foolishness it is to want to tell the biggest story! My grandfather told us once that a lie was always a lie, and that calling it a joke didn't make it any better. I think he was right."

And the Snow Buntings and Juncos, who are bright and honest, nodded their dainty little heads and said, "Nobody in our own dear north country ever spoke a truer word than that." So they became firm friends of the Ground Hog, even if he were not so large as the rock.

Among the Meadow People

The Butterfly That Went Calling

As the warm August days came, Mr. Yellow Butterfly wriggled and pushed in his snug little green chrysalis and wished he could get out to see the world. He remembered the days when he was a hairy little Caterpillar, crawling slowly over grass and leaves, and he remembered how beautiful the sky and all the flowers were. Then he thought of the new wings which had been growing from his back, and he tried to move them, just to see how it would feel. He had only six legs since his wings grew, and he missed all the sticky feet which he had to give up when he began to change into a Butterfly.

The more he thought about it the more he squirmed, until suddenly he heard a faint little sound, too faint for larger people to hear, and found a tiny slit in the wall of his chrysalis. It was such a dainty green chrysalis with white wrinkles, that it seemed almost a pity to have it break. Still it had held him for eight days already and that was as long as any of his family ever hung in the chrysalis, so it was quite time for it to be torn open and left empty. Mr. Yellow Butterfly belonged to the second brood that had hatched that year and he wanted to be out while the days were still fine and hot. Now he crawled out of the newly-opened doorway to take his first flight.

Poor Mr. Butterfly! He found his wings so wet and crinkled that they wouldn't work at all, so he had to sit quietly in the sunshine all day drying them. And just as they got big, and smooth, and dry, it grew dark, and Mr. Butterfly had to crawl under a leaf to sleep.

The next morning, bright and early, he flew away to visit the flowers. First he stopped to see the Daisies by the roadside. They were all dancing in the wind, and their bright faces looked as cheerful as anyone could wish. They were glad to see Mr. Butterfly, and wished him to stay all day with them. He said; "You are very kind, but I really couldn't think of doing it. You must excuse my saying it, but I am surprised to think you will grow here. It is very dusty and dry, and then there is no shade. I am sure I could have chosen a better place."

The Daisies smiled and nodded to each other, saying, "This is the kind of place we were made for, that's all."

Mr. Butterfly shook his head very doubtfully, and then bade them a polite "Good-morning," and flew away to call on the Cardinals.

The Cardinals are a very stately family, as everybody knows. They hold their heads very high, and never make deep bows, even to the wind, but for all that they are a very pleasant family to meet. They gave Mr. Butterfly a dainty lunch of honey, and seemed much pleased when he told them how beautiful the river looked in the sunlight.

"It is a delightful place to grow," said they.

"Ye-es," said Mr. Butterfly, "it is very pretty, still I do not think it can be healthful. I really cannot understand why you flowers choose such strange homes.

Now, there are the Daisies, where I just called. They are in a dusty, dry place, where there is no shade at all. I spoke to them about it, and they acted quite uppish."

"But the Daisies always do choose such places," said the Cardinals.

"And your family," said Mr. Butterfly, "have lived so long in wet places that it is a wonder you are alive. Your color is good, but to stand with one's roots in water all the time! It is shocking."

"Cardinals and Butterflies live differently," said the flowers. "Good-morning."

Mr. Butterfly left the river and flew over to the woods. He was very much out of patience. He was so angry that his feelers quivered, and now you know how angry he must have been. He knew that the Violets were a very agreeable family, who never put on airs, so he went at once to them.

He had barely said "Good-morning" to them when he began to explain what had displeased him.

"To think," he said, "what notions some flowers have! Now, you have a pleasant home here in the edge of the woods. I have been telling the Daisies and the Cardinals that they should grow in such a place, but they wouldn't listen to me. The Daisies were quite uppish about it, and the Cardinals were very stiff."

"My dear friend," answered a Violet, "they could never live if they moved up into our neighborhood. Every flower has his own place in this world, and is happiest in that place. Everything has its own place and its own work, and every flower that is wise will stay in the place for which it was intended. You were exceedingly kind to want to help the flowers, but suppose they had been telling you what to do. Suppose the Cardinals had told you that flying around was not good for your health, and that to be truly well you ought to grow planted with your legs in the mud and water."

"Oh!" said Mr. Butterfly, "Oh! I never thought of that. Perhaps Butterflies don't know everything."

"No," said the Violet, "they don't know everything, and you haven't been out of your chrysalis very long. But those who are ready to learn can always find someone to tell them. Won't you eat some honey?"

And Mr. Butterfly sipped honey and was happy.

The Robins Build A Nest

When Mr. and Mrs. Robin built in the spring, they were not quite agreed as to where the nest should be. Mr. Robin was a very decided bird, and had made up his mind that the lowest crotch of a maple tree would be the best place. He even went so far as to take three billfuls of mud there, and stick in two blades of dry grass. Mrs. Robin wanted it on the end of the second rail from the top of the split-rail fence. She said it was high enough from the ground to be safe and dry, and not so high that a little bird falling out of it would hurt himself very much. Then, too, the top rail was broad at the end and would keep the rain off so well.

"And the nest will be just the color of the rails," said she, "so that even a Red Squirrel could hardly see it." She disliked Red Squirrels, and she had reason to, for she had been married before, and if it had not been for a Red Squirrel, she might already have had children as large as she was.

"I say that the tree is the place for it," said Mr. Robin, "and I wear the brightest breast feathers." He said this because in bird families the one who wears the brightest breast feathers thinks he has the right to decide things.

Mrs. Robin was wise enough not to answer back when he spoke in this way. She only shook her feathers, took ten quick running steps, tilted her body forward, looked hard at the ground, and pulled out something for supper. After that she fluttered around the maple tree crotch as though she had never thought of any other place. Mr. Robin wished he had not been quite so decided, or reminded her of his breast feathers. "After all," thought he, "I don't know but the fence-rail would have done." He thought this, but he didn't say it. It is not always easy for a Robin to give up and let one with dull breast feathers know that he thinks himself wrong.

That night they perched in the maple-tree and slept with their heads under their wings. Long before the sun was in sight, when the first beams were just touching the tops of the forest trees, they awakened, bright-eyed and rested, preened their feathers, sang their morning song, "Cheerily, cheerily, cheer-up," and flew off to find food. After breakfast they began to work on the nest. Mrs. Robin stopped often to look and peck at the bark. "It will take a great deal of mud," said she, "to fill in that deep crotch until we reach a place wide enough for the nest."

At another time she said: "My dear, I am afraid that the dry grass you are bringing is too light-colored. It shows very plainly against the maple bark. Can't you find some that is darker?"

Mr. Robin hunted and hunted, but could find nothing which was darker. As he flew past the fence, he noticed that it was almost the color of the grass in his bill.

After a while, soft gray clouds began to cover the sky. "I wonder," said Mrs. Robin, "if it will rain before we get this done. The mud is soft enough now to work well, and this place is so open that the rain might easily wash away all that we have done."

It did rain, however, and very soon. The great drops came down so hard that one could only think of pebbles falling. Mr. and Mrs. Robin oiled their feathers as quickly as they could, taking the oil from their back pockets and putting it onto their feathers with their bills. This made the finest kind of waterproof and was not at all heavy to wear. When the rain was over they shook themselves and looked at their work.

"I believe," said Mrs. Robin to her husband, "that you are right in saying that we might better give up this place and begin over again somewhere else."

Now Mr. Robin could not remember having said that he thought anything of the sort, and he looked very sharply at his wife, and cocked his black head on one side until all the black and white streaks on his throat showed. She did not seem to know that he was watching her as she hopped around the partly built nest, poking it here and pushing it there, and trying her hardest to make it look right. He thought she would say something, but she didn't. Then he knew he must speak first. He flirted his tail and tipped his head and drew some of his brown wing-feathers through his bill. Then he held himself very straight and tall, and said, "Well, if you do agree with me, I think you might much better stop working here and begin in another place."

"It seems almost too bad," said she. "Of course there are other places, but——"

By this time Mr. Robin knew exactly what to do. "Plenty of them," said he. "Now don't fuss any longer with this. That place on the rail fence is an excellent one. I wonder that no other birds have taken it." As he spoke he flew ahead to the very spot which Mrs. Robin had first chosen.

She was a very wise bird, and knew far too much to say, "I told you so." Saying that, you know, always makes things go wrong. She looked at the rail fence, ran along the top of it, toeing in prettily as she ran, looked around in a surprised way, and said, "Oh, *that* place?"

"Yes, Mrs. Robin," said her husband, "*that* place. Do you see anything wrong about it?"

"No-o," she said. "I think I could make it do."

Before long another nest was half built, and Mrs. Robin was working away in the happiest manner possible, stopping every little while to sing her afternoon song: "Do you think what you do? Do you think what you do? Do you thi-ink?"

Mr. Robin was also at work, and such billfuls of mud, such fine little twigs, and such big wisps of dry grass as went into that home! Once Mr. Robin was gone a long time, and when he came back he had a beautiful piece of white cotton string dangling from his beak. That they put on the outside. "Not that we care to show off," said they, "but somehow that seemed to be the best place to put it."

Mr. Robin was very proud of his nest and of his wife. He never went far away if he could help it. Once she heard him tell Mr. Goldfinch that, "Mrs. Robin was very sweet about building where he chose, and that even after he insisted on changing places from the tree to the fence she was perfectly good-natured."

"Yes," said Mrs. Robin to Mrs. Goldfinch, "I was perfectly good-natured." Then she gave a happy, chirpy little laugh, and Mrs. Goldfinch laughed, too. They were perfectly contented birds, even if they didn't wear the brightest breast feathers or insist on having their own way. And Mrs. Robin had been married before.

The Selfish Tent-Caterpillar

One could hardly call the Tent-Caterpillars meadow people, for they did not often leave their trees to crawl upon the ground. Yet the Apple-Tree Tent-Caterpillars would not allow anybody to call them forest people. "We live on apple and wild cherry trees," they said, "and you will almost always find us in the orchards or on the roadside trees. There are Forest Tent-Caterpillars, but please don't get us mixed with them. We belong to another branch of the family, the Apple-Tree branch."

The Tree Frog said that he remembered perfectly well when the eggs were laid on the wild cherry tree on the edge of the meadow. "It was early last summer," he said, "and the Moth who laid them was a very agreeable reddish-brown person, about as large as a common Yellow Butterfly. I remember that she had two light yellow lines on each forewing. Another Moth came with her, but did not stay. He was smaller than she, and had the same markings. After he had gone, she asked me if we were ever visited by the Yellow-Billed Cuckoos."

"Why did she ask that?" said the Garter Snake.

"Don't you know?" exclaimed the Tree Frog. And then he whispered something to the Garter Snake.

The Garter Snake wriggled with surprise and cried, "Really?"

All through the fall and winter the many, many eggs which the reddish-brown Moth had laid were kept snug and warm on the twig where she had put them. They were placed in rows around the twig, and then well covered to hold them together and keep them warm. The winter winds had blown the twig to and fro, the cold rain had frozen over them, the soft snowflakes had drifted down from the clouds and covered them, only to melt and trickle away again in shining drops. One morning the whole wild cherry tree was covered with beautiful long, glistening crystals of hoar-frost; and still the ring of eggs stayed in its place around the twig, and the life in them slept until spring sunbeams should shine down and quicken it.

But when the spring sunbeams did come! Even before the leaf-buds were open, tiny Larvæ, or Caterpillar babies, came crawling from the ring of eggs and began feeding upon the buds. They took very, very small bites, and that looked as though they were polite children. Still, you know, their mouths were so small that they could not take big ones, and it may not have been politeness after all which made them eat daintily.

When all the Tent-Caterpillars were hatched, and they had eaten every leaf-bud near the egg-ring, they began to crawl down the tree toward the trunk. Once they stopped by a good-sized crotch in the branches. "Let's build here," said the leader; "this place is all right."

Then some of the Tent-Caterpillars said, "Let's!" and some of them said, "Don't let's!" One young fellow said, "Aw, come on! There's a bigger crotch farther down." Of course he should have said, "I think you will like a larger crotch better," but he was young, and, you know, these Larvæ had no father or mother to help them speak in the right way. They were orphans, and it is wonderful how they ever learned to talk at all.

After this, some of the Tent-Caterpillars went on to the larger crotch and some stayed behind. More went than stayed, and when they saw this, those by the smaller crotch gave up and joined their brothers and sisters, as they should have done. It was right to do that which pleased most of them.

It took a great deal of work to make the tent. All helped, spinning hundreds and thousands of white silken threads, laying them side by side, criss-crossing them, fastening the ends to branches and twigs, not forgetting to leave places through which one could crawl in and out. They never worked all day at this, because unless they stopped to eat they would soon have been weak and unable to spin. There were nearly always a few Caterpillars in the tent, but only in the early morning or late afternoon or during the night were they all at home. The rest of the time they were scattered around the tree feeding. Of course there were some cold days when they stayed in. When the weather was chilly they moved slowly and cared very little for food.

There was one young Tent-Caterpillar who happened to be the first hatched, and who seemed to think that because he was a minute older than any of the other children he had the right to his own way. Sometimes he got it, because the others didn't want to have any trouble. Sometimes he didn't get it, and then he was very sulky and disagreeable, even refusing to answer when he was spoken to.

One cold day, when all the Caterpillars stayed in the tent, this oldest brother wanted the warmest place, that in the very middle. It should have belonged to the younger brothers and sisters, for they were not so strong, but he pushed and wriggled his hairy black and brown and yellow body into the very place he wanted, and then scolded everybody around because he had to push to get there. It happened as it always does when a Caterpillar begins to say mean things, and he went on until he was saying some which were really untrue. Nobody answered back, so he scolded and fussed and was exceedingly disagreeable.

All day long he thought how wretched he was, and how badly they treated him, and how he guessed they'd be sorry enough if he went away. The next morning he went. As long as the warm sunshine lasted he did very well. When it began to grow cool, his brothers and sisters crawled past him on their way to the tent. "Come on!" they cried. "It's time to go home."

"Uh-uh!" said the eldest brother (and that meant "No"), "I'm not going."

"Why not?" they asked.

"Oh, because," said he.

When the rest were all together in the tent they talked about him. "Do you suppose he's angry?" said one.

"What should he be angry about?" said another.

"I just believe he is," said a third. "Did you notice the way his hairs bristled?"

"Don't you think we ought to go to get him?" asked two or three of the youngest Caterpillars.

"No," said the older ones. "We haven't done anything. Let him get over it."

So the oldest brother, who had thought that every other Caterpillar in the tent would crawl right out and beg and coax him to come back, waited and waited and waited, but nobody came. The tent was there and the door was open. All he had to do was to crawl in and be at home. He waited so long that at last he had to leave the tree and spin his cocoon without ever having gone back to his brothers and sisters in the tent. He spun his cocoon and mixed the silk with a yellowish-white powder, then he lay down in it to sleep twenty-one days and grow his wings. The last thought he had before going to sleep was an unhappy and selfish one. Probably he awakened an unhappy and selfish Moth.

His brothers and sisters were sad whenever they thought of him. But, they said, "what could we do? It wasn't fair for him to have the best of everything, and we never answered when he said mean things. He might have come back at any time and we would have been kind to him."

And they were right. What could they have done? It was very sad, but when a Caterpillar is so selfish and sulky that he cannot live happily with other people, it is much better that he should live quite alone.

The Lazy Snail

In the lower part of the meadow, where the grass grew tall and tender, there lived a fine and sturdy young Snail; that is to say, a fine-looking Snail. His shell was a beautiful soft gray, and its curves were regular and perfect. His body was soft and moist, and just what a Snail's body should be. Of course, when it came to travelling, he could not go fast, for none of his family are rapid travellers, still, if he had been plucky and patient, he might have seen much of the meadow, and perhaps some of the world outside. His friends and neighbors often told him that he ought to start out on a little journey to see the sights, but he would always answer, "Oh, it is too hard work!"

There was nobody who liked stories of meadow life better than this same Snail, and he would often stop some friendly Cricket or Snake to ask for the news. After they had told him, they would say, "Why, don't you ever get out to see these things for yourself?" and he would give a little sigh and answer, "It is too far to go."

"But you needn't go the whole distance in one day," his visitor would say, "only a little at a time."

"Yes, and then I would have to keep starting on again every little while," the Snail would reply. "What of that?" said the visitor; "you would have plenty of resting spells, when you could lie in the shade of a tall weed and enjoy yourself."

"Well, what is the use?" the Snail would say. "I can't enjoy resting if I know I've got to go to work again," and he would sigh once more.

So there he lived, eating and sleeping, and wishing he could see the world, and meet the people in the upper part of the meadow, but just so lazy that he wouldn't start out to find them.

He never thought that the Butterflies and Beetles might not like it to have him keep calling them to him and making them tell him the news. Oh, no indeed! If he wanted them to do anything for him, he asked them quickly enough, and they, being happy, good-natured people, would always do as he asked them to.

There came a day, though, when he asked too much. The Grasshoppers had been telling him about some very delicious new plants that grew a little distance away, and the Snail wanted some very badly. "Can't you bring me some?" he said. "There are so many of you, and you have such good, strong legs. I should think you might each bring me a small piece in your mouths, and then I should have a fine dinner of it."

The Grasshoppers didn't say anything then, but when they were so far away that he could not hear them, they said to each other, "If the Snail wants the food so much, he might better go for it. We have other things to do," and they hopped off on their own business.

The Snail sat there, and wondered and wondered that they did not come. He kept thinking how he would like some of the new food for dinner, but there it ended. He didn't want it enough to get it for himself.

The Grasshoppers told all their friends about the Snail's request, and everybody thought, "Such a lazy, good-for-nothing fellow deserves to be left quite alone." So it happened that for a very long time nobody went near the Snail.

The weather grew hotter and hotter. The clouds, which blew across the sky, kept their rain until they were well past the meadow, and so it happened that the river grew shallower and shallower, and the sunshine dried the tiny pools and rivulets which kept the lower meadow damp. The grass began to turn brown and dry, and, all in all, it was trying weather for Snails.

One day, a Butterfly called some of her friends together, and told them that she had seen the Snail lying in his old place, looking thin and hungry. "The grass is all dried around him," she said; "I believe he is starving, and too lazy to go nearer the river, where there is still good food for him."

They all talked it over together, and some of them said it was of no use to help a Snail who was too lazy to do anything for himself. Others said, "Well, he is too weak to help himself now, at all events, and we might help him this once." And that is exactly what they did. The Butterflies and the Mosquitoes flew ahead to find the best place to put the Snail, and all the Grasshoppers, and Beetles, and other strong crawling creatures took turns in rolling the Snail down toward the river.

They left him where the green things were fresh and tender, and he grew strong and plump once more. It is even said that he was not so lazy afterward, but one cannot tell whether to believe it or not, for everybody knows that when people let themselves grow up lazy, as he did, it is almost impossible for them to get over it when they want to. One thing is sure: the meadow people who helped him were happier and better for doing a kind thing, no matter what became of the Snail.

The Ant The Wore Wings

In one of the Ant-hills in the highest part of the meadow, were a lot of young Ants talking together. "I," said one, "am going to be a soldier, and drive away anybody who comes to make us trouble. I try biting hard things every day to make my jaws strong, so that I can guard the home better."

"I," said another and smaller Ant, "want to be a worker. I want to help build and repair the home. I want to get the food for the family, and feed the Ant babies, and clean them off when they crawl out of their old coats. If I can do those things well, I shall be the happiest, busiest Ant in the meadow."

"We don't want to live that kind of life," said a couple of larger Ants with wings. "We don't mean to stay around the Ant-hill all the time and work. We want to use our wings, and then you may be very sure that you won't see us around home any more."

The little worker spoke up: "Home is a pleasant place. You may be very glad to come back to it some day." But the Ants with the wings turned their backs and wouldn't listen to another word.

A few days after this there were exciting times in the Ant-hill. All the winged Ants said "Good-bye" to the soldiers and workers, and flew off through the air, flew so far that the little ones at home could no longer see them. All day long they were gone, but the next morning when the little worker (whom we heard talking) went out to get breakfast, she found the poor winged Ants lying on the ground near their home. Some of them were dead, and the rest were looking for food.

The worker Ant ran up to the one who had said she didn't want to stay around home, and asked her to come back to the Ant-hill. "No, I thank you," she answered. "I have had my breakfast now, and am going to fly off again." She raised her wings to go, but after she had given one flutter, they dropped off, and she could never fly again.

The worker hurried back to the Ant-hill to call some of her sister workers, and some of the soldiers, and they took the Ant who had lost her wings and carried her to another part of the meadow. There they went to work to build a new home and make her their queen.

First, they looked for a good, sandy place, on which the sun would shine all day. Then the worker Ants began to dig in the ground and bring out tiny round pieces of earth in their mouths. The soldiers helped them, and before night they had a cosy little home in the earth, with several rooms, and some food already stored. They took their queen in, and brought her food to eat, and waited on her, and she was happy and contented.

By and by the Ant eggs began to hatch, and the workers had all they could do to take care of their queen and her little Ant babies, and the soldier Ants had to help. The Ant babies were little worms or grubs when they first came out of the eggs; after a while they curled up in tiny, tiny cases, called pupa-cases, and after another while they came out of these, and then they looked like the older Ants, with their six legs, and their slender little waists. But whatever they were, whether eggs, or grubs, or curled up in the pupa-cases, or lively little Ants, the workers fed and took care of them, and the soldiers fought for them, and the queen-mother loved them, and they all lived happily together until the young Ants were ready to go out into the great world and learn the lessons of life for themselves.

The Cheerful Harvestmen

Some of the meadow people are gay and careless, and some are always worrying. Some work hard every day, and some are exceedingly lazy. There, as everywhere else, each has his own way of thinking about things. It is too bad that they cannot all learn to think brave and cheerful thoughts, for these make life happy. One may have a comfortable home, kind neighbors, and plenty to eat, yet if he is in the habit of thinking disagreeable thoughts, not even all these good things can make him happy. Now there was the young Frog who thought herself sick—but that is another story.

Perhaps the Harvestmen were the most cheerful of all the meadow people. The old Tree Frog used to say that it made him feel better just to see their knees coming toward him. Of course, when he saw their knees, he knew that the whole insect was also coming. He spoke in that way because the Harvestmen always walked or ran with their knees so much above the rest of their bodies that one could see those first.

The Harvestmen were not particularly fine-looking, not nearly so handsome as some of their Spider cousins. One never thought of that, however. They had such an easy way of moving around on their eight legs, each of which had a great many joints. It is the joints, or bending-places, you know, which make legs useful. Besides being graceful, they had very pleasant manners. When a Harvestman said "Good-morning" to you on a rainy day, you always had a feeling that the sun was shining. It might be that the drops were even then falling into your face, but for a moment you were sure to feel that everything was bright and warm and comfortable.

Sometimes the careless young Grasshoppers and Crickets called the Harvestmen by their nicknames, "Daddy Long-Legs" or "Grandfather Graybeard." Even then the Harvestmen were good-natured, and only said with a smile that the young people had not yet learned the names of their neighbors. The Grasshoppers never seemed to think how queer it was to call a young Harvestman daughter "Grandfather Graybeard." When they saw how good-natured they were, the Grasshoppers soon stopped trying to tease the Harvestmen. People who are really good-natured are never teased very long, you know.

The Walking-Sticks were exceedingly polite to the Harvestmen. They thought them very slender and genteel-looking. Once the Five-Legged Walking-Stick said to the largest Harvestman, "Why do you talk so much with the common people in the meadow?"

The Harvestman knew exactly what the Walking-Stick meant, but he was not going to let anybody make fun of his kind and friendly neighbors, so he said: "I think we Harvestmen are rather common ourselves. There are a great, great many of us here. It must be very lonely to be uncommon."

After that the Walking-Stick had nothing more to say. He never felt quite sure whether the Harvestman was too stupid to understand or too wise to gossip. Once he thought he saw the Harvestman's eyes twinkle. The Harvestman didn't care if people thought him stupid. He knew that he was not stupid, and he would rather seem dull than to listen while unkind things were said about his neighbors.

Some people would have thought it very hard luck to be Harvestmen. The Garter Snake said that if he were one, he should be worried all the time about his legs. "I'm thankful I haven't any," he said, "for if I had I should be forever thinking I should lose some of them. A Harvestman without legs would be badly off. He could never in the world crawl around on his belly as I do."

How the Harvestmen did laugh when they heard this! The biggest one said, "Well, if that isn't just like some people! Never want to have anything for fear they'll lose it. I wonder if he worries about his head? He might lose that, you know, and then what would he do?"

It was only the next day that the largest Harvestman came home on seven legs. His friends all cried out, "Oh, how did it ever happen?"

"Cows," said he.

"Did they step on you?" asked the Five-Legged Walking-Stick. He had not lived long enough in the meadow to understand all that the Harvestman meant. He was sorry for him, though, for he knew what it was to lose a leg.

"Huh!" said a Grasshopper, interrupting in a very rude way, "aren't any Cows in this meadow now!"

Then the other Harvestmen told the Walking-Stick all about it, how sometimes a boy would come to the meadow, catch a Harvestman, hold him up by one leg, and say to him, "Grandfather Graybeard, tell me where the Cows are, or I'll kill you." Then the only thing a Harvestman could do was to struggle and wriggle himself free, and he often broke off a leg in doing so.

"How terrible!" said the three Walking-Sticks all together. "But why don't you tell them?"

"We do," answered the Harvestmen. "We point with our seven other legs, and we point every way there is. Sometimes we don't know where they are, so we point everywhere, to be sure. But it doesn't make any difference. Our legs drop off just the same."

"Isn't a boy clever enough to find Cows alone?" asked the Walking-Sticks.

"Oh, it isn't that," cried all the meadow people together. "Even after you tell, and sometimes when the Cows are right there, they walk off home without them."

"I'd sting them," said a Wasp, waving his feelers fiercely and raising and lowering his wings. "I'd sting them as hard as I could."

"You wouldn't if you had no sting," said the Tree Frog.

"N-no," stammered the Wasp, "I suppose I wouldn't."

"You poor creature!" said the biggest Katydid to the biggest Harvestman. "What will you do? Only seven legs!"

"Do?" answered the biggest Harvestman, and it was then one could see how truly brave and cheerful he was. "Do? I'll walk on those seven. If I lose one of them I'll walk on six, and if I lose one of them I'll walk on five. Haven't I my mouth and my stomach and my eyes and my two feelers, and my two food-pincers? I may not be so good-looking, but I am a Harvestman, and I shall enjoy the grass and the sunshine and my kind neighbors as long as I live. I must leave you now. Good-day."

He walked off rather awkwardly, for he had not yet learned to manage himself since his accident. The meadow people looked after him very thoughtfully. They were not noticing his awkwardness, or thinking of his high knees or of his little low body. Perhaps they thought what the Cicada said, "Ah, that is the way to live!"

The Little Spider's First Web

The first thing our little Spider remembered was being crowded with a lot of other little Spiders in a tiny brown house. This tiny house had no windows, and was very warm and dark and stuffy. When the wind blew, the little Spiders would hear it rushing through the forest near by, and would feel their round brown house swinging like a cradle. It was fastened to a bush by the edge of the forest, but they could not know that, so they just wiggled and pushed and ate the food that they found in the house, and wondered what it all meant. They didn't even guess that a mother Spider had made the brown house and put the food in it for her Spider babies to eat when they came out of their eggs. She had put the eggs in, too, but the little Spiders didn't remember the time when they lay curled up in the eggs. They didn't know what had been nor what was to be—they thought that to eat and wiggle and sleep was all of life. You see they had much to learn.

One morning the little Spiders found that the food was all gone, and they pushed and scrambled harder than ever, because they were hungry and wanted more. Exactly what happened nobody knew, but suddenly it grew light, and some of them fell out of the house. All the rest scrambled after, and there they stood, winking and blinking in the bright sunshine, and feeling a little bit dizzy, because they were on a shaky web made of silvery ropes.

Just then the web began to shake even more, and a beautiful great mother Spider ran out on it. She was dressed in black and yellow velvet, and her eight eyes glistened and gleamed in the sunlight. They had never dreamed of such a wonderful creature.

"Well, my children," she exclaimed, "I know you must be hungry, and I have breakfast all ready for you." So they began eating at once, and the mother Spider told them many things about the meadow and the forest, and said they must amuse themselves while she worked to get food for them. There was no father Spider to help her, and, as she said, "Growing children must have plenty of good plain food."

You can just fancy what a good time the baby Spiders had. There were a hundred and seventy of them, so they had no chance to grow lonely, even when their mother was away. They lived in this way for quite a while, and grew bigger and stronger every day. One morning the mother Spider said to her biggest daughter, "You are quite old enough to work now, and I will teach you to spin your web."

The little Spider soon learned to draw out the silvery ropes from the pocket in her body where they were made and kept, and very soon she had one fastened at both ends to branches of the bush. Then her mother made her walk out to the middle of her rope bridge, and spin and fasten two more, so that it looked like a shining cross. After that was done, the mother showed her something like a comb, which is part of a Spider's foot, and taught her how to measure, and put more ropes out from the middle of the cross, until it looked like the spokes of a wheel.

The little Spider got much discouraged, and said, "Let me finish it some other time; I am tired of working now."

The mother Spider answered, "No, I cannot have a lazy child."

The little one said, "I can't ever do it, I know I can't."

"Now," said the mother, "I shall have to give you a Spider scolding. You have acted as lazy as the Tree Frog says boys and girls sometimes do. He has been up near the farm-house, and says that he has seen there children who do not like to work. The meadow people could hardly believe such a thing at first. He says they were cross and unhappy children, and no wonder! Lazy people are never happy. You try to finish the web, and see if I am not right. You are not a baby now, and you must work and get your own food."

So the little Spider spun the circles of rope in the web, and made these ropes sticky, as all careful spiders do. She ate the loose ends and pieces that were left over, to save them for another time, and when it was done, it was so fine and perfect that her brothers and sisters crowded around, saying, "Oh! oh! oh! how beautiful!" and asked the mother to teach them. The little web-spinner was happier than she had ever been before, and the mother began to teach her other children. But it takes a long time to teach a hundred and seventy children.

The Beetle Who Did Not Like Caterpillars

One morning early in June, a fat and shining May Beetle lay on his back among the grasses, kicking his six legs in the air, and wriggling around while he tried to catch hold of a grass-blade by which to pull himself up. Now, Beetles do not like to lie on their backs in the sunshine, and this one was hot and tired from his long struggle. Beside that, he was very cross because he was late in getting his breakfast, so when he did at last get right side up, and saw a brown and black Caterpillar watching him, he grew very ill-mannered, and said some things of which he should have been ashamed.

"Oh, yes," he said, "you are quick enough to laugh when you think somebody else is in a fix. I often lie on my back and kick, just for fun." (Which was not true, but when Beetles are cross they are not always truthful.)

"Excuse me," said the Caterpillar, "I did not mean to hurt your feelings. If I smiled, it was because I remembered being in the same plight myself yesterday, and what a time I had smoothing my fur afterwards. Now, you won't have to smooth your fur, will you?" she asked pleasantly.

"No, I'm thankful to say I haven't any fur to smooth," snapped the Beetle. "I am not one of the crawling, furry kind. My family wear dark brown, glossy coats, and we always look trim and clean. When we want to hurry, we fly; and when tired of flying, we walk or run. We have two kinds of wings. We have a pair of dainty, soft ones, that carry us through the air, and then we have a pair of stiff ones to cover over the soft wings when we come down to the earth again. We are the finest family in the meadow."

"I have often heard of you," said the Caterpillar, "and am very glad to become acquainted."

"Well," answered the Beetle, "I am willing to speak to you, of course, but we can never be at all friendly. A May Beetle, indeed, in company with a Caterpillar! I choose my friends among the Moths, Butterflies, and Dragon-flies,—in fact, *I* move in the upper circles."

"Upper circles, indeed!" said a croaking voice beside him, which made the Beetle jump, "I have hopped over your head for two or three years, when you were nothing but a fat, white worm. *You'd* better not put on airs. The fine family of May Beetles were all worms once, and they had to live in the earth and eat roots, while the Caterpillars were in the sunshine over their heads, dining on tender green leaves and flower buds."

The May Beetle began to look very uncomfortable, and squirmed as though he wanted to get away, but the Tree Frog, for it was the Tree Frog, went on: "As for your not liking Caterpillars, they don't stay Caterpillars. Your new acquaintance up there will come out with wings one of these days, and you will be glad enough to know him." And the Tree Frog hopped away.

The May Beetle scraped his head with his right front leg, and then said to the Caterpillar, who was nibbling away at the milkweed: "You know, I wasn't really in earnest about our not being friends. I shall be very glad to know you, and all your family."

"Thank you," answered the Caterpillar, "thank you very much, but I have been thinking it over myself, and I feel that I really could not be friendly with a May Beetle. Of course, I don't mind speaking to you once in a while, when I am eating, and getting ready to spin my cocoon. After that it will be different. You see, then I shall belong to one of the finest families in the meadow, the Milkweed Butterflies. *We* shall eat nothing but honey, and dress in soft orange and black velvet. *We* shall not blunder and bump around when we fly. *We* shall enjoy visiting with the Dragon-flies and Moths. I shall not forget you altogether, I dare say, but I shall feel it my duty to move in the upper circles, where I belong. Good-morning."

The Young Robin Who Was Afraid To Fly

During the days when the four beautiful green-blue eggs lay in the nest, Mrs. Robin stayed quite closely at home. She said it was a very good place, for she could keep her eggs warm and still see all that was happening. The rail-end on which they had built was on the meadow side of the fence, over the tallest grasses and the graceful stalks of golden-rod. Here the Garter Snake drew his shining body through the tangled green, and here the Tree Frog often came for a quiet nap.

Just outside the fence the milkweeds grew, with every broad, pale green leaf slanting upward in their spring style. Here the Milkweed Caterpillars fed, and here, too, when the great balls of tiny dull pink blossoms dangled from the stalks, the Milkweed Butterflies hung all day long. All the teams from the farm-house passed along the quiet, grass-grown road, and those which were going to the farm as well. When Mrs. Robin saw a team coming, she always settled herself more deeply into her nest, so that not one of her brick-red breast feathers showed. Then she sat very still, only turning her head enough to watch the team as it came near, passed, and went out of sight down the road. Sometimes she did not even have to turn her head, for if she happened to be facing the road, she could with one eye watch the team come near, and with the other watch it go away. No bird, you know, ever has to look at anything with both eyes at once.

After the young Robins had outgrown their shells and broken and thrown them off, they were naked and red and blind. They lay in a heap in the bottom of the nest, and became so tangled that nobody but a bird could tell which was which. If they heard their father or their mother flying toward them, they would stretch up their necks and open their mouths. Then each would have some food poked down his throat, and would lie still until another mouthful was brought to him.

When they got their eyes open and began to grow more down, they were good little Robins and did exactly as they were told. It was easy to be good then, for they were not strong enough to want to go elsewhere, and they had all they wanted to eat. At night their mother sat in the nest and covered them with her soft feathers. When it rained she also did this. She was a kind and very hard-working mother. Mr. Robin worked quite as hard as she, and was exceedingly proud of his family.

But when their feathers began to grow, and each young Robin's sharp quills pricked his brothers and sisters if they pushed against him, then it was not so easy to be good. Four growing children in one little round bed sometimes found themselves rather crowded. One night Mrs. Robin said to her husband: "I am all tired out. I work as long as daylight lasts getting food for those children, and I cannot be here enough to teach them anything."

"Then they must learn to work for themselves," said Mr. Robin decidedly. "They are surely old enough."

"Why, they are just babies!" exclaimed his wife. "They have hardly any tails yet."

"They don't need tails to eat with," said he, "and they may as well begin now. I will not have you get so tired for this one brood."

Mrs. Robin said nothing more. Indeed, there was nothing more to be said, for she knew perfectly well that her children would not eat with their tails if they had them. She loved her babies so that she almost disliked to see them grow up, yet she knew it was right for them to leave the nest. They were so large that they spread out over the edges of it already, and they must be taught to take care of themselves before it was time for her to rear her second brood.

The next morning all four children were made to hop out on to the rail. Their legs were not very strong and their toes sprawled weakly around. Sometimes they lurched and almost fell. Before leaving the nest they had felt big and very important; now they suddenly felt small and young and helpless. Once in a while one of them would hop feebly along the rail for a few steps. Then he would chirp in a frightened way, let his head settle down over his speckled breast, slide his eyelids over his eyes, and wait for more food to be brought to him.

Whenever a team went by, the oldest child shut his eyes. He thought they couldn't see him if he did that. The other children kept theirs open and watched to see what happened. Their father and mother had told them to watch, but the timid young Robin always shut his eyes in spite of that.

"We shall have trouble with him," said Mrs. Robin, "but he must be made to do as he is told, even if he is afraid." She shut her bill very tightly as she spoke, and Mr. Robin knew that he could safely trust the bringing-up of his timid son to her.

Mrs. Robin talked and talked to him, and still he shut his eyes every time that he was frightened. "I can't keep them open," he would say, "because when I am frightened I am always afraid, and I can't be brave when I am afraid."

"That is just when you must be brave," said his mother. "There is no use in being brave when there is nothing to fear, and it is a great deal braver to be brave when you are frightened than to be brave when you are not." You can see that she was a very wise Robin and a good mother. It would have been dreadful for her to let him grow up a coward.

At last the time came when the young birds were to fly to the ground and hop across the road. Both their father and their mother were there to show them how. "You must let go of the rail," they said. "You will never fly in the world unless you let go of the rail."

Three of the children fluttered and lurched and flew down. The timid young Robin would not try it. His father ordered and his mother coaxed, yet he only clung more closely to his rail and said, "I can't! I'm afraid!"

At last his mother said: "Very well. You shall stay there as long as you wish, but we cannot stay with you."

Then she chirped to her husband, and they and the three brave children went across the road, talking as they went. "Careful!" she would say. "Now another hop! That was fine! Now another!" And the father fluttered around and said: "Good! Good! You'll be grown-up before you know it." When they were across, the parents hunted food and fed their three brave children, tucking the mouthfuls far into their wide-open bills.

The timid little Robin on the fence felt very, very lonely. He was hungry, too. Whenever he saw his mother pick up a mouthful of food, he chirped loudly: "Me! Me! Me!" for he wanted her to bring it to him. She paid no attention to him for a long time. Then she called: "Do you think you can fly? Do you think you can fly? Do you think?"

The timid little Robin hopped a few steps and chirped but never lifted a wing. Then his mother gave each of the other children a big mouthful.

The Robin on the fence huddled down into a miserable little bunch, and thought: "They don't care whether I ever have anything to eat. No, they don't!" Then he heard a rush of wings, and his mother stood before him with a bunch in her bill for him. He hopped toward her and she ran away. Then he sat down and cried. She hopped back and looked lovingly at him, but couldn't speak because her bill was so full. Across the road the Robin father stayed with his brave children and called out, "Earn it, my son, earn it!"

The young Robin stretched out his neck and opened his bill—but his mother flew to the ground. He was so hungry—so very, very hungry,—that for a minute he quite forgot to be afraid, and he leaned toward her and toppled over. He fluttered his wings without thinking, and the first he knew he had flown to the ground. He was hardly there before his mother was feeding him and his father was singing: "Do you know what you did? Do you know what you did? Do you know?"

Before his tail was grown the timid Robin had become as brave as any of the children, for, you know, after you begin to be brave you always want to go on. But the Garter Snake says that Mrs. Robin is the bravest of the family.

The Crickets' School

In one corner of the meadow lived a fat old Cricket, who thought a great deal of himself. He had such a big, shining body, and a way of chirping so very loudly, that nobody could ever forget where he lived. He was a very good sort of Cricket, too, ready to say the most pleasant things to everybody, yet, sad to relate, he had a dreadful habit of boasting. He had not always lived in the meadow, and he liked to tell of the wonderful things he had seen and done when he was younger and lived up near the white farm-house.

When he told these stories of what he had done, the big Crickets around him would not say much, but just sit and look at each other. The little Crickets, however, loved to hear him talk, and would often come to the door of his house (which was a hole in the ground), to beg him to tell them more.

One evening he said he would teach them a few things that all little Crickets should know. He had them stand in a row, and then began: "With what part of your body do you eat?"

"With our mouths," all the little Crickets shouted.

"With what part of your body do you run and leap?"

"Our legs," they cried.

"Do you do anything else with your legs?"

"We clean ourselves with them," said one.

"We use them and our mouths to make our houses in the ground," said another.

"Oh yes, and we hear with our two front legs," cried one bright little fellow.

"That is right," answered the fat old Cricket. "Some creatures hear with things called ears, that grow on the sides of their heads, but for my part, I think it much nicer to hear with one's legs, as we do."

"Why, how funny it must be not to hear with one's legs, as we do," cried all the little Crickets together.

"There are a great many queer things to be seen in the great world," said their teacher. "I have seen some terribly big creatures with only two legs and no wings whatever."

"How dreadful!" all the little Crickets cried. "We wouldn't think they could move about at all."

"It must be very hard to do so," said their teacher; "I was very sorry for them," and he spread out his own wings and stretched his six legs to show how he enjoyed them.

"But how can they sing if they have no wings?" asked the bright little Cricket.

"They sing through their mouths, in much the same way that the birds have to. I am sure it must be much easier to sing by rubbing one's wings together, as we do," said the fat old teacher. "I could tell you many queer things about these two-legged creatures, and the houses in which they live, and perhaps some day I will. There are other large four-legged creatures around their homes that are very terrible, but, my children, I was never afraid of any of them. I am one of the truly brave people who are never frightened, no matter how terrible the sight. I hope, children, that you will always be brave, like me. If anything should scare you, do not jump or run away. Stay right where you are, and——"

But the little Crickets never heard the rest of what their teacher began to say, for at that minute Brown Bess, the Cow, came through a broken fence toward the spot where the Crickets were. The teacher gave one shrill "chirp," and scrambled down his hole. The little Crickets fairly tumbled over each other in their hurry to get away, and the fat old Cricket, who had been out in the great world, never again talked to them about being brave.

The Contented Earthworms

After a long and soaking rain, the Earthworms came out of their burrows, or rather, they came part way out, for each Earthworm put out half of his body, and, as there were many of them and they lived near to each other, they could easily visit without leaving their own homes. Two of these long, slimy people were talking, when a Potato Bug strolled by. "You poor things," said he, "what a wretched life you must lead. Spending one's days in the dark earth must be very dreary."

"Dreary!" exclaimed one of the Earthworms, "it is delightful. The earth is a snug and soft home. It is warm in cold weather and cool in warm weather. There are no winds to trouble us, and no sun to scorch us."

"But," said the Potato Bug, "it must be very dull. Now, out in the grass, one finds beautiful flowers, and so many families of friends."

"And down here," answered the Worm, "we have the roots. Some are brown and woody, like those of the trees, and some are white and slender and soft. They creep and twine, until it is like passing through a forest to go among them. And then, there are the seeds. Such busy times as there are in the ground in spring-time! Each tiny seed awakens and begins to grow. Its roots must strike downward, and its stalk upward toward the light. Sometimes the seeds are buried in the earth with the root end up, and then they have a great time getting twisted around and ready to grow."

"Still, after the plants are all growing and have their heads in the air, you must miss them."

"We have the roots always," said the Worm. "And then, when the summer is over, the plants have done their work, helping to make the world beautiful and raise their seed babies, and they wither and droop to the earth again, and little by little the sun and the frost and the rain help them to melt back into the earth. The earth is the beginning and the end of plants."

"Do you ever meet the meadow people in it?" asked the Potato Bug.

"Many of them live here as babies," said the Worm. "The May Beetles, the Grasshoppers, the great Humming-bird Moths, and many others spend their babyhood here, all wrapped in eggs or cocoons. Then, when they are strong enough, and their legs and wings are grown, they push their way out and begin their work. It is their getting-ready time, down here in the dark. And then, there are the stones, and they are so old and queer. I am often glad that I am not a stone, for to have to lie still must be hard to bear. Yet I have heard that they did not always lie so, and that some of the very pebbles around us tossed and rolled and ground for years in the bed of a river, and that some of them were rubbed and broken off of great rocks. Perhaps they are glad now to just lie and rest."

"Truly," said the Potato Bug, "you have a pleasant home, but give me the sunshine and fresh air, my six legs, and my striped wings, and you are welcome to it all."

"You are welcome to them all," answered the Worms. "We are contented with smooth and shining bodies, with which we can bore and wriggle our way through the soft, brown earth. We like our task of keeping the earth right for the plants, and we will work and rest happily here."

The Potato Bug went his way, and said to his brothers, "What do you think? I have been talking with Earthworms who would not be Potato Bugs if they could." And they all shook their heads in wonder, for they thought that to be Potato Bugs was the grandest and happiest thing in the world.

The Measuring Worm's Joke

One day there crawled over the meadow fence a jolly young Measuring Worm. He came from a bush by the roadside, and although he was still a young Worm he had kept his eyes open and had a very good idea how things go in this world. "Now," thought he, as he rested on the top rail of the fence, "I shall meet some new friends. I do hope they will be pleasant. I will look about me and see if anyone is in sight." So he raised his head high in the air and, sure enough, there were seven Caterpillars of different kinds on a tall clump of weeds near by.

The Measuring Worm hurried over to where they were, and making his best bow said: "I have just come from the roadside and think I shall live in the meadow. May I feed with you?"

The Caterpillars were all glad to have him, and he joined their party. He asked many questions about the meadow, and the people who lived there, and the best place to find food. The Caterpillars said, "Oh, the meadow is a good place, and the people are nice enough, but they are not at all fashionable—not at all."

"Why," said the Measuring Worm, "if you have nice people and a pleasant place in which to live, I don't see what more you need."

"That is all very well," said a black and yellow Caterpillar, "but what we want is fashionable society. The meadow people always do things in the same way, and one gets so tired of that. Now can you not tell us something different, something that Worms do in the great world from which you come?"

Just at this minute the Measuring Worm had a funny idea, and he wondered if the Caterpillars would be foolish enough to copy him. He thought it would be a good joke if they did, so he said very soberly, "I notice that when you walk you keep your body quite close to the ground. I have seen many Worms do the same thing, and it is all right if they wish to, but none of my family ever do so. Did you notice how I walk?"

"Yes, yes," cried the Caterpillars, "show us again."

So the Measuring Worm walked back and forth for them, arching his body as high as he could, and stopping every little while to raise his head and look haughtily around.

"What grace!" exclaimed the Caterpillars. "What grace, and what style!" and one black and brown one tried to walk in the same way.

The Measuring Worm wanted to laugh to see how awkward the black and brown Caterpillar was, but he did not even smile, and soon every one of the Caterpillars was trying the same thing, and saying "Look at me. Don't I do well?" or, "How was that?"

You can just imagine how those seven Caterpillars looked when trying to walk like the Measuring Worm. Every few minutes one of them would tumble over, and they all got warm and tired. At last they thought they had learned it very well, and took a long rest, in which they planned to take a long walk and show the other meadow people the fashion they had received from the outside world.

"We will walk in a line," they said, "as far as we can, and let them all see us. Ah, it will be a great day for the meadow when we begin to set the fashions!"

The mischievous young Measuring Worm said not a word, and off they started. The big black and yellow Caterpillar went first, the black and brown one next, and so on down to the smallest one at the end of the line, all arching their bodies as high as they could. All the meadow people stared at them, calling each other to come and look, and whenever the Caterpillars reached a place where there were many watching them, they would all raise their heads and look around exactly as the Measuring Worm had done. When they got back to their clump of bushes, they had the most dreadful backaches, but they said to each other, "Well, we have been fashionable for once."

And, at the same time, out in the grass, the meadow people were saying, "Did you ever see anything so ridiculous in your life?" All of which goes to show how very silly people sometimes are when they think too much of being fashionable.

A Puzzled Cicada

Seventeen years is a long, long time to be getting ready to fly; yet that is what the Seventeen-year Locusts, or Cicadas, have to expect. First, they lie for a long time in eggs, down in the earth. Then, when they awaken, and crawl out of their shells, they must grow strong enough to dig before they can make their way out to where the beautiful green grass is growing and waving in the wind.

The Cicada who got so very much puzzled had not been long out of his home in the warm, brown earth. He was the only Cicada anywhere around, and it was very lonely for him. However, he did not mind that so much when he was eating, or singing, or resting in the sunshine, and as he was either eating, or singing, or resting in the sunshine most of the time, he got along fairly well.

Because he was young and healthy he grew fast. He grew so very fast that after a while he began to feel heavy and stiff, and more like sitting still than like crawling around. Beside all this, his skin got tight, and you can imagine how uncomfortable it must be to have one's skin too tight. He was sitting on the branch of a bush one day, thinking about the wonderful great world, when—pop!—his skin had cracked open right down the middle of his back! The poor Cicada was badly frightened at first, but then it seemed so good and roomy that he took a deep breath, and—pop!—the crack was longer still!

The Cicada found that he had another whole skin under the outside one which had cracked, so he thought, "How much cooler and more comfortable I shall be if I crawl out of this broken covering," and out he crawled.

It wasn't very easy work, because he didn't have anybody to help him. He had to hook the claws of his outer skin into the bark of the branch, hook them in so hard that they couldn't pull out, and then he began to wriggle out of the back of his own skin. It was exceedingly hard work, and the hardest of all was the pulling his legs out of their cases. He was so tired when he got free that he could hardly think, and his new skin was so soft and tender that he felt limp and queer. He found that he had wings of a pretty green, the same color as his legs. He knew these wings must have been growing under his old skin, and he stretched them slowly out to see how big they were. This was in the morning, and after he had stretched his wings he went to sleep for a long time.

When he awakened, the sun was in the western sky, and he tried to think who he was. He looked at himself, and instead of being green he was a dull brown and black. Then he saw his old skin clinging to the branch and staring him in the face. It was just the same shape as when he was in it, and he thought for a minute that he was dreaming. He rubbed his head hard with his front legs to make sure he was awake, and then he began to wonder which one he was. Sometimes he thought that the old skin which clung to the bush was the Cicada that had lain so long in the ground, and sometimes he thought that the soft, fat, new-looking one was the Cicada. Or were both of them the Cicada? If he were only one of the two, what would he do with the other?

While he was wondering about this in a sleepy way, an old Cicada from across the river flew down beside him. He thought he would ask her, so he waved his feelers as politely as he knew how, and said, "Excuse me, Madam Cicada, for I am much puzzled. It took me seventeen years to grow into a strong, crawling Cicada, and then in one day I separated. The thinking, moving part of me is here, but the outside shell of me is there on that branch. Now, which part is the real Cicada?"

"Why, that is easy enough," said the Madam Cicada; "You are *you*, of course. The part that you cast off and left clinging to the branch was very useful once. It kept you warm on cold days and cool on warm days, and you needed it while you were only a crawling creature. But when your wings were ready to carry you off to a higher and happier life, then the skin that had been a help was in your way, and you did right to wriggle out of it. It is no longer useful to you. Leave it where it is and fly off to enjoy your new life. You will never have trouble if you remember that the thinking part is the real *you*."

And then Madam Cicada and her new friend flew away to her home over the river, and he saw many strange sights before he returned to the meadow.

The Tree Frog's Story

In all the meadow there was nobody who could tell such interesting stories as the old Tree Frog. Even the Garter Snake, who had been there the longest, and the old Cricket, who had lived in the farm-yard, could tell no such exciting tales as the Tree Frog. All the wonderful things of which he told had happened before he came to the meadow, and while he was still a young Frog. None of his friends had known him then, but he was an honest fellow, and they were sure that everything he told was true: besides, they must be true, for how could a body ever think out such remarkable tales from his own head?

When he first came to his home by the elm tree he was very thin, and looked as though he had been sick. The Katydids who stayed near said that he croaked in his sleep, and that, you know, is not what well and happy Frogs should do.

One day when many of the meadow people were gathered around him, he told them his story. "When I was a little fellow," he said, "I was strong and well, and could leap farther than any other Frog of my size. I was hatched in the pond beyond the farm-house, and ate my way from the egg to the water outside like any other Frog. Perhaps I ought to say, 'like any other Tadpole,' for, of course, I began life as a Tadpole. I played and ate with my brothers and sisters, and little dreamed what trouble was in store for me when I grew up. We were all in a hurry to be Frogs, and often talked of what we would do and how far we would travel when we were grown.

"Oh, how happy we were then! I remember the day when my hind legs began to grow, and how the other Tadpoles crowded around me in the water and swam close to me to feel the two little bunches that were to be legs. My fore legs did not grow until later, and these bunches came just in front of my tail."

"Your tail!" cried a puzzled young Cricket; "why, you haven't any tail!"

"I did have when I was a Tadpole," said the Tree Frog. "I had a beautiful, wiggly little tail with which to swim through the waters of the pond; but as my legs grew larger and stronger, my tail grew littler and weaker, until there wasn't any tail left. By the time my tail was gone I had four good legs, and could breathe through both my nose and my skin. The knobs on the ends of my toes were sticky, so that I could climb a tree, and then I was ready to start on my travels. Some of the other Frogs started with me, but they stopped along the way, and at last I was alone.

"I was a bold young fellow, and when I saw a great white thing among the trees up yonder, I made up my mind to see what it was. There was a great red thing in the yard beside it, but I liked the white one better. I hopped along as fast as I could, for I did not then know enough to be afraid. I got close up to them both, and saw strange, big creatures going in and out of the red thing—the barn, as I afterward found it was called. The largest creatures had four legs, and some of them had horns. The smaller creatures had only two legs on which to walk, and two other limbs of some sort with which they lifted and carried things. The queerest thing about it was, that the smaller creatures seemed to make the larger ones do whatever they wanted them to. They even made some of them help do their work. You may not believe me, but what I tell you is true. I saw two of the larger ones tied to a great load of dried grass and pulling it into the barn.

"As you may guess, I stayed there a long time, watching these strange creatures work. Then I went over toward the white thing, and that, I found out, was the farm-house. Here were more of the two-legged creatures, but they were dressed differently from those in the barn. There were some bright-colored flowers near the house, and I crawled in among them. There I rested until sunset, and then began my evening song. While I was singing, one of the people from the house came out and found me. She picked me up and carried me inside. Oh, how frightened I was! My heart thumped as though it would burst, and I tried my best to get away from her. She didn't hurt me at all, but she would not let me go.

"She put me in a very queer prison. At first, when she put me down on a stone in some water, I did not know that I was in prison. I tried to hop away, and—bump! went my head against something. Yet when I drew back, I could see no wall there. I tried it again and again, and every time I hurt my head. I tell you the truth, my friends, those walls were made of something which one could see through."

"Wonderful!" exclaimed all the meadow people; "wonderful, indeed!"

"And at the top," continued the Tree Frog, "was something white over the doorway into my prison. In the bottom were water and a stone, and from the bottom to the top was a ladder. There I had to live for most of the summer. I had enough to eat; but anybody who has been free cannot be happy shut in. I watched my chance, and three times I got out when the little door was not quite closed. Twice I was caught and put back. In the pleasant weather, of course, I went to the top of the ladder, and when it was going to rain I would go down again. Every time that I went up or down, those dreadful creatures would put their faces up close to my prison, and I could hear a roaring sound which meant they were talking and laughing.

"The last time I got out, I hid near the door of the house, and although they hunted and hunted for me, they didn't find me. After they stopped hunting, the wind blew the door open, and I hopped out."

"You don't say!" exclaimed a Grasshopper.

"Yes, I hopped out and scrambled away through the grass as fast as ever I could. You people who have never been in prison cannot think how happy I was. It seemed to me that just stretching my legs was enough to make me wild with joy. Well, I came right here, and you were all kind to me, but for a long time I could not sleep without dreaming that I was back in prison, and I would croak in my sleep at the thought of it."

"I heard you," cried the Katydid, "and I wondered what was the matter."

"Matter enough," said the Tree Frog. "It makes my skin dry to think of it now. And, friends, the best way I can ever repay your kindness to me, is to tell you to never, never, never, never go near the farm-house."

And they all answered, "We never will."

The Day When The Grass Was Cut

There came a day when all the meadow people rushed back and forth, waving their feelers and talking hurriedly to each other. The fat old Cricket was nowhere to be seen. He said that one of his legs was lame and he thought it best to stay quietly in his hole. The young Crickets thought he was afraid. Perhaps he was, but he said that he was lame.

All the insects who had holes crawled into them carrying food. Everybody was anxious and fussy, and some people were even cross. It was all because the farmer and his men had come into the meadow to cut the grass. They began to work on the side nearest the road, but every step which the Horses took brought the mower nearer to the people who lived in the middle of the meadow or down toward the river.

"I have seen this done before," said the Garter Snake. "I got away from the big mower, and hid in the grass by the trees, or by the stumps where the mower couldn't come. Then the men came and cut that grass with their scythes, and I had to wriggle away over the short, sharp grass-stubble to my hole. When they get near me this time, I shall go into my hole and stay there."

"They are not so bad after all," said the Tree Frog. "I like them better out-of-doors than I did in the house. They saw me out here once and didn't try to catch me."

A Meadow Mouse came hurrying along. "I must get home to my babies," she said. "They will be frightened if I am not there."

"Much good you can do when you are there!" growled a voice down under her feet. She was standing over the hole where the fat old Cricket was with his lame leg.

The mother Meadow Mouse looked rather angry for a minute, and then she answered: "I'm not so very large and strong, but I can squeak and let the Horses know where the nest is. Then they won't step on it. Last year I had ten or twelve babies there, and one of the men picked them up and looked at them and then put them back. I was so frightened that my fur stood on end and I shook like June grass in the wind."

"Humph! Too scared to run away," said the voice under her feet.

"Mothers don't run away and leave their children in danger," answered the Meadow Mouse. "I think it is a great deal braver to be brave when you are afraid than it is to be brave when you're not afraid." She whisked her long tail and scampered off through the grass. She did not go the nearest way to her nest because she thought the Garter Snake might be watching. She didn't wish him to know where she lived. She knew he was fond of young Mice, and didn't want him to come to see her babies while she was away. She said he was not a good friend for young children.

"We don't mind it at all," said the Mosquitoes from the lower part of the meadow. "We are unusually hungry today anyway, and we shall enjoy having the men come."

"Nothing to make such a fuss over," said a Milkweed Butterfly. "Just crawl into your holes or fly away."

"Sometimes they step on the holes and close them," said an Ant. "What would you do if you were in a hole and it stopped being a hole and was just earth?"

"Crawl out, I suppose," answered the Milkweed Butterfly with a careless flutter.

"Yes," said the Ant, "but I don't see what there would be to crawl out through."

The Milkweed Butterfly was already gone. Butterflies never worry about anything very long, you know.

"Has anybody seen the Measuring Worm?" asked the Katydid. "Where is he?"

"Oh, I'm up a tree," answered a pleasant voice above their heads, "but I sha'n't be up a tree very long. I shall come down when the grass is cut."

"Oh, dear, dear, dear!" cried the Ants, hurrying around. "We can't think what we want to do. We don't know what we ought to do. We can't think and we don't know, and we don't think that we ought to!"

"Click!" said a Grasshopper, springing into the air. "We must hurry, hurry, hurry!" He jumped from a stalk of pepper-grass to a plantain. "We *must* hurry," he said, and he jumped from the plantain back to the pepper-grass.

Up in the tree where the Measuring Worm was, some Katydids were sitting on a branch and singing shrilly: "Did you ever? Did you ever? Ever? Ever? Ever? Did you ever?" And this shows how much excited they were, for they usually sang only at night.

Then the mower came sweeping down the field, drawn by the Blind Horse and the Dappled Gray, and guided by the farmer himself. The dust rose in clouds as they passed, the Grasshoppers gave mighty springs which took them out of the way, and all the singing and shrilling stopped until the mower had passed. The nodding grasses swayed and fell as the sharp knives slid over the ground. "We are going to be hay," they said, "and live in the big barn."

"Now we shall grow some more tender green blades," said the grass roots.

"Fine weather for haying," snorted the Dappled Gray. "We'll cut all the grass in this field before noon."

"Good feeling ground to walk on," said the Blind Horse, tossing his head until the harness jingled.

Then the Horses and the farmer and the mower passed far away, and the meadow people came together again.

"Well," said the Tree Frog. "That's over for a while."

The Ants and the Grasshoppers came back to their old places. "We did just the right thing," they cried joyfully. "We got out of the way."

The Measuring Worm and the Katydids came down from their tree as the Milkweed Butterfly fluttered past. "The men left the grass standing around the Meadow Mouse's nest," said the Milkweed Butterfly, "and the Cows up108 by the barn are telling how glad they will be to have the hay when the cold weather comes."

"Grass must grow and hay be cut," said the wise old Tree Frog, "and when the time comes we always know what to do. Puk-rup! Puk-r-r-rup!"

"I think," said the fat old Cricket, as he crawled out of his hole, "that my lame leg is well enough to use. There is nothing like rest for a lame leg."

The Grasshopper And The Measuring Worm Run A Race

A few days after the Measuring Worm came to the meadow he met the Grasshoppers. Everybody had heard of the Caterpillars' wish to be fashionable, and some of the young Grasshoppers, who did not know that it was all a joke, said they would like to teach the Measuring Worm a few things. So when they met him the young Grasshoppers began to make fun of him, and asked him what he did if he wanted to run, and whether he didn't wish his head grew on the middle of his back so that he could see better when walking.

The Measuring Worm was good-natured, and only said that he found his head useful where it was. Soon one fine-looking Grasshopper asked him to race. "That will show," said the Grasshopper, "which is the better traveller."

The Measuring Worm said: "Certainly, I will race with you to-morrow, and we will ask all our friends to look on." Then he began talking about something else. He was a wise young fellow, as well as a jolly one, and he knew the Grasshoppers felt sure that he would be beaten. "If I cannot win the race by swift running," thought he, "I must try to win it by good planning." So he got the Grasshoppers to go with him to a place where the sweet young grass grew, and they all fed together.

The Measuring Worm nibbled only a little here and there, but he talked a great deal about the sweetness of the grass, and how they would not get any more for a long time because the hot weather would spoil it. And the Grasshoppers said to each other: "He is right, and we must eat all we can while we have it." So they ate, and ate, and ate, and ate, until sunset, and in the morning they awakened and began eating again. When the time for the race came, they were all heavy and stupid from so much eating,—which was exactly what the Measuring Worm wanted.

The Tree Frog, the fat, old Cricket, and a Caterpillar were chosen to be the judges, and the race was to be a long one,—from the edge of the woods to the fence. When the meadow people were all gathered around to see the race, the Cricket gave a shrill chirp, which meant "Go!" and off they started. That is to say, the Measuring Worm started. The Grasshopper felt so sure he could beat that he wanted to give the Measuring Worm a little the start, because then, you see, he could say he had won without half trying.

The Measuring Worm started off at a good, steady rate, and when he had gone a few feet the Grasshopper gave a couple of great leaps, which landed him far ahead of the Worm. Then he stopped to nibble a blade of grass and visit with some Katydids who were looking on. By and by he took a few more leaps and passed the Measuring Worm again. This time he began to show off by jumping up straight into the air, and when he came down he would call out to those who stood near to see how strong he was and how easy it would be for him to win the race. And everybody said, "How strong he is, to be sure!" "What wonderful legs he has!" and "He could beat the Measuring Worm with his eyes shut!" which made the Grasshopper so exceedingly vain that he stopped more and more often to show his strength and daring.

That was the way it went, until they were only a short distance from the end of the race course. The Grasshopper was more and more pleased to think how easily he was winning, and stopped for a last time to nibble grass and make fun of the Worm. He gave a great leap into the air, and when he came down there was the Worm on the fence! All the meadow people croaked, and shrilled, and chirped to see the way in which the race ended, and the Grasshopper was very much vexed. "You shouldn't call him the winner," he said; "I can travel ten times as fast as he, if I try."

"Yes," answered the judges, "we all know that, yet the winning of the race is not decided by what you might do, but by what you did do." And the meadow people all cried: "Long live the Measuring Worm! Long live the Measuring Worm!"

Mr. Green Frog And His Visitors

One day a young Frog who lived down by the river, came hopping up through the meadow. He was a fine-looking fellow, all brown and green, with a white vest, and he came to see the sights. The oldest Frog on the river bank had told him that he ought to travel and learn to know the world, so he had started at once.

Young Mr. Green Frog had very big eyes, and they stuck out from his head more than ever when he saw all the strange sights and heard all the strange sounds of the meadow. Yet he made one great mistake, just as bigger and better people sometimes do when they go on a journey; he didn't try to learn from the things he saw, but only to show off to the meadow people how much he already knew, and he boasted a great deal of the fine way in which he lived when at home.

Mr. Green Frog told those whom he met that the meadow was dreadfully dry, and that he really could not see how they lived there. He said they ought to see the lovely soft mud that there was in the marsh, and that there the people could sit all day with their feet in water in among the rushes where the sunshine never came. "And then," he said, "to eat grass as the Grasshoppers did! If they would go home with him, he would show them how to live."

The older Grasshoppers and Crickets and Locusts only looked at each other and opened their funny mouths in a smile, but the young ones thought Mr. Green Frog must be right, and they wanted to go back with him. The old Hoppers told them that they wouldn't like it down there, and that they would be sorry that they had gone; still the young ones teased and teased and teased and teased until everybody said: "Well, let them go, and then perhaps they will be contented when they return."

At last they all set off together,—Mr. Green Frog and the young meadow people. Mr. Green Frog took little jumps all the way and bragged and bragged. The Grasshoppers went in long leaps, the Crickets scampered most of the way, and the Locusts fluttered. It was a very gay little party, and they kept saying to each other, "What a fine time we shall have!"

When they got to the marsh, Mr. Green Frog went in first with a soft "plunk" in the mud. The rest all followed and tried to make believe that they liked it, but they didn't—they didn't at all. The Grasshoppers kept bumping against the tough, hard rushes when they jumped, and then that would tumble them over on their backs in the mud, and there they would lie, kicking their legs in the air, until some friendly Cricket pushed them over on their feet again. The Locusts couldn't fly at all there, and the Crickets got their shiny black coats all grimy and horrid.

They all got cold and wet and tired—yes, and hungry too, for there were no tender green things growing in among the rushes. Still they pretended to have a good time, even while they were thinking how they would like to be in their dear old home.

After the sun went down in the west it grew colder still, and all the Frogs in the marsh began to croak to the moon, croaking so loudly that the tired little travellers could not sleep at all. When the Frogs stopped croaking and went to sleep in the mud, one tired Cricket said: "If you like this, *stay*. I am going home as fast as my six little legs will carry me." And all the rest of the travellers said: "So am I," "So am I," "So am I."

Mr. Green Frog was sleeping soundly, and they crept away as quietly as they could out into the silvery moonlight and up the bank towards home. Such a tired little party as they were, and so hungry that they had to stop and eat every little while. The dew was on the grass and they could not get warm.

The sun was just rising behind the eastern forest when they got home. They did not want to tell about their trip at all, but just ate a lot of pepper-grass to make them warm, and then rolled themselves in between the woolly mullein leaves to rest all day long. And that was the last time any of them ever went away with a stranger.

The Dignified Walking-Sticks

Three Walking-Sticks from the forest had come to live in the big maple tree near the middle of the meadow. Nobody knew exactly why they had left the forest, where all their sisters and cousins and aunts lived. Perhaps they were not happy with their relatives. But then, if one is a Walking-Stick, you know, one does not care so very much about one's family.

These Walking-Sticks had grown up the best way they could, with no father or mother to care for them. They had never been taught to do anything useful, or to think much about other people. When they were hungry they ate some leaves, and never thought what they should eat the next time that they happened to be hungry. When they were tired they went to sleep, and when they had slept enough they awakened. They had nothing to do but to eat and sleep, and they did not often take the trouble to think. They felt that they were a little better than those meadow people who rushed and scrambled and worked from morning until night, and they showed very plainly how they felt. They said it was not genteel to hurry, no matter what happened.

One day the Tree Frog was under the tree when the large Brown Walking-Stick decided to lay some eggs. He saw her dropping them carelessly around on the ground, and asked, "Do you never fix a place for your eggs?"

"A place?" said the Brown Walking-Stick, waving her long and slender feelers to and fro. "A place? Oh, no! I think they will hatch where they are. It is too much trouble to find a place."

"Puk-r-r-rup!" said the Tree Frog. "Some mothers do not think it too much trouble to be careful where they lay eggs."

"That may be," said the Brown Walking-Stick, "but they do not belong to our family." She spoke as if those who did not belong to her family might be good but could never be genteel. She had once told her brother, the Five-Legged Walking-Stick, that she would not want to live if she could not be genteel. She thought the meadow people very common.

The Five-Legged Walking-Stick looked much like his sister. He had the same long, slender body, the same long feelers, and the same sort of long, slender legs. If you had passed them in a hay-field, you would surely have thought each a stem of hay, unless you happened to see them move. The other Walking-Stick, their friend, was younger and green. You would have thought her a blade of grass.

It is true that the brother had the same kind of legs as his sister, but he did not have the same number. When he was young and green he had six, then came a dreadful day when a hungry Nuthatch saw him, flew down, caught him, and carried him up a tree. He knew just what to expect, so when the Nuthatch set him down on the bark to look at him, he unhooked his feet from the bark and tumbled to the ground. The Nuthatch tried to catch him and broke off one of his legs, but she never found him again, although she looked and looked and looked and looked. That was because he crawled into a clump of ferns and kept very still.

His sister came and looked at him and said, "Now if you were only a Spider it would not be long before you would have six legs again."

Her brother waved first one feeler and then the other, and said: "Do you think I would be a Spider for the sake of growing legs? I would rather be a Walking-Stick without any legs than to be a Spider with a hundred." Of course, you know, Spiders never do have a hundred, and a Walking-Stick wouldn't be walking without any, but that was just his way of speaking, and it showed what kind of insect he was. His relatives all waved their feelers, one at a time, and said, "Ah, he has the true Walking-Stick spirit!" Then they paid no more attention to him, and after a while he and his sister and their green little friend left the forest for the meadow.

On the day when the grass was cut, they had sat quietly in their trees and looked genteel. Their feelers were held quite close together, and they did not move their feet at all, only swayed their bodies gracefully from side to side. Now they were on the ground, hunting through the flat piles of cut grass for some fresh and juicy bits to eat. The Tree Frog was also out, sitting in a cool, damp corner of the grass rows. The young Grasshoppers were kicking up their feet, the Ants were scrambling around as busy as ever, and life went on quite as though neither men nor Horses had ever entered the meadow.

"See!" cried a Spider who was busily looking after her web, "there comes a Horse drawing something, and the farmer sitting on it and driving."

When the Horse was well into the meadow, the farmer moved a bar, and the queer-looking machine began to kick the grass this way and that with its many stiff and shining legs. A frisky young Grasshopper kicked in the same way, and happened—just happened, of course—to knock over two of his friends. Then there was a great scrambling and the Crickets frolicked with them. The young Walking-Stick thought it looked like great fun and almost wished herself some other kind of insect, so that she could tumble around in the same way. She did not quite wish it, you understand, and would never have thought of it if she had turned brown.

"Ah," said the Five-Legged Walking-Stick, "what scrambling! How very common!"

"Yes, indeed!" said his sister. "Why can't they learn to move slowly and gracefully? Perhaps they can't help being fat, but they might at least act genteel."

"What is it to be genteel?" asked a Grasshopper suddenly. He had heard every word that the Walking-Stick said.

"Why," said the Five-Legged Walking-Stick, "it is just to be genteel. To act as you see us act, and to——"

Just here the hay-tedder passed over them, and every one of the Walking-Sticks was sent flying through the air and landed on his back. The Grasshoppers declare that the Walking-Sticks tumbled and kicked and flopped around in a dreadfully common way until they were right side up. "Why," said the Measuring Worm, "you act like anybody else when the hay-tedder comes along!"

The Walking-Sticks looked very uncomfortable, and the brother and sister could not think of anything to say. It was the young green one who spoke at last. "I think," said she, "that it is much easier to act genteel when one is right side up."

The Day Of The Great Storm

Everything in the meadow was dry and dusty. The leaves on the milkweeds were turning yellow with thirst, the field blossoms drooped their dainty heads in the sunshine, and the grass seemed to fairly rattle in the wind, it was so brown and dry.

All of the meadow people when they met each other would say, "Well, this *is* hot," and the Garter Snake, who had lived there longer than anyone else, declared that it was the hottest and driest time that he had ever known. "Really," he said, "it is so hot that I cannot eat, and such a thing never happened before."

The Grasshoppers and Locusts were very happy, for such weather was exactly what they liked. They didn't see how people could complain of such delightful scorching days. But that, you know, is always the way, for everybody cannot be suited at once, and all kinds of weather are needed to make a good year.

The poor Tree Frog crawled into the coolest place he could find—hollow trees, shady nooks under the ferns, or even beneath the corner of a great stone. "Oh," said he, "I wish I were a Tadpole again, swimming in a shady pool. It is such a long, hot journey to the marsh that I cannot go. Last night I dreamed that I was a Tadpole, splashing in the water, and it was hard to awaken and find myself only an uncomfortable old Tree Frog."

Over his head the Katydids were singing, "Lovely weather! Lovely weather!" and the Tree Frog, who was a good-natured old fellow after all, winked his eye at them and said: "Sing away. This won't last always, and then it will be my turn to sing."

Sure enough, the very next day a tiny cloud drifted across the sky, and the Tree Frog, who always knew when the weather was about to change, began his rain-song. "Pukr-r-rup!" sang he, "Pukr-r-rup! It will rain! It will rain! R-r-r-rain!"

The little white cloud, grew bigger and blacker, and another came following after, then another, and another, and another, until the sky was quite covered with rushing black clouds. Then came a long, low rumble of thunder, and all the meadow people hurried to find shelter. The Moths and Butterflies hung on the under sides of great leaves. The Grasshoppers and their cousins crawled under burdock and mullein plants. The Ants scurried around to find their own homes. The Bees and Wasps, who had been gathering honey for their nests, flew swiftly back. Everyone was hurrying to be ready for the shower, and above all the rustle and stir could be heard the voice of the old Frog, "Pukr-r-rup! Pukr-r-rup! It will rain! It will rain! R-r-r-rain!"

The wind blew harder and harder, the branches swayed and tossed, the leaves danced, and some even blew off of their mother trees; the hundreds of little clinging creatures clung more and more tightly to the leaves that sheltered them, and then the rain came, and such a rain! Great drops hurrying down from the sky, crowding each other, beating down the grass, flooding the homes of the Ants and Digger Wasps until they were half choked with water, knocking over the Grasshoppers and tumbling them about like leaves. The lightning flashed, and the thunder pealed, and often a tree would crash down in the forest near by when the wind blew a great blast.

When everybody was wet, and little rivulets of water were trickling through the grass and running into great puddles in the hollows, the rain stopped, stopped suddenly. One by one the meadow people crawled or swam into sight.

The Digger Wasp was floating on a leaf in a big puddle. He was too tired and wet to fly, and the whirling of the leaf made him feel sick and dizzy, but he stood firmly on his tiny boat and tried to look as though he enjoyed it.

The Ants were rushing around to put their homes in shape, the Spiders were busily eating their old webs, which had been broken and torn in the storm, and some were already beginning new ones. A large family of Bees, whose tree-home had been blown down, passed over the meadow in search for a new dwelling, and everybody seemed busy and happy in the cool air that followed the storm.

The Snake went gliding through the wet grass, as hungry as ever, the Tree Frog was as happy as when he was a Tadpole, and only the Grasshoppers and their cousins, the Locusts and Katydids, were cross. "Such a horrid rain!" they grumbled, "it spoiled all our fun. And after such lovely hot weather too."

"Now don't be silly," said the Tree Frog, who could be really severe when he thought best, "the Bees and the Ants are not complaining, and they had a good deal harder time than you. Can't you make the best of anything? A nice, hungry, cross lot you would be if it didn't rain, because then you would have no good, juicy food. It's better for you in the end as it is, but even if it were not, you might make the best of it as I did of the hot weather. When you have lived as long as I have, you will know that neither Grasshoppers nor Tree Frogs can have their way all the time, but that it always comes out all right in the end without their fretting about it."

The Story Of Lily Pad Island

This is the story of a venturesome young Spider, who left his home in the meadow to seek his fortune in the great world.

He was a beautiful Spider, and belonged to one of the best families in the country around. He was a worker, too, for, as he had often said, there wasn't a lazy leg on his body, and he could spin the biggest, strongest, and shiniest web in the meadow. All the young people in the meadow liked him, and he was invited to every party, or dance, or picnic that they planned. If he had been content to stay at home, as his brothers and sisters were, he would in time have become as important and well known as the Tree Frog, or the fat, old Cricket, or even as the Garter Snake.

But that would not satisfy him at all, and one morning he said "Good-by" to all his friends and relatives, and set sail for unknown lands. He set sail, but not on water. He crawled up a tree, and out to the end of one of its branches. There he began spinning a long silken rope, and letting the wind blow it away from the tree. He held fast to one end, and when the wind was quite strong, he let go of the branch and sailed off through the air, carried by his rope balloon, and blown along by the wind.

The meadow people, on the ground below, watched him until he got so far away that he looked about as large as a Fly, and then he looked no bigger than an Ant, and then no bigger than a clover seed, and then no bigger than the tiniest egg that was ever laid, and then—well, then you could see nothing but sky, and the Spider was truly gone. The other young Spiders all wished that they had gone, and the old Spiders said, "They might much better stay at home, as their fathers and mothers had done." There was no use talking about it when they disagreed so, and very little more was said.

Meanwhile, the young traveller was having a very fine time. He was carried past trees and over fences, down toward the river. Under him were all the bright flowers of the meadow, and the bushes which used to tower above his head. After a while, he saw the rushes of the marsh below him, and wondered if the Frogs there would see him as he passed over them.

Next, he saw a beautiful, shining river, and in the quiet water by the shore were great white water-lilies growing, with their green leaves, or pads, floating beside them. "Ah," thought he, "I shall pass over the river, and land on the farther side," and he began to think of eating his rope balloon, so that he might sink slowly to the ground, when—the wind suddenly stopped blowing, and he began falling slowly down, down, down, down.

How he longed for a branch to cling to! How he shivered at the thought of plunging into the cold water! How he wished that he had always stayed at home! How he thought of all the naughty things that he had ever done, and was sorry that he had done them! But it was of no use, for still he went down, down, down. He gave up all hope and tried to be brave, and at that very minute he felt himself alight on a great green lily-pad.

~ 171 ~

This was indeed an adventure, and he was very joyful for a little while. But he got hungry, and there was no food near. He walked all over the leaf, Lily-Pad Island he named it, and ran around its edges as many as forty times. It was just a flat, green island, and at one side was a perfect white lily, which had grown, so pure and beautiful, out of the darkness and slime of the river bottom. The lily was so near that he jumped over to it. There he nestled in its sweet, yellow centre, and went to sleep.

When he fell asleep it was late in the afternoon, and, as the sun sank lower and lower in the west, the lily began to close her petals and get ready for the night. She was just drawing under the water when the Spider awakened. It was dark and close, and he felt himself shut in and going down. He scrambled and pushed, and got out just in time to give a great leap and alight on Lily Pad-Island once more. And then he was in a sad plight. He was hungry and cold, and night was coming on, and, what was worst of all, in his great struggle to free himself from the lily he had pulled off two of his legs, so he had only six left.

He never liked to think of that night afterward, it was so dreadful. In the morning he saw a leaf come floating down the stream; he watched it; it touched Lily-Pad Island for just an instant and he jumped on. He did not know where it would take him, but anything was better than staying where he was and starving. It might float to the shore, or against one of the rushes that grew in the shallower parts of the river. If it did that, he would jump off and run up to the top and set sail again, but the island, where he had been, was too low to give him a start.

He went straight down-stream for a while, then the leaf drifted into a little eddy, and whirled around and around, until the Spider was almost too dizzy to stand on it. After that, it floated slowly, very slowly, toward the shore, and at last came the joyful minute when the Spider could jump to some of the plants that grew in the shallow water, and, by making rope bridges from one to another, get on solid ground.

After a few days' rest he started back to the meadow, asking his way of every insect that he met. When he got home they did not know him, he was so changed, but thought him only a tramp Spider, and not one of their own people. His mother was the first one to find out who he was, and when her friends said, "Just what I expected! He might have known better," she hushed them, and answered: "The poor child has had a hard time, and I won't scold him for going. He has learned that home is the best place, and that home friends are the dearest. I shall keep him quiet while his new legs are growing, and then, I think, he will spin his webs near the old place."

And so he did, and is now one of the steadiest of all the meadow people. When anybody asks him his age, he refuses to tell, "For," he says, "most of me is middle-aged, but these two new legs of mine are still very young."

The Grasshopper Who Wouldn't Be Scared

There were more Ants in the meadow than there were of any other kind of insects. In their family there were not only Ants, but great-aunts, cousins, nephews, and nieces, until it made one sleepy to think how many relatives each Ant had. Yet they were small people and never noisy, so perhaps the Grasshoppers seemed to be the largest family there.

There were many different families of Grasshoppers, but they were all related. Some had short horns, or feelers, and red legs; and some had long horns. Some lived in the lower part of the meadow where it was damp, and some in the upper part. The Katydids, who really belong to this family, you know, stayed in trees and did not often sing in the daytime. Then there were the great Road Grasshoppers who lived only in places where the ground was bare and dusty, and whom you could hardly see unless they were flying. When they lay in the dust their wide wings were hidden and they showed only that part of their bodies which was dust-color. Let the farmer drive along, however, and they rose into the air with a gentle, whirring sound and fluttered to a safe place. Then one could see them plainly, for their large under wings were black with yellow edges.

Perhaps those Grasshoppers who were best known in the meadow were the Clouded Grasshoppers, large dirty-brown ones with dark spots, who seemed to be everywhere during the autumn. The fathers and brothers in this family always crackled their wings loudly when they flew anywhere, so one could never forget that they were around.

It was queer that they were always spoken of as Grasshoppers. Their great-great-great-grandparents were called Locusts, and that was the family name, but the Cicadas liked that name and wanted it for themselves, and made such a fuss about it that people began to call them Seventeen-Year-Locusts; and then because they had to call the real Locusts something else, they called them Grasshoppers. The Grasshoppers didn't mind this. They were jolly and noisy, and as they grew older were sometimes very pompous. And you know what it is to be pompous.

When the farmer was drawing the last loads of hay to his barn and putting them away in the great mows there, three young Clouded Grasshopper brothers were frolicking near the wagon. They had tried to see who could run the fastest, crackle the loudest, spring the highest, flutter the farthest, and eat the most. There seemed to be nothing more to do. They couldn't eat another mouthful, the other fellows wouldn't play with them, they wouldn't play with their sisters, and they were not having any fun at all.

They were sitting on a hay-cock, watching the wagon as it came nearer and nearer. The farmer was on top and one of his men was walking beside it. Whenever they came to a hay-cock the farmer would stop the Horses, the man would run a long-handled, shining pitch-fork into the hay on the ground and throw it up to the farmer. Then it would be trampled down on to the load, the farmer's wife would rake up the scattering hay which was left on the ground, and that would be thrown up also.

The biggest Clouded Grasshopper said to his brothers, "You dare not sit still while they put this hay on the load!"

The smallest Clouded Grasshopper said, "I do too!"

The second brother said, "Huh! Guess I dare do anything you do!" He said it in a rather mean way, and that may have been because he had eaten too much. Overeating will make any insect cross.

Now every one of them was afraid, but each waited for the others to back out. While they were waiting, the wagon stopped beside them, the shining fork was run into the hay, and they were shaken and stood on their heads and lifted through the air on to the wagon. There they found themselves all tangled up with hay in the middle of the load. It was dark and they could hardly breathe. There were a few stems of nettles in the hay, and they had to crawl away from them. It was no fun at all, and they didn't talk very much.

When the wagon reached the barn, they were pitched into the mow with the hay, and then they hopped and fluttered around until they were on the floor over the Horses' stalls. They sat together on the floor and wondered how they could ever get back to the meadow. Because they had come in the middle of the load, they did not know the way.

"Oh!" said they. "Who are those four-legged people over there?"

"Kittens!" sang a Swallow over their heads. "Oh, tittle-ittle-ittle-ee!"

The Clouded Grasshoppers had never seen Kittens. It is true that the old Cat often went hunting in the meadow, but that was at night, when Grasshoppers were asleep.

"Meouw!" said the Yellow Kitten. "Look at those queer little brown people on the floor. Let's each catch one."

So the Kittens began crawling slowly over the floor, keeping their bodies and tails low, and taking very short steps. Not one of them took his eyes off the Clouded Grasshopper whom he meant to catch. Sometimes they stopped and crouched and watched, then they went on, nearer, nearer, nearer, still, while the Clouded Grasshoppers were more and more scared and wished they had never left the meadow where they had been so safe and happy.

At last the Kittens jumped, coming down with their sharp little claws just where the Clouded Grasshoppers—had been. The Clouded Grasshoppers had jumped too, but they could not stay long in the air, and when they came down the Kittens jumped again. So it went until the poor Clouded Grasshoppers were very, very tired and could not jump half so far as they had done at first. Sometimes the Kittens even tried to catch them while they were fluttering, and each time they came a little nearer than before. They were so tired that they never thought of leaping up on the wall of the barn where the Kittens couldn't reach them.

At last the smallest Clouded Grasshopper called to his brothers, "Let us chase the Kittens."

The brothers answered, "They're too big."

The smallest Clouded Grasshopper, who had always been the brightest one in the family, called back, "We may scare them if they are big."

Then all the Clouded Grasshoppers leaped toward the Kittens and crackled their wings and looked very, very fierce. And the Kittens ran away as fast as they could. They were in such a hurry to get away that the Yellow Kitten tumbled over the White Kitten and they rolled on the floor in a furry little heap. The Clouded Grasshoppers leaped again, and the Kittens scrambled away to their nest in the hay, and stood against the wall and raised their backs and their pointed little tails, and opened their pink mouths and spat at them, and said, "Ha-ah-h-h!"

"There!" said the smallest Clouded Grasshopper to them, "we won't do anything to you this time, because you are young and don't know very much, but don't you ever bother one of us again. We might have hopped right on to you, and then what could you have done to help yourselves?"

The Clouded Grasshoppers started off to find their way back to the meadow, and the frightened Kittens looked at each other and whispered: "Just supposing they had hopped on to us! What *could* we have done!"

The Earthworm Half-Brothers

Early one wet morning, a long Earthworm came out of his burrow. He did not really leave it, but he dragged most of his body out, and let just the tip-end of it stay in the earth. Not having any eyes, he could not see the heavy, gray clouds that filled the sky, nor the milkweed stalks, so heavy with rain-drops that they drooped their pink heads. He could not see these things, but he could feel the soft, damp grass, and the cool, clear air, and as for seeing, why, Earthworms never do have eyes, and never think of wanting them, any more than you would want six legs, or feelers on your head.

This Earthworm had been out of his burrow only a little while, when there was a flutter and a rush, and Something flew down from the sky and bit his poor body in two. Oh, how it hurt! Both halves of him wriggled and twisted with pain, and there is no telling what might have become of them if another and bigger Something had not come rushing down to drive the first Something away. So there the poor Earthworm lay, in two aching, wriggling pieces, and although it had been easy enough to bite him in two, nothing in the world could ever bite him into one.

After a while the aching stopped, and he had time to think. It was very hard to decide what he ought to do. You can see just how puzzling it must have been, for, if you should suddenly find yourself two people instead of one, you would not know which one was which. At this very minute, who should come along but the Cicada, and one of the Earthworm pieces asked his advice. The Cicada thought that he was the very person to advise in such a case, because he had had such a puzzling time himself. So he said in a very knowing way: "Pooh! That is a simple matter. I thought I was two Cicadas once, but I wasn't. The thinking, moving part is the real one, whatever happens, so that part of the Worm which thinks and moves is the real Worm."

"I am the thinking part," cried each of the pieces.

The Cicada rubbed his head with his front legs, he was so surprised.

"And I am the moving part," cried each of the pieces, giving a little wriggle to prove it.

"Well, well, well, well!" exclaimed the Cicada, "I believe I don't know how to settle this. I will call the Garter Snake," and he flew off to get him.

A very queer couple they made, the Garter Snake and the Cicada, as they came hurrying back from the Snake's home. The Garter Snake was quite excited. "Such a thing has not happened in our meadow for a long time," he said, "and it is a good thing there is somebody here to explain it to you, or you would be dreadfully frightened. My family is related to the Worms, and I know. Both of you pieces are Worms now. The bitten ends will soon be well, and you can keep house side by side, if you don't want to live together."

"Well," said the Earthworms, "if we are no longer the same Worm, but two Worms, are we related to each other? Are we brothers, or what?"

"Why," answered the Garter Snake, with a funny little smile, "I think you might call yourselves half-brothers." And to this day they are known as "the

Earthworm half-brothers." They are very fond of each other and are always seen together.

A jolly young Grasshopper, who is a great eater and thinks rather too much about food, said he wouldn't mind being bitten into two Grasshoppers, if it would give him two stomachs and let him eat twice as much.

The Cicada told the Garter Snake this one day, and the Garter Snake said: "Tell him not to try it. The Earthworms are the only meadow people who can live after being bitten in two that way. The rest of us have to be one, or nothing. And as for having two stomachs, he is just as well off with one, for if he had two, he would get twice as hungry."

A Gossiping Fly

Of all the people who lived and worked in the meadow by the river, there was not one who gave so much thought to other people's business as a certain Blue-bottle Fly. Why this should be so, nobody could say; perhaps it was because he had nothing to do but eat and sleep, for that is often the way with those who do little work.

Truly his cares were light. To be sure, he ate much, but then, with nearly sixty teeth for nibbling and a wonderful long tongue for sucking, he could eat a great deal in a very short time. And as for sleeping—well, sleeping was as easy for him as for anyone else.

However it was, he saw nearly everything that happened, and thought it over in his queer little three-cornered head until he was sure that he ought to go to talk about it with somebody else. It was no wonder that he saw so much, for he had a great bunch of eyes on each side of his head, and three bright, shining ones on the very top of it. That let him see almost everything at once, and beside this his neck was so exceedingly slender that he could turn his head very far around.

This particular Fly, like all other Flies, was very fond of the sunshine and kept closely at home in dark or wet weather. He had no house, but stayed in a certain elder bush on cloudy days and called that his home. He had spent all of one stormy day there, hanging on the under side of a leaf, with nothing to do but think. Of course, his head was down and his feet were up, but Blue-bottle Flies think in that position as well as in any other, and the two sticky pads on each side of his six feet held him there very comfortably.

He thought so much that day, that when the next morning dawned sunshiny and clear, he had any number of things to tell people, and he started out at once.

First he went to the Tree Frog. "What do you suppose," said he, "that the Garter Snake is saying about you? It is very absurd, yet I feel that you ought to know. He says that your tongue is fastened at the wrong end, and that the tip of it points down your throat. Of course, I knew it couldn't be true, still I thought I would tell you what he said, and then you could see him and put a stop to it."

For an answer to this the Tree Frog ran out his tongue, and, sure enough, it was fastened at the front end. "The Snake is quite right," he said pleasantly, "and my tongue suits me perfectly. It is just what I need for the kind of food I eat, and the best of all is that it never makes mischief between friends."

After that, the Fly could say nothing more there, so he flew away in his noisiest manner to find the Grasshopper who lost the race. "It was a shame," said the Fly to him, "that the judges did not give the race to you. The idea of that little green Measuring Worm coming in here, almost a stranger, and making so much trouble! I would have him driven out of the meadow, if I were you."

"Oh, that is all right," answered the Grasshopper, who was really a good fellow at heart; "I was very foolish about that race for a time, but the Measuring Worm and I are firm friends now. Are we not?" And he turned to a leaf just back of him, and there, peeping around the edge, was the Measuring Worm himself.

The Blue-bottle Fly left in a hurry, for where people were so good-natured he could do nothing at all. He went this time to the Crickets, whom he found all together by the fat, old Cricket's hole.

"I came," he said, "to find out if it were true, as the meadow people say, that you were all dreadfully frightened when the Cow came?"

The Crickets answered never a word, but they looked at each other and began asking him questions.

"Is it true," said one, "that you do nothing but eat and sleep?"

"Is it true," said another, "that your eyes are used most of the time for seeing other people's faults?"

"And is it true," said another, "that with all the fuss you make, you do little but mischief?"

The Blue-bottle Fly answered nothing, but started at once for his home in the elder bush, and they say that his three-cornered head was filled with very different thoughts from any that had been there before.

The Frog-Hoppers Go Out
Into The World

Along the upper edge of the meadow and in the corners of the rail fence there grew golden-rod. During the spring and early summer you could hardly tell that it was there, unless you walked close to it and saw the slender and graceful stalks pushing upward through the tall grass and pointing in many different ways with their dainty leaves. The Horses and Cows knew it, and although they might eat all around it they never pulled at it with their lips or ate it. In the autumn, each stalk was crowned with sprays of tiny bright yellow blossoms, which nodded in the wind and scattered their golden pollen all around. Then it sometimes happened that people who were driving past would stop, climb over the fence, and pluck some of it to carry away. Even then there was so much left that one could hardly miss the stalks that were gone.

It may have been because the golden-rod was such a safe home that most of the Frog-Hoppers laid their eggs there. Some laid eggs in other plants and bushes, but most of them chose the golden-rod. After they had laid their eggs they wandered around on the grass, the bushes, and the few trees which grew in the meadow, hopping from one place to another and eating a little here and a little there.

Nobody knows why they should have been called Frog-Hoppers, unless it was because when you look them in the face they seem a very little like tiny Frogs. To be sure, they have six legs, and teeth on the front pair, as no real Frog ever thought of having. Perhaps it was only a nickname because their own name was so long and hard to speak.

The golden-rod was beginning to show small yellow-green buds on the tips of its stalks, and the little Frog-Hoppers were now old enough to talk and wonder about the great world. On one stalk four Frog-Hopper brothers and sisters lived close together. That was much pleasanter than having to grow up all alone, as most young Frog-Hoppers do, never seeing their fathers and mothers or knowing whether they ever would.

These four little Frog-Hoppers did not know how lucky they were, and that, you know, happens very often when people have not seen others lonely or unhappy. They supposed that every Frog-Hopper family had two brothers and two sisters living together on a golden-rod stalk. They fed on the juice or sap of the golden-rod, pumping it out of the stalk with their stout little beaks and eating or drinking it. After they had eaten it, they made white foam out of it, and this foam was all around them on the stalk. Any one passing by could tell at once by the foam just where the Frog-Hoppers lived.

One morning the oldest Frog-Hopper brother thought that the sap pumped very hard. It may be that it did pump hard, and it may be that he was tired or lazy. Anyway, he began to grumble and find fault. "This is the worst stalk of golden-rod I ever saw in my life," he said. "It doesn't pay to try to pump any more sap, and I just won't try, so there!"

He was quite right in saying that it was the worst stalk he had ever seen, because he had never seen any other, but he was much mistaken in saying that it didn't pay to pump sap, and as for saying that "it didn't pay, so there!" we all know that when insects begin to talk in that way the best thing to do is to leave them quite alone until they are better-natured.

The other Frog-Hopper children couldn't leave him alone, because they hadn't changed their skins for the last time. They had to stay in their foam until that was done. After the big brother spoke in this way, they all began to wonder if the sap didn't pump hard. Before long the big sister wiggled impatiently and said, "My beak is dreadfully tired."

Then they all stopped eating and began to talk. They called their home stuffy, and said there wasn't room to turn around in it without hitting the foam. They didn't say why they should mind hitting the foam. It was soft and clean, and always opened up a way when they pushed against it.

"I tell you what!" said the big brother, "after I've changed my skin once more and gone out into the great world, you won't catch me hanging around this old golden-rod."

"Nor me!" "Nor me!" "Nor me!" said the other young Frog-Hoppers.

"I wonder what the world is like," said the little sister. "Is it just bigger foam and bigger golden-rod and more Frog-Hoppers?"

"Huh!" exclaimed her big brother. "What lots you know! If I didn't know any more than that about it, I'd keep still and not tell anybody." That made her feel badly, and she didn't speak again for a long time.

Then the little brother spoke. "I didn't know you had ever been out into the world," he said.

"No," said the big brother, "I suppose you didn't. There are lots of things you don't know." That made him feel badly, and he went off into the farthest corner of the foam and stuck his head in between a golden-rod leaf and the stalk. You see the big brother was very cross. Indeed, he was exceedingly cross.

For a long time nobody spoke, and then the big sister said, "I wish you would tell us what the world is like."

The big brother knew no more about the world than the other children, but after he had been cross and put on airs he didn't like to tell the truth. He might have known that he would be found out, yet he held up his head and answered: "I don't suppose that I can tell you so that you will understand, because you have never seen it. There are lots of things there—whole lots of them—and it is very big. Some of the things are like golden-rod and some of them are not. Some of them are not even like foam. And there are a great many people there. They all have six legs, but they are not so clever as we are. We shall have to tell them things."

This was very interesting and made the little sister forget to pout and the little brother come out of his foam-corner. He even looked as though he might ask a few questions, so the big brother added, "Now don't talk to me, for I must think about something."

It was not long after this that the young Frog-Hoppers changed their skins for the last time. The outside part of the foam hardened and made a little roof over them while they did this. Then they were ready to go out into the meadow. The big brother felt rather uncomfortable, and it was not his new skin which made him so. It was remembering what he had said about the world outside.

When they had left their foam and their golden-rod, they had much to see and ask about. Every little while one of the smaller Frog-Hoppers would exclaim, "Why, you never told us about this!" or, "Why didn't you tell us about that?"

Then the big brother would answer: "Yes, I did. That is one of the things which I said were not like either golden-rod or foam."

For a while they met only Crickets, Ants, Grasshoppers, and other six-legged people, and although they looked at each other they did not have much to say. At last they hopped near to the Tree Frog, who was sitting by the mossy trunk of a beech tree and looked so much like the bark that they did not notice him at first. The big brother was very near the Tree Frog's head.

"Oh, see!" cried the others. "There is somebody with only four legs, and he doesn't look as though he ever had any more. Why, Brother, what does this mean? You said everybody had six."

At this moment the Tree Frog opened his eyes a little and his mouth a great deal, and shot out his quick tongue. When he shut his mouth again, the big brother of the Frog-Hoppers was nowhere to be seen. They never had a chance to ask him that question again. If they had but known it, the Tree Frog at that minute had ten legs, for six and four are ten. But then, they couldn't know it, for six were on the inside.

The Mosquito Tries To Teach His Neighbors

In this meadow, as in every other meadow since the world began, there were some people who were always tired of the way things were, and thought that, if the world were only different, they would be perfectly happy. One of these discontented ones was a certain Mosquito, a fellow with a whining voice and disagreeable manners. He had very little patience with people who were not like him, and thought that the world would be a much pleasanter place if all the insects had been made Mosquitoes.

"What is the use of Spiders, and Dragon-flies, and Beetles, and Butterflies?" he would say, fretfully; "a Mosquito is worth more than any of them."

You can just see how unreasonable he was. Of course, Mosquitoes and Flies do help keep the air pure and sweet, but that is no reason why they should set themselves up above the other insects. Do not the Bees carry pollen from one flower to another, and so help the plants raise their Seed Babies? And who would not miss the bright, happy Butterflies, with their work of making the world beautiful?

But this Mosquito never thought of those things, and he said to himself: "Well, if they cannot all be Mosquitoes, they can at least try to live like them, and I think I will call them together and talk it over." So he sent word all around, and his friends and neighbors gathered to hear what he had to say.

"In the first place," he remarked, "it is unfortunate that you are not Mosquitoes, but, since you are not, one must make the best of it. There are some things, however, which you might learn from us fortunate creatures who are. For instance, notice the excellent habit of the Mosquitoes in the matter of laying eggs. Three or four hundred of the eggs are fastened together and left floating on a pond in such a way that, when the babies break their shells, they go head first into the water. Then they——"

"Do you think I would do that if I could?" interrupted a motherly old Grasshopper. "Fix it so my children would drown the minute they came out of the egg? No, indeed!" and she hurried angrily away, followed by several other loving mothers.

"But they don't drown," exclaimed the Mosquito, in surprise.

"They don't if they're Mosquitoes," replied the Ant, "but I am thankful to say my children are land babies and not water babies."

"Well, I won't say anything more about that, but I must speak of your voices, which are certainly too heavy and loud to be pleasant. I should think you might speak and sing more softly, even if you have no pockets under your wings like mine. I flutter my wings, and the air strikes these pockets and makes my sweet voice."

"Humph!" exclaimed a Bee, "it is a very poor place for pockets, and a very poor use to make of them. Every Bee knows that pockets are handiest on the hind legs, and should be used for carrying pollen to the babies at home."

"My pocket is behind," said a Spider, "and my web silk is kept there. I couldn't live without a pocket."

Some of the meadow people were getting angry, so the Garter Snake, who would always rather laugh than quarrel, glided forward and said: "My friends and neighbors; our speaker here has been so kind as to tell us how the Mosquitoes do a great many things, and to try to teach us their way. It seems to me that we might repay some of his kindness by showing him our ways, and seeing that he learns by practice. I would ask the Spiders to take him with them and show him how to spin a web. Then the Bees could teach him how to build comb, and the Tree Frog how to croak, and the Earthworms how to burrow, and the Caterpillars how to spin a cocoon. Each of us will do something for him. Perhaps the Measuring Worm will teach him to walk as the Worms of his family do. I understand he does that very well." Here everybody laughed, remembering the joke played on the Caterpillars, and the Snake stopped speaking.

The Mosquito did not dare refuse to be taught, and so he was taken from one place to another, and told exactly how to do everything that he could not possibly do, until he felt so very meek and humble that he was willing the meadow people should be busy and happy in their own way.

The Frog Who Thought Herself Sick

By the edge of the marsh lived a young Frog, who thought a great deal about herself and much less about other people. Not that it was wrong to think so much of herself, but it certainly was unfortunate that she should have so little time left in which to think of others and of the beautiful world.

Early in the morning this Frog would awaken and lean far over the edge of a pool to see how she looked after her night's rest. Then she would give a spring, and come down with a splash in the cool water for her morning bath. For a while she would swim as fast as her dainty webbed feet would push her, then she would rest, sitting in the soft mud with just her head above the water.

When her bath was taken, she had her breakfast, and that was the way in which she began her day. She did nothing but bathe and eat and rest, from sunrise to sunset. She had a fine, strong body, and had never an ache or a pain, but one day she got to thinking, "What if sometime I should be sick?" And then, because she thought about nothing but her own self, she was soon saying, "I am afraid I shall be sick." In a little while longer it was, "I certainly am sick."

She crawled under a big toadstool, and sat there looking very glum indeed, until a Cicada came along. She told the Cicada how sick she felt, and he told his cousins, the Locusts, and they told their cousins, the Grasshoppers, and they told their cousins, the Katydids, and then everybody told somebody else, and started for the toadstool where the young Frog sat. The more she had thought of it, the worse she felt, until, by the time the meadow people came crowding around, she was feeling very sick indeed.

"Where do you feel badly?" they cried, and, "How long have you been sick?" and one Cricket stared with big eyes, and said, "How dr-r-readfully she looks!" The young Frog felt weaker and weaker, and answered in a faint little voice that she had felt perfectly well until after breakfast, but that now she was quite sure her skin was getting dry, and "Oh dear!" and "Oh dear!"

Now everybody knows that Frogs breathe through their skins as well as through their noses, and for a Frog's skin to get dry is very serious, for then he cannot breathe through it; so, as soon as she said that, everybody was frightened and wanted to do something for her at once. Some of the timid ones began to weep, and the others bustled around, getting in each other's way and all trying to do something different. One wanted to wrap her in mullein leaves, another wanted her to nibble a bit of the peppermint which grew near, a third thought she should be kept moving, and that was the way it went.

Just when everybody was at his wits' end, the old Tree Frog came along. "Pukr-r-rup! What is the matter with you?" he said.

"Oh!" gasped the young Frog, weakly, "I am sure my skin is getting dry, and I feel as though I had something in my head."

"Umph!" grunted the Tree Frog to himself, "I guess there isn't enough in her head to ever make her sick; and, as for her skin, it isn't dry yet, and nobody knows that it ever will be."

But as he was a wise old fellow and had learned much about life, he knew he must not say such things aloud. What he did say was, "I heard there was to be a great race in the pool this morning."

The young Frog lifted her head quite quickly, saying: "You did? Who are the racers?"

"Why, all the young Frogs who live around here. It is too bad that you cannot go."

"I don't believe it would hurt me any," she said.

"You might take cold," the Tree Frog said; "besides, the exercise would tire you."

"Oh, but I am feeling much better," the young Frog said, "and I am certain it will do me good."

"You ought not to go," insisted all the older meadow people. "You really ought not."

"I don't care," she answered, "I am going anyway, and I am just as well as anybody."

And she did go, and it did seem that she was as strong as ever. The people all wondered at it, but the Tree Frog winked his eyes at them and said, "I knew that it would cure her." And then he, and the Garter Snake, and the fat, old Cricket laughed together, and all the younger meadow people wondered at what they were laughing.

The Katydids' Quarrel

The warm summer days were past, and the Katydids came again to the meadow. Everybody was glad to see them, and the Grasshoppers, who are cousins of the Katydids, gave a party in their honor.

Such a time as the meadow people had getting ready for that party! They did not have to change their dresses, but they scraped and cleaned themselves, and all the young Grasshoppers went off by the woods to practise jumping and get their knees well limbered, because there might be games and dancing at the party, and then how dreadful it would be if any young Grasshopper should find that two or three of his legs wouldn't bend easily!

The Grasshoppers did not know at just what time they ought to have the party. Some of the meadow people whom they wanted to invite were used to sleeping all day, and some were used to sleeping all night, so it really was hard to find an hour at which all would be wide-awake and ready for fun. At last the Tree Frog said: "Pukr-r-rup! Pukr-r-rup! Have it at sunset!" And at sunset it was.

Everyone came on time, and they hopped and chattered and danced and ate a party supper of tender green leaves. Some of the little Grasshoppers grew sleepy and crawled among the plantains for a nap. Just then a big Katydid said he would sing a song—which was a very kind thing for him to do, because he really did it to make the others happy, and not to show what a fine musician he was. All the guests said, "How charming!" or, "We should be delighted!" and he seated himself on a low swinging branch. You know Katydids sing with the covers of their wings, and so when he alighted on the branch he smoothed down his pale green suit and rubbed his wing-cases a little to make sure that they were in tune. Then he began loud and clear, "Katy did! Katy did!! Katy did!!!"

Of course he didn't mean any real Katy, but was just singing his song. However, there was another Katydid there who had a habit of contradicting, and he had eaten too much supper, and that made him feel crosser than ever; so when the singer said "Katy did!" this cross fellow jumped up and said, "Katy didn't! Katy didn't!! Katy didn't!!!" and they kept at it, one saying that she did and the other that she didn't, until everybody was ashamed and uncomfortable, and some of the little Grasshoppers awakened and wanted to know what was the matter.

Both of the singers got more and more vexed until at last neither one knew just what he was saying—and that, you know, is what almost always happens when people grow angry. They just kept saying something as loud and fast as possible and thought all the while that they were very bright—which was all they knew about it.

Suddenly somebody noticed that the one who began to say "Katy did!" was screaming "Katy didn't!" and the one who had said "Katy didn't!" was roaring "Katy did!" Then they all laughed, and the two on the branch looked at each other in a very shamefaced way.

The Tree Frog always knew the right thing to do, and he said "Pukr-r-rup!" so loudly that all stopped talking at once. When they were quiet he said: "We will now listen to a duet, 'Katy,' by the two singers who are up the tree. All please join in the chorus." So it was begun again, and both the leaders were good-natured, and all the Katydids below joined in with "did or didn't, did or didn't, did or didn't." And that was the end of the quarrel.

The Last Party Of The Season

Summer had been a joyful time in the meadow. It had been a busy time, too, and from morning till night the chirping and humming of the happy people there had mingled with the rustle of the leaves, and the soft "swish, swish," of the tall grass, as the wind passed over it.

True, there had been a few quarrels, and some unpleasant things to remember, but these little people were wise enough to throw away all the sad memories and keep only the glad ones. And now the summer was over. The leaves of the forest trees were turning from green to scarlet, orange, and brown. The beech and hickory nuts were only waiting for a friendly frost to open their outer shells, and loosen their stems, so that they could fall to the earth.

The wind was cold now, and the meadow people knew that the time had come to get ready for winter. One chilly Caterpillar said to another, "Boo-oo! How cold it is! I must find a place for my cocoon. Suppose we sleep side by side this winter, swinging on the same bush?"

And his friend replied: "We must hurry then, or we shall be too old and stiff to spin good ones."

The Garter Snake felt sleepy all the time, and declared that in a few days he would doze off until spring.

The Tree Frog had chosen his winter home already, and the Bees were making the most of their time in visiting the last fall flowers, and gathering every bit of honey they could find for their cold-weather stock.

The last eggs had been laid, and the food had been placed beside many of them for the babies that would hatch out in the spring. Nothing was left but to say "Good-by," and fall asleep. So a message was sent around the meadow for all to come to a farewell party under the elm tree.

Everybody came, and all who could sing did so, and the Crickets and Mosquitoes made music for the rest to dance by.

The Tree Frog led off with a black and yellow Spider, the Garter Snake followed with a Potato Bug, and all the other crawling people joined in the dance on the grass, while over their heads the Butterflies and other light-winged ones fluttered to and fro with airy grace.

The Snail and the fat, old Cricket had meant to look on, and really did so, for a time, from a warm corner by the tree, but the Cricket couldn't stand it to not join in the fun. First, his eyes gleamed, his feelers waved, and his feet kept time to the music, and, when a frisky young Ant beckoned to him, he gave a great leap and danced with the rest, balancing, jumping, and circling around in a most surprising way.

When it grew dark, the Fireflies' lights shone like tiny stars, and the dancing went on until all were tired and ready to sing together the last song of the summer, for on the morrow they would go to rest. And this was their song:

The autumn leaves lying

So thick on the ground,
The summer Birds flying
The meadow around,
      Say, "Good-by."

The Seed Babies dropping
    Down out of our sight,
The Dragon-flies stopping
    A moment in flight,
      Say, "Good-by."

The red Squirrels bearing
    Their nuts to the tree,
The wild Rabbits caring
    For babies so wee,
      Say, "Good-by."

The sunbeams now showing
Are hazy and pale,
The warm breezes blowing
Have changed to a gale,
So, "Good-by."

The season for working
    Is passing away.
Both playing and shirking
    Are ended to day,
      So, "Good-by."

The Garter Snake creeping
    So softly to rest,
The fuzzy Worms sleeping
    Within their warm nest,
      Say, "Good-by."

The Honey Bees crawling
    Around the full comb,
The tiny Ants calling
    Each one to the home,
      Say, "Good-by."

We've ended our singing,
    Our dancing, and play,
And Nature's voice ringing
    Now tells us to say
      Our "Good-by."

Among the Night People

The Black Spanish Chickens

When the Speckled Hen wanted to sit there was no use in trying to talk her out of the idea, for she was a very set Hen. So, after the farmer's wife had worked and worked, and barred her out of first one nesting-place and then another, she gave up to the Speckled Hen and fixed her a fine nest and put thirteen eggs into it. They were Black Spanish eggs, but the Speckled Hen did not know that. The Hens that had laid them could not bear to sit, so, unless some other Hen did the work which they left undone, there would have been no Black Spanish Chickens. This is always their way, and people have grown used to it. Now nobody thinks of asking a Black Spanish Hen to sit, although it does not seem right that a Hen should be unwilling to bring up chickens. Supposing nobody had been willing to bring her up?

Still, the Black Spanish Hens talk very reasonably about it. "We will lay plenty of eggs," they say, "but some of the common Hens must hatch them." They do their share of the farmyard work, only they insist on choosing what that share shall be.

When the Speckled Hen came off the nest with eleven Black Chickens (two of the eggs did not hatch), she was not altogether happy. "I wanted them to be speckled," said she, "and not one of the whole brood is." That was why she grew so restless and discontented in her coop, although it was roomy and clean and she had plenty given her to eat and drink. She was quite happy only when they were safely under her wings at night. And such a time as they always had getting settled!

When the sunbeams came more and more slantingly through the trees, the Chickens felt less and less like running around. Their tiny legs were tired and they liked to cuddle down on the grass in the shadow of the coop. Then the Speckled Hen often clucked to them to come in and rest, but they liked it better in the open air. The Speckled Hen would also have liked to be out of the coop, yet the farmer kept her in. He knew what was best for Hens with little Chickens, and also what was best for the tender young lettuce and radishes in his garden.

When the sun was nearly down, the Speckled Hen clucked her come-to-bed cluck, which was quite different from her food cluck or her Hawk cluck, and the little Black Chickens ran between the bars and crawled under her feathers. Then the Speckled Hen began to look fatter and fatter and fatter for each Chicken who nestled beneath her. Sometimes one little fellow would scramble up on to her back and stand there, while she turned her head from side to side, looking at him with first one and then the other of her round yellow eyes, and scolding him all the time. It never did any good to scold, but she said she had to do something, and with ten other children under her wings it would never do for her to stand up and tumble him off.

All the time that they were getting settled for the night the Chickens were talking in sleepy little cheeps, and now and then one of them would poke his head out between the feathers and tell the Speckled Hen that somebody was pushing him. Then she would be more puzzled than ever and cluck louder still. Sometimes, too, the Chickens would run out for another mouthful of cornmeal mush or a few more drops of water. There was one little fellow who always wanted something to drink just when he should have been going to sleep. The Speckled Hen used to say that it took longer for a mouthful of water to run down his throat than it would for her to drink the whole panful. Of course it did take quite a while, because he couldn't hurry it by swallowing. He had to drink, as all birds do, by filling his beak with water and then holding it up until the last drop had trickled down into his stomach.

When the whole eleven were at last safely tucked away for the night, the Speckled Hen was tired but happy. "They are good children," she often said to herself, "if they are Black Spanish. They might be just as mischievous if they were speckled; still, I do wish that those stylish-looking, white-eared Black Spanish Hens would raise their own broods. I don't like to be hatch-mother to other Hens' chickens." Then she would slide her eyelids over her eyes, and doze off, and dream that they were all speckled like herself.

There came a day when the coop was raised and they were free to go where they chose. There was a fence around the vegetable garden now and netting around the flower-beds, but there were other lovely places for scratching up food, for nipping off tender young green things, for picking up the fine gravel which every Chicken needs, and for wallowing in the dust. Then the Black Spanish Chickens became acquainted with the other fowls whom they had never met before. They were rather afraid of the Shanghai Cock because he had such a gruff way of speaking, and they liked the Dorkings, yet the ones they watched and admired and talked most about were the Black Spanish Cock and Hen. There were many fowls on the farm who did not have family names, and the Speckled Hen was one of these. They had been there longer than the rest and did not really like having new people come to live in the poultry-yard. It was trying, too, when the older Hens had to hatch the eggs laid by the newcomers.

It is said that this was what made the Speckled Hen leave the eleven little Black Spanish Chickens after she had been out of the coop for a while. They had been very mischievous and disobedient one day, and she walked off and left them to care for themselves while she started to raise a family of her own in a stolen nest under the straw-stack.

When night came, eleven little Black Spanish Chickens did not know what to do. They went to look for their old coop, but that had been given to another Hen and her family. They walked around looking very small and lonely, and wished they had minded the Speckled Hen and made her love them more. At last they found an old potato-crate which reminded them of a coop and so seemed rather homelike. It stood, top down, upon the ground and they were too big to crawl through its barred sides, so they did the best they could and huddled together on top of it. If there had not been a stone-heap near, they could not have done that, for their wing-feathers were not yet large enough to help them flutter. The bravest Chicken went first, picking his way from stone to stone until he reached the highest one, balancing himself awhile on that, stretching his neck toward the potato-crate, looking at it as though he were about to jump, and then seeming to change his mind and decide not do so after all.

The Chickens on the ground said he was afraid, and he said he wasn't any more afraid than they were. Then, after a while, he did jump, a queer, floppy, squawky kind of jump, but it landed him where he wanted to be. After that it was his turn to laugh at the others while they stood teetering uncertainly on the top stone. They were very lonely without the Speckled Hen, and each Chicken wanted to be in the middle of the group so that he could have others to keep him warm on all sides.

Somebody laughed at the most mischievous Chicken and told him he could stand on the potato-crate's back without being scolded, and he pouted his bill and said: "Much fun that would be! All I cared about standing on the Speckled Hen's back was to make her scold." It is very shocking that he should say such things, but he did say exactly that.

They slept safely that night, and only awakened when the Cocks crowed a little while after midnight. After that they slept until sunrise, and when the Shanghais and Dorkings came down from the apple-tree where they had been roosting, the Black Spanish Chickens stirred and cheeped, and looked at their feathers to see how much they had grown during the night. Then they pushed and squabbled for their breakfast.

Every night they came back to sleep on the potato-crate. At last they were able to spring up into their places without standing on the stone-pile, and that was a great day. They talked about it long after they should have been asleep, and were still chattering when the Shanghai Cock spoke: "If you Black Spanish Chickens don't keep still and let us sleep," said he, "some Owl or Weasel will come for you, and I shall be glad to have him!"

That scared the Chickens and they were very quiet. It made the Black Spanish Hen uneasy though, and she whispered to the Black Spanish Cock and wouldn't let him sleep until he had promised to fight anybody who might try to carry one of the Chickens away from the potato-crate.

The next night first one Chicken and then another kept tumbling off the potato-crate. They lost their patience and said such things as these to each other:

"You pushed me! You know you did!"

"Well, he pushed me!"

"Didn't either!"

"Did too!"

"Well, I couldn't help it if I did!"

The Shanghai Cock became exceedingly cross because they made so much noise, and even the Black Spanish Cock lost his patience. "You may be my children," said he, "but you do not take your manners from me. Is there no other place on this farm where you can sleep excepting that old crate?"

"We want to sleep here," answered the Chicken on the ground. "There is plenty of room if those fellows wouldn't push." Then he flew up and clung and pushed until some other Chicken tumbled off.

"Well!" said the Black Spanish Cock. And he would have said much more if the Black Spanish Hen had not fluttered down from the apple-tree to see what was the matter. When he saw the expression of her eyes he decided to go back to his perch.

"There is not room for you all," said the Black Spanish Hen. "One must sleep somewhere else."

"There *is* room," said the Chickens, contradicting her. "We have always roosted on here."

"There is *not* room," said the Black Spanish Hen once more. "How do your feathers grow?"

"Finely," said they.

"And your feet?"

"They are getting very big," was the answer.

"Do you think the Speckled Hen could cover you all with her wings if she were to try it now?"

The Chickens looked at each other and laughed. They thought it would take three Speckled Hens to cover them.

"But she used to," said the Black Spanish Hen. She did not say anything more. She just looked at the potato-crate and at them and at the potato-crate again. Then she walked off.

After a while one of the Chickens said: "I guess perhaps there isn't room for us all there."

The mischievous one said: "If you little Chickens want to roost there you may. I am too large for that sort of thing." Then he walked up the slanting board to the apple-tree branch and perched there beside the young Shanghais. You should have seen how beautifully he did it. His toes hooked themselves around the branch as though he had always perched there, and he tucked his head under his wing with quite an air. Before long his brothers and sisters came also, and heard him saying to one of his new neighbors, "Oh, yes, I much prefer apple-trees, but when I was a Chicken I used to sleep on a potato-crate."

"Just listen to him!" whispered the Black Spanish Cock. "And he hasn't a tail-feather worth mentioning!"

"Never mind," answered the Black Spanish Hen. "Let them play that they are grown up if they want to. They will be soon enough." She sighed as she put her head under her wing and settled down for the night. It made her feel old to see her children roosting in a tree.

The Wigglers Become Mosquitoes

It was a bright moonlight night when the oldest Wigglers in the rain-barrel made up their mind to leave the water. They had always been restless and discontented children, but it was not altogether their fault. How could one expect any insect with such a name to float quietly? When the Mosquito Mothers laid their long and slender eggs in the rain-barrel, they had fastened them together in boat-shaped masses, and there they had floated until the Wigglers were strong enough to break through the lower ends of the eggs into the water. It had been only a few days before they were ready to do this.

Then there had been a few more days and nights when the tiny Wigglers hung head downward in the water, and all one could see by looking across the barrel was the tips of their breathing tubes. Sometimes, if they were frightened, a young Wiggler would forget and get head uppermost for a minute, but he was always ashamed to have this happen, and made all sorts of excuses for himself when it did. Well-bred little Wigglers tried to always have their heads down, and Mosquitoes who stopped to visit with them and give good advice told them such things as these: "The Wiggler who keeps his head up may never have wings," and, "Up with your tails and down with your eyes, if you would be mannerly, healthy, and wise."

When they were very young they kept their heads way down and breathed through a tube that ran out near the tail-end of their bodies. This tube had a cluster of tiny wing-like things on the very tip, which kept it floating on the top of the water. They had no work to do, so they just ate food which they found in the water, and wiggled, and played tag, and whenever they were at all frightened they dived to the bottom and stayed there until they were out of breath. That was never very long.

There were many things to frighten them. Sometimes a stray Horse stopped by the barrel to drink, sometimes a Robin perched on the edge for a few mouthfuls of water, and once in a while a Dragon-Fly came over to visit from the neighboring pond. It was not always the biggest visitor who scared them the worst. The Horses tried not to touch the Wigglers, while a Robin was only too glad if he happened to get one into his bill with the water. The Dragon-Flies were the worst, for they were the hungriest, and they were so much smaller that sometimes the Wigglers didn't see them coming. Sometimes, too, when they thought that a Dragon-Fly was going the other way, some of them stayed near the top of the water, only to find when it was too late that a Dragon-Fly can go backward or sidewise without turning around.

When they were a few days old the Wigglers began to change their skins. This they did by wiggling out of their old ones and wearing the new ones which had been growing underneath. This made them feel exceedingly important, and some of them became disgracefully vain. One Wiggler would not dive until he was sure a certain Robin had seen his new suit. It was because of that vanity he never lived to be a Mosquito.

After they had changed their skins a few times, they had two breathing-tubes apiece instead of one, and these two grew out near their heads. And their heads were much larger. At the tail-end of his body each Wiggler now had two leaf-like things with which he swam through the water. Because they used different breathing-tubes, those Wigglers who had moulted or cast their skins several times now floated in the water with their heads just below the surface and their tails down. When a Wiggler is old enough for this, he is called a Pupa, or half-grown one.

There are often young Mosquito children of all ages in the same barrel—eggs, Wigglers, and Pupæ all together. There is plenty of room and plenty of food, but because they have no work to do there is much time for quarrelling and talking about each other.

This year the Oldest Brother had put on so many airs that nobody liked it at all, and several of the Wigglers had been heard to say that they couldn't bear the sight of him. He had such a way of saying, "When I was a young Wiggler and had to keep my head down," or repeating, "Up with your tails and down with your eyes, if you would be mannerly, healthy, and wise." One little Wiggler crossed his feelers at him, and they say that it is just as bad to do that as to make faces. Besides, it is so much easier—if you have the feelers to cross.

Now the Oldest Brother and those of his brothers and sisters who had hatched from the same egg-mass were talking of leaving the rain-barrel forever. It was a bright moonlight night and they longed to get their wings uncovered and dried, for then they would be full-grown Mosquitoes, resting most of the day and having glorious times at night.

The Oldest Brother was jerking himself through the water as fast as he could, giving his jointed body sudden bends, first this way and then that, and when he met anyone nearly his own age he said, "Come with me and cast your skin. It is a fine evening for moulting."

Sometimes they answered, "All right," and jerked or wiggled or swam along with him, and sometimes a Pupa would answer, "I'm afraid I'm not old enough to slip out of my skin easily."

Then the Oldest Brother would reply, "Don't stop for that. You'll be older by the time we begin." That was true, of course, and all members of Mosquito families grow old very fast. So it happened that when the moon peeped over the farmhouse, showing her bright face between the two chimneys, twenty-three Pupæ were floating close to each other and making ready to change their skins for the last time.

It was very exciting. All the young Wigglers hung around to see what was going on, and pushed each other aside to get the best places. The Oldest Brother was much afraid that somebody else would begin to moult before he was ready, and all the brothers were telling their sisters to be careful to split their skins in the right place down the back, and the sisters were telling them that they knew just as much about moulting as their brothers did. Every little while the Oldest Brother would say, "Now wait! Don't one of you fellows split his old skin until I say so."

Then two or three of his brothers would become impatient, because their outer skins were growing tighter every minute, and would say, "Why not?" and would grumble because they had to wait. The truth was that the Oldest Brother could not get his skin to crack, although he jerked and wiggled and took very deep breaths. And he didn't want any one else to get ahead of him. At last it did begin to open, and he had just told the others to commence moulting, when a Mosquito Mother stopped to lay a few eggs in the barrel.

"Dear me!" said she. "You are not going to moult to-night, are you?"

"Yes, we are," answered the Oldest Brother, giving a wiggle that split his skin a little farther. "We'll be biting people before morning."

"You?" said the Mosquito Mother, with a queer little smile. "I wouldn't count on doing that. But you young people may get into trouble if you moult now, for it looks like rain."

She waved her feelers upward as she spoke, and they noticed that heavy black clouds were piling up in the sky. Even as they looked the moon was hidden and the wind began to stir the branches of the trees. "It will rain," she said, "and then the water will run off the roof into this barrel, and if you have just moulted and cannot fly, you will be drowned."

"Pooh!" answered the Oldest Brother. "Guess we can take care of ourselves. I'm not afraid of a little water." Then he tried to crawl out of his old skin.

The Mosquito Mother stayed until she had laid all the eggs she wanted to, and then flew away. Not one of the Pupæ had been willing to listen to her, although some of the sisters might have done so if their brothers had not made fun of them.

At last, twenty-three soft and tired young Mosquitoes stood on their cast-off pupa-skins, waiting for their wings to harden. It is never easy work to crawl out of one's skin, and the last moulting is the hardest of all. It was then, when they could do nothing but wait, that these young Mosquitoes began to feel afraid. The night was now dark and windy, and sometimes a sudden gust blew their floating pupa skins toward one side of the barrel. They had to cling tightly to them, for they suddenly remembered that if they fell into the water they might drown. The oldest one found himself wishing to be a Wiggler again. "Wigglers are never drowned," thought he.

"Who are you going to bite first?" asked one of his brothers.

He answered very crossly: "I don't know and I don't care. I'm not hungry. Can't you think of anything but eating?"

"Why, what else is there to think about?" cried all the floating Mosquitoes.

"Well, there is flying," said he.

"Humph! I don't see what use flying would be except to carry us to our food," said one Mosquito Sister. She afterward found out that it was good for other reasons.

After that they didn't try to talk with their Oldest Brother. They talked with each other and tried their legs, and wished it were light enough for them to see their wings. Mosquitoes have such interesting wings, you know, thin and gauzy, and with delicate fringes around the edges and along the line of each vein. The sisters, too, were proud of the pockets under their wings, and were in a hurry to have their wings harden, so that they could flutter them and hear the beautiful singing sound made by the air striking these pockets. They knew that their brothers could never sing, and they were glad to think that they were ahead of them for once. It was not really their fault that they felt so, for the brothers had often put on airs and laughed at them.

Then came a wonderful flash of lightning and a long roll of thunder, and the trees tossed their beautiful branches to and fro, while big rain-drops pattered down on to the roof overhead and spattered and bounded and rolled toward the edge under which the rain-barrel stood.

"Fly!" cried the Oldest Brother, raising his wings as well as he could.

"We can't. Where to?" cried the rest.

"Fly any way, anywhere!" screamed the Oldest Brother, and in some wonderful way the whole twenty-three managed to flutter and crawl and sprawl up the side of the building, where the rain-drops fell past but did not touch them. There they found older Mosquitoes waiting for the shower to stop. Even the Oldest Brother was so scared that he shook, and when he saw that same Mosquito Mother who had told him to put off changing his skin, he got behind two other young Mosquitoes and kept very still. Perhaps she saw him, for it was lighter then than it had been. She did not seem to see him, but he heard her talking to her friends. "I told him," she said, "that he might better put off moulting, but he answered that he could take care of himself, and that he would be out biting people before morning."

"Did he say that?" cried the other old Mosquitoes.

"He did," she replied.

Then they all laughed and laughed and laughed again, and the young Mosquito found out why. It was because Mosquito brothers have to eat honey, and only the sisters may bite people and suck their blood. He had thought so often how he would sing around somebody until he found the nicest, juiciest spot, and then settle lightly down and bite and suck until his slender little body was fat and round and red with its stomachful of blood. And that could never be! He could never sing, and he would have to sit around with his stomach full of honey and see his eleven sisters gorged with blood and hear them singing sweetly as they flew. If Mosquito Fathers had ever come to the barrel he might have found this out, but they never did. He sneaked off by himself until he met an early bird and then—well, you know birds must eat something, and the Mosquito was right there. Of course, after that, his brothers and sisters had a chance to do as they wanted to, and the eleven sisters bit thirteen people the very next night and had the loveliest kind of Mosquito time.

The Naughty Raccoon Children

There was hardly a night of his life when the Little Brother of the Raccoon family was not reproved by his mother for teasing. Mrs. Raccoon said she didn't know what she had done to deserve such a child. When she spoke like this to her neighbors they sighed and said, "It must be trying, but he may outgrow it."

The Oldest Wolverene, though, told the Skunk that his cousin, Mrs. Raccoon's husband, had been just as bad as that when he was young. "I do not want you to say that I said so," he whispered, "because he might hear of it and be angry, but it is true." The Oldest Wolverene didn't say whether Mr. Raccoon outgrew this bad habit, yet it would seem that his wife had never noticed it.

You must not think that Mr. Raccoon was dead. Oh, no, indeed! Every night he was prowling through the forest on tiptoe looking for food. But Mrs. Raccoon was a very devoted mother and gave so much time and attention to her children that she was not good company for her husband. He did not care much for home life, and the children annoyed him exceedingly, so he went away and found a hole in another tree which he fitted up for himself. There he slept through the day and until the setting of the sun told him that it was time for his breakfast. Raccoons like company, and he often had friends in to sleep with him. Sometimes these friends were Raccoons like himself with wives and children, and then they would talk about their families and tell how they thought their wives were spoiling the children.

The four little Raccoons, who lived with their mother in the dead branch of the big oak-tree, had been born in April, when the forest was sweet with the scent of wild violets and every one was happy. Beautiful pink and white trilliums raised their three-cornered flowers above their threefold leaves and nodded with every passing breeze. Yellow adder's-tongue was there, with cranesbill geraniums, squirrel-corn, and spring beauties, besides hepaticas and windflowers and the dainty bishop's-cap. The young Raccoons did not see these things, for their eyes would not work well by daylight, and when, after dark, their mother let them put their heads out of the hole and look around, they were too far from the ground to see the flowers sleeping in the dusk below. They could only sniff, sniff, sniff with their sharp little turned-up noses, and wonder what flowers look like, any way.

When their mother was with them for a time, and that was while they were drinking the warm milk that she always carried for them, she told them stories of the flowers and trees. She had begun by telling them animal stories, but she found that it made them cowardly. "Just supposing," one young Raccoon had said, "a great big, dreadful Snail should come up this tree and eat us all!"

The mother told them that Snails were small and slow and weak, and never climbed trees or ate people, but it did no good, and her children were always afraid of Snails until they had seen one for themselves. After that she told them stories of the flowers, and when they asked if the flowers would ever come to see them, she said, "No, indeed! You will never see them until you can climb down the tree and walk among them, for they grow with their feet in the ground and never go anywhere." There were many stories which they wanted over and over again, but the one they liked best of all was that about the wicked, wicked Poison Ivy and the gentle Spotted Touch-me-not who grew near him and undid all the trouble that the Ivy made.

When the night came for the young Raccoons to climb down from their tree and learn to hunt, all the early spring blossoms were gone, and only the ripening seed-vessels showed where nodding flowers had been. You would have expected the Raccoon children to be disappointed, yet there were so many other things to see and learn about that it was not until three nights later that they thought much of the flowers. They might not have done so then if Little Sister had not lost her hold upon the oak-tree bark and fallen with her forepaws on a scarlet jack-in-the-pulpit berry.

They had to learn to climb quickly and strongly up all sorts of trees. Perhaps Mrs. Raccoon had chosen an oak for her nest because that was rough and easily climbed. There were many good places for Raccoons to grip with their twenty strong claws apiece. After they had learned oaks they took maples, ironwoods, and beeches—each a harder lesson than the one before.

"When you climb a tree," said their mother, "always look over the trunk and the largest branches for hiding-places, whether you want to use one then or not."

"Why?" asked three of the four children. Big Brother, who was rather vain, was looking at the five beautiful black rings and the beautiful black tip of his wonderful bushy tail. Between the black rings were whitish ones, and he thought such things much more interesting than holes in trees.

"Because," said the Mother Raccoon, "you may be far from home some night and want a safe place to sleep in all day. Or if a man and his Dogs are chasing you, you must climb into the first hiding-place you can. We Raccoons are too fat and slow to run away from them, and the rings on our tails and the black patches on our broad faces might show from the ground. If the hole is a small one, make it cover your head and your tail anyway, and as much of your brown body fur as you can."

Mother Raccoon looked sternly at Big Brother because he had not been listening, and he gave a slight jump and asked, "W-what did you say?"

"What did I say?" she replied. "You should have paid better attention."

"Yes 'm," said Big Brother, who was now very meek.

"I shall not repeat it," said his mother, "but I will tell you not to grow vain of your fur. It is very handsome, and so is that of your sisters and your brother. So is mine, and so was your father's the last time I saw him. Yet nearly all the trouble that Raccoons have is on account of their fur. Never try to show it off."

The time came for the young Raccoons to stop drinking milk from their mother's body, and when they tried to do so she only walked away from them.

"I cannot work so hard to care for you," said she. "I am so tired and thin, now, that my skin is loose, and you must find your own food. You are getting forty fine teeth apiece, and I never saw a better lot of claws on any Raccoon family, if I do say it."

They used to go hunting together, for it is the custom for Raccoons to go in parties of from five to eight, hunt all night, and then hide somewhere until the next night. They did not always come home at sunrise, and it made a pleasant change to sleep in different trees. One day they all cuddled down in the hollow of an old maple, just below where the branches come out. Mother Raccoon had climbed the tree first and was curled away in the very bottom of the hole. The four children were not tired and hadn't wanted to go to bed at all. Little Sister had made a dreadful face when her mother called her up the tree, and if it had not already been growing light, Mrs. Raccoon would probably have seen it and punished her.

Big Sister curled down beside her mother and Little Sister was rather above them and beside mischievous Little Brother. Last of all came Big Brother, who had stopped to scratch his ear with his hind foot. He was very proud of his little round ears, and often scratched them in this way to make sure that the fur lay straight on them. He was so slow in reaching the hole that before he got into it a Robin had begun his morning song of "Cheerily, cheerily, cheerup!" and a Chipmunk perched on a stump to make his morning toilet.

He got all settled, and Little Brother was half asleep beside him, when he remembered his tail and sat up to have one more look at it. Little Brother growled sleepily and told him to "let his old tail alone and come to bed, as long as they couldn't hunt any more." But Big Brother thought he saw a sand-burr on his tail, and wanted to pull it out before it hurt the fur. Then he began to look at the bare, tough pads on his feet, and to notice how finely he could spread his toes. Those of his front feet he could spread especially wide. He balanced himself on the edge of the hole and held them spread out before him. It was still dark enough for him to see well. "Come here, Little Brother," he cried. "Wake up, and see how big my feet are getting."

Mother Raccoon growled at them to be good children and go to sleep, but her voice sounded dreamy and far away because she had to talk through part of her own fur and most of her daughters'.

Little Brother lost his patience, unrolled himself with a spring, jumped to the opening, and knocked his brother down. It was dreadful. Of course Big Brother was not much hurt, for he was very fat and his fur was both long and thick, but he turned over and over on his way to the ground before he alighted on his feet. He turned so fast and Little Brother's eyes hurt him so that it looked as though Big Brother had about three heads, three tails, and twelve feet. He called out as he fell, and that awakened the sisters, who began to cry, and Mother Raccoon, who was so scared that she began to scold.

Such a time! Mother Raccoon found out what had happened, and then she said to Little Brother, "Did you mean to push him down?"

"No, ma'am," answered Little Brother, hanging his head. "Anyhow I didn't mean to after I saw him going. Perhaps I did mean to before that." You see he was a truthful Raccoon even when he was most naughty, and there is always hope for a Raccoon who will tell the truth, no matter how hard it is to do so.

Big Brother climbed slowly up the trunk of the oak-tree, while more and more of the daytime people came to look at him. He could not see well now, and so was very awkward. When he reached the hole he was hot and cross, and complained to his mother. "Make him quit teasing me," he said, pointing one forepaw at Little Brother.

"I will," answered Mother Raccoon; "but you were just as much to blame as he, for if you had cuddled down quietly when I told you to, you would have been dreaming long ago. Now you must sleep where I was, at the lower end of the hole. Little Brother must go next, and I do not want to hear one word from either of you. Sisters next, and I will sleep by the opening. You children must remember that it is no time for talking to each other, or looking at claws, or getting sand-burrs out of your tails after you have been sent to bed. Go to sleep, and don't awaken until the sun has gone down and you are ready to be my good little Raccoons again."

Her children were asleep long before she was, and she talked softly to herself after they were dreaming. "They do not mean to be naughty," she said. "Yet it makes my fur stand on end to think what might have happened.... I ought not to have curled up for the day until they had done so.... Mothers should always be at the top of the heap." Then she fixed herself for a long, restful day's sleep.

The Timid Little Ground Hog

It was not often that the little Ground Hogs were left alone in the daytime. Before they were born their mother had been heard to say that she had her opinion of any Ground Hog who would be seen out after sunrise. Mr. Ground Hog felt in the same way, and said if he ever got to running around by daylight, like some of his relatives, people might call him a Woodchuck. He thought that any one who ate twigs, beets, turnips, young tree-bark, and other green things from sunset to sunrise ought to be able to get along until the next sunset without a lunch. He said that any Ground Hog who wanted more was a Pig.

After the baby Ground Hogs were born, matters were different. They could not go out at night to feed for themselves, and their stomachs were so tiny and held so little at a time that they had to be filled very often. Mr. Ground Hog was never at home now, and the care all fell upon his hard-working wife.

"You know, my dear," he had said, "that I should only be in the way if I were to stay at home, for I am not clever and patient with children as you are. No, I think I will go away and see to some matters which I have rather neglected of late. When the children are grown up and you have more time to give me, I will come back to you."

Then Mr. Ground Hog trotted away to join a party of his friends who had just told their wives something of the same sort, and they all went together to the farmer's turnip patch and had a delightful time until morning. Mrs. Ground Hog looked after him as he trotted away and wished that she could go too. He looked so handsome with the moonlight shining down on his long, thick, reddish fur, and showing the black streak on his back where the fur was tipped with gray. He was fat and shaky, with a baggy skin, and when he stopped to sit up on his haunches and wave his paws at her and comb his face-fur, she thought him just as handsome as he had been in the early spring when they first met. That had been in a parsnip patch where there was good feeding until the farmer found that the Ground Hogs were there, and dug the rest of his vegetables and stored them in his cellar. Such midnight meals as they had eaten there together! Mrs. Ground Hog said she never saw a parsnip afterward without thinking of their courtship.

She had been as handsome as he, and there were many other Ground Hogs who admired her. But now she was thin and did not have many chances to comb her fur with her fore paws. She could not go with him to the turnip patch because she did not wish to go so far from her babies. Thinking of that reminded her to go into her sidehill burrow and see what they were doing. Then she lay down and let them draw the warm milk from her body. While they were feeding she felt of them, and thought how fast they were growing. It would be only a short time before they could trot around the fields by themselves and whistle shrilly as they dodged down into their own burrows. "Ah!" said she, "this is better than turnip patches or even parsnips."

When they had finished, their mother left them and went out to feed. She had always been a hearty eater, but now she had to eat enough more to make the milk for her babies. She often thought that if Ground Hog babies could eat anything else their father might have learned to help feed them. She thought of this especially when she saw the Great Horned Owl carrying food home to his son and daughter. "It is what comes of being four-legged," said she, "and I wouldn't be an Owl for anything, so I won't grumble." After this she was more cheerful.

When she left the burrow she always said: "I am going out to feed, and I shall not be gone very long. Don't be afraid, for you have a good burrow, and it is nice and dark outside."

The children would cry: "And you will surely come home before sunrise?"

"Surely," she always answered as she trotted away. Then the children would rest happily in their burrow-nest.

But now Mrs. Ground Hog was hungry, and it was broad daylight. She knew that it was because her children grew bigger every day and had to have more and more milk. This meant that she must eat more, or else when they wanted milk there would not be enough ready. She knew that she must begin to feed by day as well as by night, and she was glad that she could see fairly well if the sun were not shining into her eyes.

"Children," said she to them, just as they finished their morning lunch, "I am very hungry and I am going out to feed. You will be quite safe here and I want you to be good while I am gone."

The young Ground Hogs began to cry and clutch at her fur with their weak little paws. "Oh, don't go," they said. "Please don't go. We don't want to stay alone in the daytime. We're afraid."

"I must," said she, "or I shall have no milk for you. And then, you wouldn't have me lie here all day too hungry to sleep, would you?"

"N-no," said they; "but you'll come back soon, won't you?"

"Yes," said she, and she shook off their clinging paws and poked back the daughter who caught on again, and trotted away as fast as she could. It was the first time that she had been out by daylight, and everything looked queer. The colors looked too bright, and there seemed to be more noise than usual, and she met several people whom she had never seen before. She stopped for a minute to look at an Ovenbird's nest. The mother-bird was inside, sitting there very still and brave, although she was much frightened.

"Good-morning," said Mrs. Ground Hog. "I was just admiring your nest. I have never seen it by daylight."

"Good-morning," answered the Ovenbird. "I'm glad you fancy my nest, but I hope you don't like to eat meat."

"Meat?" answered Mrs. Ground Hog. "I never touch it." And she smiled and showed all her teeth.

"Oh," exclaimed the Ovenbird, "I see you don't, for you have gnawing-teeth, rather like those of the Rabbits." Then she hopped out of the nest and let Mrs. Ground Hog peep in to see how the inside was finished and also to see the four speckled eggs which lay there.

"It is a lovely nest," said Mrs. Ground Hog, "and those eggs are beauties. But I promised the children that I would hurry. Good-by." She trotted happily away, while Mrs. Ovenbird settled herself upon her eggs again and thought what a pleasant call she had had and what an excellent and intelligent person Mrs. Ground Hog was!

All this time the children at home were talking together about themselves and what their mother had told them. Once there was a long pause which lasted until the brother said: "I'm not afraid, are you?"

"Of course not," said they.

"Because there isn't anything to be afraid of," said he.

"Not anything," said they.

"And I wouldn't be afraid anyway," said he.

"Neither would we," answered the sisters.

There was another long pause.

"She said we'd be just as safe as if it were dark," said the big sister.

"Of course," said the brother.

"And she said she'd come back as soon as she could," said the second sister.

"I wish she'd come now," said the smallest sister.

There was another long pause.

"You don't suppose anybody would come here just to scare us, do you?" asked the second sister.

"See here," said the brother, "I wish you'd quit saying things to make a fellow afraid."

"You don't mean that you are frightened!" exclaimed the three sisters together. And the smallest one added: "Why, you are, too! I can feel you tremble."

"Well, I don't care," said the brother. "I'm not afraid of people, anyhow. If it were only dark I wouldn't mind."

"Oh, are you afraid of the daylight too?" cried each of the sisters. "So am I!" Then they all trembled together.

"I tell you what let's do," said the smallest sister. "Let's all stop looking toward the light end of the burrow, and cuddle up together and cover our eyes and make believe it's night." They did this and felt better. They even played that they heard the few noises of the night-time. A Crow cawed outside, and the brother said, "Did you hear that Owl? That was the Great Horned Owl, the one who had to hatch the eggs, you know."

When another Crow cawed, the smallest sister said, "Was that his cousin, the Screech Owl?"

"Yes," answered the big sister. "He is the one who used to bring things for the Great Horned Owl to eat."

So they amused themselves and each other, and really got along very well except when, once in a while, they opened their eyes a little crack to see if it were not getting really dark. Then they had to begin all over again. At last their mother came, and what a comfort it was! How glad she was to be back, and how much she had to tell them! All about the Ovenbird's nest and the four eggs in it, and how the Ovenbirds spent their nights in sleeping and their days in work and play.

"I wonder if the little Ovenbirds will be scared when they have to stay alone in the daytime?" said the smallest sister.

"They would be more scared if they had to stay alone at night," said their mother.

"At night!" exclaimed all the young Ground Hogs. "Why, it is dark then!"

"They might be afraid of the darkness," said their mother. Then the children laughed and thought she was making fun of them. They drank some milk and went to sleep like good little Ground Hogs, but even after he was half asleep the big brother laughed out loud at the thought of the Ovenbird babies being scared at night. He could understand any one's being afraid of daylight, but darkness——!

The Young Raccoons Go To A Party

It was not very many nights after Big Brother had tumbled from the maple-tree, when he and the other children were invited to a Raccoon party down by the pond. The water was low, and in the small pools by the shore there were many fresh-water clams and small fishes, such as Raccoons like best of all. A family of six young Raccoons who lived very near the pond had found them just before sunrise, when they had to climb off to bed. They knew there was much more food there than they could eat alone, so their mother had let them invite their four friends who lived in the hollow of the oak-tree. The party was to begin the next evening at moonrise, and the four children who lived in the oak-tree got their invitation just as they were going to sleep for the day. They were very much excited over it, for they had never been to a party.

"I wish we could go now," said Big Brother.

"Yes, lots of fun it would be now!" answered Little Brother. "The sun is almost up, and there are no clouds in the sky. We couldn't see a thing unless we shaded our eyes with our fore paws, and if we had to use our fore paws in that way we couldn't eat."

"You do eat at parties, don't you?" asked Little Sister, who had not quite understood what was said.

"Of course," shouted her brothers. "That is what parties are for."

"I thought maybe you talked some," said Big Sister.

"I suppose you do have to, some," said Big Brother, "but I know you eat. I've heard people tell about parties lots of times, and they always began by telling what they ate. That's what makes it a party."

"Oh, I wish it were night and time to go," sighed Little Brother.

"I don't," said Little Sister. "I wouldn't have any fun if I were to go now. I'd rather wait until my stomach is empty."

"There!" said their mother. "You children have talked long enough. Now curl down and go to sleep. The birds are already singing their morning songs, and the Owls and Bats were dreaming long ago. It will make night-time come much sooner if you do not stay awake."

"We're not a bit sleepy," cried all the young Raccoons together.

"That makes no difference at all," said their mother, and she spoke quite sternly. "Cuddle down for the day now, cover your eyes, and stop talking. I do not say you must sleep, but you must stop talking."

They knew that when she spoke in that way and said "must," there was nothing to do but to mind. So they cuddled down, and every one of them was asleep before you could drop an acorn. Mother Raccoon had known it would be so.

When they awakened, early the next night, each young Raccoon had to make himself look as neat as possible. There were long fur to be combed, faces and paws to be washed, and twenty-three burrs to be taken out of Little Brother's tail. He began to take them out himself, but his mother found that whenever he got one loose he stuck it onto one of the other children, so she scolded him and made him sit on a branch by himself while she worked at the burrs. Sometimes she couldn't help pulling the fur, and then he tried to wriggle away.

"You've got enough out," he cried. "Let the rest go."

"You should have thought sooner how it would hurt," she said. "You have been told again and again to keep away from the burrs, and you are just as careless as you were the first night you left the tree." Then she took out another burr and dropped it to the ground.

"Ouch!" said he. "Let me go!"

"Not until I am done," she answered. "No child of mine shall ever go to a party looking as you do."

After that Little Brother tried to hold still, and he had time to think how glad he was that he hadn't stuck any more burrs on the other children. If he had gotten more onto them, he would have had to wait while they were pulled off again, and then they might have been late for the party. If he had been very good, he would have been glad they didn't have to be hurt as he was. But he was not very good, and he never thought of that.

When he was ready at last, Mother Raccoon made her four children sit in a row while she talked to them. "Remember to walk on your toes," said she, "although you may stand flat-footed if you wish. Don't act greedy if you can help it. Go into the water as much as you choose, but don't try to dive, even if they dare you to. Raccoons can never learn to dive, no matter how well they swim. And be sure to wash your food before you eat it."

All the young Raccoons said "Yes'm," and thought they would remember every word. The first moonbeam shone on the top of the oak-tree, and Mrs. Raccoon said: "Now you may go. Be good children and remember what I told you. Don't stay too long. Start home when you see the first light in the east."

"Yes'm," said the young Raccoons, as they walked off very properly toward the pond. After they were well away from the oak-tree, they heard their mother calling to them: "Remember to walk on your toes!"

Raccoons cannot go very fast, and the moon was shining brightly when they reached the pond and met their six friends. Such frolics as they had in the shallow water, swimming, twisting, turning, scooping up food with their busy fore paws, going up and down the beach, and rolling on the sand! They never once remembered what their mother had told them, and they acted exactly as they had been in the habit of doing every day. Big Brother looked admiringly at his own tail every chance he got, although he had been told particularly not to act as if he thought himself fine-looking. Little Brother rolled into a lot of sand-burrs and got his fur so matted that he looked worse than ever. Big Sister snatched food from other Raccoons, and not one of them remembered about walking on tiptoe. Little Sister ate half the time without washing her food. Of course that didn't matter when the food was taken from the pond, but when they found some on the beach and ate it without washing—that was dreadful. No Raccoon who is anybody at all will do that.

The mother of the family of six looked on from a tree near by. The children did not know that she was there. "What manners!" said she. "I shall never have them invited here again." Just then she saw one of her own sons eat without washing his food, and she groaned out loud. "My children are forgetting too," she said. "I have told him hundreds of times that if he did that way every day he would do so at a party, but he has always said he would remember."

The mother of the four young Raccoons was out hunting and found herself near the pond. "How noisy those children are!" she said to herself. "Night people should be quiet." She tiptoed along to a pile of rocks and peeped between them to see what was going on. She saw her children's footprints on the sand. "Aha!" said she. "So they did walk flat-footed after all."

She heard somebody scrambling down a tree near by. "Good-evening," said a pleasant Raccoon voice near her. It was the mother of the six. "Are you watching the children's party?" asked the newcomer. "I hope you did not notice how badly my son is behaving. I have tried to teach my children good manners, but they will be careless when I am not looking, and then, of course, they forget in company."

That made the mother of the four feel more comfortable. "I know just how that is," said she. "Mine mean to be good, but they are so careless. It is very discouraging."

The two mothers talked for a long time in whispers and then each went to her hole.

When the four young Raccoons came home, it was beginning to grow light, and they kept close together because they were somewhat afraid. Their mother was waiting to see them settled for the day. She asked if they had a good time, and said she was glad they got home promptly. They had been afraid she would ask if they had washed their food and walked on their toes. She even seemed not to notice Little Brother's matted coat.

When they awakened the next night, the mother hurried them off with her to the same pond where they had been to the party. "I am going to visit with the mother of your friends," said she, "and you may play around and amuse yourselves."

The young Raccoons had another fine time, although Little Brother found it very uncomfortable to wear so many burrs. They played tag in the trees, and ate, and swam, and lay on the beach. While they were lying there, the four from the oak-tree noticed that their mother was walking flat-footed. There was bright moonlight and anybody might see her. They felt dreadfully about it. Then they saw her begin to eat food which she had not washed. They were so ashamed that they didn't want to look their friends in the eye. They didn't know that their friends were feeling in the same way because they had seen their mother doing ill-mannered things.

After they reached home, Big Brother said, very timidly, to his mother: "Did you know you ate some food without washing it?"

"Oh, yes," she answered; "it is such a bother to dip it all in water."

"And you walked flat-footed," said Little Brother.

"Well, why shouldn't I, if I want to?" said she.

The children began to cry: "P-people will think you don't know any b-better," said they. "We were d-dreadfully ashamed."

"Oh!" said their mother. "Oh! Oh! So you think that my manners are not so good as yours! Is that it?"

The young Raccoons looked at each other in a very uncomfortable way. "We suppose we don't always do things right ourselves," they answered, "but you are grown up."

"Yes," replied their mother. "And you will be."

For a long time nobody spoke, and Little Sister sobbed out loud. Then Mrs. Raccoon spoke more gently: "The sun is rising," said she. "We will go to sleep now, and when we awaken to-morrow night we will try to have better manners, so that we need not be ashamed of each other at parties or at home."

Long after the rest were dreaming, Big Sister nudged Big Brother and awakened him. "I understand it now," she said. "She did it on purpose."

"Who did what?" asked he.

"Why, our mother. She was rude on purpose to let us see how it looked."

Big Brother thought for a minute. "Of course," said he. "Of course she did! Well she won't ever have to do it again for me."

"Nor for me," said Big Sister. Then they went to sleep.

The Skunks And The Oven-Bird's Nest

The Skunks did not go into society at all. They were very unpopular, and so many people feared or disliked them that nobody would invite them to a party. Indeed, if they had been invited to a party and had gone, the other guests would have left at once. The small people of the forest feared them because they were meat-eaters, and the larger ones disliked them because of their disagreeable habits. The Skunks were handsome and quiet, but they were quick-tempered, and as soon as one of them became angry he threw a horrible smelling liquid on the people who displeased him. It was not only horrible smelling, but it made those who had to smell it steadily quite sick, and would, indeed, have killed them if they had not kept in the fresh air. If a drop of this liquid got on to a person, even his wife and children had to keep away from him for a long time.

And the Skunks were so unreasonable. They would not stop to see what was the real trouble, but if anybody ran into them by mistake in the darkness, they would just as likely as not throw the liquid at once. Among themselves they seemed to be quite happy. There were from six to ten children born at a time in each family. These children lived in the burrow with their father and mother until the next spring, sleeping steadily through the coldest weather of winter, and only awakening when it was warm enough for them to enjoy life. When spring came, the children found themselves grown-up and went off to live their own lives in new holes, while their mothers took care of the six or seven or eight or nine or ten new babies.

There was one very interesting Skunk family in the forest, with the father, mother, and eight children living in one hole. No two of them were marked in exactly the same way, although all were stoutly built, had small heads, little round ears, and beautiful long tails covered with soft, drooping hair. Their fur was rather long and handsome and they were dark brown or black nearly all over. Most of them had a streak of white on the forehead, a spot of it on the neck, some on the tail, and a couple of stripes of it on their backs. One could see them quite easily by starlight on account of the white fur.

The Skunks were really very proud of their white stripes and spots. "It is not so much having the white fur," Mrs. Skunk had been heard to say, "as it is having it where all can see it. Most animals wear the dark fur on their backs and the light on their bellies, and that is to make them safer from enemies. But we dare to wear ours in plain sight. *We* are never afraid."

And what she said was true, although it hardly seemed modest for her to talk about it in that way. It would have been more polite to let other people tell how brave her family were. Perhaps, however, if somebody else had been telling it, he would have said that part of their courage was rudeness.

Father Skunk always talked to his children as his father had talked to him, and probably as his grandfather had also talked when he was raising a family. "Never turn out of your way for anybody," said he. "Let the other fellow step aside. Remember that, no matter whom you meet and no matter how large the other people may be. If they see you, they will get out of your path, and if they can't it is not your fault. Don't speak to them and don't hurry. Always take your time."

Father Skunk was slow and stately. It was a sight worth seeing when he started off for a night's ramble, walking with a slow and measured gait and carrying his fine tail high over his back. He always went by himself. "One is company, two is a crowd," he would say as he walked away. When they were old enough, the young Skunks began to walk off alone as soon as it was dark. Mother Skunk also went alone, and perhaps she had the best time of all, for it was a great rest not to have eight babies tumbling over her back and getting under her feet and hanging on to her with their thirty-two paws, and sometimes even scratching her with their one hundred and sixty claws. They still slept through the days in the old hole, so they were together much of the time, but they did not hunt in parties, as Raccoons and Weasels do.

One of the brothers had no white whatever on his tail, so they called him the Black-tailed Skunk. He had heard in some way that there was an Ovenbird's nest on the ground by the fern bank, and he made up his mind to find it the very next night and eat the eggs which were inside.

Another brother was called the Spotted Skunk, because the spot on his neck was so large. He had found the Ovenbird's nest himself, while on his way home in the early morning. He would have liked to rob it then, but he had eaten so much that night that he thought it better to wait.

So it happened that when the family awakened the next night two of the children had important plans of their own. Neither of them would have told for anything, but they couldn't quite keep from hinting about it as they made themselves ready to go out.

"Aha!" said the Black-tailed Skunk. "I know something you don't know."

"Oh, tell us!" cried four or five of the other children, while the Spotted Skunk twisted his head and said, "You don't either!"

"I do too!" replied the Black-tailed Skunk.

"Children! Children!" exclaimed Mrs. Skunk, while their father said that he couldn't see where his children got their quarrelsome disposition, for none of his people had ever contradicted or disputed. His wife told him that she really thought them very good, and that she was sure they behaved much better than most Skunks of their age. Then their father walked off in his most stately manner, putting his feet down almost flat, and carrying his tail a little higher than usual.

"I do know something that you don't," repeated the Black-tailed Skunk, "and it's something nice, too."

"Aw!" said the Spotted Skunk. "I don't believe it, and I don't care anyhow."

"I know you don't know, and I know you'd want to know if you knew what I know," said the Black-tailed Skunk, who was now getting so excited that he could hardly talk straight.

"Children!" exclaimed their mother. "Not another word about that. I do wish you would wake up good-natured."

"He started it," said the Spotted Skunk, "and we're not quarrelling anyhow. But I guess he'd give a good deal to know where I'm going."

"Children!" repeated their mother. "Go at once. I will not have you talking in this way before your brothers and sisters. Do not stop to talk, but go!"

So the two brothers started out for the night and each thought he would go a roundabout way to fool the other. The Black-tailed Skunk went to the right, and the Spotted Skunk went to the left, but each of them, you know, really started to rob the Ovenbird's nest. It was a very dark night. Even the stars were all hidden behind thick clouds, and one could hardly see one's forepaws while walking. But, of course, the night-prowlers of the forest are used to this, and four-footed people are not so likely to stumble and fall as two-footed ones. Besides, young Skunks have to remember where logs and stumps of trees are, just as other people have to remember their lessons.

So it happened that, while Mrs. Ovenbird was sleeping happily with her four eggs safe and warm under her breast, two people were coming from different ways to rob her. Such a snug nest as it was! She had chosen a tiny hollow in the fern bank and had cunningly woven dry grasses and leaves into a ball-shaped nest, which fitted neatly into the hollow and had a doorway on one side.

The Black-tailed Skunk sneaked up to the nest from one side. The Spotted Skunk sneaked up from the other side. Once the Black-tailed Skunk thought he heard some other creature moving toward him. At the same minute the Spotted Skunk thought he heard somebody, so he stopped to listen. Neither heard anything. Mrs. Ovenbird was sure that she heard a leaf rustle outside, and it made her anxious until she remembered that a dead twig might have dropped from the beech-tree overhead and hit the dry leaves below.

Slowly the two brothers crept toward the nest and each other. They moved very quietly, because each wanted to catch the mother-bird if he could. Close to the nest hollow they crouched and sprang with jaws open and sharp teeth ready to bite. There was a sudden crashing of leaves and ferns. The two brothers had sprung squarely at each other, each was bitten, growled, and ran away. And how they did run! It is not often, you know, that Skunks go faster than a walk, but when they are really scared they move very, very swiftly.

Mrs. Ovenbird felt her nest roof crush down upon her for a minute as two people rolled and growled outside. Then she heard them running away in different directions and knew that she was safe, for a time at least. In the morning she repaired her nest and told her bird friends about it. They advised her to take her children away as soon as possible after they were hatched. "If the Skunks have found your nest," they said, "you may have another call from them."

When the Black-tailed Skunk came stealing home in the first faint light just before sunrise, he found the Spotted Skunk telling the rest of the family how some horrible great fierce beast had pounced upon him in the darkness and bitten him on the shoulder. "It was so dark," said he, "that I couldn't see him at all, but I am sure it must have been a Bear."

They turned to tell the Black-tailed Skunk about his brother's misfortune, and saw that he limped badly. "Did the Bear catch you, too?" they cried.

"Yes," answered he. "It must have been a Bear. It was so big and strong and fierce. But I bit him, too. I wouldn't have run away from him, only he was so much bigger than I."

"That was just the way with me," said the Spotted Skunk. "I wouldn't have run if he hadn't been so big."

"You should have thrown liquid on him," said their father. "Then he would have been the one to run."

The brothers hung their heads. "We never thought," they cried. "We think it must have been because we were so surprised and didn't see him coming."

"Well," said their father sternly, "I suppose one must be patient with children, but such unskunklike behavior makes me very much ashamed of you both." Then the two bitten brothers went to bed in disgrace, although their mother was sorry for them and loved them, as mothers will do, even when their children are naughty or cowardly.

One night, some time later, these two brothers happened to meet down by the fern bank. It was bright moonlight and they stopped to visit, for both were feeling very good-natured. The Black-tailed Skunk said: "Come with me and I'll show you where there is an Ovenbird's nest."

"All right," answered the Spotted Skunk, "and then I'll show you one."

"I've just been waiting for a bright night," said the Black-tailed Skunk, "because I came here once in the dark and had bad luck."

"It was near here," said the Spotted Skunk, "that I was bitten by the Bear."

They stopped beside a tiny hollow. "There is the nest," said the Black-tailed Skunk, pointing with one of his long forefeet.

"Why, that is the one I meant," exclaimed the Spotted Skunk.

"I found it first," said the Black-tailed Skunk, "and I'd have eaten the eggs before if that Bear hadn't bitten me."

Just at that minute the two Skunks had a new idea. "We do believe," cried they, "that we bit each other!"

"We certainly did," said the Spotted Skunk.

"But we'll never tell," said the Black-tailed Skunk.

"Now," they added together, "let's eat everything."

But they didn't. In fact, they didn't eat anything, for the eggs were hatched, and the young birds had left the nest only the day before.

The Lazy Cut-Worms

Now that spring had come and all the green things were growing, the Cut-Worms crawled out of their winter sleeping-places in the ground, and began to eat the tenderest and best things that they could find. They felt rested and hungry after their quiet winter, for they had slept without awakening ever since the first really cold days of fall.

There were many different kinds of Cut-Worms, brothers and sisters, cousins and second cousins, so, of course, they did not all look alike. They had hatched the summer before from eggs laid by the Owlet Moths, their mothers, and had spent the time from then until cold weather in eating and sleeping and eating some more. Of course they grew a great deal, but then, you know, one can grow without taking time especially for it. It is well that this is so. If people had to say, "I can do nothing else now. I must sit down and grow awhile," there would not be so many large people in the world as there are. They would become so interested in doing other things that they would not take the time to grow as they should.

Now the Cut-Worms were fine and fat and just as heedless as Cut-Worms have been since the world began. They had never seen their parents, and had hatched without any one to look after them. They did not look like their parents, for they were only worms as yet, but they had the same habit of sleeping all day and going out at night, and never thought of eating breakfast until the sun had gone down. They were quite popular in underground society, and were much liked by the Earthworms and May Beetle larvæ, who enjoyed hearing stories of what the Cut-Worms saw above ground. The May Beetle larvæ did not go out at all, because they were too young, and the Earthworms never knew what was going on outside unless somebody told them. They often put their heads up into the air, but they had no eyes and could not see for themselves.

The Cut-Worms were bold, saucy, selfish, and wasteful. They were not good children, although when they tried they could be very entertaining, and one always hoped that they would improve before they became Moths. Sometimes they even told the Earthworms and May Beetle larvæ stories that were not so, and that shows what sort of children they were. It was dreadful to tell such things to people who could never find out the difference. One Spotted Cut-Worm heard a couple of Earthworms talking about Ground Moles, and told them that Ground Moles were large birds with four wings apiece and legs like a Caterpillar's. They did not take pains to be entertaining because they wanted to make the underground people happy, but because they enjoyed hearing them say: "What bright fellows those Cut-Worms are! Really exceedingly clever!" And doing it for that reason took all the goodness out of it.

One bright moonlight night the Cut-Worms awakened and crawled out on top of the ground to feed. They lived in the farmer's vegetable garden, so there were many things to choose from: young beets just showing their red-veined leaves above their shining red stems; turnips; clean-looking onions holding their slender leaves very stiff and straight; radishes with just a bit of their rosy roots peeping out of the earth; and crisp, pale green lettuce, crinkled and shaking in every passing breeze. It was a lovely growing time, and all the vegetables were making the most of the fine nights, for, you know, that is the time when everything grows best. Sunshiny days are the best for coloring leaves and blossoms, but the time for sinking roots deeper and sending shoots higher and unfolding new leaves is at night in the beautiful stillness.

Some Cut-Worms chose beets and some chose radishes. Two or three liked lettuce best, and a couple crawled off to nibble at the sweet peas which the farmer's wife had planted. They never ate all of a plant. Ah, no! And that was one way in which they were wasteful. They nibbled through the stalk where it came out of the ground, and then the plant tumbled down and withered, while the Cut-Worm went on to treat another in the same way.

"Well!" exclaimed one Spotted Cut-Worm, as he crawled out from his hole. "I must have overslept! Guess I stayed up too late this morning."

"You'd better look out," said one of his friends, "or the Ground Mole will get you. He likes to find nice fat little Cut-Worms who sleep too late in the evening."

"Needn't tell me," answered the Spotted Cut-Worm. "It's the early Mole that catches the Cut-Worm. I don't know when I have overslept myself so. Have you fellows been up ever since sunset?"

"Yes," they answered; and one saucy fellow added: "I got up too early. I awakened and felt hungry, and thought I'd just come out for a lunch. I supposed the birds had finished their supper, but the first thing I saw was a Robin out hunting. She was not more than the length of a bean-pole from me, and when I saw her cock her head on one side and look toward me, I was sure she saw me. But she didn't, after all. Lucky for me that I am green and came up beside the lettuce. I kept still and she took me for a leaf."

"St!" said somebody else. "There comes the Ground Mole." They all kept still while the Mole scampered to and fro on the dewy grass near them, going faster than one would think he could with such very, very short legs. His pink digging hands flashed in the moonlight, and his pink snout showed also, but the dark, soft fur of the rest of his body could hardly be seen against the brown earth of the garden. It may have been because he was not hungry, or it may have been because his fur covered over his eyes so, but he went back to his underground run-way without having caught a single Cut-Worm.

Then the Cut-Worms felt very much set up. They crawled toward the hole into his run-way and made faces at it, as though he were standing in the doorway. They called mean things after him and pretended to say them very loudly, yet really spoke quite softly.

Then they began to boast that they were not afraid of anybody, and while they were boasting they ate and ate and ate and ate. Here and there the young plants drooped and fell over, and as soon as one did that, the Cut-Worm who had eaten on it crawled off to another.

"Guess the farmer will know that we've been here," said they. "We don't care. He doesn't need all these vegetables. What if he did plant them? Let him plant some more if he wants to. What business has he to have so many, anyhow, if he won't share with other people?" You would have thought, to hear them, that they were exceedingly kind to leave any vegetables for the farmer.

In among the sweet peas were many little tufts of purslane, and purslane is very good to eat, as anybody knows who has tried it. But do you think the Cut-Worms ate that? Not a bit of it. "We can have purslane any day," they said, "and now we will eat sweet peas."

One little fellow added: "You won't catch me eating purslane. It's a weed." Now, Cut-Worms do eat weeds, but they always seem to like best those things which have been carefully planted and tended. If the purslane had been set in straight rows, and the sweet peas had just come up of themselves everywhere, it is quite likely that this young Cut-Worm would have said: "You won't catch me eating sweet peas. They are weeds."

As the moon rose higher and higher in the sky, the Cut-Worms boasted more and more. They said there were no Robins clever enough to find them, and that the Ground Mole dared not touch them when they were together, and that it was only when he found one alone underground that he was brave enough to do so. They talked very loudly now and bragged dreadfully, until they noticed that the moon was setting and a faint yellow light showed over the tree-tops in the east.

"Time to go to bed for the day," called the Spotted Cut-Worm. "Where are you going to crawl in?" They had no regular homes, you know, but crawled into the earth wherever they wanted to and slept until the next night.

"Here are some fine holes already made," said a Green Cut-Worm, "and big enough for a Garter Snake. They are smooth and deep, and a lot of us can cuddle down into each. I'm going into one of them."

"Who made those holes?" asked the Spotted Cut-Worm; "and why are they here?"

"Oh, who cares who made them?" answered the Green Cut-Worm. "Guess they're ours if we want to use them."

"Perhaps the farmer made them," said the Spotted Cut-Worm, "and if he did I don't want to go into them."

"Oh, who's afraid of him?" cried the other Cut-Worms. "Come along!"

"No," answered the Spotted Cut-Worm. "I won't. I don't want to and I won't do it. The hole I make to sleep in will not be so large, nor will it have such smooth sides, but I'll know all about it and feel safe. Good-morning." Then he crawled into the earth and went to sleep. The others went into the smooth, deep holes made by the farmer with his hoe handle.

The next night there was only one Cut-Worm in the garden, and that was the Spotted Cut-Worm. Nobody has ever seen the lazy ones who chose to use the smooth, deep holes which were ready made. The Spotted Cut-Worm lived quite alone until he was full-grown, then he made a little oval room for himself in the ground and slept in it while he changed into a Black Owlet Moth.

After that he flew away to find a wife and live among her people. It is said that whenever he saw a Cut-Worm working at night, he would flutter down beside him and whisper,—"The Cut-Worm who is too lazy to bore his own sleeping-place will never live to become an Owlet Moth."

The Night Moth's Party

From the time when she was a tiny golden-green Caterpillar, Miss Polyphemus had wanted to go into society. She began life on a maple leaf with a few brothers and sisters, who hatched at the same time from a cluster of flattened eggs which their mother had laid there ten days before. The first thing she remembered was the light and color and sound when she broke the shell open that May morning. The first thing she did was to eat the shell out of which she had just crawled. Then she got acquainted with her brothers and sisters, many of whom had also eaten their egg-shells, although two had begun at once on maple leaves. It was well that she took time for this now, for the family were soon scattered and several of her sisters she never saw again.

She found it a very lovely world to live in. There was so much to eat. Yes, and there were so many kinds of leaves that she liked,—oak, hickory, apple, maple, elm, and several others. Sometimes she wished that she had three mouths instead of one. In those days she had few visitors. It is true that other Caterpillars happened along once in a while, but they were almost as hungry as she, and they couldn't speak without stopping eating. They could, of course, if they talked with their mouths full, but she had too good manners for that, and, besides, she said that if she did, she couldn't enjoy her food so much.

You must not think that it was wrong in her to care so much about eating. She was only doing what is expected of a Polyphemus Caterpillar, and you would have to do the same if you were a Polyphemus Caterpillar. When she was ten days old she had to weigh ten times as much as she did the morning that she was hatched. When she was twenty days old she had to weigh sixty times as much; when she was a month old she had to weigh six hundred and twenty times as much; and when she was fifty days old she had to weigh four thousand times as much as she did at hatching. Every bit of this flesh was made of the food she ate. That is why eating was so important, you know, and if she had chosen to eat the wrong kind of leaves just because they tasted good, she would never have become such a fine great Caterpillar as she did. She might better not eat anything than to eat the wrong sort, and she knew it.

Still, she often wished that she had more time for visiting, and thought that she would be very gay next year, when she got her wings. "I'll make up for it then," she said to herself, "when my growing is done and I have time for play." Then she ate some more good, plain food, for she knew that there would be no happy Moth-times for Caterpillars who did not eat as they should.

She had five vacations of about a day each when she ate nothing at all. These were the times when she changed her skin, crawling out of the tight old one and appearing as fresh and clean as possible in the new one which was ready underneath. After her last change she was ready to plan her cocoon, and she was a most beautiful Caterpillar. She was about as long as a small cherry leaf, and as plump as a Caterpillar can be. She was light green, with seven slanting yellow lines on each side of her body, and a purplish-brown V-shaped mark on the back part of each side. There were many little orange-colored bunches on her body, which showed beautiful gleaming lights when she moved. Growing out of these bunches were tiny tufts of bristles.

She had three pairs of real legs and several pairs of make-believe ones. Her real legs were on the front part of her body and were slender. These she expected to keep always. The make-believe ones were called pro-legs. They grew farther back and were fat, awkward, jointless things which she would not need after her cocoon was spun. But for them, she would have had to drag the back part of her body around like a Snake. With them, the back part of her body could walk as well as the front, although not quite so fast. She always took a few steps with her real legs and then waited for her pro-legs to catch up.

As the weather grew colder the Polyphemus Caterpillar hunted around on the ground for a good place for her cocoon. She found an excellent twig lying among the dead leaves, and decided to fasten to that. Then began her hardest work, spinning a fluffy mass of gray-white silk which clung to the twig and to one of the dry leaves and was almost exactly the color of the leaf. Other Caterpillars came along and stopped to visit, for they did not have to eat at cocoon-spinning time.

"Better fasten your cocoon to a tree," said a pale bluish-green Promethea Caterpillar. "Put it inside a curled leaf, like mine, and wind silk around the stem to strengthen it. Then you can swing every time the wind blows, and the silk will keep the leaf from wearing out."

"But I don't want to swing," answered the Polyphemus Caterpillar. "I'd rather lie still and think about things."

"Fasten to the twig of a tree," advised a pale green Cecropia Caterpillar with red, yellow, and blue bunches. "Then the wind just moves you a little. Fasten it to a twig and taper it off nicely at each end, and then——"

"Yes," said the Polyphemus Caterpillar, "and then the Blue-Jays and Chickadees will poke wheat or corn or beechnuts into the upper end of it. I don't care to turn my sleeping room into a corn-crib."

Just here some other Polyphemus Caterpillars came along and agreed with their relative. "Go ahead with your tree homes," said they. "We know what we want, and we'll see next summer who knew best."

The Polyphemus cocoons were spun on the ground where the dead leaves had blown in between some stones, and no wandering Cows or Sheep would be likely to step on them. First a mass of coarse silk which it took half a day to make, then an inside coating of a kind of varnish, then as much silk as a Caterpillar could spin in four or five days, next another inside varnishing, and the cocoons were done. As the Polyphemus Caterpillars snuggled down for the long winter's sleep, each said to himself something like this: "Those poor Caterpillars in the trees! How cold they will be! I hope they may come out all right in the spring, but I doubt it very much."

And when the Cecropia and Promethea Caterpillars dozed off for the winter, they said: "What a pity that those Polyphemus Caterpillars would lie around on the ground. Well, we advised them what to do, so it isn't our fault."

They all had a lovely winter, and swung or swayed or lay still, just as they had chosen to do. Early in the spring, the farmer's wife and little girl came out to find wild flowers, and scraped the leaves away from among the stones. Out rolled the cocoon that the first Polyphemus Caterpillar had spun and the farmer's wife picked it up and carried it off. She might have found more cocoons if the little girl had not called her away.

This was how it happened that one May morning a little girl stood by the sitting-room window in the white farmhouse and watched Miss Polyphemus crawl slowly out of her cocoon. A few days before a sour, milky-looking stuff had begun to trickle into the lower end of the cocoon, softening the hard varnish and the soft silken threads until a tiny doorway was opened. Now all was ready and Miss Polyphemus pushed out. She was very wet and weak and forlorn. "Oh," said she to herself, "it is more fun to be a new Caterpillar than it is to be a new Moth. I've only six legs left, and it will be very hard worrying along on these. I shall have to give up walking."

It was discouraging. You can see how it would be. She had been used to having so many legs, and had looked forward all the summer before to the time when she should float lightly through the air and sip honey from flowers. She had dreamed of it all winter. And now here she was—wet and weak, with only six legs left, and four very small and crumpled wings. Her body was so big and fat that she could not hold it up from the window-sill. She wanted to cry—it was all so sad and disappointing. She would have done so, had she not remembered how very unbecoming it is to cry. When she remembered that, she decided to take a nap instead, and that was a most sensible thing to do, for crying always makes matters worse, while sleeping makes them better.

When she awakened she felt much stronger and more cheerful. She was drier and her body felt lighter. This was because the fluids from it were being pumped into her wings. That was making them grow, and the beautiful colors began to show more brightly on them. "I wonder," she said to herself, "if Moths always feel so badly when they first come out?"

If she had but known it, there were at that very time hundreds of Moths as helpless as she, clinging to branches, leaves, and stones all through the forest. There were many Polyphemus Moths just out, for in their family it is the custom for all to leave their cocoons at just about such a time in the morning. Perhaps she would have felt more patient if she had known this, for it does seem to make hard times easier to bear when one knows that everybody else has hard times also. Of course other people always are having trouble, but she was young and really believed for a time that she was the only uncomfortable Moth in the world.

All day long her wings were stretching and growing smooth. When it grew dark she was nearly ready to fly. Then the farmer's wife lifted her gently by the wings and put her on the inside of the wire window-screen. When the lights in the house were all put out, the moonbeams shone in on Miss Polyphemus and showed her beautiful sand-colored body and wings with the dark border on the front pair and the lighter border on the back pair.

On the back ones were dark eye-spots with clear places in the middle, through which one could see quite clearly.

"I would like to fly," sighed Miss Polyphemus, "and I believe I could if it were not for this horrid screen." She did not know that the farmer's wife had put her there to keep her safe from night birds until she was quite strong.

The wind blew in, sweet with the scent of wild cherry and shad-tree blossoms, and poor Miss Polyphemus looked over toward the forest where she had lived when she was a Caterpillar, and wished herself safely there. "Much good it does me to have wings when I cannot use them," said she. "I want something to eat. There is no honey to be sucked out of wire netting. I wish I were a happy Caterpillar again, eating leaves on the trees." She was not the first Moth who has wished herself a Caterpillar, but she soon changed her mind.

There fluttered toward her another Polyphemus Moth, a handsome fellow, marked exactly as she was, only with darker coloring. His body was more slender, and his feelers were very beautiful and feathery. She was fat and had slender feelers.

"Ah!" said he. "I thought I should find you soon."

"Indeed?" she replied. "I wonder what made you think that?"

"My feelers, of course," said he. "They always tell me where to find my friends. You know how that is yourself."

"I?" said she, as she changed her position a little. "I am just from my cocoon. This was my coming-out day."

"And so you have not met any one yet?" he asked. "Ah, this is a strange world—a very strange world. I would advise you to be very careful with whom you make friends. There are so many bad Moths, you know."

"Good-evening," said a third voice near them, and another Polyphemus Moth with feathery feelers alighted on the screen. He smiled sweetly at Miss Polyphemus and scowled fiercely at the other Moth. It would have ended in a quarrel right then and there, if a fourth Moth had not come at that minute. One after another came, until there were nine handsome fellows on the outside and Miss Polyphemus on the inside of the screen trying to entertain them all and keep them from quarrelling. It made her very proud to think so many were at her coming-out party. Still, she would have enjoyed it better, she thought, if some whom she had known as Caterpillars could be there to see how much attention she was having paid to her. There was one Caterpillar whom she had never liked. She only wished that she could see her now.

Still, society tires one very much, and it was hard to keep her guests from quarrelling. When she got to talking with one about maple-trees, another was sure to come up and say that he had always preferred beech when he was a Caterpillar. And the two outside would glare at each other while she hastily thought of something else to say.

At last those outside got to fighting. There was only one, the handsomest of all, who said he thought too much of his feelers to fight anybody. "Supposing I should fight and break them off," said he. "I couldn't smell a thing for the rest of my life." He was very sensible, and really the eight other fellows were fighting on account of Miss Polyphemus, for whenever they thought she liked one best they began to bump up against him.

Toward morning the farmer's wife awakened and looked at Miss Polyphemus. When she saw that she was strong enough to fly, she opened the screen and let her go. By that time three of those with feathery feelers were dead, three were broken-winged and clinging helplessly to the screen, and two were so busy fighting that they didn't see Miss Polyphemus go. The handsome great fellow who did not believe in fighting went with her, and they lived in the forest after that. But she never cared for society again.

The Lonely Old Bachelor Muskrat

Beyond the forest and beside the river lay the marsh where the Muskrats lived. This was the same marsh to which the young Frog had taken some of the meadow people's children when they were tired of staying at home and wanted to travel. When they went with him, you remember, they were gay and happy, the sun was shining, and the way did not seem long. When they came back they were cold and wet and tired, and thought it very far indeed. One could never get them to say much about it.

Some people like what others do not, and one's opinion of a marsh must always depend on whether he is a Grasshopper or a Frog. But whether people cared to live there or not, the marsh had always been a pleasant place to see. In the spring the tall tamaracks along the edge put on their new dresses of soft, needle-shaped green leaves, the marsh-marigolds held their bright faces up to the sun, and hundreds of happy little people darted in and out of the tussocks of coarse grass. There was a warm, wet, earthy smell in the air, and near the pussy-willows there was also a faint bitterness.

Then the Marsh Hens made their nests, and the Sand-pipers ran mincingly along by the quiet pools.

In summer time the beautiful moccasin flowers grew in family groups, and over in the higher, dryer part were masses of white boneset, tall spikes of creamy foxglove, and slender, purple vervain. In the fall the cat-tails stood stiffly among their yellow leaves, and the Red-winged Blackbirds and the Bobolinks perched upon them to plan their journey to the south.

Even when the birds were gone and the cat-tails were ragged and worn—even then, the marsh was an interesting place. Soft snow clung to the brown seed clusters of boneset and filled the open silvery-gray pods of the milkweed. In among the brown tussocks of grass ran the dainty footprints of Mice and Minks, and here and there rose the cone-shaped winter homes of the Muskrats.

The Muskrats were the largest people there, and lived in the finest homes. It is true that if a Mink and a Muskrat fought, the Mink was likely to get the better of the Muskrat, but people never spoke of this, although everybody knew that it was so. The Muskrats were too proud to do so, the Minks were too wise to, and the smaller people who lived near did not want to offend the Muskrats by mentioning it. It is said that an impudent young Mouse did say something about it once when the Muskrats could overhear him and that not one of them ever spoke to him again. The next time he said "Good-evening" to a Muskrat, the Muskrat just looked at him as though he didn't see him or as though he had been a stick or a stone or something else uneatable and uninteresting.

The Muskrats were very popular, for they were kind neighbors and never stole their food from others. That was why nobody was jealous of them, although they were so fat and happy. Their children usually turned out very well, even if they were not at all strictly brought up. You know when a father and mother have to feed and care for fifteen or so children each summer, there is not much time for teaching them to say "please" and "thank you" and "pardon me." Sometimes these young Muskrats did snatch and quarrel, as on that night when fifteen of them went to visit their old home and all wanted to go in first. You may recall how, on that dreadful night, their father had to spank them with his scaly tail and their mother sent them to bed. They always remembered it, and you may be very sure their parents did. It makes parents feel dreadfully when their children quarrel, and it is very wearing to have to spank fifteen at once, particularly when one has to use his tail with which to do it.

There was one old Bachelor Muskrat who had always lived for himself, and had his own way more than was good for him. If he had married, it would not have been so, and he would have grown used to giving up to somebody else. He was a fine-looking fellow with soft, short, reddish-brown fur, which shaded almost to black on his back, and to a light gray underneath. There were very few hairs on his long, flat, scaly tail, and most of these were in two fringes, one down the middle of the upper side, and the other down the middle of the lower side. His tiny ears hardly showed above the fur on his head, and he was so fat that he really seemed to have no neck at all. To look at his feet you would hardly think he could swim, for the webs between his toes were very, very small and his feet were not large.

He was like all other Muskrats in using a great deal of perfume, and it was not a pleasant kind, being so strong and musky. He thought it quite right, and it was better so, for he couldn't help wearing it, and you can just imagine how distressing it would be to see a Muskrat going around with his nose turned up and all the time finding fault with his own perfume.

Nobody could remember the time when there had been no Muskrats in the marsh. The Ground Hog who lived near the edge of the forest said that his grandfather had often spoken of seeing them at play in the moonlight; and there was an old Rattlesnake who had been married several times and wore fourteen joints in his rattle, who said that he remembered seeing Muskrats there before he cast his first skin. And it was not strange that, after their people had lived there so long, the Muskrats should be fond of the marsh.

One day in midsummer the farmer and his men came to the marsh with spades and grub-hoes and measuring lines. All of them had on high rubber boots, and they tramped around and measured and talked, and rooted up a few huckleberry bushes, and drove a good many stakes into the soft and spongy ground. Then the dinner-bell at the farmhouse rang and, they went away. It was a dull, cloudy day and a few of the Muskrats were out. If it had been sunshiny they would have stayed in their burrows. They paddled over to where the stakes were, and smelled of them and gnawed at them, and wondered why the men had put them there.

"I know," said one young Muskrat, who had married and set up a home of his own that spring. "I know why they put these stakes in."

"Oh, do listen!" cried the young Muskrat's wife. "He knows and will tell us all about it."

"Nobody ever told me this," said the young husband. "I thought it out myself. The Ground Hog once said that they put small pieces of potato into the ground to grow into whole big ones, and they have done the same sort of thing here. You see, the farmer wanted a fence, and so he stuck down these stakes, and before winter he will have a fence well grown."

"Humph!" said the Bachelor Muskrat. It seemed as though he had meant to say more, but the young wife looked at him with such a frown on her furry forehead that he shut his mouth as tightly as he could (he never could quite close it) and said nothing else.

"Do you mean to tell me," said one who had just sent five children out of her burrow to make room for another lot of babies, "that they will grow a fence here where it is so wet? Fences grow on high land."

"That is what I said," answered the young husband, slapping his tail on the water to make himself seem more important.

"Well," said the anxious mother, "if they go to growing fences and such things around here I shall move. Every one of my children will want to play around it, and as like as not will eat its roots and get sick."

Then the men came back and all the Muskrats ran toward their burrows, dived into the water to reach the doors of them, and then crawled up the long hallways that they had dug out of the bank until they got to the large rooms where they spent most of their days and kept their babies.

That night the young husband was the first Muskrat to come out, and he went at once to the line of stakes. He had been lying awake and thinking while his wife was asleep, and he was afraid he had talked too much. He found that the stakes had not grown any, and that the men had begun to dig a deep ditch beside them. He was afraid that his neighbors would point their paws at him and ask how the fence was growing, and he was not brave enough to meet them and say that he had been mistaken. He went down the river bank and fed alone all night, while his wife and neighbors were grubbing and splashing around in the marsh or swimming in the river near their homes. The young Muskrats were rolling and tumbling in the moonlight and looking like furry brown balls. After it began to grow light, he sneaked back to his burrow.

Every day the men came in their high rubber boots to work, and every day there were more ditches and the marsh was drier. By the time that the flowers had all ripened their seeds and the forest trees were bare, the marsh was changed to dry ground, and the Muskrats could find no water there to splash in. One night, and it was a very, very dark one, they came together to talk about winter.

"It is time to begin our cold-weather houses," said one old Muskrat, "I have never started so soon, but we are to have an early winter."

"Yes, and a long one, too," added his wife, who said that Mr. Muskrat never told things quite strongly enough.

"It will be cold," said another Muskrat, "and we shall need to build thick walls."

"Why?" asked a little Muskrat.

"Sh!" said his mother.

"The question is," said the old Muskrat who had first spoken, "where we shall build."

"Why?" asked the little Muskrat, pulling at his mother's tail.

"Sh-h!" said his mother.

"There is no water here except in the ditches," said the oldest Muskrat, "and of course we would not build beside them."

"Why not?" asked the little Muskrat. And this time he actually poked his mother in the side.

"Sh-h-h!" said she. "How many times must I speak to you? Don't you know that young Muskrats should be seen and not heard?"

"But I can't be seen," he whimpered. "It is so dark that I can't be seen, and you've just got to hear me."

Of course, after he had spoken in that way to his mother and interrupted all the others by his naughtiness, he had to be punished, so his mother sent him to bed. That is very hard for young Muskrats, for the night, you know, is the time when they have the most fun.

The older ones talked and talked about what they should do. They knew, as they always do know, just what sort of winter they were to have, and that they must begin to build at once. Some years they had waited until a whole month later, but that was because they expected a late and mild winter. At last the oldest Muskrat decided for them. "We will move to-morrow night," said he. "We will go to the swamp on the other side of the forest and build our winter homes there."

All the Muskrats felt sad about going, and for a minute it was so still that you might almost have heard a milkweed seed break loose from the pod and float away. Then a gruff voice broke the silence. "I will not go," it said. "I was born here and I will live here. I never have left this marsh and I never will leave it."

They could not see who was speaking, but they knew it was the Bachelor. The oldest Muskrat said afterward that he was so surprised you could have knocked him over with a blade of grass. Of course, you couldn't have done it, because he was so fat and heavy, but that is what he said, and it shows just how he felt.

The other Muskrats talked and talked and talked with him, but it made no difference. His brothers told him it was perfectly absurd for him to stay, that people would think it queer, and that he ought to go with the rest of his relatives. Yet it made no difference. "You should stay," he would reply. "Our family have always lived here."

When the Muskrat mothers told him how lonely he would be, and how he would miss seeing the dear little ones frolic in the moonlight, he blinked and said: "Well, I shall just have to stand it." Then he sighed, and they went away saying to each other what a tender heart he had and what a pity it was that he had never married. One of them spoke as though he had been in love with her some years before, but the others had known nothing about it.

The Muskrat fathers told him that he would have no one to help him if a Mink should pick a quarrel with him. "I can take care of myself then," said he, and showed his strong gnawing teeth in a very fierce way.

It was only when the dainty young Muskrat daughters talked to him that he began to wonder if he really ought to stay. He lay awake most of one day thinking about it and remembering the sad look in their little eyes when they said that they should miss him. He was so disturbed that he ate only three small roots during the next night. The poor old Bachelor had a hard time then, but he was so used to having his own way and doing what he had started to do, and not giving up to anybody, that he stayed after all.

The others went away and he began to build his winter house beside the biggest ditch. He placed it among some bushes, so that if the water in the ditch should ever overflow they would help hold his house in place. He built it with his mouth, bringing great mouthfuls of grass roots and rushes and dropping them on the middle of the heap. Sometimes they stayed there and sometimes they rolled down. If they rolled down he never brought them back, for he knew that they would be useful where they were. When it was done, the house was shaped like a pine cone with the stem end down, for after he had made it as high as a tall milkweed he finished off the long slope up which he had been running and made it look like the other sides.

After that he began to burrow up into it from below. The right way to do, he knew, was to have his doorway under water and dive down to it. Other winters he had done this and had given the water a loud slap with his tail as he dived. Now there was not enough water to dive into, and when he tried slapping on it his tail went through to the ditch bottom and got muddy. He had to fix the doorway as best he could, and then he ate out enough of the inside of his house to make a good room and poked a small hole through the roof to let in fresh air.

After the house was done, he slept there during the days and prowled around outside at night. He slept there, but ate none of the roots of which it was made until the water in the ditch was frozen hard. He knew that there would be a long, long time when he could not dig fresh roots and must live on those.

At night the marsh seemed so empty and lonely that he hardly knew what to do. He didn't enjoy his meals, and often complained to the Mice that the roots did not taste so good to him as those they used to have when he was young. He tried eating other things and found them no better. When there was bright moonlight, he sat upon the highest tussock he could find and thought about his grandfathers and grandmothers. "If they had not eaten their houses," he once said to a Mouse, "this marsh would be full of them."

"No it wouldn't," answered the Mouse, who didn't really mean to contradict him, but thought him much mistaken. "If the houses hadn't been eaten, they would have been blown down by the wind and beaten down by rains and washed away by floods. It is better so. Who wants things to stay the way they are forever and ever? I'd rather see the trees drop their leaves once in a while and grow new ones than to wear the same old ones after they are ragged and faded."

The Bachelor Muskrat didn't like this very well, but he couldn't forget it. When he awakened in the daytime he would think about it and at night he thought more. He was really very forlorn, and because he had nobody else to think about he thought too much of himself and began to believe that he was lame and sick. When he sat on a tussock and remembered all the houses which his grandparents had built and eaten, he became very sad and sighed until his fat sides shook. He wished that he could sleep through the winter like the Ground Hog, or through part of it like the Skunk, but just as sure as night came his eyes popped open and there he was—awake.

When spring came he thought of his friends who had gone to the swamp and he knew that last year's children were marrying and digging burrows of their own. The poor old Bachelor wanted to go to them, yet he was so used to doing what he had said he would, and disliked so much to let anybody know that he was mistaken, that he chose to stay where he was, without water enough for diving and with hardly enough for swimming. How it would have ended nobody knows, had the farmer not come to plough up the old drained marsh for planting celery.

Then the Bachelor went. He reached his new home in the early morning, and the mothers let their children stay up until it was quite light so that he might see them plainly. "Isn't it pleasant here?" they cried. "Don't you like it better than the old place?"

"Oh, it does very well," he answered, "but you must remember that I only moved because I had to."

"Oh, yes, we understand that," said one of the mothers, "but we hope you will really like it here."

Afterward her husband said to her, "Don't you know he was glad to come? What's the use of being so polite?"

"Poor old fellow," she answered. "He is so queer because he lives alone, and I'm sorry for him. Just see him eat."

And truly it was worth while to watch him, for the roots tasted sweet to him, and, although he had not meant to be, he was very happy—far happier than if he had had his own way.

The Greedy Red Fox

The Red Fox had been well brought up. His mother was a most cautious person and devoted to her children. When he did things which were wrong, he could never excuse himself by saying that he did not know better. Of course it is possible that he was like his father in being so reckless, yet none of his two brothers and three sisters were like him. They did not remember their father. In fact, they had never seen him, and their mother seldom spoke of him.

His mother had taken all the care of her six children, even pulling fur from her own belly to make a soft nest covering for them when they were first born. They were such helpless babies. Their eyes and ears were closed for some time, and all they could do was to tumble each other around and drink the warm milk that their mother had for them.

They had three burrows to live in, all of them in an open field between the forest and the farmhouse. Sometimes they lived in the first, sometimes in the second, and sometimes in the third. One night when their mother went out to hunt, she smelled along the ground near the burrow and then came back. "There has been a man near here," she said, "and I shall take you away."

That excited the little Foxes very much, and each wanted to be the first to go, but she hushed them up, and said that if they talked so loudly as that some man might catch them before they moved, and then—. She said nothing more, yet they knew from the way she moved her tail that it would be dreadful to have a man catch them.

While she was carrying them to another burrow one at a time, those who were left behind talked about men. "I wish I knew why men are so dreadful," said the first. "It must be because they have very big mouths and sharp teeth."

"I wonder what color their fur is," said another.

Now these young Foxes had seen nobody but their mother. If she had not told them that different animals wore different colored furs, they would have thought that everybody looked just like her, with long reddish-yellow fur and that on the hinder part of the back quite grizzled; throat, belly, and the tip of the tail white, and the outside of the ears black. They were very sure, however, that no other animal had such a wonderful tail as she, with each of its long, reddish hairs tipped with black and the beautiful brush of pure white at the end. In fact, she had told them so.

The next time their mother came back, the four children who were still there cried out, "Please tell us, what color is a man's fur?"

She was a sensible and prudent Fox, and knew it was much more important to keep her children from being caught than it was to answer all their questions at once. Besides, she already had one child in her mouth when they finished their question, and she would not put him down for the sake of talking. And that also was right, you know, for one can talk at any time, but the time to do work is just when it needs to be done.

After they were snugly settled in the other burrow, she lay down to feed them, and while they were drinking their milk she told them about men. "Men," she said, "are the most dreadful animals there are. Other animals will not trouble you unless they are hungry, but a man will chase you even when his stomach is full. They have four legs, of course,—all animals have,—but they use only two to walk upon. Their front legs they use for carrying things. We carry with our mouths, yet the only thing I ever saw a man have in his mouth was a short brown stick that was afire at one end. I thought it very silly, for he couldn't help breathing some of the smoke, and he let the stick burn up and then threw the fire away. However, men are exceedingly silly animals."

One of the little Red Foxes stopped drinking long enough to say, "You didn't tell us what color their fur is."

"The only fur they have," said Mother Fox, "is on their heads. They usually have fur on the top and back parts of their heads, and some of them have a little on the lower part of their faces. They may have black, red, brown, gray, or white fur. It is never spotted."

The children would have liked to ask more questions, but Mother Fox had eaten nothing since the night before, and was in a hurry to begin her hunt.

One could never tell all that happened to the little Red Foxes. They moved from burrow to burrow many times; they learned to eat meat which their mother brought them instead of drinking milk from her body, they frolicked together near the doorway of their home, and while they did this their mother watched from the edge of the forest, ready to warn them if she saw men or dogs coming.

She had chosen to dig her burrows in the middle of a field, because then there was no chance for men or Dogs to sneak up to them unseen, as there would have been in the forest, yet she feared that her children would be playing so hard that they might forget to watch. They slept most of the day, and at night they were always awake. When they were old enough, they began to hunt for themselves. Mother Fox gave them a great deal of good advice and then paid no more attention to them. After that, she took her naps on a sunny hillside, lying in a beautiful soft reddish-yellow bunch, with her bushy tail curled around to keep her feet warm and shade her eyes from the light.

The six brothers and sisters seldom saw each other after this. Foxes succeed better in life if they live alone, and of course they wanted to succeed. The eldest brother was the reckless one. His mother had done her best by him, and still he was reckless. He knew by heart all the rules that she had taught him, but he did not keep them. These were the rules:

"Always run on hard, dry things when you can. Soft, wet places take more scent from your feet, and Dogs can follow your trail better on them.

"Never go into any place unless you are sure you can get out.

"Keep your tail dry. A Fox with a wet tail cannot run well.

"If Dogs are chasing you, jump on to a rail fence and run along the top of it or walk in a brook.

"Always be willing to work for your food. That which you find all ready and waiting for you may be the bait of a trap.

"Always walk when you are hunting. The Fox who trots will pass by that which he should find."

For a while he said them over to himself every night when he started out. Then he began to skip a night once in a while. Next he got to saying them only when he had been frightened the day before. After that he stopped saying them altogether. "I am a full-grown Fox now," he said to himself, "and such things are only good for children. I guess I know how to take care of myself."

He often went toward the farmhouse to hunt, sometimes for grapes, sometimes for vegetables, and sometimes for heartier food. Collie had chased him away, but Collie was growing old and fat and had to hang his tongue out when he ran, so the Red Fox thought it only fun. He trotted along in the moonlight, his light, slender body seeming to almost float over the ground, and his beautiful tail held straight out behind. His short, slender legs were strong and did not tire easily, and as long as he could keep his tail dry he outran Collie easily. Sometimes he would get far ahead and sit down to wait for him. Then he would call out saucy things to the panting Dog, and only start on when Collie's nose had almost touched him.

"Fine evening!" he once said. "Hope your nose works better than your legs do."

That was a mean thing to say, you know, but Collie always keeps his temper and only answered, "It's sweating finely, thank you." He answered that way because it is the sweat on a Dog's nose which makes it possible for him to smell and follow scents which dry-nosed people do not even know about.

Then the Fox gave a long, light leap, and was off again, and Collie had to lie down to breathe. "I think," said he, "that I can tend Sheep better than I can chase Foxes—and it is a good deal easier." Still, Collie didn't like to be beaten and he lay awake the rest of the night thinking how he would enjoy catching that Fox. Every little while he heard the Red Fox barking off in the fields, and it made him twitch his tail with impatience.

Now the Red Fox was walking carefully toward the farmhouse and planning to catch a Turkey. He had watched the flocks of Turkeys all afternoon from his sleeping-place on the hillside. Every time he opened his eyes between naps he had looked at them as they walked to and fro in the fields, talking to each other in their gentle, complaining voices and moving their heads back and forth at every step. If his stomach had not been so full he would have tried to catch one then. He made up his mind to try it that night, and decided that he would rather have the plump, light-colored one than any of her darker sisters. He did not even think of catching the old Gobbler, for he was so big and strong and fierce-looking. He had just begun to walk with the Turkey mothers and children. During the summer they had had nothing to do with each other.

When the Red Fox reached the farmyard, he found them roosting on the low branches of an apple-tree. A long board had been placed against it to let the Chickens walk up. Now the Chickens were in the Hen-house, but the board was still there. The Red Fox looked all around. It was a starlight night. The farmhouse was dark and quiet. Collie was nowhere to be seen. Once he heard a Horse stamp in his sleep. Then all was still again.

The Red Fox walked softly up the slanting board. The Gobbler stirred. The Red Fox stopped with one foot in the air. When he thought him fast asleep he went on. The Gobbler stirred again and so did the others. The Red Fox sprang for the plump, light-colored one. She jumped also, and with the others flew far up to the top of the barn. The Red Fox ran down the board with five buff tail-feathers in his mouth. He was much out of patience with himself. "If I hadn't stopped to pick for her," he said, "I could have caught one of the others easily enough."

He sneaked around in the shadows to see if the noise made by the turkeys had awakened the farmer or Collie. The farmhouse was still and dark. Collie was not at home. "I will look at the Hen-house," said the Red Fox.

He walked slowly and carefully to the Hen-house. The big door was closed and bolted. He walked all around and into the poultry yard. There was a small opening through which the fowls could pass in and out. The Red Fox managed to crawl though, but it was not easy. It squeezed his body and crushed his fur. He had to push very hard with his hind feet to get through at all. When he was inside it took him some time to get his breath. "That's the tightest place I ever was in," said he softly, "but I always could crawl through a very small hole."

He found the fowls all roosting too high for him. Perhaps if the Hen-house had been larger, he might have leaped and caught one, but there was not room for one of his finest springs. He went to the nests and found many eggs there. These he broke and ate. They ran down in yellow streams from the corners of his mouth and made his long fur very sticky. You can just imagine how hard it would be to eat raw eggs from the shell with only your paws in which to hold them.

One egg was light and slippery. He bit hard to break that one, and when it broke it was hollow. Not a drop of anything to eat in it, and then it cut his lip a little, too, so that he could not eat more without its hurting. He jumped and said something when he was cut. The Shanghai Cock, who was awakened by the noise, said that he exclaimed, "Brambles and traps!" but it may not have been anything so bad as that. We will hope it was not.

The Shanghai Cock awakened all the other fowls. "Don't fly off your perch!" he cried. "Stay where you are! *Stay where where you are!* Stay where you are!" The other Cocks kept saying "Eru-u-u-u," as they do when Hawks are near. The Hens squawked and squawked and squawked, until they were out of breath. When they got their breath they squawked some more.

The Red Fox knew that it was time for him to go. The farmer would be sure to hear the noise. He put his head out of the hole through which he had come in, and he pushed as hard as he could with his hind feet and scrambled with his fore feet. His fur was crushed worse than ever, and he was squeezed so tightly that he could hardly breathe. You see it had been all he could do to get in through the hole, and now he had nine eggs in his stomach (excepting what had run down at the corners of his mouth), and he was too large to pass through.

The fowls saw what was the matter, and wanted to laugh. They thought it very funny, and yet the sooner he could get away the better they would like it. The Red Fox had his head outside and saw a light flash in the farmer's room. Then he heard doors open, and the farmer came toward the Hen-house with a lantern in his hand. Collie came trotting around the corner of the house. The Red Fox made one last desperate struggle and then lay still.

When the farmer picked him up and tied a rope around his neck, he had to pull him backward into the Hen-house to do it. The Red Fox was very quiet and gentle, as people of his family always are when caught. Collie pranced around on two legs and barked as loudly as he could. The fowls blinked their round yellow eyes in the lantern light, and the farmer's man ran out for an empty Chicken-coop into which to put the Red Fox. Collie was usually quite polite, but he had not forgotten how rude the Red Fox had been to him, and it was a fine chance to get even.

"Good evening!" he barked. "Oh, good evening! I'm glad you came. Don't think you must be going. Excuse me, but your mouth worked better than your legs, didn't it?"

The Red Fox shut his eyes and pretended not to hear. The dirt from the floor of the Hen-house had stuck to his egg-covered fur, and he looked very badly. They put him in a Chicken-coop with a board floor, so that he couldn't burrow out, and he curled down in a little heap and hid his face with his tail. Collie hung around for a while and then went off to sleep. After he was gone, the Red Fox cleaned his fur. "I got caught this time," he said, "but it won't happen again. Now I must watch for a chance to get away. It will surely come."

It did come. But that is another story.

The Unfortunate Fireflies

Several very large families of Fireflies lived in the marsh and were much admired by their friends who were awake at night. Once in a while some young Firefly who happened to awaken during the day would go out and hover over the heads of the daylight people. He never had any attention paid to him then, however, for during the day he seemed like a very commonplace little beetle and nobody even cared to look at him a second time. The only remarkable thing about him was the soft light that shone from his body, and that could only be seen at night.

The older Fireflies told the younger ones that they should get all the sleep they could during the daytime if they were to flutter and frisk all night. Most of them did this, but two young Fireflies, who cared more about seeing the world than they did about minding their elders, used to run away while the rest were dreaming. Each thought herself very important, and was sure that if the others missed her they wouldn't sleep a wink all day.

One night they planned to go by daylight to the farthest corner of the marsh. They had heard a couple of young Muskrats talking about it, and thought it might be different from anything they had seen. They went to bed when the rest did and pretended to fall asleep. When she was sure that the older Fireflies were dreaming, one of them reached over with her right hind leg and touched the other just below the edge of her left wing-cover. "Are you ready?" she whispered.

"Yes," answered the friend, who happened to be the smaller of the two.

"Come on, then," said the larger one, picking her way along on her six tiptoes. It was already growing light, and they could see where they stepped, but, you know, it is hard to walk over rough places on two tiptoes, so you can imagine what it must be on six. There are some pleasant things about having many legs. There are also some hard things. It is a great responsibility.

When well away from their sleeping relatives, they lifted their wing-covers, spread their wings, and flew to the farthest corner of the marsh. They were not afraid of being punished if caught, for they were orphans and had nobody to bring them up. They were afraid that if the other Fireflies awakened they would be called "silly" or "foolish young bugs." They thought that they were old enough to take care of themselves, and did not want advice.

"Oh, wouldn't they make a fuss if they knew!" exclaimed the Larger Firefly.

"They think we need to be told every single thing," said the Smaller Firefly.

"Guess we're old enough now to go off by ourselves," said the Larger Firefly.

"I guess so," answered the Smaller Firefly. "I'm not afraid if it is light, and I can see pretty near as well as I can at night."

Just then a Flycatcher darted toward them and they had to hide. He had come so near that they could look down his throat as he flew along with his beak open. The Fireflies were so scared that their feelers shook.

"I wish that bird would mind his own business," grumbled the Larger Firefly.

"That's just what he was doing," said a voice beside them, as a Garter Snake drew himself through the grass. Then their feelers shook again, for they knew that snakes do not breakfast on grass and berries.

"Did you ever see such luck?" said the Smaller Firefly. "If it isn't birds it is snakes."

"Perfectly dreadful!" answered the other. "I never knew the marsh to be so full of horrid people. Besides, my eyes are bothering me and I can't see plainly."

"So are mine," said the Smaller Firefly. "Are you going to tell the other Fireflies all about things to-night?"

"I don't know that I will," said the Larger Firefly. "I'll make them ask me first."

Then they reached the farther corner of the marsh and crawled around to see what they could find. Their eyes bothered them so that they could not see unless they were close to things, so it was useless to fly. They peeped into the cool dark corners under the skunk cabbage leaves, and lay down to rest on a bed of soft moss. A few stalks of last year's teazles stood, stiff and brown, in the corner of the fence. The Smaller Firefly alighted on one and let go in such a hurry that she fell to the ground. "Ouch!" she cried. "It has sharp hooks all over it."

While they were lying on the moss and resting, they noticed a queer plant growing near. It had a flower of green and dark red which was unlike any other blossom they had ever seen. The leaves were even queerer. Each was stiff and hollow and grew right out of the ground instead of coming from a stalk.

"I'm going to crawl into one of them," said the Larger Firefly. "There is something sweet inside. I believe it will be lots better than the skunk cabbage." She balanced herself on the top of a fresh green leaf.

"I'm going into this one," said the other Firefly, as she alighted on the edge of a brown-tipped leaf. "It looks nice and dark inside. We must tell about this at the party to-night, even if they don't ask us."

Then they repeated together the little verse that some of the pond people use when they want to start together:

"Tussock, mud, water, and log,
Muskrat, Snake, Turtle, and Frog,
Here we go into the bog!"

When they said "bog" each dropped quickly into her own leaf.

For a minute nobody made a sound. Then there was a queer sputtering, choking voice in the fresh green leaf and exactly the same in the brown-tipped one. After that a weak little voice in the green leaf said, "Abuschougerh! I fell into water."

Another weak voice from the brown-tipped one replied, "Gtschagust! So did I."

On the inside of each leaf were many stiff hairs, all pointing downward. When the Fireflies dropped in, they had brushed easily past these hairs and thought it rather pleasant. Now that they were sputtering and choking inside, and wanted to get out, these same hairs stuck into their eyes and pushed against their legs and made them exceedingly uncomfortable. The water, too, had stood for some time in the leaves and did not smell good.

Perhaps it would be just as well not to tell all the things which those two Fireflies said, for they were tired and out of patience. After a while they gave up trying to get out until they should be rested. It was after sunset when they tried the last time, and the light that shone from their bellies brightened the little green rooms where they were. They rested and went at it carefully, instead of in the angry, jerky way which they had tried before. Slowly, one foot at a time, they managed to climb out of the doorway at the top. As they came out, they heard the squeaky voice of a young Mouse say, "Oh, where did those bright things come from?"

They also heard his mother answer, "Those are only a couple of foolish Fireflies who have been in the leaves of the pitcher-plant all day."

After they had eaten something they flew toward home. They knew that it would be late for the party, and they expected to surprise and delight everybody when they reached there. On the way they spoke of this. "I'm dreadfully tired," said one, "but I suppose we shall have to dance in the air with the rest or they will make a fuss."

"Yes," said the other. "It spoils everything if we are not there. And we'll have to tell where we've been and what we've done and whom we have seen, when we would rather go to sleep and make up what we lost during the daytime."

As they came near the middle of the marsh they were surprised to see the mild summer air twinkling with hundreds of tiny lights as their friends and relatives flew to and fro in the dusk. "Well," said the Larger Firefly, "I think they might have waited for us."

"Humph!" said the Smaller Firefly. "If they can't be more polite than that, I won't play."

"After we've had such a dreadfully hard time, too," said the Larger Firefly. "Got most eaten by a Flycatcher and scared by a Garter Snake and shut up all day in the pitcher-plant. I won't move a wing to help on their old party."

So two very tired and cross young Fireflies sat on a last year's cat-tail and sulked. People didn't notice them because they were sitting and their bright bellies didn't show. After a long time an elderly Firefly came to rest on the cat-tail and found them. "Good evening," said he. "Have you danced until you are tired?"

They looked at each other, but before either could speak one of their young friends alighted beside them and said the same thing. Then the Smaller Firefly answered. "We have been away," said she, "and we are not dancing to-night."

"Going away, did you say?" asked the elderly Firefly, who was rather deaf. "I hope you will have a delightful time." Then he bowed and flew off.

"Don't stay long," added their young friend. "We shall be so lonely without you."

After he also was gone, the two runaways looked into each other's eyes. "We were not even missed!" they cried. "We had a bad time and nobody makes any fuss. They were dancing without us." Poor little Fireflies!

They were much wiser after that, for they had learned that two young Fireflies were not so wonderfully important after all. And that if they chose to do things which it was never meant young Fireflies should do, they would be likely to have a very disagreeable time, but that other Fireflies would go on eating and dancing and living their own lives. To be happy, they must keep the Firefly laws.

The Kittens Come To The Forest

One day the three big Kittens who lived with their mother in the farmer's barn had a dreadful quarrel. If their mother had been with them, she would probably have cuffed each with her fore paw and scolded them soundly. She was not with them because she had four little new Kittens lying beside her in the hay-loft over the stalls.

You would think that the older Kittens must have been very proud of their baby brothers and sisters, yet they were not. They might have done kind little things for their mother, but they didn't. They just hunted food for themselves and never took a mouthful of it to her. And this does not prove that they were bad Kittens. It just shows that they were young and thoughtless.

The Brown Kitten, the one whose fur was black and yellow mixed so finely as to look brown, had climbed the barn stairs to see them. When he reached their corner he sat down and growled at them. His mother said nothing at first, but when he went so far as to switch his tail in a threatening way, she left her new babies and sprang at him and told him not to show his whiskers upstairs again until he could behave properly.

His sisters, the Yellow Kitten and the White Kitten, stayed downstairs. They didn't dislike babies so much as their brother. They just didn't care anything about them. Cats never care much about Kittens, you know, unless they are their own, and big brothers always say that they can't bear them.

Now these three older Kittens were perfectly able to care for themselves. It was a long time since their mother stopped feeding them, and they were already excellent hunters. They had practised crouching, crawling, and springing before they left the hay-loft. Sometimes they hunted wisps of hay that moved when the wind blew in through the open door. Sometimes they pounced on each other, and sometimes they hunted the Grasshoppers who got brought in with the hay. It was when they were doing this once that they were so badly scared, but that is a story which has already been told.

There was no reason why they should feel neglected or worry about getting enough to eat. If one of them had poor luck in hunting, all he had to do was to hang around the barn when the Cows were brought up, and go into the house with the man when he carried the great pails full of foamy milk. Then if the Kittens acted hungry, mewed very loudly, and rubbed up lovingly against the farmer's wife they were sure to get a good, dishful of warm milk.

You can see how unreasonable they were. They had plenty to eat, and their mother loved them just as much as ever, but they felt hurt and sulked around in corners, and answered each other quite rudely, and would not run after a string which the farmer's little girl dangled before them. They were not cross all the time, because they had been up the whole night and had to sleep. They stopped being cross when they fell asleep and began again as soon as they awakened. The Hens who were feeding around became so used to it that as soon as they saw a Kitten twist and squirm, and act like awakening, they put their heads down and ran away as fast as they could.

They did not even keep themselves clean. Oh, they licked themselves over two or three times during the day, but not thoroughly. The Yellow Kitten did not once try to catch her tail and scrub it, and actually wore an unwashed tail all day. It didn't show very plainly because it was yellow, but that made it no cleaner. The White Kitten went around with her fore paws looking really disgraceful. The Brown Kitten scrubbed his ears in a sort of half-hearted way, and paid no attention to the place under his chin. When he did his ears, he gave his paw one lick and his ear one rub, and repeated this only six times. Everybody knows that a truly tidy Cat wets his paw with two licks, cleans his ear with two rubs, and does this over and over from twenty to forty times before he begins on the other ear.

Toward night they quarrelled over a dishful of milk which the farmer's wife gave them. There was plenty of room for them all to put their heads into the dish at once and lap until each had his share. If it had not been for their whiskers, there would have been no trouble. These hit, and each told the others to step back and wait. Nobody did, and there was such a fuss that the farmer's wife took the dish away and none of them had any more. They began to blame each other and talk so loudly that the man drove them all away as fast as they could scamper.

Now that they were separated, each began to grow more and more discontented. The Brown Kitten had crawled under the carriage house, and as soon as it was really dark he stole off to the forest.

"My mother has more Kittens," he said, "and my sisters get my whiskers all out of shape, and I'll go away and never come back. I won't say good-by to them either. I guess they'll feel badly then and wish they'd been nicer to me! If they ever find me and want me to come back, I won't go. Not if they beg and beg! I'll just turn my tail toward them and walk away."

The Brown Kitten knew that Cats sometimes went to live in the woods and got along very well. He was not acquainted with one who had done this; his mother had told him and his sisters stories of Cats who chose to live so. She said that was one thing which showed how much more clever they were than Dogs. Dogs, you know, cannot live happily away from men, although there may be the best of hunting around them.

"I will find a good hollow tree," said he, "for my home, and I will sleep there all day and hunt at night. I will eat so much that I shall grow large and strong. Then, when I go out to hunt, the forest people will say, 'Sh! Here comes the Brown Cat.'"

As he thought this he was running softly along the country road toward the forest. Once in a while he stopped to listen, and stood with his head raised and turned and one fore foot in the air. He kept his ears pointed forward all the time so as to hear better.

When he passed the marsh he saw the Fireflies dancing in the air. Sometimes they flew so low that a Kitten might catch them. He thought he would try, so he crawled through the fence and toward the place where they were dancing. He passed two tired ones sitting on a leaf and never saw them. That was because their wings covered their sides so well that no light shone past, and their bright bellies were close to the leaf. He had almost reached the dancers when he found his paws getting wet and muddy. That made him turn back at once, for mud was something he couldn't stand. "I wish I had something to eat," he said, as he took a bite of catnip. "This is very good for a relish, but not for a whole meal."

He trotted on toward the forest, thinking about milk and Fireflies and several other things, when he was stopped by some great winged person flying down toward him and then sweeping upward and alighting on a branch. The Brown Kitten drew back stiffly and said, "Ha-a-ah!"

"Who? Who? To who?" asked the person on the branch.

The Brown Kitten answered, "It is I." But the question came again: "Who? Who? To who?"

That made the Brown Kitten remember that, since his voice was not known in the forest, nobody could tell anything by his answer. This time he replied: "I am the Brown Kitten, if you please, and I have come to live in the forest."

"Who? Who? To who?" was the next question, and the Brown Kitten thought he was asked to whose home he was going.

"I am not going to anybody," he said. "I just wanted to come, and left my old home suddenly. I shall live alone and have a good time. I didn't even tell my mother."

"Who? Who? To who?" said the Great Horned Owl, for it was he.

"My m-mother," said the Brown Kitten, and then he ran away as fast as he could. He had seen the Owl more clearly as he spoke, and the Owl's face reminded him a little of his mother and made him want to see her. He ran so fast that he almost bumped into the Skunk, who was taking a dignified stroll through the forest and sniffing at nearly everything he saw. It was very lucky, you know, that he did not quite run into the Skunk, for Skunks do not like to be run into, and, if he had done so, other people would soon have been sniffing at him.

The Brown Kitten thought that the Skunk might be related to him. They were about the same size, and the Brown Kitten had been told that his relatives were not only different colors, but different shapes. His mother had told of seeing some Manx Kittens who had no tails at all, and he thought that the Skunk's elegant long-haired one needn't prevent his being a Cat.

"Good evening," said the Brown Kitten. "Would you mind telling me if you are a Cat."

"Cat? No!" growled the Skunk. "They sometimes call me a Wood-Kitty, but they have no right to. I am a Skunk, *Skunk*, Skunk, and I am related to the Weasles. Step out of my path."

A family of young Raccoons in a tree called down teasingly to him to come up, but after he had started they told him to go down, and then laughed at him because he had to go tail first. He did not know that forest climbers turn the toes of their hind feet backward and scamper down head first. Still, it would have made no difference if he had known, for his toes wouldn't turn.

He found something to eat now and then, and he looked for a hollow tree. He found only one, and that was a Bee tree, so he couldn't use it. All around him the most beautiful mushrooms were pushing up from the ground. White, yellow, orange, red, and brown they were, and looked so plump and fair that he wanted to bite them. He knew, however, that some of them were very poisonous, so he didn't even lick them with his eager, rough little pink tongue. He was just losing his Kitten teeth, and his new Cat teeth were growing, and they made him want to bite almost everything he saw. One kind of mushroom, which he thought the prettiest of all, grew only on the trunks of fallen beech trees. It was white, and had a great many little branches, all very close together.

Most of the plants which he saw were sound asleep. Every plant has to sleep, you know, and most of them take a long nap at night. Some of them, like the water-lilies, also sleep on cloudy days. He was very fond of the clovers, but they had their leaflets folded tight, and only the mushrooms, the evening primroses, and a few others were wide awake. Everybody whom he met was a stranger, and he began to feel very lonely. Cats do not usually mind being alone. Indeed, they rather like it; still, you can see how hard it would be for a Kitten who had always been loved and cared for to find himself alone in a dark forest, where great birds ask the same questions over and over, and other people make fun of him. You wouldn't like it yourself, if you were a Kitten.

At last, when he was prowling along an old forest road and hoping to meet a tender young Wood-Mouse, he saw a couple of light-colored animals ahead of him. They looked to him very much like Kittens, but he remembered how the Skunk had snubbed him when taken for a Cat, and he kept still. He ran to overtake them and see more clearly, and just as he reached them they all came to a turn in the road.

Before he could speak or they could notice that he was there, the wind roared through the branches above, and just ahead two terrible great eyes glared at them out of an old log. They all stopped with their back-fur bristling and their tails arched stiffly. Not a sound did one of them make. They lifted first one foot and then another and backed slowly and silently away. When they had gone far enough, they turned quickly and ran down the old road as fast as their twelve feet could carry them. They never stopped until they were in the road for home and could look back in the starlight and be sure that nobody was following them. Then they stared at each other—the Yellow Kitten, the White Kitten, and the Brown Kitten.

"Did you run away to live in the forest?" asked the sisters.

"Did you?" asked the Brown Kitten.

"You'll never tell?" said they.

"Never!" said he.

"Well then, we did run away, and met each other just before you came. We meant to live in the forest."

"So did I," said he. "And I couldn't find any hollow tree."

"Did you meet that dreadful bird?" said they,—"the one who never hears your answers and keeps asking you over and over?"

"Yes," said he. "Don't you ever tell!"

"Ha-ha!" screamed a laughing little Screech-Owl, who had seen what had happened in the old forest road and flapped along noiselessly behind them.

"Three big Kittens afraid of fox-fire! O-ho! O-ho!"

Now all of them had heard about fox-fire and knew it was the light which shines from some kinds of rotten wood in the dark, but they held up their heads and answered, "We're not afraid of fox-fire."

"Ha-ha!" screamed the Screech-Owl again. "Thought you saw big eyes glaring at you. Only fox-fire. Dare you to come back if you are not afraid."

"We don't want to go back," answered the Brown Kitten. "We haven't time."

"Ha-ha!" screamed the Screech-Owl. "Haven't time! Where are you going?"

"Going home, of course," answered the Brown Kitten. And then he whispered to his sisters, "Let's!"

"All right," said they, and they raced down the road as fast as they could go. To this day their mother does not know that they ever ran away from home.

But it was only fox-fire.

The Inquisitive Weasels

The Weasels were very unpopular with most of the forest people, the pond and meadow people did not like them, and those who lived in the farmyard couldn't bear them. Something went wrong there every time that a Weasel came to call. Once, you know, the Dorking Hen was so frightened that she broke her wonderful shiny egg, and there were other times when even worse things had happened. Usually there was a Chicken or two missing after the Weasel had gone.

The Weasels were very fond of their own family, however, and would tell their best secrets to each other. That meant almost as much with them as to share food, for they were very inquisitive and always wanted to know all about everything. They minded their own business, but they minded everybody's else as well. If you told a thing to one Weasel you might be sure that before the night was over every Weasel in the neighborhood would know all about it. They told other people, too, when they had a chance. They were dreadful gossips. If they saw a person do something the least unusual, they thought about it and talked about it and wondered what it meant, and decided that it meant something very remarkable and became very much excited. At such times, they made many excuses to go calling, and always managed to tell about what they had seen, what they had heard, and what they were perfectly certain it meant.

They went everywhere, and could go quietly and without being noticed. They were small people, about as long as Rats, but much more slender, and with such short legs that their bodies seemed to almost lie on the ground. All their fur was brown, except that on their bellies and the inside of their legs, which was pure white. Sometimes the fur on their feet matched their backs and sometimes it matched their bellies. That was as might happen. You can easily see how they could steal along over the brown earth or the dead leaves and grass without showing plainly. In winter they turned white, and then they did not show on the snow. The very tip of their short tails stayed a pale brown, but it was so tiny as hardly to be noticed. Any Hawk in the air, who saw just that bit of brown on the snow beneath him, would be likely to think it a leaf or a piece of bark and pay no more attention to it.

The Weasel mothers were very careful of their children and very brave. It made no difference how great the danger might be, they would stay by their babies and fight for them. And such workers as they were! It made no difference to them whether it was day or night, they would burrow or hunt just the same. When they were tired they slept, and when they awakened they began at once to do something.

Several families lived in the high bank by the edge of the forest, just where the ground slopes down to the marsh. They had lived there year after year, and had kept on adding to their burrows. There was only one doorway to each burrow and that was usually hidden by some leaves or a stone. They were hardly as large as Chipmunk's holes and easily hidden. "It is a good thing to have a fine, large home," said the Weasels, "but we build for comfort, not for show."

All the Weasel burrows began alike, with a straight, narrow hall. Then more halls branched off from this, and every little way there would be a room in which to turn around or rest. In some of these they stored food; in others they had nothing but bones and things which were left from their meals. Each burrow had one fine, large room, bigger than an Ovenbird's nest, with a soft bed of leaves and fur. Some of the rooms were so near the top of the ground that a Weasel could dig his way up in a few minutes if he needed another door. They were the loveliest sort of places for playing hide-and-seek, and that is a favorite Weasel game, only every Weasel wants to seek instead of hiding. There was never a bit of loose earth around these homes, and that is the one secret which Weasels will not tell out of the family—they never tell what they do with the earth they dig out. It just disappears.

Weasels like to hunt in parties. They say there is no fun in doing anything unless you have somebody with whom to talk it over. One night four of them went out together as soon as it was dark. They were young fellows and had planned to go to the farmer's Hen-house for the first time. They started to go there, but of course they wanted to see everything by the way. They would run straight ahead for a little while, then turn off to one side, as Ants do, poking into a Chipmunk's hole or climbing a tree to find a bird's nest, eating whatever food they found, and talking softly about everything.

"It is disgraceful the way that Chipmunk keeps house," said one of them, as he came back from going through a burrow under a tree. "Half-eaten food dropped right on the floor of the burrow in the most careless way. It was only a nut. If it had been anything I cared for, I would have eaten it myself."

Then they gossiped about Chipmunks, and said that, although they always looked trim and neat, there was no telling what sort of housekeepers they were; and that it really seemed as though they would do better to stay at home more and run about the forest less. The Chipmunk heard all this from the tree where he had hidden himself, and would have liked to speak right out and tell them what he thought of callers who entered one's home without knocking and sneaked around to see how things were kept. He knew better than to do so, however. He knew that when four hungry Weasels were out hunting their supper, it was an excellent time to keep still. He was right. And there are many times when it is better for angry people to keep still, even if they are not afraid of being eaten.

After they had gone he came down. "It was lucky for me," he said, "that I awakened hungry and ate a lunch. If I hadn't been awake to run away there's no telling where I would be now. There are some things worse than having people think you a poor housekeeper."

Just as the Chipmunk was finishing his lunch, one of the Weasels whispered to the others to stop. "There is somebody coming," said he. "Let's wait and see what he is doing."

It was the Black-tailed Skunk, who came along slowly, sniffing here and there, and once in a while stopping to eat a few mouthfuls.

"Doesn't it seem to you that he acts very queerly?" said one of the Weasels to the rest.

"Very," replied another. "And he doesn't look quite as usual. I don't know that I ever saw him carry his tail in just that way."

"I'd like to know where he is going," said another. "I guess he doesn't think anybody will see him."

"Let's follow him," said the fourth Weasel, who had not spoken before.

While he was near them they hid behind a hemlock log out of which many tiny hemlocks were growing. Once in a while they peeped between the soft fringy leaves of these to see what he was doing. They were much excited. "He is putting his nose down to the ground," one would say. "It must be that he has found something."

Then another would poke his little head up through the hemlocks and look at the Skunk. "He couldn't have found anything after all," he would say. "I can't hear him eating."

"It is very strange," the rest would murmur.

Now it just happened that the Black-tailed Skunk had scented the Weasels and knew that they were near. He had also heard the rustling behind the hemlock log. He knew what gossips Weasels are, and he guessed that they were watching him, so he decided to give them something to think about. He knew that they would often fight people larger than themselves, but he was not afraid of anybody. He did not care to fight them either, for if he got near enough to really enjoy it they would be likely to bite him badly, and when a Weasel has set his teeth into anybody it is not easy to make him let go. "I rather think," said he to himself, "that there will be four very tired young Weasels sleeping in their burrows to-morrow."

"He's walking away," whispered one of the Weasels. "Where do you suppose he is going?"

"We'll have to find out," said the others, as they crept quietly out of their hiding-places.

The Skunk went exactly where he wanted to. Whenever he found food he ate it. The Weasels who followed after found nothing left for them. They became very hungry, but if one of them began to think of going off for a lunch, the Skunk was certain to do something queer. Sometimes he would lie down and laugh. Then the Weasels would peep at him from a hiding-place and whisper together.

"What do you suppose makes him laugh?" they would ask. "It must be that he is thinking of something wonderful which he is going to do. We must not lose sight of him."

Once he met the Spotted Skunk, his brother, and they whispered together for a few minutes. Then the Spotted Skunk laughed, and as he passed on, the Black-tailed Skunk called back to him: "Be sure not to tell any one. I do not want it known what I am doing."

Then the four young Weasels nudged each other and said, "There! We knew it all the time!"

After that, nobody spoke about being hungry. All they cared for was the following of the Black-tailed Skunk. Once, when they were in the marsh, they were so afraid of being seen that they slipped into the ditch and swam for a way. They were good swimmers and didn't much mind, but it just shows how they followed the Skunk. Once he led them over to the farm and they remembered their plan of going to the Hen-house. They were very, very hungry, and each looked at the others to see what they thought about letting the Skunk go and stopping for a hearty supper. Still, nobody spoke of doing so. One Weasel whispered: "Now we shall surely see what he is about. He ought to know that he cannot do wrong or mischievous things without being found out. And since we discover it ourselves, we shall certainly feel free to speak of it."

Collie, the watch-dog, was sleeping lightly, and came rushing around the corner of the house to see what strangers were there, but when he saw who they were, he dropped his tail and walked away. He was old enough to know many things, and he knew too much to fight either a Skunk or a Weasel. Every one lets Skunks alone, and it is well to let Weasels alone also, for although they are so small they bite badly.

Now the Black-tailed Skunk turned to the forest and walked toward his hole. The Screech-Owl passed them flying homeward, and several times Bats darted over their heads. When they went by the Bats' cave they could tell by the sound that ten or twelve were inside hanging themselves up for the day. A dim light showed in the eastern sky, and the day birds were stirring and beginning to preen their feathers.

"What do you think it means?" whispered the Weasels. "He seems to be going home. Do you suppose he has changed his mind?"

When he reached his hole the Black-tailed Skunk stopped and looked around. The Weasels hid themselves under some fallen leaves. "I bid you good-morning," said the Skunk, looking toward the place where they were. "I hope you are not *too* tired. This walk has been very easy for me, but I fear it was rather long for Weasels. Besides, I have found plenty to eat and have chosen smooth paths for myself. Good-morning! I have enjoyed your company!"

When even the tip of his tail was hidden in the hole, the Weasels crawled from under the leaves and looked at each other.

"We believe he knew all the time that we were following him," they said. "He acted queerly just to fool us. The wretch!"

Yet after all, you see, he had done only what he did every night, and it was because they were watching and talking about him that they thought him going on some strange errand.

The Thrifty Deer Mouse

When the days grew short and chilly, and bleak winds blew out of the great blue-gray cloud banks in the west, many of the forest people went to sleep for the winter. And not only they, but over in the meadow the Tree Frog and the Garter Snake had already crawled out of sight and were dreaming sweetly. The song birds had long before this started south, and the banks of the pond and its bottom of comfortable soft mud held many sleepers. Under the water the Frogs had snuggled down in groups out of sight. Some of the Turtles were there also, and some were in the bank.

The Ground Hogs had grown stupid and dozy before the last leaves fluttered to the ground, and had been the first of the fur-bearers to go to bed for the winter. There were so many interesting things to see and do in the late fall days that they tried exceedingly hard to keep awake.

A Weasel was telling a Ground Hog something one day—and it was a very interesting piece of gossip, only it was rather unkind, and so might better not be told here—when he saw the Ground Hog winking very slow and sleepy winks and letting his head droop lower and lower. Once he asked him if he understood. The Ground Hog jumped and opened his eyes very wide indeed, and said: "Oh, yes, yes! Perfectly! Oh-ah-ah-ah-ah-ah." His yawn didn't look so big as it sounds, because his mouth was so small.

He tried to act politely interested, but just as the Weasel reached the most exciting part of his story, the Ground Hog rolled over sound asleep. The next day he said "good-by" to his friends, wished them a happy winter, and said he might see some of them before spring, as he should come out once to make the weather. "I only hope I shall awaken in time," he said, "but I am fat enough to sleep until the violets are up."

He had to be fat, you know, to last him through the cold weather without eating. He was so stout that he could hardly waddle, his big, loose-skinned body dragged when he walked, and was even shakier than ever. He really couldn't hurry by jumping and he was so short of breath that he could barely whistle when he went into his hole.

The Raccoons went after the Ground Hog and the Skunks were later still. They never slept so very long, and said they didn't really need to at all, and wouldn't except that they had nothing to do and it made housekeeping easier. It saved so much not to have to go out to their meals in the coldest weather.

When the large people were safely out of the way, the smaller ones had their best times. The Muskrats were awake, but they had their big houses to eat and were not likely to trouble Mice and Squirrels. There was not much to fear except Owls and Weasels. The Ground Hogs had once tried to get the Great Horned Owl to go south when the Cranes did, and he had laughed in their faces. "To-whoo!" said he. "Not I! I'm not afraid of cold weather. You don't know how warm feathers are. I never wear anything else. Furs are all right, but they are not feathers."

He and his relatives sat all day in their holes, and seldom flew out except at night. Sometimes, when the day was not too bright, they made short trips out for luncheon. It was very unfortunate for any Mouse to be near at those times.

Now the snow had fallen and the beautiful still cold days had come. The Weasels' fur had changed from brown to white, as it does in cold countries in winter. The Chipmunks had taken their last scamper until early spring, and were living, each alone, in their comfortable burrows. They were most independent and thrifty. No one ever heard of a Chipmunk lacking food unless some robber had carried off his nuts and corn. The Mice think that it must be very dull for a Chipmunk to stay by himself all winter, since he does not sleep steadily. The Chipmunks do not find it so. One of them said: "Dull? I never find it dull. When I am awake, I eat or clean my fur or think. If I had any one staying with me he might rouse me when I want to sleep, or pick the nut that I want for myself, or talk when I am thinking. No, thank you, I will go calling when I want company."

The Mice make winter their playtime. Then the last summer's babies are all grown up and able to look out for themselves, and the fathers and mother's have a chance to rest. The Meadow Mice come together in big parties and build groups of snug winter homes under the snow of the meadow, with many tiny covered walks leading from one to another. Their food is all around them—grass roots and brown seeds—and there is so much of it that they never quarrel to see who shall have this root and who shall have that. They sleep during the daytime and awaken to eat and visit and have a good time at night.

Sometimes they are awakened in the daytime, as they were when the Grouse broke through the snow near them. That was an accident, and the Grouse felt very sorry about it. They had snuggled down in a cozy family party near by, and were just starting out for a stroll one morning when the eldest son stumbled and fell and crushed through the snow into the little settlement of Meadow Mice.

The young Grouse was much ashamed of his awkwardness. "I am so sorry," he said. "I'm not used to my snow-shoes yet. This is the first winter I have worn them."

"That is all right," said the Oldest Mouse politely. "It must be hard to manage them at first. We hope you will have better luck after this." Then they bowed to each other and the Grouse walked off to join his brothers and sisters, lifting his feet with their newly grown feather snow-shoes very high at every step. The Meadow Mice went to work to make their homes neat again, yet they never looked really right until that snow had melted and more had fallen. One might think that the Meadow Mice and the Grouse would care less for each other after that, but it was not so. It never is so if people who make trouble are quick to say that they are sorry, and those who were hurt will keep patient and forgiving.

It was only the night after this happened that one of the Deer Mice had a great fright. His home was in a Bee tree in the forest. The Bees and he had always been the best of friends, and now that they were keeping close to their honeycomb all winter, the Deer Mouse had taken a small room in the same tree. It helped to keep him warm when he slept close to the Bees, for there was always some heat coming from their bodies. Once in a while, too, he took a nibble of honey, and they did not mind.

The Deer Mouse did not keep much of his own winter food where he lived. He had a few beechnuts near by, and when the weather was very stormy indeed he ate some of these. There was room for many more in the storeroom (another hole in the Bee tree), but he liked to keep food in many places. "It is wiser," said he. "Supposing I had them all here and this tree should be blown down, and it should fall in such a way that I couldn't reach the hole. What would I do then?"

He was talking to a Rabbit when he said this. The Rabbit never stored up food himself, yet he sometimes told other people how he thought it should be done. He was sure it would be better to have all the nuts in one place as the Chipmunks did. And now that the Deer Mouse had given his reasons, he was just as sure as ever. "The Bee tree is not very likely to blow down in that way," said he. "There is not much danger."

"Not much, but some," answered the Deer Mouse. "Hollow trees fall more quickly than solid ones. You may store your food where you please and I'll take care of mine."

The Deer Mouse spoke very decidedly, although he was perfectly polite. His beautiful brown eyes looked squarely at the Rabbit, and you could tell by the position of his slender long tail that he was much in earnest. The Rabbit went home.

The Deer Mouse put away hundreds and hundreds of beechnuts. These he took carefully out of their shells and laid in nicely lined holes in tree-trunks. He used leaves for lining these places. Besides keeping food in the trees, he hid little piles of nuts under stones and logs, and tucked seeds into chinks of fences or tiny pockets in the ground. He had worked in the wheatfield after the grain was cut, picking up and carrying away the stray kernels which had fallen from the sheaves. He never counted the places where food was stored, but he was happy in thinking about them. When he lay down to sleep in the morning he always knew where the next night's meals were coming from. There was not a thriftier, happier person in the forest. He was gentle, good-natured, and exceedingly businesslike. He was also very handsome, with large ears and white belly and feet.

The night after his cousins, the Meadow Mice, had been so frightened by the Grouse, this Deer Mouse started out for a good time. He called on the Meadow Mice, ate a chestnut which he dug up in the edge of the forest, scampered up a fence-post and tasted of his hidden wheat to be sure that it was keeping well, and then went to the tree where most of his beechnuts were stored. He was not quite certain that he wanted to eat one, but he wished to be sure that they were all right before he went on. He had been invited to a party by some other Deer Mice, and so, you see, it wouldn't do for him to spoil his appetite. They would be sure to have refreshments at the party.

"I suppose they are all right," said he, as he started to run up the tree; "still it is just as well to be sure."

"My whiskers!" he exclaimed, when he reached the hole. "If that isn't just like a Red Squirrel!"

The opening into the tree had been barely large enough for him to squeeze through, and now he could pass in without crushing his fur. Around the edge of it were many marks of sharp teeth. Somebody had wanted to get in and had not found the doorway large enough. The Deer Mouse went inside and sat on his beechnuts. Then he thought and thought and thought. He knew very well that it was a Red

Squirrel, for the Red Squirrels are not so thrifty as most of the nut-eaters. They make a great fuss about gathering food in the fall, and frisk and chatter and scold if anybody else comes where they are busy. For all that, the Chipmunks and the Deer Mice work much harder than they. It is not always the person who makes the greatest fuss, you know, who does the most.

A Red Squirrel is usually out of food long before spring comes, and after that he takes whatever he can lay his paws on. Sometimes the Chipmunks tell them that they should be ashamed of themselves and work harder. Then the Red Squirrels sigh and answer, "Oh, that is all very well for you to say, still you must remember that we have not such cheek pouches as you."

The Deer Mouse thought of these things. "Cheek pouches!" cried he. "I have no cheek pouches, but I lay up my own food. It is only an excuse when they say that. I don't think much of people who make excuses."

He passed through the doorway several times to see just how big it was. He found it was not yet large enough for a Red Squirrel. Then he scampered over the snow to a friend's home. "I'm not going to the party," said he. "I have some work to do."

"Work?" said the friend. "Work? In winter?" But before he had finished speaking his caller had gone.

All night long the Deer Mouse carried beechnuts from the old hiding-place to a new one. He wore quite a path in the snow between one tree and the other. His feet were tiny, but there were four of them, and his long tail dragged after him. It was not far that he had to go. The new place was one which he had looked at before. It was in a maple tree, and had a long and very narrow opening leading to the storeroom. It was having to go so far into the tree that had kept the Deer Mouse from using it before. Now he liked it all the better for having this.

"If that Red Squirrel ever gnaws his way in here," he said, "he won't have any teeth left for eating."

When the sun rose, the Deer Mouse went to sleep in the maple tree. The Red Squirrel came and gnawed at the opening into his old storeroom. If he had gnawed all day he would surely have gotten in. As it was, he had to spend much time hunting for food. He found some frozen apples still hanging in the orchard, and bit away at them until he reached the seeds inside. He found one large acorn, but it was old and tasted musty. He also squabbled with another Red Squirrel and chased him nearly to the farmyard. Then Collie heard them and chased him most of the way back.

When night came and he ran off to sleep in his hollow tree, he had made the hole almost, but not quite, large enough. He could smell the beechnuts inside, and it made him hungry to think how good they would taste. "I will get up early to-morrow morning and come here," he said. "I can gnaw my way in before breakfast, and then!"

He went off in fine leaps to his home and was soon sound asleep. In summer he often frolicked around half of the night, but now it was cold, and when the sun went down he liked to get home quickly and wrap up warmly in his tail. The Red Squirrel was hardly out of sight when the Deer Mouse came along his path in the snow and up to his old storeroom. His dainty white feet shook a little as he climbed, and he hardly dared look in for fear of finding the hole empty. You can guess how happy he was to find everything safe.

All night long he worked, and when morning came it was a very tired little Deer Mouse who carried his last beechnut over the trodden path to its safe new resting place. He was tired but he was happy.

There was just one other thing that he wanted to do. He wanted to see that Red Squirrel when he found the beechnuts gone. He waited near by for him to come. It was a beautiful, still winter morning when the hoar-frost clung to all the branches, and the shadows which fell upon the snow looked fairly blue, it was so cold. The Deer Mouse crouched down upon his dainty feet to keep them warm, and wrapped his tail carefully around to help.

Along came the Red Squirrel, dashing finely and not noticing the Deer Mouse at all. A few leaps brought him to the tree, a quick run took him to the hole, and then he began to gnaw. The Deer Mouse was growing sleepy and decided not to wait longer. He ran along near the Red Squirrel. "Oh, good-morning!" said he. "Beautiful day! I see you are getting that hole ready to use. Hope you will like it. I liked it very well for a while, but I began to fear it wasn't safe."

"Wh-what do you mean?" asked the Red Squirrel sternly. He had seen the Deer Mouse's eyes twinkle and he was afraid of a joke.

"Oh," answered the Deer Mouse with a careless whisk of his tail, "I had some beechnuts there until I moved them."

"You had!" exclaimed the Red Squirrel. He did not gnaw any after that. He suddenly became very friendly. "You couldn't tell me where to find food, I suppose," said he. "I'd eat almost anything."

The Deer Mouse thought for a minute. "I believe," said he, "that you will find plenty in the farmer's barn, but you must look out for the Dog."

"Thank you," said the Red Squirrel. "I will go."

"There!" said the Deer Mouse after he had whisked out of sight. "He has gone to steal from the farmer. Still, men have so very much that they ought to share with Squirrels."

And that, you know, is true.

The Complete Works of Clara Dillinham Pierson

The Humming-Bird And The Hawk-Moth

The Hawk-Moths are acquainted with nearly everybody and are great society people. They are invited to companies given by the daylight set, and also to parties given at night by those who sleep during the day. This is not because the Hawk-Moths are always awake. Oh dear, no! There is nobody in pond, forest, meadow, marsh, or even in houses, who can be well and strong and happy without plenty of sleep.

The Hawk-Moths were awake more or less during the day, but it was not until the sun was low in the western sky that they were busiest. When every tree had a shadow two or three times as long as the tree itself, then one heard the whir-r-r of wings and the Hawk-Moths darted past. They staid up long after the daylight people went to bed. The Catbird, who sang from the tip of the topmost maple tree branch long after most of his bird friends were asleep, said that when he tucked his head under his wing the Hawk-Moths were still flying. In that way, of course, they became acquainted with the people of the night-time.

There was one fine large Hawk-Moth who used to be a Tomato Worm when he was young, although he really fed as much upon potato vines as upon tomato plants. He was handsome from the tip of his long, slender sucking-tongue to the tip of his trim, gray body. His wings were pointed and light gray in color, with four blackish lines across the hind ones. His body was also gray, and over it and his wings were many dainty markings of black or very dark gray. On the back part of it he had ten square yellow spots edged with black. There were also twenty tiny white spots there, but he did not care so much for them. He always felt badly to think that his yellow spots showed so little. That couldn't be helped, of course, and he should have been thankful to have them at all.

Another thing which troubled him was the fact that he couldn't see his own yellow spots. He would have given a great deal to do so. He could see the yellow spots of other Hawk-Moths who had been Tomato Worms when he was, but that was not like seeing his own. He had tried and tried, and it always ended in the same way—his eyes were tired and his back ached. His body was so much stouter and stiffer than that of his butterfly cousins that he could not bend it easily.

When he got to thinking about his yellow spots he often flew away to the farmer's potato-fields, where the young Tomato Worms were feeding. He would fly around them and cry out: "Look at my yellow spots. Are they not fine?" Then he would dart away to the vegetable-garden and balance himself in the air over the tomato plants. The humming of his wings would make the Tomato Worms there look up, and he would say: "If you are good little Worms and eat a great deal, you may some day become fine Moths like me and have ten yellow spots apiece."

Sometimes he even went down to the corner where the farmer had tobacco plants growing, and showed his yellow spots to the Tomato Worms there. He never went anywhere else, for these worms do not care for other things to eat. Everywhere that he went the Tomato Worms exclaimed: "Oh! Oh! What beautiful yellow spots! What wonderful yellow spots!" When he flew away they would not eat for a while, but rested on their fat pro-legs, raised the front part of their bodies in the air, folded their six little real legs under their chins, and thought and thought and thought. They always sat in that position when they were thinking, and they had a great many cousins who did the same thing. It was a habit which ran in the family.

When other people saw them sitting in this way, with their real legs crossed under their chins, they always cried: "Look at the Sphinxes!" although not one of them knew what a Sphinx really was. And that was just one of their habits. This was why the Hawk-Moths were sometimes called Sphinx-Moths.

It was not kind in the Hawk-Moth to come and make the Tomato Worms discontented. If he had stayed away, they would have thought it the loveliest thing in the world to be fat green Tomato Worms with two sorts of legs and each with a horn standing up on the hind end of his body. That is not the usual place for horns, still it does very well, and these horns are worn only for looks. They are never used for poking or stinging.

Before the Hawk-Moth came to visit them, the Tomato Worms had thought it would be quiet, and restful, and pleasant to lie all winter in their shining brown pupa-cases in the ground, waiting for the spring to finish turning them into Moths. Now they were so impatient to get their yellow spots that they could hardly bear the idea of waiting. They did not even care about the long, slender tongue-case which every Tomato-Worm has on his pupa-case, and which looks like a handle to it.

One day the Tomato Worms told the Ruby-throated Humming-Bird about all this. The Humming-Bird was a very sensible fellow, and would no doubt have been a hard-working husband and father if his wife had not been so independent. He had been a most devoted lover, and helped build a charming nest of fern-wool and plant-down, and cover it with beautiful gray-green lichens. When done it was about as large as half of a hen's egg, and a morning-glory blossom would have more than covered it. The lichens were just the color of the branch on which it rested, and one could hardly see where it was. That is the nicest thing to be said about a nest. If a bird ever asks you what you think of his nest, and you wish to say something particularly agreeable, you must stare at the tree and ask: "Where is it?" Then, when he has shown it to you, you may speak of the soft lining, or the fine weaving, or the stout way in which it is fastened to the branches.

After this nest was finished and the two tiny white eggs laid in it, Mrs. Humming-Bird cared for nothing else. She would not go honey-hunting with her husband, or play in the air with him as she used to do. He tried to coax her by darting down toward her as she sat covering her eggs, and by squeaking the sweetest things he could think of into her ear, but she acted as though she cared more for the eggs than for him, and did not even squeak sweet things back. So, of course, he went away, and let her hatch and bring up her children as she chose. It was certainly her fault that he left her. She might not have been able to leave the eggs, but she could have squeaked.

Now that the Ruby-throated Humming-Bird had no home cares, he made many calls on his friends. They were very short calls, for he would seldom sit down, yet he heard and told much news while he balanced himself in the air with his tiny feet curled up and his wings moving so fast that one could not see them.

The Complete Works of Clara Dillinham Pierson

When the Tomato Worms told him how they felt about the Hawk-Moth's yellow spots, he became very indignant. "Those poor young worms!" he said to himself. "It is a shame, and something must be done about it."

The more he thought, the angrier he became, and his feathers fairly stood on end. He hardly knew what he was doing, and ran his long, slender bill into the same flowers several times, although he had taken all the honey from them at first.

That night, when the sun had set and the silvery moon was peeping above a violet-colored cloud in the eastern sky, the Ruby-throated Humming-Bird sat on the tip of a spruce-tree branch and waited for the Hawk-Moth.

"I hope nobody else will hear me talking," said he. "It would sound so silly if I were overheard." He sat very still, his tiny feet clutching the branch tightly. It was late twilight now and really time that he should go to sleep, but he had decided that if he could possibly keep awake he would teach the Hawk-Moth a lesson.

"I wish he would hurry," said he. "I can hardly keep my eyes open." He did not yawn because he had not the right kind of mouth for it. You know a yawn ought to be nearly round. His beak would have made one a great, great many times higher than it was wide, and that would have been exceedingly unbecoming to him.

Yellow evening primroses grew near the spruce-tree, and the tall stalks were opening their flowers for the night. Above the seed-pods and below the buds on each stalk two, three, or four blossoms were slowly unfolding. The Ruby-throated Humming-Bird did not often stay up long enough to see this, and he watched the four smooth yellow petals of one untwist themselves until they were free to spring wide open. He had watched five blossoms when he heard the Hawk-Moth coming. Then he darted toward the primroses and balanced himself daintily before one while he sucked honey from it.

Whir-r-r-r! The Hawk-Moth was there. "Good evening," said he. "Rather late for you, isn't it?"

"It is a little," answered the Humming-Bird. "Growing a bit chilly, too, isn't it? I should think you'd be cold without feathers. Mine are such a comfort. Feel as good as they look, and that is saying a great deal."

The Hawk-Moth balanced himself before another primrose and seemed to care more about sucking honey up his long tongue-tube than he did about talking.

"I think it is a great thing to have a touch of bright color, too," said the Humming-Bird. "The beautiful red spot on my throat looks particularly warm and becoming when the weather is cool. You ought to have something of the sort."

"I have yellow spots—ten of them," answered the Hawk-Moth sulkily.

"You have?" exclaimed the Humming-Bird in the most surprised way. "Oh yes! I think I do remember something about them. It is a pity they don't show more. Mrs. Humming-Bird never wears bright colors. She says it would not do. People would see her on her nest if she did. Excepting the red spot, she is dressed like me—white breast, green back and head, and black wings and tail. Green is another good color. You should wear some green."

The Hawk-Moth murmured that he didn't see any particular use in wearing green.

"Oh," said the Humming-Bird, "it is just the thing to wear—neat, never looks dusty" (here the Hawk-Moth drew back, for his own wings, you know, were almost dust color), "and matches the leaves perfectly."

The Hawk-Moth said something about having to go and thinking that the primrose honey was not so good as usual.

"I thought it excellent," said the Humming-Bird. "Perhaps you do not get it so easily as I. Ah yes, you use a tongue-tube. What different ways different people do have. Now I like honey, but I could not live many days on that alone. What I care most for is the tiny insects that I find eating it. And you cannot eat meat. What a pity! I must say that you seem to make the best of it, though, and do fairly well. Oh, must you go? Well, good night."

The Hawk-Moth flew away feeling very much disgusted. He had always thought himself the most beautiful person in the neighborhood. He rather thought so still. Yet it troubled him to know that others did not think so, and he began to remember how many times he had heard people admire the Ruby-throated Humming-Bird. He never liked him after that. But neither did he brag.

The young Tomato Worms soon forgot what the Hawk-Moth had said to them, and became happy and contented once more. The Ruby-throated Humming-Bird never cared to talk about it, yet he was once heard to say that he would rather offend the Hawk-Moth and even make him a little unhappy than to have him bothering the poor little Tomato Worms all the time.

Among the Pond People

The Biggest Frog Awakens

The Biggest Frog stretched the four toes of his right forefoot. Then he stretched the four toes of his left forefoot. Next he stretched the five toes of his right hindfoot. And last of all he stretched the four toes of his left hindfoot. Then he stretched all seventeen toes at once. He should have had eighteen toes to stretch, like his friends and neighbors, but something had happened to the eighteenth one a great many years before. None of the pond people knew what had happened to it, but *something* had, and when the Tadpoles teased him to tell them what, he only stared at them with his great eyes and said, "My children, that story is too sad to tell."

After the Biggest Frog had stretched all his toes, he stretched his legs and twitched his lips. He poked his head out of the mud a very, very little way, and saw a Minnow swimming past. "Good day!" said he. "Is it time to get up?"

"Time!" exclaimed the Minnow, looking at him with her mouth open. "I should say it was. Why, the watercress is growing!"

Now every one who lives in a pond knows that when the watercress begins to grow, it is time for all the winter sleepers to awaken. The Biggest Frog crawled out of the mud and poked this way and that all around the spot where he had spent the cold weather. "Wake up!" he said. "Wake up! Wake up!" The water grew dark and cloudy because he kicked up so much mud, but when it began to clear again he saw the heads of his friends peeping up everywhere out of that part of the pond bottom. Seven of them had huddled close to him all winter. "Come out!" he cried. "The spring is here, and it is no time for Frogs to be asleep."

"Asleep! No indeed!" exclaimed his sister, an elderly and hard-working Frog, as she swam to the shore and crawled out on it. She ate every bit of food that she found on the way, for neither she nor any of the others had taken a mouthful since the fall before.

The younger Frogs followed through the warmer shallow water until they were partly out of it. There is always a Biggest Frog in every pond. All the young Frogs thought how fine it would be to become the Biggest Frog of even a very small puddle, for then they could tell the others what to do. Now they looked at their leader and each said to himself, "Perhaps some day I shall begin the concert."

The Biggest Frog found a comfortable place and sat down. He toed in with his eight front toes, as well-bred frogs do, and all his friends toed in with their eight front toes. He toed out with his nine back toes, and all his friends toed out with their ten back toes. One young Yellow Brown Frog said, "How I wish I did not have that bothersome fifth toe on my left hindfoot! It is so in the way! Besides, there is such a style about having one's hind feet different." He spoke just loud enough for the Biggest Frog to hear. Any one would know from this remark that he was young and foolish, for when people are wise they know that the most beautiful feet and ears and bodies are just the way that they were first made to be.

Now the Biggest Frog swallowed a great deal of air, filled the sacs on each side of his neck with it, opened his big mouth, and sang croakily, "Frogs! Frogs! Frogs! Frogs! Frogs! Frogs! Frogs! Frogs!" And all the others sang, "Frogs! Frogs! Frogs!" as long as he. The Gulls heard it, and the Muskrats heard it, and all were happy because spring had come.

A beautiful young Green Brown Frog, who had never felt grown-up until now, tried to sing with the others, but she had not a strong voice, and was glad enough to stop and visit with the Biggest Frog's Sister. "Don't you wish we could sing as loudly as they can?" said she.

"No," answered the Biggest Frog's Sister. "I would rather sit on the bank and think about my spring work. Work first, you know, and pleasure afterward!"

"Oh!" said the Green Brown Frog. "Then you don't want to sing until your work is done?"

"You may be very sure I don't want to sing then," answered the older Frog. "I am too tired. Besides, after the eggs are laid, there is no reason for wanting to sing."

"Why not?" asked the Green Brown Frog. "I don't see what difference that makes."

"That," said the older Frog wisely, "is because you are young and have never laid eggs. The great time for singing is before the eggs are laid. There is some singing afterward, but that is only because people expect it of us, and not because we have the same wish to sing." After she had said all this, which was a great deal for a Frog to say at once, she shut her big mouth and slid her eyelids over her eyes.

There was another question which the Green Brown Frog wanted very much to ask, but she had good manners and knew that it was impolite to speak to any Frog whose eyes were not open. So she closed her own eyes and tried to think what the answer would be. When she opened them again, the Biggest Frog's Sister had hopped away, and in her place sat the Yellow Brown Frog, the same handsome young fellow who had found one of his toes in the way. It quite startled her to find him sitting so close to her and she couldn't think of anything to say, so she just looked at him with her great beautiful eyes and toed in a little more with her front feet. That made him look at them and see how pretty they were, although of course this was not the reason why she had moved them.

The Yellow Brown Frog hopped a little nearer and sang as loudly as he could, "Frogs! Frogs! Frogs! Frogs! Frogs! Frogs! Frogs! Frogs!" Then she knew that he was singing just for her, and she was exceedingly happy. She swallowed air very fast because she seemed to be out of breath from thinking what she should answer. She had wanted to ask the Biggest Frog's Sister what she should say if any one sang to her alone. She knew that if she wanted to get away from him, all she had to do was to give a great jump and splash into the water. She didn't want to go away, yet she made believe that she did, for she hopped a little farther from him.

He knew she was only pretending, though, for she hadn't hopped more than the length of a grass-blade. So he followed her and kept on singing. Because she knew that she must say something, she just opened her mouth and sang the first words that she could think of; and what she sang was, "Eggs! Eggs! Eggs! Eggs! Eggs! Eggs! Eggs! Eggs!" As it happened, this was exactly what she should have sung, so he knew that she liked him. They stayed together for a long, long time, and he sang a great deal and very loudly, and she sang a little and very softly.

After a while she remembered that she was now a fully grown Frog and had spring work to do, and she said to him, "I really must lay some eggs. I am going into the water."

"Then I will go too," said he. And they gave two great leaps and came down with two great splashes.

The Green Brown Frog laid eggs for four days, and the Yellow Brown Frog stayed with her all that time and took care of the eggs after she had laid them. They were covered with a sort of green jelly which made them stick to each other as they floated in little heaps on the water. The Frogs thought that a good thing, for then, when the Tadpoles hatched, each would have playmates near.

One day, after the eggs were all laid and were growing finely (for Frogs' eggs grow until the Tadpoles are ready to eat their way out), the Green Brown Frog sat alone on the bank of the pond and the Biggest Frog's Sister came to her. She had a queer smile around the corners of her mouth. Frogs have excellent mouths for smiling, but it takes a very broad smile to go way across, so when they smile a little it is only at the corners. "How are your eggs growing?" she asked.

"Oh," answered the Green Brown Frog sadly, "I can't tell which ones they are."

"That's just like a young Frog," said the Biggest Frog's Sister. "Is there any reason why you should know which ones they are? It isn't as though you were a bird and had to keep them warm, or as though you were a Mink and had to feed your children. The sun will hatch them and they will feed themselves all they need."

"I think," said the Green Brown Frog, "that my eggs were a little better than the rest."

"Yes," croaked the Biggest Frog's Sister, "every Frog thinks that."

"And I wanted to have my own Tadpoles to look after," sighed the Green Brown Frog.

"Why?" asked the Biggest Frog's Sister. "Can't you take any comfort with a Tadpole unless you laid the egg from which he was hatched? I never know one of my own eggs a day after it is laid. There are such a lot floating around that they are sure to get mixed. But I just make the best of it."

"How?" asked the Green Brown Frog, looking a little more cheerful.

"Oh, I swim around and look at all the eggs, and whenever I see any Tadpoles moving in them I think, 'Those may be mine!' As they are hatched I help any one who needs it. Poor sort of Frog it would be who couldn't like other people's Tadpoles!"

"I believe I'll do that way," said the Green Brown Frog. "And then," she added, "what a comfort it will be if any of them are cross or rude, to think, 'I'm glad I don't know that they are mine.'"

"Yes," said the Biggest Frog's Sister. "I often tell my brother that I pity people who have to bring up their own children. It is much pleasanter to let them grow up as they do and then adopt the best ones. Do you know, I have almost decided that you are my daughter? My brother said this morning that he thought you looked like me."

The Dance Of The Sand-Hill Cranes

One fine day in spring, a great flock of Sand-hill Cranes came from the south. They were flying high and quietly because the weather was bright. If it had been stormy, or if they had been flying by night, as they usually did, they would have stayed nearer the ground, and their leader would have trumpeted loudly to let his followers know which way he was going. They would also have trumpeted, but more softly, to tell him that they were coming after.

They were a fine company to look upon, orderly, strong, and dignified. Their long necks were stretched out straight ahead, their long legs straight behind, and they beat the air with slow, regular strokes of the strong wings. As they came near the pond, they flew lower and lower, until all swept down to the earth and alighted, tall and stately, by the edge of the water.

They had eaten nothing for several days, and were soon hunting for food, some on land, and some in the water, for they had stopped to feed and rest. Those who hunted in the water, did so very quietly. A Crane would stand on one leg, with his head against his breast, so quietly that one might think him asleep: but as soon as anything eatable came near, he would bend his body, stretch out his neck, open his long, slender bill, and swallow it at one gulp. Then he would seem to fall asleep again.

While most of the Cranes were still feeding, some of them were stalking through the woods and looking this way and that, flying up to stand on a tree, and then flying down to stand on the ground. They were those who thought of staying there for the summer.

When the flock arose to fly on again, eight Cranes stayed behind. They watched their friends fly away, and stood on the ground with their necks and bills uplifted and mouths open, while they trumpeted or called out, "Good-bye! Stop for us in the fall!" The flying Cranes trumpeted back, "We will! Don't forget us!"

That night they slept near together, as they had done when with the large flock, and one Crane kept awake to watch for danger while the others tucked their heads under their wings. They were fine looking, even when they slept, and some people never look well unless they are awake. They were brownish-gray, with no bright markings at all, and their long legs gave them a very genteel look. The tops of their heads were covered with warty red skin, from which grew short black feathers that looked more like hairs.

One morning, when the Cranes awakened, a fine young fellow began to strut up and down before the rest, bowing low, and leaping high into the air, and every now and then whooping as loudly as he could. The Gulls, who had spent the winter by the pond, screamed to each other, "The Crane dance has begun!" Even the Frogs, who are afraid of Cranes, crept quietly near to look on.

It was not long before another young Crane began to skip and hop and circle around, drooping his wings and whooping as he went. Every Crane danced, brothers, and sisters, and all, and as they did so, they looked lovingly at each other, and admired the fine steps and enjoyed the whooping. This went on until they were so tired they could hardly stand, and had to stop to eat and rest.

When they were eating, the young fellow who had begun the dance, stalked up to the sister of one of his friends, as she stood in the edge of the pond, gracefully balanced on one leg. She did not turn her head towards him, although, having such a long and slender neck, she could have done so with very little trouble. She stood with her head on her breast and looked at the water. After a while, he trumpeted softly, as though he were just trying his voice. Then she gave a pretty little start, and said, "Oh, are you here? How you did frighten me!"

"I am sorry," he said. "I did not want to frighten you." And he looked at her admiringly.

"It was just for a minute," she answered. "Of course I am not frightened now that I know who it is."

Then they stood and fished for a long time without saying anything. When she flew away, she said, "That is a very pleasant fishing-place." He stood on the other leg for a while, and thought how sweet her voice sounded as she said it. Then he thought that, if she liked the place so well, she might come there again the next day. He wondered why he could not come too, although everybody knows that a Crane catches more if he fishes alone.

The next morning, when the Cranes danced, he bowed to her oftener than to any of the rest, and he thought she noticed it. They danced until they were almost too tired to move, and indeed he had to rest for a while before he went to feed. As she stalked off toward the pond, she passed him, and she said over her shoulder, "I should think you would be hungry. I am almost starved." After she had gone, he wondered why she had said that. If he had been an older Crane, and understood the ways of the world a little better, he would have known that she meant, "Aren't you coming to that fishing-place? I am going now." Still, although he was such a young Crane and had never danced until this year, he began to think that she liked him and enjoyed having him near. So he flew off to the fishing-place where he had seen her the day before, and he stalked along to where she was, and stood close to her while she fished. Once, when he caught something and swallowed it at one gulp, she looked admiringly at him and said, "What fine, big mouthfuls you can take!"

That pleased him, of course, because Cranes think that big mouthfuls are the best kind, so he tipped his head to one side, and watched his neck as the mouthful slid down to his stomach. He could see it from the outside, a big bunch slowly moving downward. He often did this while he was eating. He thought it very interesting. He pitied short-necked people. Then he said, "Pooh! I can take bigger mouthfuls than that. You ought to see what big mouthfuls I can take."

She changed, and stood on her other leg. "I saw you dancing this morning," she said. Now it was not at all queer that she should have seen him dancing, for all the eight Cranes had danced together, but he thought it very wonderful.

"Did you notice to whom I bowed?" he asked. He was so excited that his knees shook, and he had to stand on both legs at once to keep from falling. When a Crane is as much excited as that, it is pretty serious.

"To my sister?" she asked carelessly, as she drew one of her long tail-feathers through her beak.

"No," said he. "I bowed to her sister." He thought that was a very clever thing to say. But she suddenly raised her head, and said, "There! I have forgotten something," and flew off, as she had done the day before. He wondered what it was. Long afterward he asked her what she had forgotten and she said she couldn't remember—that she never could remember what she had forgotten.

It made him feel very badly to have her leave him so. He wanted a chance to tell her something, yet, whenever he tried to, it seemed to stick in his bill. He began to fear that she didn't like him; and the next time the Cranes danced he didn't bow to her so much, but he strutted and leaped and whooped even more. And she strutted and leaped and whooped almost as loudly as he. When they were all tired out and had stopped dancing, she said to him, "I am so tired! Let us go off into the woods and rest."

You may be very sure he was glad to go, and as he stalked off with her, he led the way to a charming nesting-place. He didn't know just how to tell what he wanted to, but he had seen another Crane bowing to her, and was afraid she might marry him if he was not quick. Now he pointed with one wing to this nesting-place, and said, "How would you like to build a nest there?"

She looked where he had pointed, "I?" she said. "Why, it is a lovely place, but I could never have a nest alone."

"Let me help you," he said. "I want to marry and have a home."

"Why," said she, as she preened her feathers, "that is a very good plan. When did you think of it?"

So they were married, and Mrs. Sand-Hill Crane often told her friends afterward that Mr. Crane was so much in love with her that she just *had* to marry him. They were very, very happy, and after a while—but that is another story.

The Young Minnow Who Would Not Eat When He Should

"When I grow up," said one young Minnow, "I am going to be a Bullhead, and scare all the little fishes."

"I'm not," said his sister. "I'm going to be a Sucker, and lie around in the mud."

"Lazy! Lazy!" cried the other young Minnows, wiggling their front fins at her.

"What is the matter?" asked a Father Minnow, swimming in among them with a few graceful sweeps of his tail, and stopping himself by spreading his front fins. He had the beautiful scarlet coloring on the under part of his body which Father Minnows wear in the summer-time. That is, most of them do, but some wear purple. "What is the matter?" he asked again, balancing himself with his top fin and his two hind ones.

Then all the little Minnows spoke at once. "He says that when he grows up he is going to be a Bullhead, and frighten all the small fishes; and she says that she is going to be a Sucker, and lie around in the mud; and we say that Suckers are lazy, and they *are* lazy, aren't they?"

"I am surprised at you," began the Father Minnow severely, "to think that you should talk such nonsense. You ought to know——"

But just then a Mother Minnow swam up to him. "The Snapping Turtle is looking for you," she said. Father Minnow hurried away and she turned to the little ones. "I heard what you were saying," she remarked, with a twinkle in her flat, round eyes. "Which of you is going to be a Wild Duck? Won't somebody be a Frog?" She had had more experience in bringing up children than Father Minnow, and she didn't scold so much. She did make fun of them though, sometimes; and you can do almost anything with a young Minnow if you love him a great deal and make fun of him a little.

"Why-ee!" said the young Minnows. "We wouldn't think of being Wild Ducks, and we couldn't be Frogs, you know. Frogs have legs—four of them. A fish couldn't be a Frog if he wanted to!"

"No," said Mother Minnow. "A fish cannot be anything but a fish, and a Minnow cannot be anything but a Minnow. So if you will try to be just as good Minnows as you can, we will let the little Bullheads and Suckers do their own growing up."

She looked at them all again with her flat, round eyes, which saw so much and were always open, because there was nothing to make them shut. She saw one tiny fellow hiding behind his brother. "Have you torn your fin again?" she asked.

"Yes'm, just a little," said he. "A boy caught me when he was in wading, and I tore it when I flopped away from him."

"Dreadful!" said she. "How you do look! If you are so careless, you will soon not have a whole fin to your back—or your front either. Children, you must remember to swim away from boys. When the Cows wade in to drink, you may stay among them, if you wish. They are friendly. We pond people are afraid of boys, although some of them are said not to be dangerous."

"Pooh!" said one young Minnow. "All the pond people are not so afraid! The Bloodsuckers say they like them."

The Mother Minnow looked very severe when he said this, but she only replied, "Very well. When you are a Bloodsucker you may stay near boys. As long as you are a Minnow, you must stay away."

"Now," she added, "swim along, the whole school of you! I am tired and want a nap in the pondweed." So they all swam away, and she wriggled her silvery brown body into the soft green weeds and had a good sleep. She was careful to hide herself, for there were some people in the pond whom she did not want to have find her; and, being a fish, she could not hear very distinctly if they came near. Of course her eyes were open even when she was asleep, because she had no eyelids, but they were not working although they were open. That is an uncomfortable thing about being a fish—one cannot hear much. One cannot taste much either, or feel much, yet when one has always been a fish and is used to it, it is not so hard.

She slept a long time, and then the whole school of young Minnows came to look for her. "We are afraid," they cried. "We feel so very queerly. We don't know how we feel, either, and that is the worst part of it. It might be in our stomachs, or it might be in our fins, and perhaps there is something wrong with our gill-covers. Wake up and tell us what is the matter."

The Mother Minnow awakened and she felt queerly too, but, being older, she knew what was the matter. "That," she said, "is the storm feeling."

"But," said the young Minnows, "there isn't any storm."

"No," she answered wisely. "Not now."

"And there hasn't been any," they said.

"No," she answered again. "The storm you feel is the storm that is going to be."

"And shall we always feel it so?" they asked.

"Always before a storm," she said.

"Why?" asked the young Minnows.

"Because," said she. "There is no answer to that question, but just 'because.' When the storm comes you cannot smell your food and find it, so you must eat all you can before then. Eat *everything* you can find and be quick." As she spoke she took a great mouthful of pondweed and swallowed it.

All but one of the young Minnows swam quickly away to do as she had told them to. This young Minnow wanted to know just how and why and all about it, so he stayed to ask questions. You know there are some questions which fishes cannot answer, and some which Oxen cannot answer, and some which nobody can answer; and when the Mother Minnow told the young Minnows what she did, she had nothing more to tell. But there are some young Minnows who never will be satisfied, and who tease, and tease, and tease, and tease.

"Hurry along and eat all you can," said the Mother Minnow to him again.

"I want to know," said he, opening his mouth very wide indeed and breathing in a great deal of water as he spoke, "I want to know where I feel queerly."

"I can't tell," said the Mother Minnow, between mouthfuls. "No fish can tell."

"Well, what makes me feel queerly there?"

"The storm," said she.

"How does it make me feel queerly?"

"I don't know," said the Mother Minnow.

"Who does know?" asked the young Minnow.

"Nobody," said she, swallowing some more pondweed of one kind and then beginning on another. "Do eat something or you will be very hungry by and by."

"Well, why does a storm make me feel so?" asked he.

"Because!" said she. She said it very firmly and she was quite right in saying it then, for there was a cause, yet she could not tell what it was. There are only about seven times in one's life when it is right to answer in this way, and what the other six are you must decide for yourself.

Just then there was a peal of thunder which even a Minnow could hear, and the wind blew until the slender forest trees bent far over. The rain came down in great drops which pattered on the water of the pond and started tiny circles around each drop, every circle spreading wider and wider until it touched other circles and broke. Down in the darkened water the fishes lay together on the bottom, and wondered how long it would last, and hoped it would not be a great, great while before they could smell their food again.

One little fellow was more impatient than the others. "Didn't you eat enough to last you?" they said.

"I didn't eat anything," he answered.

"Not anything!" they exclaimed. "Why not?"

"Because!" said he. And that was not right, for he did know the reason. His mother looked at him, and he looked at her, and she had a twinkle in her round, flat eyes. "Poor child!" she thought. "He must be hungry." But she said nothing.

The Stickleback Father

Nobody can truthfully say that the Sticklebacks are not good fathers. There are no other fish fathers who work so hard for their children as the Sticklebacks do. As to the Stickleback Mothers—well, that is different.

This particular Stickleback Father had lived, ever since he had left the nest, with a little company of his friends in a quiet place near the edge of the pond. Sometimes, when they tired of staying quietly at home, they had made short journeys up a brook that emptied into the pond. It was a brook that flowed gently over an even bed, else they would never have gone there, for Sticklebacks like quiet waters. When they swam in this little stream, they met the Brook Trout, who were much larger than they, and who were the most important people there.

Now this Stickleback was a year old and knew much more than he did the summer before. When the alder tassels and pussy willows hung over the edge of the pond in the spring-time, he began to think seriously of life. He was no longer really young, and the days were past in which he was contented to just swim and eat and sleep. It was time he should build a home and raise a family if he wanted to ever be a grandfather. He had a few relatives who were great-grandfathers, and one who was a great-great-grandfather. That does not often happen, because to be a Stickleback Great-great-grandfather, one must be four years old, and few Sticklebacks live to that age.

As he began to think about these things, he left the company of his friends and went to live by himself. He chose a place near the edge of the pond to be his home; and he brushed the pond-bottom there with his tail until he had swept away all the loose sticks and broken shells. He told some Pond Snails, who were there, that they must move away because he wanted the place. At first they didn't want to go, but when they saw how fierce he looked, they thought about it again and decided that perhaps there were other places which would suit them quite as well—indeed, they might find one that they liked even better. Besides, as one of them said to his brother, they had to remember that in ponds it is always right for the weak people to give up to the strong people.

"It will take us quite a while to move," they said to him, "for you know we cannot hurry, but we will begin at once."

All the rest of that day each Snail was lengthening and shortening his one foot, which was his only way of walking. You can see how slow that must be, for a Snail cannot lift his foot from one place and put it down in another, or he would have nothing to stand on while he was lifting it. This was a very hard day for them, yet they were cheerful and made the best of it.

"Well," said one, as he stopped to rest his foot, "I'm glad we don't have to build a home when we do find the right place. How I pity people who have to do that!"

"Yes," said his brother. "There are not many so sure of their homes as we. And what people want of so much room, I can't understand! A Muskrat told me he wanted room to turn around in his house. I don't see what use there is in turning round, do you?"

"No," answered the other Snail, beginning to walk again. "It is just one of his silly ideas. My shell is big enough to let me draw in my whole body, and that is house room enough for any person!"

The Stickleback had not meant to look fierce at the Pond Snails. He had done so because he couldn't help it. All his fins were bristling with sharp points of bone, and he had extra bone-points sticking out of his back, besides wearing a great many of his flat bones on the outside. All his family had these extra bones, and that was why they were called Sticklebacks. They were a brave family and not afraid of many things, although they were so small. There came a time when the Stickleback Father wanted to look fierce, but that was later. Now he went to work to build his nest.

First he made a little hollow in the pond-bottom, and lined it with watergrass and tiny pieces of roots. Next, he made the side-walls of the same things, and last of all, the roof. When it was done, he swam carefully into it and looked around. Under and beside and over him were soft grasses and roots. At each end was an open doorway. "It is a good nest," he said, "a very good nest for my first one. Now I must ask some of my friends to lay eggs in it for me."

Before doing this, he went to look at the homes built by his neighbors. After he left the company in the quiet pool, many others did the same, until the only Sticklebacks left there were the dull-colored ones, the egg-layers. The nest-builders had been dull-colored, too, but in the spring-time there came beautiful red and blue markings on their bodies, until now they were very handsome fellows. It is sad to tell, still it is true, that they also became very cross at this time. Perhaps it was the work and worry of nest-building that made them so, yet, whatever it was, every bright-colored Stickleback wanted to fight every other bright-colored Stickleback. That was how it happened that, when this one went to look at the nest of an old friend, with whom he had played ever since he was hatched, this same friend called out, "Don't you come near my nest!"

The visiting Stickleback replied, "I shall if I want to!" Then they swam at each other and flopped and splashed and pushed and jabbed until both were very tired and sore, and each was glad to stay by his own home. This was the time when they wanted to look fierce.

Soon the dull-colored Sticklebacks came swimming past, waving their tails gracefully, and talking to each other. Now this fine fellow, who had sent the Snails away and built his nest, who had fought his old friend and come home again, swam up to a dull-colored Stickleback, and said, "Won't you lay a few eggs in my nest? I'm sure you will find it comfortable."

She answered, "Why, yes! I wouldn't mind laying a few there." And she tried to look as though she had not expected the invitation. While she was carefully laying the eggs in the nest, he stood ready to fight anybody who disturbed her. She came out after a while and swam away. Before she went, she said, "Aren't you ashamed to fight so? We dull-colored ones never fight." She held her fins very stiff as she spoke, because she thought it her duty to scold him. The dull-colored Sticklebacks often did this. They thought that they were a little better than the others; so they swam around together and talked about things, and sometimes forgot how hard it was to be the nest-builder and stay at home and work. Then they called upon the bright-colored Sticklebacks, for they really liked them very much, and told them what they should do. That was why this one said, "We dull-colored ones never fight."

"Have you ever been red and blue?" asked the nest-builder.

"N—no," said she. "But I don't see what difference that makes."

"Well, it does make a difference," said he. "When a fellow is red and blue, he can't help fighting. I'll be as good-natured as any of you after I stop being red and blue."

Of course she could not say anything more after that, so she swam off to her sisters. The bright-colored Stickleback looked at the eggs she had laid. They were sticky, like the eggs of all fishes, so that they stuck to the bottom of the nest. He covered them carefully, and after that he was really a Stickleback Father. It is true that he did not have any Stickleback children to swim around him and open their dear little mouths at him, but he knew that the eggs would hatch soon, and that after he had built a nest and covered the eggs in it, the tiny Sticklebacks were beginning to grow.

However, he wanted more eggs in his nest, so he watched for another dull-colored Stickleback and called her in to help him. He did this until he had almost an hundred eggs there, and all this time he had fought every bright-colored Stickleback who came near him. He became very tired indeed; but he had to fight, you know, because he was red and blue. And he had covered all the eggs and guarded them, else they would never have hatched.

The dull-colored Sticklebacks were also tired. They had been swimming from nest to nest, laying a few eggs in each. Now they went off together to a quiet pool and ate everything they could find to eat, and visited with each other, and said it was a shame that the bright-colored Sticklebacks had fought so, and told how they thought little Sticklebacks should be brought up.

And now the red and blue markings on the Stickleback Father grew paler and paler, until he did not have to fight at all, and could call upon his friends and see how their children were hatching. One fine day, his first child broke the shell, and then another and another, until he had an hundred beautiful Stickleback babies to feed. He worked hard for them, and some nights, when he could stop and rest, his fins ached as though they would drop off. But they never did.

As the Stickleback children grew stronger, they swam off to take care of themselves, and he had less to do. When the last had gone, he left the old nest and went to the pool where the dull-colored Sticklebacks were. They told him he was not looking well, and that he hadn't managed the children right, and that they thought he tried to do too much.

He was too tired to talk about it, so he just said, "Perhaps," and began to eat something. Yet, down in his fatherly heart he knew it was worth doing. He knew, too, that when spring should come once more, he would become red and blue again, and build another nest, and fight and work and love as he had done before. "There is nothing in the world better than working for one's own little Sticklebacks," said he.

The Careless Caddis Worm

When the Caddis Fly felt like laying eggs, she crawled down the stalk of one of the pond plants and laid them there. She covered them with something sticky, so that they were sure to stay where she put them. "There!" she said, as she crawled up to the air again. "My work is done." Soon after this, she lay down for a long, long rest. What with flying, and visiting, and laying eggs, she had become very tired; and it was not strange, for she had not eaten a mouthful since she got her wings.

This had puzzled the Dragon-Flies very much. They could not understand it, because they were always eating. They would have liked to ask her about it, but they went to sleep for the night soon after she got up, and whenever she saw them coming she flew away. "I do not seem to feel hungry," said she, "so why should I eat? Besides," she added, "I couldn't eat if I wanted to, my mouth is so small and weak. I ate a great deal while I was growing—quite enough to last me—and it saves time not to bother with hunting food now."

When her eggs hatched, the larvæ were slender, soft, six-footed babies called Caddis Worms. They were white, and they showed as plainly in the water as a pond-lily does on the top of it. It is not safe to be white if one is to live in the water; certainly not unless one can swim fast and turn quickly. And there is a reason for this, as any one of the pond people will tell you. Even the fishes wear all their white on the under side of their bodies, so that if they swim near the top of the water, a hungry Fish Hawk is not so likely to see them and pounce down on them.

The Caddis Worms soon found that white was not a good color to wear, and they talked of it among themselves. They were very bright larvæ. One day the biggest one was standing on a stem of pickerel-weed, when his sister came toward him. She did not come very fast, because she was neither swimming nor walking, but biting herself along. All the Caddis Worms did this at times, for their legs were weak. She reached as far forward as she could, and fastened her strong jaws in the weed, then she gave a jerk and pulled her body ahead. "It is a very good way to travel," said she, "and such a saving of one's legs." Now she was in so great a hurry that sometimes when she pulled herself ahead, she turned a half-somersault and came down on her back.

"What is the matter?" called the Biggest Caddis Worm. "Don't hurry so. There is lots of time." That was just him, for he was lazy. Everybody said so.

"I must hurry," said she, and she breathed very fast with the white breathing hairs that grew on both sides of her body. She picked herself up from her last somersault and stood beside her brother, near enough to speak quite softly. "I have been getting away from Belostoma," she said, "and I was dreadfully afraid he would catch me."

"Well, you're all right now, aren't you?" asked her brother. And that was also like him. As long as he could have enough to eat and was comfortable, he did not want to think about anything unpleasant.

"No, I'm not," she answered, "and I won't be so long as any hungry fish or water-bug can see me so plainly. I'm tired of being white."

"You are not so white as you were," said her brother. "None of us children are. Our heads and the front part of our bodies are turning brown and getting harder." That was true, and he was particularly hard-headed.

"Yes, but what about the rest of us?" said she, and surely there was some excuse for her if she was impatient. "If Belostoma can see part of me and chase that, he will find the rest of me rather near by."

"Keep quiet then, and see if you don't get hard and brown all over," said he.

"I never shall," said she. "I went to the Clams and asked them if I would, and they said 'No.' I'm going to build a house to cover the back part of my body, and you'd better do the same thing."

The Biggest Caddis Worm looked very much surprised. "Whatever made you think of that?" said he.

"I suppose because there wasn't anything else to think of," said she. "One has to think of something."

"I don't," said he.

She started away to where her other brothers and sisters were. "Where are you going?" cried he.

"Going to build my house," answered she. "You'd better come too."

"Not now," said he. "I am waiting to get the rest of my breakfast. I'll come by and by."

The Biggest Caddis Worm stood on the pickerel-weed and ate his breakfast. Then he stood there a while longer. "I do not think it is well to work right after eating," he said. Below him in the water, his brothers and sisters were busily gathering tiny sticks, stones, and bits of broken shell, with which to make their houses. Each Caddis Worm found his own, and fastened them together with a sort of silk which he pulled out of his body. They had nobody to show them how, so each planned to suit himself, and no two were exactly alike.

"I'm going to make my house big enough so I can pull in my head and legs when I want to," said one.

"So am I," cried all the other Caddis Worms.

After a while, somebody said, "I'm going to have an open door at the back of my house." Then each of his busy brothers and sisters cried, "So am I."

When the tiny houses were done, each Caddis Worm crawled inside of his own, and lay with head and legs outside the front door. The white part of their bodies did not show at all, and, if they wanted to do so, they could pull their heads in. Even Belostoma, the Giant Water-Bug, might have passed close to them then and not seen them at all.

"Let's hook ourselves in!" cried one Caddis Worm, and all the others answered, "Let's."

So each hooked himself in with the two stout hooks which grew at the end of his body, and there they were as snug and comfortable as Clams. About this time the Big Brother came slowly along the stem of pickerel-weed. "What," said he, "you haven't got your houses done already?"

"Yes," answered the rest joyfully. "See us pull in our heads." And they all pulled in their heads and poked them out again. He was the only white-bodied person in sight.

"I must have a home," said he. "I wish one of you Worms would give me yours. You could make yourself another, you know. There is lots more stuff."

"Make it yourself," they replied. "Help yourself to stuff."

"But I don't know how," he said, "and you do."

"Whose fault is that?" asked his sister. Then she was afraid that he might think her cross, and she added quickly, "We'll tell you how, if you'll begin."

The Biggest Caddis Worm got together some tiny sticks and stones and pieces of broken shell, but it wasn't very much fun working alone. Then they told him what to do, and how to fasten them to each other with silk. "Be sure you tie them strongly," they said.

"Oh, that's strong enough," he answered. "It'll do, anyhow. If it comes to pieces I can fix it." His brothers and sisters thought he should make it stouter, yet they said nothing more, for he would not have liked it if they had; and they had already said so once. When he crawled into his house and hooked himself in, there was not a Caddis Worm in sight, and they were very proud to think how they had planned and built their houses. They did not know that Caddis Worms had always done so, and they thought themselves the first to ever think of such a thing.

The Biggest Caddis Worm's house was not well fastened together, and every day he said, "I really must fix it to-morrow." But when to-morrow came, it always proved to be to-day, and, besides, he usually found something more interesting to be done. It took him a great deal of time to change his skin, and that could not be easily put off. He grew so fast that he was likely to awaken almost any morning and find his head poking through the top of his skin, and, lazy as he was, he would not have the pond people see him around with a crack in the skin of his head, right where it showed. So when this happened, he always pulled his body through the crack, and threw the old skin away. There was sure to be a whole new one underneath, you know.

When they had changed their skin many times, the Caddis Worms became more quiet and thoughtful. At last the sister who had first planned to build houses, fastened hers to a stone, and spun gratings across both its front and its back doors. "I am going to sleep," she said, "to grow my feelers and get ready to fly and breathe air. I don't want anybody to awaken me. All I want to do is to sleep and grow and breathe. The water will come in through the gratings, so I shall be all right. I couldn't sleep in a house where there was not plenty of fresh water to breathe." Then she cuddled down and dozed off, and when her brothers and sisters spoke of her, they called her "the Caddis Nymph."

They did not speak of her many times, however, for they soon fastened their houses to something solid, and spun gratings in their doorways and went to sleep.

One day a Water-Adder came around where all the Caddis houses were. "Um-hum," said he to himself. "There used to be a nice lot of Caddis Worms around here, and now I haven't seen one in ever so long. I suppose they are hidden away somewhere asleep. Well, I must go away from here and find my dinner. I am nearly starved. The front half of my stomach hasn't a thing in it." He whisked his tail and went away, but that whisk hit a tiny house of sticks, stones, and bits of broken shell, and a fat sleeping Caddis Nymph rolled out. It was the Biggest Brother.

Soon Belostoma, the Giant Water-Bug, came that way. "What is this?" he exclaimed, as he saw the sleeping Caddis Nymph. "Somebody built a poor house to sleep in. You need to be cared for, young Caddis." He picked up the sleeping Caddis Nymph in his stout forelegs and swam off. Nobody knows just what happened after that.

When the other Caddis Nymphs awakened, they bit through their gratings and had a good visit before they crawled out of the pond into their new home, the air. "Has anybody seen my biggest brother?" asked one Nymph of another, but everybody answered, "No."

Each looked all around with his two far-apart eyes, and then they decided that he must have awakened first and left the water before them. But you know that he could not have done so, because he could never be a Caddis Fly unless he finished the Nymph-sleep in his house, and he did not do that. He had stopped being a Caddis Worm when he turned into a Caddis Nymph. Nobody will ever know just what did become of him unless Belostoma tells—and Belostoma is not likely to tell.

The Tadpole Who Wanted To Be Grown-Up

It was a bright, warm April day when the First Tadpole of the season ate his way out of the jelly-covered egg in which he had come to life. He was a very tiny, dark brown fellow. It would be hard to tell just what he did look like, for there is nothing in the world that one Tadpole looks like unless it is another Tadpole. He had a very small head with a busy little mouth opening on the front side of it: just above each end of this mouth was a shining black eye, and on the lower side of his head was a very wiggly tail. Somewhere between his head and the tip of this were his small stomach and places for legs, but one could not see all that in looking at him. It seemed as if what was not head was tail, and what was not tail was head.

When the First Tadpole found himself free in the water, he swam along by the great green floating jelly-mass of Frogs' eggs, and pressed his face up close to first one egg and then another. He saw other Tadpoles almost as large as he, and they were wriggling inside their egg homes. He couldn't talk to them through the jelly-mass—he could only look at them, and they looked greenish because he saw them through green jelly. They were really dark brown, like him. He wanted them to come out to play with him and he tried to show them that it was more interesting where he was, so he opened and shut his hard little jaws very fast and took big Tadpole-mouthfuls of green jelly.

Perhaps it was seeing this, and perhaps it was because the warm sunshine made them restless—but for some reason the shut-in Tadpoles nibbled busily at the egg-covering and before long were in the water with their brother. They all looked alike, and nobody except that one particular Tadpole knew who had been the first to hatch. He never forgot it, and indeed why should he? If one has ever been the First Tadpole, he is quite sure to remember the loneliness of it all his life.

Soon they dropped to the bottom of the pond and met their neighbors. They were such little fellows that nobody paid much attention to them. The older pond people often seemed to forget that the Tadpoles heard what they said, and cared too. The Minnows swam in and out among them, and hit them with their fins, and slapped them with their tails, and called them "little-big-mouths," and the Tadpoles couldn't hit back because they were so little. The Minnows didn't hurt the Tadpoles, but they made fun of them, and even the smallest Minnow would swim away if a Tadpole tried to play with him.

Then the Eels talked among themselves about them. "I shall be glad," said one old Father Eel, "when these youngsters hide their breathing-gills and go to the top of the water."

"So shall I," exclaimed a Mother Eel. "They keep their tails wiggling so that it hurts my eyes to look at them. Why can't they lie still and be good?"

Now the Tadpoles looked at each other with their shining black eyes. "What are our breathing-gills?" they asked. "They must be these little things on the sides of our heads."

"They are!" cried the First Tadpole. "The Biggest Frog said so. But I don't see where we can hide them, because they won't come off. And how could we ever breathe water without them?"

"Hear the children talk," exclaimed the Green Brown Frog, who had come down to look the Tadpoles over and decide which were hers. "Why, you won't always want to breathe water. Before long you will have to breathe air by swallowing it, and then you cannot stay long under water. I must go now. I am quite out of breath. Good-bye!"

Then the Tadpoles looked again at each other. "She didn't tell us what to do with our breathing-gills," they said. One of the Tadpoles who had hatched last, swam up to the First Tadpole. "Your breathing-gills are not so large as mine," she said.

"They surely are!" he exclaimed, for he felt very big indeed, having been the first to hatch.

"Oh, but they are not!" cried all his friends. "They don't stick out as they used to." And that was true, for his breathing-gills were sinking into his head, and they found that this was happening to all the older Tadpoles.

The next day they began going to the top to breathe air, the oldest ones first, and so on until they were all there. They thought it much pleasanter than the bottom of the pond, but it was not so safe. There were more dangers to be watched for here, and some of the careless young Tadpoles never lived to be Frogs. It is sad, yet it is always so.

Sometimes the Frogs came to see them, and once—once, after the Tadpoles had gotten their hindlegs, the Biggest Frog sat in the marsh near by and told them stories of his Tadpolehood. He said that he was always a very good little Tadpole, and always did as the Frogs told him to do; and that he was such a promising little fellow that every Mother Frog in the pond was sure that he had been hatched from one of her eggs.

"And were you?" asked one Tadpole, who never listened carefully, and so was always asking stupid questions.

The Biggest Frog looked at him very sternly. "No," said he, "I was not. Each wanted me as her son, but I never knew to which I belonged. I never knew! Still," he added, "it does not so much matter who a Frog's mother is, if the Frog is truly great." Then he filled the sacs on each side of his neck with air, and croaked loudly. His sister afterward told the Tadpoles that he was thinking of one of the forest people, the Ground Hog, who was very proud because he could remember his grandfather.

The Green Brown Frog came often to look at them and see how they were growing. She was very fond of the First Tadpole. "Why, you have your forelegs!" she exclaimed one morning. "How you do grow!"

"What will I have next?" he asked, "more legs or another tail?"

The Green Brown Frog smiled the whole length of her mouth, and that was a very broad smile indeed. "Look at me," she said. "What change must come next to make you look like a Frog?"

"You haven't any tail," he said slowly. "Is that all the difference between us Tadpoles and Frogs?"

"That is all the difference now," she answered, "but it will take a long, long time for your tail to disappear. It will happen with that quite as it did with your breathing-gills. You will grow bigger and bigger and bigger, and it will grow smaller and smaller and smaller, until some day you will find yourself a Frog." She shut her mouth to get her breath, because, you know, Frogs can only breathe a little through their skins, and then only when they are wet. Most of their air they take in through their noses and swallow with their mouths closed. That is why they cannot make long speeches. When their mouths are open they cannot swallow air.

After a while she spoke again. "It takes as many years to make a newly hatched Tadpole into a fully grown Frog," she said, "as there are toes on one of your hindfeet."

The First Tadpole did not know what a year was, but he felt sure from the way in which she spoke that it was a long, long time, and he was in a hurry to grow up. "I want to be a Frog sooner!" he said, crossly. "It isn't any fun at all being a Tadpole." The Green Brown Frog swam away, he was becoming so disagreeable.

The First Tadpole became crosser and crosser, and was very unreasonable. He did not think of the pleasant things which happened every day, but only of the trying ones. He did not know that Frogs often wished themselves Tadpoles again, and he sulked around in the pondweed all day. Every time he looked at one of his hindfeet it reminded him of what the Green Brown Frog had said, and he even grew out of patience with his tail—the same strong wiggly little tail of which he had been so proud.

"Horrid old thing!" he said, giving it a jerk. "Won't I be glad to get rid of you?" Then he thought of something—foolish, vain little First Tadpole that he was. He thought and he thought and he thought and he thought, and when his playmates swam around him he wouldn't chase them, and when they asked him what was the matter, he just answered, "Oh nothing!" as carelessly as could be.

The truth was that he wanted to be a Frog right away, and he thought he knew how he could be. He didn't want to tell the other Tadpoles because he didn't want any one else to become a Frog as soon as he. After a while he swam off to see the Snapping Turtle. He was very much afraid of the Snapping Turtle, and yet he thought him the best one to see just now. "I came to see if you would snap off my tail," said he.

"Your what?" said the Snapping Turtle, in his most surprised way.

"My tail," answered the First Tadpole, who had never had a tail snapped off, and thought it could be easily done. "I want to be a Frog to-day and not wait."

"Certainly," said the Snapping Turtle. "With pleasure! No trouble at all! Anything else I can do for you?"

"No, thank you," said the First Tadpole, "only you won't snap off too much, will you?"

"Not a bit," answered the Snapping Turtle, with a queer look in his eyes. "And if any of your friends are in a hurry to grow up, I shall be glad to help them." Then he swam toward the First Tadpole and did as he had been asked to do.

The next morning all the other Tadpoles crowded around to look at the First Tadpole. "Why-ee!" they cried. "Where is your tail?"

"I don't know," he answered, "but I think the Snapping Turtle could tell you."

"What is this?" asked the Green Brown Frog, swimming up to them. "Did the Snapping Turtle try to catch you? You poor little fellow! How did it happen?" She was very fond of the First Tadpole, and had about decided that he must be one of her sons.

"Well," he said slowly, for he didn't want the other Tadpoles to do the same thing, "I met him last evening and he—"

"Snapped at you!" exclaimed the Green Brown Frog. "It is lucky for you that he doesn't believe in eating hearty suppers, that is all I have to say! But you are a very foolish Tadpole not to keep out of his way, as you have always been told you must."

Then the First Tadpole lost his temper. "I'm not foolish, and I'm not a Tadpole," he said. "I asked him to snap it off, and now I am a Frog!"

"Oho!" said the voice of the Yellow Brown Frog behind him. "You are a Frog, are you? Let's hear you croak then. Come out on the bank and have a hopping match with me."

"I—I don't croak yet," stammered the First Tadpole, "a—and I don't care to hop."

"You are just a tailless Tadpole," said the Yellow Brown Frog sternly. "Don't any more of you youngsters try such a plan, or some of you will be Tadpole-less tails and a good many of you won't be anything."

The old Snapping Turtle waited all morning for some more Tadpoles who wanted to be made into Frogs, but none came. The Biggest Frog croaked hoarsely when he heard of it. "Tails! Tails! Tails! Tails! Tails! Tails! Tails! Tails!" said he. "That youngster will never be a strong Frog. Tadpoles must be Tadpoles, tails and all, for a long time, if they hope to ever be really fine Frogs like me." And that is so, as any Frog will tell you.

The Green Brown Frog sighed as she crawled out on the bank. "What a silly Tadpole," she said; "I'm glad he isn't my child!"

The Runaway Water Spiders

When the little Water Spiders first opened their eyes, and this was as soon as they were hatched, they found themselves in a cosy home of one room which their mother had built under the water. This room had no window and only one door. There was no floor at all. When Father Stickleback had asked Mrs. Spider why she did not make a floor, she had looked at him in great surprise and said, "Why, if I had built one, I should have no place to go in and out." She really thought him quite stupid not to think of that. It often happens, you know, that really clever people think each other stupid, just because they live in different ways. Afterward, Mrs. Water Spider saw Father Stickleback's nest, and understood why he asked that question.

When her home was done, it was half as large as a big acorn and a charming place for Water Spider babies. The side walls and the rounding ceiling were all of the finest Spider silk, and the bottom was just one round doorway. The house was built under the water and fastened down by tiny ropes of Spider silk which were tied to the stems of pond plants. Mrs. Water Spider looked at it with a happy smile. "Next I must fill it with air," said she, "and then it will be ready. I am out of breath now."

She crept up the stem of the nearest plant and sat in the air for a few minutes, eating her lunch and resting. Next she walked down the stem until just the end of her body was in the air. She stood so, with her head down, then gave a little jerk and dove to her home. As she jerked, she crossed her hindlegs and caught a small bubble of air between them and her body. When she reached her home, she went quickly in the open doorway and let go of her bubble. It did not fall downward to the floor, as bubbles do in most houses, and there were two reasons for this. In the first place, there was no floor. In the second place, air always falls upward in the water. This fell up until it reached the rounded ceiling and had to stop. Just as it fell, a drop of water went out through the open doorway. The home had been full of water, you know, but now that Mrs. Spider had begun to bring in air something had to be moved to make a place for it.

She brought down thirteen more bubbles of air and then the house was filled with it. On the lower side of the open doorway there was water and on the upper side was air, and each stayed where it should. When Mrs. Spider came into her house, she always had some air caught in the hairs which covered her body, even when she did not bring a bubble of it in her hindlegs. She had to have plenty of it in her home to keep her from drowning, for she could not breathe water like a fish. "Side doors may be all right for Sticklebacks," said she, "for they do not need air, but I must have bottom doors, and I will have them too!"

After she had laid her eggs, she had some days in which to rest and visit with the Water-Boatmen who lived near. They were great friends. Belostoma used to ask the Water-Boatmen, who were his cousins, why they were so neighborly with the Water Spiders. "I don't like to see you so much with eight-legged people," he said. "They are not our kind." Belostoma was very proud of his family.

"We know that they have rather too many legs to look well," said Mrs. Water-Boatman, "but they are pleasant, and we are interested in the same things. You know we both carry air about with us in the water, and so few of our neighbors seem to care anything for it." She was a sensible little person and knew that people who are really fond of their friends do not care how many legs they have. She carried her air under her wings, but there were other Water-Boatmen, near relatives, who spread theirs over their whole bodies, and looked very silvery and beautiful when they were under water.

One day, when Mrs. Water Spider was sitting on a lily-pad and talking with her friends, a Water-Boatman rose quickly from the bottom of the pond. As soon as he got right side up (and that means as soon as he got to floating on his back), he said to her, "I heard queer sounds in your house; I was feeding near there, and the noise startled me so that I let go of the stone I was holding to, and came up. I think your eggs must be hatching."

"Really?" exclaimed Mrs. Water Spider. "I shall be so glad! A house always seems lonely to me without children." She dove to her house, and found some very fine Water Spider babies there. You may be sure she did not have much time for visiting after that. She had to hunt food and carry it down to her children, and when they were restless and impatient she stayed with them and told them stories of the great world.

Sometimes they teased to go out with her, but this she never allowed. "Wait until you are older," she would say. "It will not be so very long before you can go safely." The children thought it had been a long, long time already, and one of them made a face when his mother said this. She did not see him, and it was well for him that she did not. He should have been very much ashamed of himself for doing it.

The next time Mrs. Water Spider went for food, one of the children said, "I tell you what let's do! Let's all go down to the doorway and peek out." They looked at each other and wondered if they dared. That was something their mother had forbidden them to do. There was no window to look through and they wanted very much to see the world. At last the little fellow who had made a face said, "I'm going to, anyway." After that, his brothers and sisters went, too. And this shows how, if good little Spiders listen to naughty little Spiders, they become naughty little Spiders themselves.

All the children ran down and peeked around the edge of the door, but they couldn't see much besides water, and they had seen that before. They were sadly disappointed. Somebody said, "I'm going to put two of my legs out!" Somebody else said, "I'll put four out!" A big brother said, "I'm going to put six out!" And then another brother said "I'll put eight out! Dare you to!"

You know what naughty little Spiders would be likely to do then. Well, they did it. And, as it happened, they had just pulled their last legs through the open doorway when a Stickleback Father came along. "Aren't you rather young to be out of the nest?" said he, in his most pleasant voice.

Poor little Water Spiders! They didn't know he was one of their mother's friends, and he seemed so big to them, and the bones on his cheeks made him look so queer, and the stickles on his back were so sharp, that every one of them was afraid and let go of the wall of the house—and then!

Every one of them rose quickly to the top, into the light and the open air. They crawled upon a lily-pad and clung there, frightened, and feeling weak in all their knees. The Dragon Flies flew over them, the Wild Ducks swam past them, and on a log not far away they saw a long row of Mud Turtles sunning themselves. Why nothing dreadful happened, one cannot tell. Perhaps it was bad enough as it was, for they were so scared that they could only huddle close together and cry, "We want our mother."

Here Mrs. Water Spider found them. She came home with something for dinner, and saw her house empty. Of course she knew where to look, for, as she said, "If they stepped outside the door, they would be quite sure to tumble up into the air." She took them home, one at a time, and how she ever did it nobody knows.

When they were all safely there and had eaten the food that was waiting for them, Mrs. Spider, who had not scolded them at all, said, "Look me straight in the eye, every one of you! Will you promise never to run away again?"

Instead of saying at once, "Yes, mother," as they should have done, one of them answered, "Why, we didn't run away. We were just peeking around the edge of the doorway, and we got too far out, and somebody came along and scared us so that we let go, and then we couldn't help falling up into the air."

"Oh, no," said their mother, "you couldn't help it then, of course. But who told you that you might peep out of the door?"

The little Water Spiders hung their heads and looked very much ashamed. Their mother went on, "You needn't say that you were not to blame. You were to blame, and you began to run away as soon as you took the first step toward the door, only you didn't know that you were going so far. Tell me," she said, "whether you would ever have gone to the top of the water if you had not taken that first step?"

The little Water Spiders were more ashamed than ever, but they had to look her in the eye and promise to be good.

It is very certain that not one of those children even peeped around the edge of the doorway from that day until their mother told them that they might go into the world and build houses for themselves. "Remember just one thing," she said, as they started away. "Always take your food home to eat." And they always did, for no Water Spider who has been well brought up will ever eat away from his own home.

The Slow Little Mud Turtle

When the twenty little Mud Turtles broke their egg-shells one hot summer day, and poked their way up through the warm sand in which they had been buried, they looked almost as much alike as so many raindrops. The Mother Turtle who was sunning herself on the bank near by, said to her friends, "Why! There are my children! Did you ever see a finer family? I believe I will go over and speak to them."

Most of the young Mud Turtles crawled quickly out of the sand and broken shells, and began drying themselves in the sunshine. One slow little fellow stopped to look at the broken shells, stubbed one of his front toes on a large piece and then sat down until it should stop aching. "Wait for me!" he called out to his brothers and sisters. "I'm coming in a minute."

The other little Turtles waited, but when his toe was comfortable again and he started toward them, he met a very interesting Snail and talked a while with him. "Come on," said the Biggest Little Turtle. "Don't let's wait any longer. He can catch up."

So they sprawled along until they came to a place where they could sit in a row on an old log, and they climbed onto it and sat just close enough together and not at all too close. Then the Slow Little Turtle came hurrying over the sand with a rather cross look in his eyes and putting his feet down a little harder than he needed to—quite as though he were out of patience about something. "Why didn't you Turtles wait for me?" he grumbled. "I was coming right along."

Just then the Mother Turtle came up. "Good morning," said she. "I believe you are my children?"

The little Mud Turtles looked at each other and didn't say a word. This was not because they were rude or bashful, but because they did not know what to say. And that, you know, was quite right, for unless one has something worth saying, it is far better to say nothing at all.

She drew a long Mud Turtle breath and answered her own question. "Yes," she said, "you certainly are, for I saw you scrambling out of the sand a little while ago, and you came from the very place where I laid my eggs and covered them during the first really warm nights this year. I was telling your father only yesterday that it was about time for you to hatch. The sun has been so hot lately that I was sure you would do well."

The Mother Turtle stretched her head this way and that until there was hardly a wrinkle left in her neck-skin, she was so eager to see them all. "Why are you not up here with your brothers and sisters?" she asked suddenly of the Slow Little Turtle, who was trying to make a place for himself on the log.

"They didn't wait for me," he said. "I was coming right along but they wouldn't wait. I think they are just as mea——"

The Mother Turtle raised one of her forefeet until all five of its toes with their strong claws were pointing at him. She also raised her head as far as her upper shell would let her. "So you *are* the one," she said. "I thought you were when I heard you trying to make the others wait. It is too bad."

She looked so stern that the Slow Little Turtle didn't dare finish what he had begun to say, yet down in his little Turtle heart he thought, "Now they are going to catch it!" He was sure his mother was going to scold the other Turtle children for leaving him. He wanted to see what they would do, so he looked out of his right eye at the ten brothers and sisters on that side, and out of his left eye at the nine brothers and sisters on that side. He could do this very easily, because his eyes were not on the front of his head like those of some people, but one on each side.

"I have raised families of young Turtles every year," said the Mother Turtle. "The first year I had only a few children, the next year I had more, and so it has gone—every year a few more children than the year before—until now I never know quite how many I do have. But there is always one Slow Little Turtle who lags behind and wants the others to wait for him. That makes him miss his share of good things, and then he is quite certain to be cross and think it is somebody else's fault."

The Slow Little Turtle felt the ten brothers and sisters on his right side looking at him out of their left eyes, and the nine brothers and sisters on his left side looking at him out of their right eyes. He drew in his head and his tail and his legs, until all they could see was his rounded upper shell, his shell side-walls, and the yellow edge of his flat lower shell. He would have liked to draw them in too, but of course he couldn't do that.

"I did hope," said the Mother Turtle, "that I might have one family without such a child in it. I cannot help loving even a slow child who is cross, if he is hatched from one of my eggs, yet it makes me sad—very, very sad."

"Try to get over this," she said to the Slow Little Turtle, "before it is too late. And you," she added, turning to his brothers and sisters, "must be patient with him. We shall not have him with us long."

"What do you mean?" asked the Slow Little Turtle, peeping out from between his shells. "I'm not going away."

"You do not want to," said his mother, "but you will not be with us long unless you learn to keep up with the rest. Something always happens to pond people who are too slow. I cannot tell you what it will be, yet it is sure to be *something*. I remember so well my first slow child—and how he—" She began to cry, and since she could not easily get her forefeet to her eyes, she sprawled to the pond and swam off with only her head and a little of her upper shell showing above the water.

The Slow Little Turtle was really frightened by what his mother had said, and for a few days he tried to keep up with the others. Nothing happened to him, and so he grew careless and made people wait for him just because he was not quite ready to go with them, or because he wanted to do this or look at that or talk to some other person. He was a very trying little Turtle, yet his mother loved him and did not like it when the rest called him a Land Tortoise. It is all right, you know, to be a Land Tortoise when your father and mother are Land Tortoises, and these cousins of the Turtles look so much like them that some people cannot tell them apart. That is because they forget that the Tortoises live on land, have higher back shells, and move very, very slowly. Turtles live more in the water and can move quickly if they will. This is why other Turtles sometimes make fun of a slow brother by calling him a Land Tortoise.

One beautiful sunshiny afternoon, when most of the twenty little Turtles were sitting on a floating log by the edge of the pond, their mother was with some of her friends on another log near by. She looked often at her children, and thought how handsome their rounded-up back shells were in the sunshine with the little red and yellow markings showing on the black. She could see their strong little pointed tails too, and their webbed feet with a stout claw on each toe. She was so proud that she could not help talking about them. "Is there any sight more beautiful," she said, "than a row of good little Turtles?"

"Yes," said a fine old fellow who was floating near her, "a row of their mothers!" He was a Turtle whom she had never liked very well, but now she began to think that he was rather agreeable after all. She was just noticing how beautifully the skin wrinkled on his neck, when she heard a splash and saw two terrible great two-legged animals wading into the pond from the shore.

"Boys!" she cried, "Boys!" And she sprawled off the end of her log and slid into the water, all her friends following her. The Biggest Little Turtle saw these great animals coming toward him. He sprawled off the end of his log and slid into the water, and all his brothers and sisters followed him except the Slow Little Turtle. "Wait for me," he said. "I'm coming in just a——"

Then one of these great animals stooped over and picked him up, and held him bottom side uppermost and rapped on that side, which was flat; and on the other side, which was rounded; and stared at him with two great eyes. Next the other great animal took him and turned him over and rapped on his shells and stared at him. The poor Slow Little Turtle drew in his head and tail and legs and kept very, very still. He wished that he had side-pieces of shell all around now, instead of just one on each side between his legs. He was thinking over and over, "Something has happened! Something has happened!" And he knew that back in the pond his mother would be trying to find him and could not.

The boys carried him to the edge of the meadow and put him down on the grass. He lay perfectly still for a long, long time, and when he thought they had forgotten about him he tried to run away. Then they laughed and picked him up again, and one of them took something sharp and shiny and cut marks into his upper shell. This did not really give him pain, yet, as he said afterward, "It hurts almost as much to think you are going to be hurt, as it does to be hurt."

It was not until the sun went down that the boys let the Slow Little Turtle go. Then he was very, very tired, but he wanted so much to get back to his home in the pond that he started at once by moonlight. This was the first time he had ever seen the moon, for, except when they are laying eggs, Turtles usually sleep at night. He was not quite sure which way he should go, and if it had not been for the kindness of the Tree Frog he might never have seen his brothers and sisters again. You know the Tree Frog had been carried away when he was young, before he came to live with the meadow people, so he knew how to be sorry for the Slow Little Turtle.

The Tree Frog hopped along ahead to show the way, and the Turtle followed until they reached a place from which they could see the pond. "Good night!" said the Tree Frog. "You can find your way now."

"Good night!" said the Turtle. "I wish I might help you some time."

"Never mind me," said the Tree Frog. "Help somebody else and it will be all right." He hopped back toward his home, and for a long time afterward the Turtle heard his cheerful "Pukr-r-rup! Pukr-r-rup!" sounding over the dewy grass and through the still air. At the edge of the pond the Slow Little Turtle found his nineteen brothers and sisters sound asleep. "I'm here!" he cried joyfully, poking first one and then another of them with his head.

The Biggest Little Turtle moved without awakening. "I tell you I'm not hungry," he murmured. "I don't want to get up." And again he fell fast asleep.

So the Slow Little Turtle did not disturb him, but cuddled inside his two shells and went to sleep also. He was so tired that he did not awaken until the sun was high in the sky. When he did open his eyes, his relatives were sitting around looking at him, and he remembered all that had happened before he slept. "Does my shell look very bad?" he cried. "I wish I could see it. Oh, I am so glad to get back! I'll never be slow again, Never! Never!"

His mother came and leaned her shell lovingly against his. "If you will only learn to keep up with your brothers and sisters," she said "I shall not be sorry that the boys carried you off."

"You just wait and see," said the Slow Little Turtle. And he was as good as his word. After that he was always the first to slip from the log to the water if anything scared them; and when, one day, a strange Turtle from another pond came to visit, he said to the Turtles who had always lived there, "Why do you call that young fellow with the marked shell 'The Slow Little Turtle?' He is the quickest one in his family."

The pond people looked at each other and laughed. "That is queer!" they said. "After this we will call him 'The Quick Little Turtle.'"

This made him very happy, and when, once in a while, somebody forgot and by mistake called him "The Quick Slow Little Turtle," he said he rather liked it because it showed that a Turtle needn't keep his faults if he did have them.

The Dragon-Fly Children And The Snapping Turtle

The Dragon-Flies have always lived near the pond. Not the same ones that are there now, of course, but the great-great-great-grandfathers of these. A person would think that, after a family had lived so long in a place, all the neighbors would be fond of them, yet it is not so. The Dragon-Flies may be very good people—and even the Snapping Turtle says that they are—still, they are so peculiar that many of their neighbors do not like them at all. Even when they are only larvæ, or babies, they are not good playmates, for they have such a bad habit of putting everything into their mouths. Indeed, the Stickleback Father once told the little Sticklebacks that they should not stir out of the nest, unless they would promise to keep away from the young Dragon-Flies.

The Stickleback Mothers said that it was all the fault of the Dragon-Fly Mothers. "What can you expect," exclaimed one of them, "when Dragon-Fly eggs are so carelessly laid? I saw a Dragon-Fly Mother laying some only yesterday, and how do you suppose she did it? Just flew around in the sunshine and visited with her friends, and once in a while flew low enough to touch the water and drop one in. It is disgraceful!"

The Minnow Mothers did not think it was so much in the way the eggs were laid, "although," said one, "I always lay mine close together, instead of scattering them over the whole pond." They thought the trouble came from bad bringing up or no bringing up at all. Each egg, you know, when it is laid, drops to the bottom of the pond, and the children are hatched and grow up there, and do not even see their fathers and mothers.

Now most of the larvæ were turning into Nymphs, which are half-grown Dragon Flies. They had been short and plump, and now they were longer and more slender, and there were little bunches on their shoulders where the wings were growing under their skin. They had outgrown their old skins a great many times, and had to wriggle out of them to be at all comfortable. When a Dragon-Fly child became too big for his skin, he hooked the two sharp claws of each of his six feet firmly into something, unfastened his skin down the back, and wriggled out, leaving it to roll around in the water until it became just part of the mud.

Like most growing children, the Dragon-Fly larvæ and Nymphs had to eat a great deal. Their stomachs were as long as their bodies, and they were never really happy unless their stomachs were full. They always ate plain food and plenty of it, and they never ate between meals. They had breakfast from the time they awakened in the morning until the sun was high in the sky, then they had dinner until the sun was low in the sky, and supper from that time until it grew dark and they went to sleep: but never a mouthful between meals, no matter how hungry they might be. They said this was their only rule about eating, and they *would* keep it.

They were always slow children. You would think that, with six legs apiece and three joints in each leg, they might walk quite fast, yet they never did. When they had to, they hurried in another way by taking a long leap through the water. Of course they breathed water like their neighbors, the fishes and the Tadpoles. They did not breathe it into their mouths, or through gills, but took it in through some openings in the back part of their bodies. When they wanted to hurry, they breathed this water out so suddenly that it sent them quickly ahead.

The Snapping Turtle had called them "bothering bugs" one day when he was cross (and that was the day after he had been cross, and just before the day when he was going to be cross again), and they didn't like him and wanted to get even. They all put their queer little three-cornered heads together, and there was an ugly look in their great staring eyes.

"Horrid old thing!" said one larva. "I wish I could sting him."

"Well, you can't," said a Nymph, turning towards him so suddenly that he leaped. "You haven't any sting, and you never will have, so you just keep still." It was not at all nice in her to speak that way, but she was not well brought up, you know, and that, perhaps, is a reason why one should excuse her for talking so to her little brother. She was often impatient, and said she could never go anywhere without one of the larvæ tagging along.

"I tell you what let's do," said another Nymph. "Let's all go together to the shallow water where he suns himself, and let's all stand close to each other, and then, when he comes along, let's stick out our lips at him!"

"Both lips?" asked the larvæ.

"Well, our lower lips anyway," answered the Nymph. "Our upper lips are so small they don't matter."

"We'll do it," exclaimed all the Dragon-Fly children, and they started together to walk on the pond-bottom to the shallow water. They thought it would scare the Snapping Turtle dreadfully. They knew that whenever they stuck out their lower lips at the small fishes and bugs, they swam away as fast as they could. The Giant Water-Bug (Belostoma), was the only bug who was not afraid of them when they made faces. Indeed, the lower lip of a Dragon-Fly child might well frighten people, for it is fastened on a long, jointed, arm-like thing, and has pincers on it with which it catches and holds its food. Most of the time, the Dragon-Fly child keeps the joint bent, and so holds his lip up to his face like a mask. But sometimes he straightens the joint and holds his lip out before him, and then its pincers catch hold of things. He does this when he is hungry.

When they reached the shallow water, the Dragon-Fly children stood close together, with the larvæ in the middle and the Nymphs all around them. The Snapping Turtle was nowhere to be seen, so they had to wait. "Aren't you scared?" whispered one larva to another.

"Scared? Dah! Who's afraid," answered he.

"Oh, look!" cried a Nymph. "There go some grown-up Dragon-Flies over our heads. Just you wait until I change my skin once more, and then won't I have a good time! I'll dry my wings and then I'll——"

"Sh-h!" said one of the larvæ. "Here comes the Snapping Turtle."

Sure enough, there he came through the shallow water, his wet back-shell partly out of it and shining in the sunlight. He came straight toward the Dragon-Fly children, and they were glad to see that he did not look hungry. They thought he might be going to take a nap after his dinner. Then they all stood even closer together and stuck out their lower lips at him. They thought he might run away when they did this. They felt sure that he would at least be very badly frightened.

The Snapping Turtle did not seem to see them at all. It was queer. He just waddled on and on, coming straight toward them. "Ah-h-h!" said he. "How sleepy I do feel! I will lie down in the sunshine and rest." He took a few more steps, which brought his great body right over the crowd of Dragon-Fly children. "I think I will draw in my head," said he (the Dragon-Fly children looked at each other), "and my tail (here two of the youngest larvæ began to cry) and lie down." He began to draw in his legs very, very slowly, and just as his great hard lower shell touched the mud, the last larva crawled out under his tail. The Nymphs had already gotten away.

"Oh," said the Dragon-Fly children to each other, "Wasn't it awful!"

"Humph," said the Snapping Turtle, talking to himself—he had gotten into the way of doing that because he had so few friends—"How dreadfully they did scare me!" Then he laughed a grim Snapping Turtle laugh, and went to sleep.

The Snappy Snapping Turtle

There was but one Snapping Turtle in the pond, and he was the only person there who had ever been heard to wish for another. He had not always lived there, and could just remember leaving his brothers and sisters when he was young. "I was carried away from my people," he said, "and kept on land for a few days. Then I was brought here and have made it my home ever since."

One could tell by looking at him that he was related to the Mud Turtles. He had upper and lower shells like them, and could draw in his head and legs and tail when he wanted to. His shells were gray, quite the color of a clay-bank, and his head was larger than those of the Mud Turtles. His tail was long and scaly and pointed, and his forelegs were large and warty. There were fine, strong webs between his toes, as there were between the toes of his relatives, the Mud Turtles.

When he first came to live in the pond, people were sorry for him, and tried to make him feel at home. He had a chance to win many friends and have all his neighbors fond of him, but he was too snappy. When the water was just warm enough, and his stomach was full, and he had slept well the night before, and everything was exactly as he wished it to be,—ah, then he was a very agreeable Turtle, and was ready to talk in the most gracious way to his neighbors. That was all very well. Anybody can be good-natured when everything is exactly right and he can have his own way. But the really delightful people, you know, are the ones who are pleasant when things go wrong.

It was a Mud Turtle Father who first spoke to him. "I hope you'll like the pond," said he. "We think it very homelike and comfortable."

"Humph! Shallow little hole!" snapped the one who had just come. "I bump my head on the bottom every time I dive."

"That is too bad," exclaimed the Mud Turtle Father. "I hope you dive where there is a soft bottom."

"Sometimes I do and sometimes I don't," answered the Snapping Turtle. "I can't bother to swim down slowly and try it, and then go back to dive. When I want to dive, I *want* to dive, and that's all there is to it."

"Yes," said the Mud Turtle Father. "I know how it is when one has the diving feeling. I hope your head will not trouble you much, and that you will soon be used to our waters." He spread his toes and swam strongly away, pushing against the water with his webbed feet.

"Humph!" said the Snapping Turtle to himself. "It is all very well to talk about getting used to these waters, but I never shall. I can hardly see now for the pain in the right side of my head, where I bumped it. Or was it the left side I hit? Queer I can't remember!" Then he swam to shallow water, and drew himself into his shell, and lay there and thought how badly he felt, and how horrid the pond was, and what poor company his neighbors were, and what a disagreeable world this is for Snapping Turtles.

The Mud Turtle Father went home and told his wife all about it. "What a disagreeable fellow!" she said. "But then, he is a bachelor, and bachelors are often queer."

"I never was," said her husband.

"Oh!" said she. And, being a wise wife, she did not say anything else. She knew, however, that Mr. Mud Turtle was a much more agreeable fellow since he had married and learned to think more of somebody else than of himself. It is the people who think too much of themselves you know, who are most unhappy in this world.

The Eels also tried to be friendly, and, when he dove to the bottom, called to him to stay and visit with them. "You must excuse us from making the first call," they said. "We go out so little in the daytime."

"Humph!" said the Snapping Turtle. "Do you good to get away from home more. No wonder your eyes are weak, when you lie around in the mud of the dark pond-bottom all day. Indeed, I'll not stay. You can come to see me like other people."

Then he swam away and told the Clams what he had said, and he acted quite proud of what was really dreadful rudeness. "It'll do them good to hear the truth," said he. "I always speak right out. They are as bad as the Water-Adder. They have no backbone."

The Clams listened politely and said nothing. They never did talk much. The Snapping Turtle was mistaken though, when he said that the Eels and the Water-Adder had no backbone. They really had much more than he, but they wore theirs inside, while his was spread out in the shape of a shell for everybody to see.

He did not even try to keep his temper. He became angry one day because Belostoma, the Giant Water-Bug, ate something which he wanted for himself. His eyes glared and his horny jaws snapped, and he waved his long, pointed, scaly tail in a way which was terrible to see. "You are a good-for-nothing bug," he said. "You do no work, and you eat more than any other person of your size here. Nobody likes you, and there isn't a little fish in the pond who would be seen with you if he could help it. They all hide if they see you coming. I'll be heartily glad when you get your wings and fly away. Don't let any of your friends lay their eggs in this pond. I've seen enough of your family."

Of course this made Belostoma feel very badly. He was not a popular bug, and it is possible that if he could have had his own way, he would have chosen to be a Crayfish or a Stickleback, rather than what he was. As for his not working—there was nothing for him to do, so how could he work? He had to eat, or he would not grow, and since the Snapping Turtle was a hearty eater himself, he should have had the sense to keep still about that. Belostoma told the Mud Turtles what the Snapping Turtle had said, and the Mud Turtle Father spoke of it to the Snapping Turtle.

By that time the Snapping Turtle was feeling better natured and was very gracious. "Belostoma shouldn't remember those things," said he, moving one warty foreleg. "When I am angry, I often say things that I do not mean; but then, I get right over it. I had almost forgotten my little talk with him. I don't see any reason for telling him I am sorry. He is very silly to think so much of it." He lifted his big head quite high, and acted as though it was really a noble thing to be ugly and then forget about it. He might just as sensibly ask people to admire him for not eating when his stomach was full, or for lying still when he was too tired to swim.

When the Mud Turtle Mother heard of this, she was quite out of patience. "All he cares for," said she, "is just Snapping Turtle, Snapping Turtle, Snapping Turtle. When he is good-natured, he thinks everybody else ought to be; and when he is bad-tempered he doesn't care how other people feel. He will never be any more agreeable until he does something kind for somebody, and I don't see any chance of that happening."

There came a day, though, when the pond people were glad that the Snapping Turtle lived there. Two boys were wading in the edge of the pond, splashing the water and scaring all the people who were near them. The Sticklebacks turned pale all over, as they do when they are badly frightened. The Yellow Brown Frog was so scared that he emptied out the water he had saved for wetting his skin in dry weather. He had a great pocket in his body filled with water, for if his skin should get dry he couldn't breathe through it, and unless he carried water with him he could not stay ashore at all.

The boys had even turned the Mud Turtle Father onto his back in the sunshine, where he lay, waving his feet in the air, but not strong enough to get right side up again. The Snapping Turtle was taking a nap in deep water, when the frightened fishes came swimming toward him as fast as their tails would take them. "What is the matter?" said he.

"Boys!" cried they. "Boys! The dreadful, splashing, Turtle-turning kind."

"Humph!" said the Snapping Turtle. "I'll have to see about that. How many are there?"

"Two!" cried the Sticklebacks and Minnows together.

"And there is only one of me," said the Snapping Turtle to himself. "I must have somebody to help me. Oh, Belostoma," he cried, as the Giant Water-Bug swam past. "Help me drive those boys away."

"With pleasure," said Belostoma, who liked nothing better than this kind of work. Off they started for the place where the boys were wading. The Snapping Turtle took long, strong strokes with his webbed feet, and Belostoma could not keep up with him. The Snapping Turtle saw this. "Jump onto my back," cried he. "You are a light fellow. Hang tight."

Belostoma jumped onto the Snapping Turtle's clay-colored shell, and when he found himself slipping off the back end of it, he stuck his claws into the Snapping Turtle's tail and held on in that way. He knew that he was not easily hurt, even if he did make a fuss when he bumped his head. As soon as they got near the boys, the Snapping Turtle spoke over his back-shell to Belostoma. "Slide off now," said he, "and drive away the smaller boy. Don't stop to talk with these Bloodsuckers."

So Belostoma slid off and swam toward the smaller boy, and he ran out his stout little sucking tube and stung him on the leg. Just then the Snapping Turtle brought his horny jaws together on one of the larger boy's feet. There was a great splashing and dashing as the boys ran to the shore, and three Bloodsuckers, who had fastened themselves to the boy's legs, did not have time to drop off, and were carried ashore and never seen again.

"There!" said the Snapping Turtle. "That's done. I don't know what the pond people would do, if you and I were not here to look after them, Belostoma."

"I'm glad I happened along," said the Giant Water-Bug quietly, "but you will have to do it all after this. I'm about ready to leave the pond. I think I'll go to-morrow."

"Going to-morrow!" exclaimed the Snapping Turtle. "I'm sorry. Of course I know you can never come back, but send your friends here to lay their eggs. We mustn't be left without some of your family."

"Thank you," said Belostoma, and he did not show that he remembered some quite different things which the Snapping Turtle had said before, about his leaving the pond. And that showed that he was a very wise bug as well as a brave one.

"Humph!" said the Snapping Turtle. "There is the Mud Turtle Father on his back." And he ran to him and pushed him over onto his feet. "Oh, thank you," cried the Mud Turtle Mother. "I was not strong enough to do that."

"Always glad to help my neighbors," said the Snapping Turtle. "Pleasant day, isn't it? I must tell the fishes that the boys are gone. The poor little fellows were almost too scared to swim." And he went away with a really happy look on his face.

"There!" said the Mud Turtle Mother to her husband. "He has begun to help people, and now he likes them, and is contented, I always told you so!"

The Clever Water-Adder

None of the pond people were alone more than the Water-Adders. The Snapping Turtle was left to himself a great deal until the day when he and Belostoma drove away the boys. After that his neighbors began to understand him better and he was less grumpy, so that those who wore shells were soon quite fond of him.

Belostoma did not have many friends among the smaller people, and only a few among the larger ones. They said that he was cruel, and that he had a bad habit of using his stout sucking tube to sting with. Still, Belostoma did not care; he said, "A Giant Water-Bug does not always live in the water. I shall have my wings soon, and leave the water and marry. After that, I shall fly away on my wedding trip. Mrs. Belostoma may go with me, if she feels like doing so after laying her eggs here. I shall go anyway. And I shall flutter and sprawl around the light, and sting people who bother me, and have a happy time." That was Belostoma's way. He *would* sting people who bothered him, but then he always said that they need not have bothered him. And perhaps that was so.

With the Water-Adders it was different. They were good-natured enough, yet the Mud Turtles and Snapping Turtle were the only ones who ever called upon them and found them at home. The small people without shells were afraid of them, and the Clams and Pond Snails never called upon any one. The Minnows said they could not bear the looks of the Adders—they had such ugly mouths and such quick motions. The larger fishes kept away on account of their children, who were small and tender.

One might think that the Sand-Hill Cranes, the Fish Hawks, and the other shore families would have been good friends for them, but when they called, the Adders were always away. People said that the Adders were afraid of them.

The Yellow Brown Frog wished that the Adders could be scared, badly scared, some time: so scared that a chilly feeling would run down their backs from their heads clear to the tips of their tails. "I wish," said he, "that the chilly feeling would be big enough to go way through to their bellies. Their bellies are only the front side of their backs, anyway," he added, "because they are so thin." Of course this was a dreadful wish to make, but people said that one of the Adders had frightened the Yellow Brown Frog so that he never got over it, and this was the reason he felt so.

The Water-Adders were certainly the cleverest people in the pond, and there was one Mother Adder who was so very bright that they called her "the Clever Water-Adder." She could do almost anything, and she knew it. She talked about it, too, and that showed bad taste, and was one reason why she was not liked better. She could swim very fast, could creep, glide, catch hold of things with her tail, hang herself from the branch of a tree, lift her head far into the air, leap, dart, bound, and dive. All her family could do these things, but she could do them a little the best.

One day she was hanging over the pond in a very graceful position, with her tail twisted carelessly around a willow branch. The Snapping Turtle and a Mud Turtle Father were in the shallow water below her. Her slender forked tongue was darting in and out of her open mouth. She was using her tongue in this way most of the time. "It is useful in feeling of things," she said, "and then, I have always thought it quite becoming." She could see herself reflected in the still water below her, and she noticed how prettily the dark brown of her back shaded into the white of her belly. You see she was vain as well as clever.

The Snapping Turtle felt cross to-day, and had come to see if a talk with her would not make him feel better. The Mud Turtle was tired of having the children sprawl around him, and of Mrs. Mud Turtle telling about the trouble she had to get the right kind of food.

The Clever Water-Adder spoke first of the weather. "It must be dreadfully hot for the shore people," she said. "Think of their having to wear the same feathers all the year and fly around in the sunshine to find food for their children."

"Ah yes," said the Mud Turtle. "How they must wish for shells!"

"Humph!" said the Snapping Turtle. "What for? To fly with? Let them come in swimming with their children, if they are warm and tired."

The Water-Adder laughed in her snaky way, and showed her sharp teeth. "I have heard," she said, "that when the Wild Ducks bring their children here to swim, they do not always take so many home as they brought."

The Snapping Turtle became very much interested in his warty right foreleg, and did not seem to hear what she said. The Mud Turtle smiled. "I have heard," she went on, "that when young Ducks dive head first, they are quite sure to come up again, but that when they dive feet first, they never come up."

"What do you mean?" asked the Snapping Turtle, and he was snappy about it.

"Oh, nothing," replied the Water-Adder, swinging her head back and forth and looking at the scales on her body.

"I know what you mean," said the Snapping Turtle, "and you know what you mean, but I have to eat something, and if I am swimming under the water and a Duckling paddles along just above me and sticks his foot into my mouth, I am likely to swallow him before I think."

The Water-Adder saw that he was provoked by what she had said, so she talked about something else. "I think the Ducks spoil their children," said she. "They make such a fuss over them, and they are not nearly so bright as my children. Why, mine hatch as soon as the eggs are laid, and go hunting at once. They are no trouble at all."

"I never worry about mine," said the Mud Turtle, "although their mother thinks it is not safe for them all to sleep at once, as they do on a log in the sunshine."

"It isn't," said the Adder decidedly. "I never close my eyes. None of us Adders do. Nobody can ever say that we close our eyes to danger." They couldn't shut their eyes if they wanted to, because they had no eyelids, but she did not speak of that. "How stupid people are," she said.

"Most of them," remarked the Turtles.

"All of them," she said, "except us Adders and the Turtles. I even think that some of the Turtles are a little queer, don't you?"

"We have thought so," said the Mud Turtle.

"They certainly are," agreed the Snapping Turtle, who was beginning to feel much better natured.

"What did you say?" asked the Adder who, like all her family, was a little deaf.

"Ouch!" exclaimed the Snapping Turtle. "Ouch! Ouch!"

"What is the matter?" asked the Mud Turtle. Then he began to slap the water with his short, stout tail, and say "Ouch!"

Two naughty young Water-Boatmen had swum quietly up on their backs, and stung the Turtles on their tails. Then they swam away, pushing themselves quickly through the water with swift strokes of their hairy oar-legs.

"Ah-h-h!" exclaimed the Snapping Turtle, and he backed into the mud, knowing that fine, soft mud is the best thing in the world for stings.

"Ah-h-h!" exclaimed the Mud Turtle, "if I could only reach my tail with my head, or even with one of my hind feet!"

"Reach your tail with your head?" asked the Water-Adder in her sweetest voice. "Nothing is easier." And she wound herself around the willow branch in another graceful position, and took the tip of her tail daintily between her teeth.

"Humph!" said the Snapping Turtle, and he pulled his tail out of the mud and swam away.

"Ugh!" said the Mud Turtle, and he swam away with the Snapping Turtle.

"What a rude person she is!" they said. "Always trying to show how much more clever she is than other people. We would rather be stupid and polite."

After a while the Snapping Turtle said, "But then, you know, we are not stupid."

"Of course not," replied the Mud Turtle, "not even queer."

The Good Little Cranes Who Were Bad

When the Sand-Hill Cranes were married, they began to work for a home of their own. To be sure, they had chosen a place for it beforehand, yet there were other things to think about, and some of their friends told them it would be very foolish to build on the ground. "There are so many accidents to ground nests," these friends said. "There are Snakes, you know, and Rats, and a great many other people whom you would not want to have look in on your children. Besides, something might fall on it."

The young couple talked this all over and decided to build in a tree. "We are not afraid of Snakes and Rats," they said, "but we would fear something falling on the nest." They were talking to quite an old Crane when they said this.

"Do you mean to build in a tree?" said he. "My dear young friends, don't do that. Just think, a high wind might blow the nest down and spoil everything. Do whatever you wish, but don't build in a tree." Then he flew away.

"Dear me!" exclaimed young Mrs. Crane, "one tells me to do this and never to do that. Another tells me to do that and never to do this. I shall just please myself since I cannot please my friends."

"And which place do you choose?" asked her husband, who always liked whatever she did.

"I shall build on the ground," she said decidedly. "If the tree falls, it may hit the nest and it may not, but if we build in the tree and it falls, we are sure to hit the ground."

"How wise you are!" exclaimed her husband. "I believe people get in a way of building just so, and come to think that no other way can be right." Which shows that Mr. Sand-Hill Crane was also wise.

Both worked on the nest, bringing roots and dried grasses with which to build it up. Sometimes they went to dance with their friends, and when they did they bowed most of the time to each other. They did not really care very much about going, because they were so interested in the nest. This they had to build quite high from the ground, on account of their long legs. "If I were a Duck," said Mrs. Sand-Hill Crane, "it would do very well for me to sit on the nest, but with my legs? Never! I would as soon sit on two bare branches as to have them doubled under me." So she tried the nest until it was just as high as her legs were long.

When it was high enough, she laid in it two gray eggs with brown spots. After that she did no more dancing, but stood with a leg on either side of the nest, and her soft body just over the eggs to keep them warm. It was very tiresome work, and sometimes Mr. Crane covered the eggs while she went fishing. The Cranes are always very kind to their wives.

This, you know, was the first time that either had had a nest, and it was all new and wonderful to them. They thought that there never had been such a beautiful home. They often stood on the ground beside it, and poked it this way and that with their bills, and said to each other, "Just look at this fine root that I wove in," or, "Have you noticed how well that tuft of dried grass looks where I put it?" As it came near the time for their eggs to hatch, they could hardly bear to be away long enough to find food.

One day young Mr. Sand-Hill Crane came home much excited. "Our neighbors, the Cranes who live across the pond," said he, "had two children hatched this morning."

"Oh, how glad I am!" cried his wife. "How glad I am! Those eggs were laid just before ours, which must hatch very soon now."

"That is what I thought," said he. "I feel so sorry for them, though, for I saw their children, and they are dreadfully homely,—not at all like their parents, who are quite good-looking."

"I must see them myself," said his wife, "and if you will cover the eggs while I go for food, I will just peep in on them. I will hurry back." She flew steadily across the pond, which was not very wide, and asked to see the babies. She had never seen any Crane children, you know, since she herself was little. She thought them very ugly to look at, and wondered how their mother could seem bright and cheerful with two such disappointing children. She said all the polite things that she honestly could, then got something to eat, and flew home. "They are very, very homely," she said to her husband, "and I think it queer. All their older children are good-looking."

She had hardly said this when she heard a faint tapping sound in the nest. She looked, and there was the tip of a tiny beak showing through the shell of one egg. She stood on one side of the nest, watching, and her husband stood on the other while their oldest child slowly made his way out. They dared not help for fear of hurting him, and besides, all the other Cranes had told them that they must not.

"Oh, look!" cried the young mother. "What a dear little bill!"

"Ah!" said the young father. "Did you ever see such a neck?"

"Look at those legs," cried she. "What a beautiful child he is!"

"He looks just like you," said the father, "and I am glad of it."

"Ah, no," said she. "He is exactly like you." And she began to clear away the broken egg-shell.

Soon the other Crane baby poked her bill out, and again the young parents stood around and admired their child. They could not decide which was the handsomer, but they were sure that both were remarkable babies. They felt more sorry than ever for their neighbors across the pond, who had such homely children. They took turns in covering their own damp little Cranes, and were very, very happy.

Before this, it had been easy to get what food they wanted, for there had been two to work for two. Now there were two to work for four, and that made it much harder. There was no time for dancing, and both father and mother worked steadily, yet they were happier than ever, and neither would have gone back to the careless old days for all the food in the pond or all the dances on the beach.

The little Cranes grew finely. They changed their down for pin-feathers, and then these grew into fine brownish gray feathers, like those which their parents wore. They were good children, too, and very well brought up. They ate whatever food was given to them, and never found fault with it. When they left the nest for the first time, they fluttered and tumbled and had trouble in learning to walk. A Mud Turtle Father who was near, told them that this was because their legs were too long and too few.

"Well," said the brother, as he picked himself up and tried to stand on one leg while he drew the other foot out of the tangled grass, "they may be too long, but I'm sure there are enough of them. When I'm thinking about one, I never can tell what the other will do."

Still, it was not long before they could walk and wade and even fly. Then they met the other pond people, and learned to tell a Stickleback from a Minnow. They did not have many playmates. The saucy little Kingfishers sat on branches over their heads, the Wild Ducks waddled or swam under their very bills, the Fish Hawks floated in air above them, and the Gulls screamed hoarsely to them as they circled over the pond, yet none of them were long-legged and stately. The things that the other birds enjoyed most, they could not do, and sometimes they did not like it very well. One night they were talking about the Gulls, when they should have been asleep, and their father told them to tuck their heads right under their wings and not let him hear another word from them. They did tuck their heads under their wings, but they peeped out between the feathers, and when they were sure their father and mother were asleep, they walked softly away and planned to do something naughty.

"I'm tired of being good," said the brother. "The Gulls never are good. They scream, and snatch, and contradict, and have lots of fun. Let's be bad just for fun."

"All right," said his sister. "What shall we do?"

"That's the trouble," said he. "I can't think of anything naughty that I really care for."

Each stood on one leg and thought for a while. "We might run away," said she. "Where would we go?" asked he.

"We might go to the meadow," said she. So they started off in the moonlight and went to the meadow, but all the people there were asleep, except the Tree Frog, and he scrambled out of the way as soon as he saw them coming, because he thought they might want a late supper.

"This isn't any fun!" said the brother. "Let's go to the forest."

They went to the forest, and saw the Bats flitting in and out among the trees, and the Bats flew close to the Cranes and scared them. The Great Horned Owl stood on a branch near them, and stared at them with his big round eyes, and said, "Who? Who? Waugh-ho-oo!" Then the brother and sister stood closer together and answered, "If you please, sir, we are the Crane children."

But the Great Horned Owl kept on staring at them and saying "Who? Who? Waugh-ho-oo!" until they were sure he was deaf, and answered louder and louder still.

The Screech Owls came also, and looked at them, and bent their bodies over as if they were laughing, and nodded their heads, and shook themselves. Then the Crane children were sure that they were being made fun of, so they stalked away very stiffly, and when they were out of sight of the Owls, they flew over toward the farmhouse. They were not having any fun at all yet, and they meant to keep on trying, for what was the good of being naughty if they didn't?

They passed Horses and Cows asleep in the fields, and saw the Brown Hog lying in the pen with a great many little Brown Pigs and one White Pig sleeping beside her. Nobody was awake except Collie, the Shepherd Dog, who was sitting in the farmyard with his nose in the air, barking at the moon.

"Go away!" he said to the Crane children, who were walking around the yard. "Go away! I must bark at the moon, and I don't want anybody around." They did not start quite soon enough to please him, so he dashed at them, and ran around them and barked at them, instead of at the moon, until they were glad enough to fly straight home to the place where their father and mother were sleeping with their heads under their wings.

"Are you going to tell them?" asked the brother.

"I don't know," answered the sister. When morning came, they looked tired, and their father and mother seemed so worried about them that they told the whole story.

"We didn't care so very much about what we did," they said, "but we thought it would be fun to be naughty."

The father and mother looked at each other in a very knowing way. "A great many people think that," said the mother gently. "They are mistaken after all. It is really more fun to be good."

"Well, I wish the Gulls wouldn't scream, 'Goody-goody' at us," said the brother.

"What difference does that make?" asked his father. "Why should a Crane care what a Gull says?"

"Why, I—I don't know," stammered the brother. "I guess it doesn't make any difference after all."

The next day when the Crane children were standing in the edge of the pond, a pair of young Gulls flew down near them and screamed out, "Goody-goody!"

Then the Crane brother and sister lifted their heads and necks and opened their long bills, and trumpeted back, "Baddy-baddy!"

"There!" they said to each other. "Now we are even."

The Oldest Dragon-Fly Nymph

When the Oldest Dragon-Fly Nymph felt that the wings under her skin were large enough, she said good-bye to her water friends, and crawled slowly up the stem of a tall cat-tail. All the other Dragon-Fly Nymphs crowded around her and wished that their wings were more nearly ready, and the larvæ talked about the time when they should become Nymphs. The Oldest Nymph, the one who was going away, told them that if they would be good little larvæ, and eat a great deal of plain food and take care not to break any of their legs, or to hurt either of their short, stiff little feelers, they would some day be fine great Nymphs like her. Then she crawled slowly up the cat-tail stem, and when she drew the tenth and last joint of her body out of the water, her friends turned to each other and said, "She is really gone." They felt so badly about it that they had to eat something at once to keep from crying.

The Oldest Nymph now stopped breathing water and began to breathe air. She waited to look at the pond before she went any farther. She had never seen it from above, and it looked very queer to her. It was beautiful and shining, and, because the sky above it was cloudless, the water was a most wonderful blue. There was no wind stirring, so there were no tiny waves to sparkle and send dancing bits of light here and there. It was one of the very hot and still summer days, which Dragon-Flies like best.

A sad look came into the Nymph's great eyes as she stood there. "The pond is beautiful," she said; "but when one looks at it from above, it does not seem at all homelike." She shook her three-cornered head sadly, and rubbed her eyes with her forelegs. She thought she should miss the happy times in the mud with the other children.

A Virgin Dragon-Fly lighted on the cat-tail next to hers. She knew it was a Virgin Dragon-Fly because he had black wings folded over his back, and there were shimmering green and blue lights all over his body and wings. He was very slender and smaller than she. "Good morning," said he. "Are you just up?"

"Yes," said she, looking bashfully down at her forefeet. She did not know how to behave in the air, it was so different from the water.

"Couldn't have a finer day," said he. "Very glad you've come. Excuse me. There is a friend to whom I must speak." Then he flew away with another Virgin Dragon-Fly.

"Hurry up and get your skin changed," said a voice above her, and there was a fine great fellow floating in the air over her head. "I'll tell you a secret when you do."

Dragon-Flies care a great deal for secrets, so she quickly hooked her twelve sharp claws into the cat-tail stem, and unfastened her old skin down the back, and wriggled and twisted and pulled until she had all her six legs and the upper part of her body out. This made her very tired and she had to rest for a while. The old skin would only open down for a little way by her shoulders, and it was hard to get out through such a small place. Next she folded her legs close to her body, and bent over backward, and swayed this way and that, until she had drawn her long, slender body from its outgrown covering.

She crawled away from the empty skin and looked it over. It kept the shape of her body, but she was surprised to find how fast she was growing slender. Even then, and she had been out only a short time, she was much longer and thinner than she had been, and her old skin looked much too short for her. "How styles do change," she said. "I remember how proud I was of that skin when I first got it, and now I wouldn't be seen in it."

Her beautiful gauzy wings with their dark veinings, were drying and growing in the sunshine. She was weak now, and had them folded over her back like those of the Virgin Dragon-Fly, but, as soon as she felt rested and strong, she meant to spread them out flat.

The fine Big Dragon-Fly lighted beside her. "How are your wings?" said he.

"Almost dry," she answered joyfully, and she quivered them a little to show him how handsome they were.

"Well," said he. "I'll tell you the secret now, and of course you will never speak of it. I saw you talking with a Virgin Dragon-Fly. He may be all right, but he isn't really in our set, you know, and you'd better not have anything to do with him."

"Thank you," she said. "I won't." She thought it very kind in him to tell her.

He soon flew away, and, as she took her first flight into the air, a second Big Dragon-Fly overtook her. "I'll tell you a secret," said he, "if you will never tell."

"I won't," said she.

"I saw you talking to a Virgin Dragon-Fly a while ago. You may have noticed that he folded his wings over his back. The Big Dragon-Flies never do this, and you must never be seen with yours so."

"Thank you," she said. "I won't. But when they were drying I had to hold them in that way."

"Of course," said he. "We all do things then that we wouldn't afterward."

Before long she began egg-laying, flying low enough to touch her body to the water now and then and drop a single egg. This egg always sank at once to the bottom, and she took no more care of it.

A third Big Dragon-Fly came up to her. "I want to tell you something," he said. "Put your head close to mine."

She put her head close to his, and he whispered, "I saw you flying with my cousin a few minutes ago. I dislike to say it, but he is not a good friend for you. Whatever you do, don't go with him again. Go with me."

"Thank you," said she, yet she began to wonder what was the matter. She saw that just as soon as she visited with anybody, somebody else told her that she must not do so again. Down in the pond they had all been friends. She wondered if it could not be so in the air. She rubbed her head with her right foreleg, and frowned as much as she could. You know she couldn't frown very much, because her eyes were so large and close together that there was only a small frowning-place left.

She turned her head to see if any one else was coming to tell her a secret. Her neck was very, very slender and did not show much, because the back side of her head was hollow and fitted over her shoulders. No other Dragon-Fly was near. Instead, she saw a Swallow swooping down on her. She sprang lightly into the air and the Swallow chased her. When he had his beak open to catch her as he flew, she would go backward or sidewise without turning around. This happened many times, and it was well for her that it was so, for the Swallow was very hungry, and if he had caught her—well, she certainly would never have told any of the secrets she knew.

The Swallow quite lost his patience and flew away grumbling. "I won't waste any more time," he said, "on trying to catch somebody who can fly backward without turning around. Ridiculous way to fly!"

The Dragon-Fly thought it an exceedingly good way, however, and was even more proud of her wings than she had been. "Legs are all very well," she said to herself, "as far as they go, and one's feet would be of very little use without them; but I like wings better. Now that I think of it," she added, "I haven't walked a step since I began to fly. I understand better the old saying, 'Make your wings save your legs.' They certainly are very good things to stand on when one doesn't care to fly."

Night came, and she was glad to sleep on the under side of a broad leaf of pickerel-weed. She awakened feeling stupid and lazy. She could not think what was the matter, until she heard her friends talking about the weather. Then she knew that Dragon-Flies are certain to feel so on dark and wet days. "I don't see what difference that should make," she said. "I'm not afraid of rain. I've always been careless about getting my feet wet and it never hurt me any."

"Ugh!" said one of her friends. "You've never been wet in spots, or hit on one wing by a great rain-drop that has fallen clear down from a cloud. I had a rain-drop hit my second right knee once, and it has hurt me ever since. I have only five good knees left, and I have to be very careful about lighting on slippery leaves."

It was very dull. Nobody seemed to care about anybody or anything. The fine Big Dragon-Flies, who had been so polite to her the day before, hardly said "Good morning" to her now. When she asked them questions, they would say nothing but "Yes" or "No" or "I don't know," and one of them yawned in her face. "Oh dear!" she said. "How I wish myself back in the pond where the rain couldn't wet me. I'd like to see my old friends and some of the dear little larvæ. I wish more of the Nymphs would come up."

She looked all around for them, and as she did so she saw the shining back-shell of the Snapping Turtle, showing above the shallow water. "I believe I'll call on him," she said. "He may tell me something about my old friends, and anyway it will cheer me up." She lighted very carefully on the middle of his back-shell and found it very comfortable. "Good morning," said she. "Have you—"

"No," snapped he. "I haven't, and I don't mean to!"

"Dear me," said she. "That is too bad."

"I don't see why," said he. "Is there any particular reason why I should?"

"I thought you might have just happened to," said she, "and I should like to know how they are."

"What are you talking about?" snapped he.

"I was going to ask if you had seen the Dragon-Fly children lately," she said. And as she spoke she made sure that she could not slip. She felt perfectly safe where she was, because she knew that, no matter how cross he might be, he could not reach above the edges of his back-shell.

"Well, why didn't you say so in the first place," he snapped, "instead of sitting there and talking nonsense! They are all right. A lot of the Nymphs are going into the air to-day!" Now that he had said a few ugly things, he began to feel better natured. "You've changed a good deal since the last time I saw you."

"When was that?" asked she.

"It was one day when I came remarkably near sitting down on a lot of you Dragon-Fly children," he chuckled. "You were a homely young Nymph then, and you stuck out your lower lip at me."

"Oh!" said she. "Then you did see us?"

"Of course I did," answered he. "Haven't I eyes? I'd have sat down on you, too, if I hadn't wanted to see you scramble away. The larvæ always are full of mischief, but then they are young. You Nymphs were old enough to know better."

"I suppose we were," she said. "I didn't think you saw us. Why didn't you tell us?"

"Oh," said the Snapping Turtle, "I thought I'd have a secret. If I can't keep a secret for myself, I know that nobody can keep it for me. Secrets can swim faster than any fish in the pond if you once let them get away from you. I thought I'd better not tell. I might want to sit on you some other time, you know."

"You'll never have the chance," said she, with a twinkle in her big eyes. "It is my turn to sit on you." And after that they were very good friends—as long as she sat on the middle of his shell.

The Eels' Moving-Night

The Eels were as different from the Clams as people well could be. It was not alone that they looked unlike, but that they had such different ways of enjoying life. The Clams were chubby people, each comfortably settled in his own shell, which he could open or shut as he chose. They never wanted to live anywhere else, or to get beyond the edges of their own pearl-lined shells.

The Eels were long, slender, and slippery people, looking even more like snakes than they did like fishes. They were always careful to tell new acquaintances, though, that they were not even related to the snakes. "To be sure," they would say, "we do not wear our fins like most fishes, but that is only a matter of taste after all. We should find them dreadfully in the way if we did." And that was just like the Eels—they were always so ready to explain everything to their friends.

They were great talkers. They would talk about themselves, and their friends, and the friends of their friends, and the pond, and the weather, and the state of the mud, and what everything was like yesterday, and what it would be likely to be like to-morrow, and did you really think so, and why? The Water-Adder used to say that they were the easiest people in the pond to visit with, for all one had to do was to keep still and look very much interested. Perhaps that may have been why the Clams and they were such good friends.

The Clams, you know, were a quiet family. Unless a Clam was very, very much excited, he never said more than "Yes," "No," or "Indeed?" They were excellent listeners and some of the most popular people in the pond. Those who were in trouble told the Clams, and they would say, "Indeed," or "Ah," in such a nice way that their visitor was sure to leave feeling better. Others who wanted advice would go to them, and talk over their plans and tell them what they wanted to do, and the Clams would say, "Yes," and then the visitors would go away quite decided, and say, "We really didn't know what to do until we spoke to the Clams about it, but they agree with us perfectly." The Clams were also excellent people to keep secrets, and as the Eels were forever telling secrets, that was all very well.

Mother Eel was fussy. She even said so herself. And if a thing bothered her, she would talk and talk and talk until even her own children were tired of hearing about it. Now she was worrying over the pond water.

"I do not think it nearly so clean as it was last year," she said, "and the mud is getting positively dirty. Our family are very particular about that, and I think we may have to move. I do dread the moving, though. It is so much work with a family the size of mine, and Mr. Eel is no help at all with the children."

She was talking with Mother Mud Turtle when she said this, and the little Eels were wriggling all around her as she spoke. Then they began teasing her to go, until she told them to swim away at once and play with the young Minnows. "I'm afraid I shall have to go," said she, "if only on account of the children. I want them to see something of the world. It is so dull in this pond. Were you ever out of it?" she asked, turning suddenly to Mrs. Mud Turtle.

"Oh, yes," answered she. "I go quite often, and one of my sons took a very long trip to the meadow. He went with some boys. It was most exciting."

"Is that the one with the—peculiar back-shell?" asked Mother Eel.

"Yes," replied Mother Mud Turtle sweetly. "He is very modest and does not care to talk about it much, but I am really quite pleased. Some people travel and show no sign of it afterward. One would never know that they had left home (Mother Eel wondered if she meant her), but with him it is different. He shows marks of having been in the great world outside."

Mother Eel wriggled a little uneasily. "I think I must tell you after all," she said. "I have really made up my mind to go. Mr. Eel thinks it foolish, and would rather stay here, but I am positive that we can find a better place, and we must consider the children. He thinks he cares as much for them as I do, yet he would be willing to have them stay here forever. He was hatched here, and thinks the pond perfect. We get to talking about it sometimes, and I say to him, 'Mr. Eel, where would those children be now if it were not for me?'"

"And what does he say then?" asked the Mud Turtle Mother.

"Nothing," answered Mother Eel, with a smart little wriggle. "There is nothing for him to say. Yes, we shall certainly move. I am only waiting for the right kind of night. It must not be too light, or the land people would see us; not too dark, or we could not see them. And then the grass must be dewy. It would never do for us to get dry, you know, or we should all be sick. But please don't speak of this, dear Mrs. Turtle. I would rather leave quietly when the time comes."

So the Mud Turtle Mother remembered that it was a secret, and told nobody except the Mud Turtle Father, and he did not speak of it to anybody but the Snapping Turtle.

"Did you say that it was a secret?" asked the Snapping Turtle.

"Yes," said the Mud Turtle Father, "It is a great secret."

"Humph!" said the Snapping Turtle. "Then why did you tell me?"

That same day when the Stickleback Father came to look for nineteen or twenty of his children who were missing, Mother Eel told him about her plans. "I thought you would be interested in hearing of it," she said, "but I shall not mention it to anybody else."

"You may be sure I shall not speak of it," said he. And probably he would not have told a person, if it had not been that he forgot and talked of it with the Snails. He also forgot to say that it was a secret, and so they spoke freely of it to the Crayfishes and the Caddis Worms.

The Caddis Worms were playing with the Tadpoles soon after this, and one of them whispered to a Tadpole right before the others, although he knew perfectly well that it was rude for him to do so. "Now, don't you ever tell," said he aloud.

"Uh-uh!" answered the Tadpole, and everybody knew that he meant "No," even if they hadn't seen him wave his hindlegs sidewise. Of course, not having the right kind of neck for it, he couldn't shake his head.

Then the other Tadpoles and Caddis Worms wanted to tell secrets, and they kept whispering to each other and saying out loud, "Now don't you *ever* tell." When a Caddis Worm told a Tadpole anything, he said, "The Eels are going to move away." And when a Tadpole told a secret to a Caddis Worm, he just moved his lips and said, "Siss-el, siss-el, siss-el-siss. I'm only making believe, you know." But he was sure to add out loud, "Now don't you *tell*." And the Caddis Worm would answer, "Uh-uh!"

The Eel Mother also spoke to the Biggest Frog, asking him to watch the grass for her and tell her when it was dewy enough for moving. He was afraid he might forget it, and so told his sister and asked her to help him remember. And she was afraid that she might forget, so she spoke to her friend, the Green Brown Frog, about it. The Yellow Brown Frog afterward said that he heard it from her.

One night it was neither too dark nor too light, and the dew lay heavy on the grass. Then Mother Eel said to her children, "Now stop your wriggling and listen to me, every one of you! We shall move because the mud here is so dirty. You are going out into the great world, and I want you to remember everything you feel and see. You may never have another chance."

The little Eels were so excited that they couldn't keep still, and she had to wait for them to stop wriggling. When they were quiet, she went on. "All the Eels are going—your uncles and aunts and cousins—and you children must keep with the older ones. Be careful where you wriggle to, and don't get on anybody else's tail."

She led the way out of the water and wriggled gracefully up the bank, although it was quite steep at that place. "I came this way," she said, "because I felt more as though this was the way to come." She closed her mouth very firmly as she spoke. Mr. Eel had thought another way better. They had to pass through crowds of pond people to reach the shore, for everybody had kept awake and was watching. The older ones cried out, "Good-bye; we shall miss you," and waved their fins or their legs, or their tails, whichever seemed the handiest. The younger ones teased the little Eels and tried to hold them back, and told them they'd miss lots of fun, and that they guessed they'd wish themselves back in the pond again. When they got onto the shore, the Frogs and the Mud Turtles were there, and it was a long time before they could get started on their journey. One of the little Eels was missing, and his mother had to go back for him. She found that a mischievous young Stickleback had him by the tail.

When at last they were all together on the bank, the Eel Father said to his wife, "Are you sure that the Cranes and Fish Hawks don't know about our moving? Because if they did—"

"I know," she said. "It would be dreadful if they found out; and we have been so late in getting started. We shall have to stop at the very first water we find now, whether we like it or not." She lay still and thought. "I have a feeling," said she, "that we should go this way." So that way they went, dragging their yellow bellies over the ground as carefully as they could, their dark green backs with their long fringes of back fins hardly showing in the grass. It was a good thing that their skin was so fat and thick, for sometimes they had to cross rough places that scraped it dreadfully and even rumpled the tiny scales that were in it, while their long fringes of belly fins became worn and almost ragged. "If your scales were on the outside," said their father, "like those of other fishes, you wouldn't have many left."

Mother Eel was very tired and did not say much. Her friends began to fear that she was ill. At last she spoke, "I do not see," she said, "how people found out that we were to move."

"You didn't tell anybody?" said Mr. Eel.

"No indeed!" said she; and she really believed it. That was because she had talked so much that she couldn't remember what she did say. It is always so with those that talk too much.

The Crayfish Mother

Three Stickleback Mothers and several Clams were visiting under the lily-pads in the early morning. Mother Eel was also there. "Yes," she said "I am glad to come back and be among my old friends, and the children are happier here. As I often tell Mr. Eel, there is no place like one's home. We had a hard journey, but I do not mind that. We are rested now, and travel does teach people so much. I should think you would get dreadfully tired of being in the water all the time. I want my children to see the world. Now they know grass, and trees, and air, and dry ground. There are not many children of their age who know more than they. We stayed in a brook the one day we were gone, so they have felt running water too. It was clean—I will say that for it—but it was no place for Eels, and so we came back."

There is no telling how long she would have kept on talking if she had not been called away. As soon as she left, the Sticklebacks began to talk about her.

"So she thinks we must be tired of staying in the water all the time," said one. "It doesn't tire me nearly so much as it would to go dragging myself over the country, wearing out my fins on the ground."

"Indeed?" said a Clam, to whom she turned as she spoke.

"Well, I'll tell you what I think," said another Stickleback Mother. "I think that if she didn't care so much for travel herself, she would not be dragging her family around to learn grass and trees. Some night they will be learning Owls or men, and that will be the end of them!"

"I do not believe in it at all," said the first speaker. "I certainly would not want my sons to learn these things, for they must grow up to be good nest-builders and baby-tenders. I have told their fathers particularly to bring them up to be careful housekeepers. With my daughters, it is different."

For a long time nobody spoke; then a Clam said, "What a difference there is in mothers!" It quite startled the Sticklebacks to hear a Clam say so much. It showed how interested he was, and well he might be. The Clam who brings up children has to do it alone, and be both father and mother to them, and of course that is hard work. It is hard, too, because when a little Clam is naughty, his parent can never say that he takes his naughtiness from any one else.

"And there is a difference in fathers too," exclaimed one fine-looking Stickleback Mother. "*I* say that a father's place is by the nest, and that if he does his work there well, he will not have much time to want to travel, or to loaf around by the shore." The Clams looked at each other and said nothing. Some people thought that the Stickleback Mothers were lazy.

Just then a Crayfish Mother came swimming slowly along, stopping often to rest. Her legs were almost useless, there were so many little Crayfishes clinging to them.

"Now look at her," said one Stickleback. "Just look at her. She laid her eggs at the beginning of last winter and fastened them to her legs. Said she was so afraid something would happen if she left them, and that this was a custom in her family anyway. Now they have hatched, and her children hang on to her in the same way."

The Crayfish Mother stopped with a sigh. "Isn't it dreadfully warm?" said she.

"We haven't found it so," answered the Sticklebacks, while the Clams murmured "No."

"Let me take some of your children," said one Stickleback. "Perhaps carrying them has made you warm and tired."

The Crayfish stuck her tail-paddles into the mud, and spread her pinching-claws in front of her family. "Oh no, thank you," said she. "They won't be contented with any one but me."

"That must make it hard for you," said another Stickleback politely. She was thinking how quickly she would shake off the little Crayfishes if they were her children.

"It does," answered their mother. "It is hard, for I carried the eggs on my legs all through the cold weather and until it was very warm again; and now that they are hatched, the children hang on with their pinching-claws. Still, I can't bear to shake them off, poor little things!" She held up first one leg and then another to show off her dangling babies.

"I don't know what will happen to them when I cast my shell," said she. "I shall have to soon, for I can hardly breathe in it. My sister changed hers some time ago, and her new one is getting hard already."

"Oh, they'll be all right," said a Stickleback cheerfully. "Their fathers tell me that my children learn remarkably fast how to look out for themselves."

"But my children can't walk yet," said the Crayfish Mother, "and they don't know how to swim."

"What of that?" asked a Stickleback, who was beginning to lose her patience. "They can learn, can't they? They have eight legs apiece, haven't they, besides the ones that have pincers? Isn't that enough to begin on? And haven't they tail-paddles?"

"I suppose so," said their mother, with a sigh, "but they don't seem to want to go. I must put them to sleep now and try to get a little rest myself, for the sun is well up."

The next night she awakened and remembered what the Sticklebacks had said, so she thought she would try shaking her children off. "It is for your own good," she said, and she waved first one leg and then another. When she got four of her legs free, and stood on them to shake the other four, her children scrambled back to her and took hold again with their strong little pinching-claws. Then she gave it up. "You dear tiny things!" she said. "But I do wish you would walk instead of making me carry you."

"We don't want to!" they cried; "we don't know how."

"There, there!" said their mother. "No, to be sure you don't."

The next night, though, they had to let go, for their mother was casting her shell. When it was off she lay weak and helpless on the pond-bottom, and her children lay around her. They behaved very badly indeed. "Come here and let me catch hold of you," cried one. "I can't walk," said another, "because I don't know how."

Some of them were so cross that they just lay on their backs and kicked with all their eight feet, and screamed, "I *won't* try!" It was dreadful!

The Crayfish Mother was too weak to move, and when the Wise Old Crayfish came along she spoke to him. "My children will not walk," said she, "even when I tell them to." He knew that it was because when she had told them to do things before, she had not made them mind.

"I will see what I can do," said he, "but you must not say a word." He walked backward to where they were, and kept his face turned toward their mother, which was polite of him. "Do you want the Eels to find you here?" he said, in his gruffest voice. "If you don't, you'd better run."

What a scrambling there was! In one way or another, every little Crayfish scampered away. Some went forward, some went sidewise, and some went backward. Some didn't keep step with themselves very well at first, but they soon found out how. Even the crossest ones, who were lying on their backs flopped over and were off.

The Wise Old Crayfish turned to their mother. "It is no trouble to teach ten-legged children to walk," said he, "if you go at it in the right way."

The little Crayfishes soon got together again, and while they were talking, one of their many aunts came along with all her children hanging to her legs. Then the little Crayfishes who had just learned to walk, pointed their pinching-claws at their cousins, and said, "Sh-h-h! 'Fore I'd let my mother carry me! Babies!"

Two Little Crayfishes Quarrel

The day after the Eels left, the pond people talked of nothing else. It was not that they were so much missed, for the Eels, you know, do not swim around in the daytime. They lie quietly in the mud and sleep or talk. It is only at night that they are really lively. Still, as the Mother Mud Turtle said, "They had known that they were there, and the mud seemed empty without them."

The larger people had been sorry to have them go, and some of them felt that without the Eels awake and stirring, the pond was hardly a safe place at night.

"I think it is a good deal safer," remarked a Minnow, who usually said what she thought. "I have always believed that the Eels knew what became of some of my brothers and sisters, although, of course, I do not know."

"Why didn't you ask them?" said a Stickleback.

"Why?" replied the Minnow. "If I had gone to the Eels and asked them that, my other brothers and sisters would soon be wondering what had become of me."

"I have heard some queer things about the Eels myself," said the Stickleback, "but I have never felt much afraid of them. I suppose I am braver because I wear so many of my bones on the outside."

Just then a Wise Old Crayfish came along walking sidewise. "What do you think about the Eels?" asked the Stickleback, turning suddenly to him.

The Crayfish stuck his tail into the mud. He often did this when he was surprised. It seemed to help him think. When he had thought for a while, he waved his big pinching-claws and said, "It would be better for me not to tell what I think. I used to live near them."

This showed that the Wise Old Crayfish had been well brought up, and knew he should not say unpleasant things about people if he could help it. When there was need of it, he could tell unpleasant truths, and indeed that very evening he did say what he thought of the Eels. That was when he was teaching some young Crayfishes, his pupils. Their mother had brought up a large family, and was not strong. She had just cast the shell which she had worn for a year, and now she was weak and helpless until the new one should harden on her. "It is such a bother," she said, "to keep changing one's shell in this way, but it is a comfort to think that the new one will last a year when I do get it."

While their mother was so weak, the Wise Old Crayfish amused the children, and taught them things which all Crayfishes should know. Every evening they gathered around him, some of them swimming to him, some walking forward, some sidewise, and some backward. It made no difference to them which way they came. They were restless pupils, and their teacher could not keep them from looking behind them. Each one had so many eyes that he could look at the teacher with a few, and at the other little Crayfishes with a few more, and still have a good many eyes left with which to watch the Tadpoles. These eyes were arranged in two big bunches, and, unless you looked very closely, you might think that they had only two eyes apiece. They had good ears, and there were also fine smelling-bristles growing from their heads. The Wise Old Crayfish sometimes said that each of his pupils should sit in a circle of six teachers, so that he might be taught on all sides at once.

"That is the way in which children should learn," he said, "all around at once. But I do the best I can, and I at least teach one side of each."

This evening the Wise Old Crayfish was very sleepy. There had been so much talking and excitement during the day that he had not slept so much as usual; and now, when he should have been wide awake, he felt exceedingly dull and stupid. When he tried to walk, his eight legs stumbled over each other, and the weak way in which he waved his pinching-claw legs showed how tired he was.

After he had told his pupils the best way to hold their food with their pinching-claws, and had explained to them how it was chewed by the teeth in their stomachs, one mischievous little fellow called out, "I want to know about the Eels. My mother would never let me go near them, and now they've moved away, and I won't ever see them, and I think it's just horrid."

"Eels, my children," said their teacher, "are long, slender, sharp-nosed, slippery people, with a fringe of fins along their backs, and another fringe along their bellies. They breathe through very small gill-openings in the backs of their heads. They have large mouths, and teeth in their mouths, and they are always sticking out their lower jaws."

"And how do—" began the Biggest Little Crayfish.

"Ask me that to-morrow," said their teacher, stretching his eight walking legs and his two pinching-claw legs and his tail paddles, "but remember this one thing:—if you ever see an Eel, *get out of his way*. Don't stop to look at him."

"We won't," said one little Crayfish, who thought it smart to be saucy. "We'll look to stop at him." All of which meant nothing at all and was only said to annoy his teacher.

They scrambled away over the pond-bottom, upsetting Snails, jiggling the young Clams, and racing with each other where the bottom was smooth. "Beat you running backward!" cried the Saucy Crayfish to the Biggest Little Crayfish, and they scampered along backward in the moonlit water. There was an old log on the bottom of the pond, and they sat on that to rest. The Biggest Little Crayfish had beaten. "I would like to see an Eel," said he.

"I'd like to see them running on the land," said the saucy one.

"Pooh!" said the biggest one. "That's all you know! They don't run on land."

"Well, I guess they do," replied the saucy one. "I know as much about it as you do!"

"Eels swim. They don't run," said the biggest one. "Guess I know!"

"Well, they don't swim in air," said the saucy one. "That's the stuff that lies on top of the water and the ground, and people can't swim in it. So there!"

"Well, I've seen the Wild Ducks swim in it! They swim with their legs in the water, and with their wings in the air," said the biggest one.

"I don't believe it," said the saucy one. "Anyhow, Eels run on land."

"Eels swim on land," said the biggest one.

"Eels run!"

"Eels swim!"

"Run!"

"Swim!"

Then the two little Crayfishes, who had been talking louder and louder and becoming more and more angry, glared at each other, and jerked their feelers, and waved their pinching-claws in a very, very ugly way.

They did not notice a great green and yellow person swimming gently toward them, and they did not know that the Eels had come back to live in the old pond again. Mother Eel opened her big mouth very wide. "On land," she said decidedly, as she swallowed the Biggest Little Crayfish, "Eels wriggle." Then she swallowed the Saucy Crayfish.

"There!" said she. "I've stopped that dreadful quarrel." And she looked around with a satisfied smile.

The Lucky Mink

During the warm weather, the Minks did not come often to the pond. Then they had to stay nearer home and care for their babies. In the winter, when food was not so plentiful and their youngest children were old enough to come with them, they visited there every day. It was not far from their home.

The Minks lived by a waterfall in the river, and had burrows in the banks, where the young Minks stayed until they were large enough to go out into the world. Then the fathers and mothers were very busy, for in each home there were four or five or six children, hungry and restless, and needing to be taught many things.

They were related to the Weasels who lived up by the farmyard, and had the same slender and elegant bodies and short legs as they. Like the Weasels, they sometimes climbed trees, but that was not often. They did most of their hunting in the river, swimming with their bodies almost all under water, and diving and turning and twisting gracefully and quickly. When they hunted on land, they could tell by smelling just which way to go for their food.

The Minks were a very dark brown, and scattered through their close, soft fur were long, shining hairs of an even darker shade, which made their coats very beautiful indeed. The fur was darker on their backs than on the under part of their bodies, and their tapering, bushy tails were almost black. Their under jaws were white, and they were very proud of them. Perhaps it was because they had so little white fur that they thought so much of it. You know that is often the way—we think most of those things which are scarce or hard to get.

There was one old Mink by the river who had a white tip on his tail, and that is something which many people have never seen. It is even more uncommon than for Minks to have white upper lips, and that happens only once in a great while. This Mink was a bachelor, and nobody knew why. Some people said it was because he was waiting to find a wife with a white tip on her tail, yet that could not have been, for he was too wise to wait for something which might never happen. However it was he lived alone, and fished and hunted just for himself. He could dive more quickly, stay under water longer, and hunt by scent better than any other Mink round there. His fur was sleeker and more shining than that of his friends, and it is no wonder that the sisters of his friends thought that he ought to marry.

When the Minks visited together, somebody was sure to speak of the Bachelor's luck. They said that, whatever he did, he was always lucky. "It is all because of a white tip on his tail," they said. "That makes him lucky."

The young Minks heard their fathers and mothers talking, and wished that they had been born with white tips on their tails so that they could be lucky too. Once the Bachelor heard them wishing this, and he smiled and showed his beautiful teeth, and told them that it was not the tip of his tail but his whole body that made him lucky. He did not smile *to* show his teeth, because he was not at all vain. He just smiled *and* showed his teeth.

There was a family of young Minks who lived at the foot of the waterfall, where the water splashed and dashed in the way they liked best. There were four brothers and two sisters in this family, and the brothers were bigger than the sisters (as Mink Brothers always are), although they were all the same age. One was very much larger than any of the rest, and so they called him Big Brother. He thought there was never such a fine Mink as the Bachelor, and he used to follow him around, and look at the tip on his tail, and wish that he was lucky like him. He wished to be just like him in every way but one; he did not want to be a bachelor.

The other young Minks laughed at Big Brother, and asked him if he thought his tail would turn white if he followed the Bachelor long enough. Big Brother stood it very patiently for a while; then he snarled at them, and showed his teeth without smiling, and said he would fight anybody who spoke another word about it. Minks are very brave and very fierce, and never know when to stop if they have begun to fight; so, after that, nobody dared tease Big Brother by saying anything more about the Bachelor. Sometimes they did look at his tail and smile, but they never spoke, and he pretended not to know what they meant by it.

A few days after this, the Bachelor was caught in a trap—a common, clumsy, wooden trap, put together with nails and twine. It was not near the river, and none of his friends would have found him, if Big Brother had not happened along. He could hardly believe what he saw. Was it possible that a trap had dared to catch a Mink with a white-tipped tail? Then he heard the Bachelor groan, and he knew that it was so. He hurried up to where the trap was.

"Can't you get out?" said he.

"No," said the Bachelor. "I can't. The best way to get out is not to get in—and I've gotten in."

"Can't you do something with your lucky tail to make the trap open?" asked Big Brother.

"I could do something with my teeth," answered the Bachelor, "if they were only where the tip of my tail is. Why are Minks always walking into traps?" He was trying hard not to be cross, but his eyes showed how he felt, and that was very cross indeed.

Then Big Brother became much excited. "I have good teeth," said he, "Tell me what to do."

"If you will help me out," said the Bachelor, "I will give you my luck."

"And what shall I do with the tail I have?" asked the young Mink, who thought that the Bachelor was to give him his white-tipped tail.

"Never mind now," answered the Bachelor, and he told the young Mink just where to gnaw. For a long time there was no sound but that of the young Mink's teeth on the wood of the trap. The Bachelor was too brave to groan or make a fuss, when he knew there was anybody around to hear. Big Brother's mouth became very sore, and his stomach became very empty, but still he kept at work. He was afraid somebody would come for the trap and the Mink in it, before he finished.

"Now try it," said he, after he had gnawed for quite a while. The Bachelor backed out as far as he could, but his body stuck in the hole. "You are rumpling your beautiful fur," cried the young Mink.

"Never mind the fur," answered the Bachelor. "I can smooth that down afterward. You will have to gnaw a little on this side." And he raised one of his hind feet to show where he meant. It was a beautiful hindfoot, thickly padded, and with short partly webbed toes, and no hair at all growing between them. The claws were short, sharp, and curved.

Big Brother gnawed away. "Now try it," said he. The Bachelor backed carefully out through the opening and stood there, looking tired and hungry and very much rumpled.

"You are a fine young Mink," said he. "We will get something to eat, and then we will see about making you lucky."

They went to the river bank and had a good dinner. The Bachelor ate more than Big Brother, for his mouth was not sore. But Big Brother was very happy. He thought how handsome he would look with a white-tipped tail, and how, after he had that, he could surely marry whoever he wished. It was the custom among his people to want to marry the best looking and strongest. Indeed it is so among all the pond people, and that is one reason why they care so much about being good-looking. It is very hard for a young Mink to have the one he loves choose somebody else, just because the other fellow has the bushiest tail, or the longest fur, or the thickest pads on his feet.

"Now," said the Bachelor, "we will talk about luck. We will go to a place where nobody can hear what we say." They found such a place and lay down. The Bachelor rolled over three times and smoothed his fur; he was still so tired from being in the trap. Then he looked at the young Mink very sharply. "So you want my tail?" said he.

"You said you would give me your luck," answered Big Brother, "and everybody knows that your luck is in your tail."

The Bachelor smiled. "What will you do with the tail you have?" said he.

"I don't know," answered Big Brother.

"You wouldn't want to wear two?" asked the Bachelor.

"Oh, no," answered Big Brother. "How that would look!"

"Well, how will you put my tail in place of yours?" asked the Bachelor.

"I don't know," answered the young Mink, "but you are so wise that I thought you might know some way." He began to feel discouraged, and to think that the Bachelor's offer didn't mean very much after all.

"Don't you think?" said the Bachelor slowly, "don't you think that, if you could have my luck, you could get along pretty well with your own tail?"

"Why, yes," said the young Mink, who had begun to fear he was not going to get anything. "Yes, but how could that be?"

The Bachelor smiled again. "I always tell people," said he, "that my luck is not in my tail, and they never believe it. I will tell you the secret of my luck, and you can have luck like it, if you really care enough." He looked all around to make sure that nobody was near, and he listened very carefully with the two little round ears that were almost hidden in his head-fur. Then he whispered to Big Brother, "This is the secret: *always do everything a little better than anybody else can*."

"Is that all?" asked the young Mink.

"That is enough," answered the Bachelor. "Keep trying and trying and trying, until you can dive deeper, stay under water longer, run faster, and smell farther than other Minks. Then you will have good luck when theirs is poor. You will have plenty to eat when they are hungry. You can beat in every fight. You can have sleek, shining fur when theirs is dull. Luck is not a matter of white-tipped tails."

The more the young Mink thought about it, the happier he became. "I don't see that I am to have your luck after all," said he. "When I have learned to do everything in the very best way, it will be luck of my own."

"Of course," answered the Bachelor. "Then it is a kind of luck that cannot be lost. If I carried mine in the tip of my tail, somebody might bite it off and leave me unlucky."

Big Brother kept the secret, and worked until he had learned to be as lucky as the Bachelor. Then he married the person he wanted, and she was very, very handsome. It is said that one of their sons has a white-tipped tail, but that may not be so.

The Playful Muskrats

One warm day in winter, when some of the pussy-willows made a mistake and began to grow because they thought spring had come, a party of Muskrats were visiting in the marsh beside the pond. All around them were their winter houses, built of mud and coarse grasses. These homes looked like heaps of dried rushes, unless one went close to them. If one did that, he could plainly see what they were; and if one happened to be a Muskrat, and could dive and go into them through their watery doorways, he would find under the queer roof of each, a warm, dry room in which to pass the cold days.

"Fine weather!" said every Muskrat to his neighbor. "Couldn't sleep all of such a day as this." They spoke in that way, you know, because they usually sleep in the daytime and are awake at night.

"We wish it would always be warm weather," said the young Muskrats. "What's the use of winter?"

"Hard to tell," answered one Muskrat, who had lived in the marsh longer than the rest. "Hard to tell: I know it always gives me a good appetite, though." Then all the Muskrats laughed. They were a jolly, good-natured company, and easy to get along with. The other pond people liked them much better than they did their neighbors, the Minks. The Wild Ducks who nested in the sedges, were quite willing that the young Muskrats should play with their children, and the Mud Hens were not afraid of them. Mud Hens cannot bear Minks. They say that when a Mud Chicken is missing from the nest, there is quite sure to be a Mink somewhere near with a full stomach and down around the corners of his mouth.

Perhaps if the Wild Ducks and the Mud Hens were raising their families in the winter time it might be different, for then the Muskrats get hungry enough to eat almost anything. In spring and summer, when they can find fresh grasses and young rushes, or a few parsnips, carrots, and turnips from the farmers' fields, other animals are quite safe. In the winter they live mostly on roots.

"Fine day!" screamed the Gulls, as they swept through the air. "Pity the Frogs don't come out to enjoy it!"

"Yes, great pity," chuckled the old Muskrat. "How glad you would be to see them!" He smiled all around his little mouth and showed his gnawing teeth. He knew that the Frogs were better off asleep in the mud at the bottom of the pond, than they would be sitting in the sunshine with a few hungry Gulls above them. The Turtles were sleeping all winter, too, in the banks of the pond. The Eels were lying at the bottom, stupid and drowsy, and somewhere the Water-Adders were hidden away, dreaming of spring. Of all the birds who lived by the water, only the Gulls were there, and they were not popular. It is true that they helped keep the pond sweet and clean, and picked up and carried away many things which made the shore untidy, still, they were rude, and talked too loudly, and wore their feathers in such a way that they looked like fine large birds, when really they were lean and skinny and small. The other pond people said that was just like them, always pretending to be more than they really were.

Fifteen young Muskrats, all brothers and sisters, and all born the summer before, started off to look at the old home where they were children together. That is to say, they were not all there at once, but there were five born early in the season; and when they were old enough to look out for themselves, five more came to live in the old nest; and when these were old enough to leave the nest, another five were born.

It doesn't mean so much to Muskrats to be brothers and sisters as it does to some people, still they remembered that they were related, and they played more with each other than with those young Muskrats who were only their cousins or friends. Their mother was very proud of them, and loved to watch them running around on their short legs, and to hear them slap their long, scaly tails on the water when they dove. They had short, downy fur, almost black on the back, soft gray underneath, and a reddish brown everywhere else. There was very little fur on their tails or on their feet, and those parts were black.

These fifteen children had been fairly well brought up, but you can see that their mother had many cares; so it is not strange if they sometimes behaved badly. In some other families, where there were only nine or ten babies all the season, they had been brought up more strictly. Like all young Muskrats, they were full of fun, and there were few pleasanter sights than to see them frolicking on a warm moonlight evening, when they looked like brown balls rolling and bounding around on the shore or plunging into the water. If they had all been exactly the same age, it would have been even pleasanter, for the oldest five would put on airs and call the others "the children"; and the next five would call the youngest five "babies"; although they were all well grown. There was no chance for the youngest five to call other Muskrats "babies," so when they were warm and well fed and good-natured they laughed and said, "Who cares?" When they were cold and hungry, they slapped their tails on the ground or on the water and said, "Don't you think you're smart!"

When they got to talking so and their mother heard it, she would say, "Now, children!" in such a way that they had to stop. Their father sometimes slapped them with his tail. Teasing is not so very bad, you know, although it is dreadfully silly, but when people begin by teasing they sometimes get to saying things in earnest— even really hateful, mean things. And that was what made the Muskrat father and mother stop it whenever they could.

Now the whole fifteen crowded around the old summer home, and some of them went in one way, and some of them went in another, for every Muskrat's summer house has several burrows leading to it. When they reached the old nest at the end, all of them tried to get in at once, and they pushed each other around with their broad little heads, scrambled and clutched and held on with their strong little feet. Five of them said, "It's our turn first. We're the oldest." And five more said, "Well, it's our turn next anyway, 'cause we're next oldest." The others said, "You might give up to us, because we're the youngest."

They pushed and scrambled some more, and one of the youngest children said to one of the oldest, "Well, I don't care. I'm just as big as you are" (which was so). And the older one answered back, "Well, you're not so good-looking" (which was also true).

Then part of the brothers and sisters took sides with one, and part took sides with the other. What had been a lovely frolic became an unpleasant, disgraceful quarrel, and they said such things as these:

"'Fore I'd make such a fuss!"

"Who's making any more fuss than you are, I'd like to know?"

"Oh, yes. You're big enough, but you're just as homely as you can be. So there!"

"Quit poking me!"

"You slapped your tail on my back!"

"I'm going to tell on you fellows!"

"I dare you to!"

"Won't you catch it though!"

And many more things which were even worse. Think of it. Fifteen young Muskrats who really loved each other, talking like that because they couldn't decide whether the oldest or the youngest or the half-way-between brothers and sisters should go first into the old nest. And it didn't matter a bit who was oldest or who was youngest, and it never would have happened had it not been for their dreadful habit of teasing.

Just as they had become very hot and angry, they heard their mother's voice say, "Now, children!" but they were too much excited to mind, and they did not stop until their father came and slapped them with his tail. Then they kept still and listened to their mother. She told them that they should leave the place at once, and not one of them should even set foot in the old nest. "Suppose somebody had gotten hurt," she said. This made the young Muskrats look very sober, for they knew that the Muskrat who is hurt in winter never gets well.

After she had let them think about this for a while, she said, "I shall punish you all for this." Then there was no quarrel among her children to see who should have the first turn—not at all.

One young Muskrat said, "Aren't you going to let us play any more?"

"Yes," said she. "I shall let you play all the rest of the day, but I shall choose the games. The oldest five will play 'Mud Turtles in winter,' the next five will play 'Frogs in winter,' and the youngest five will play 'Snakes in winter.' The way to play these games is to lie perfectly still in some dark place and not say a word."

The young Muskrats looked at each other sorrowfully. They thought it sounded very much the same as being sent to bed for being naughty. They did not dare say anything, for they knew that, although their mother was gentle, as Muskrats are most of the time, she could be very severe. So they went away quietly to play what she had told them they must. But it was not much fun to play those games when all the others were having a fine time in the sunshine.

There were nine of the young Muskrats who did not tease any after that. Even the other six were more careful.

The Meaning of Life and Other Useless Crap is perhaps our generations greatest work as it answers the age old question "What is the meaning of life?" Written simply and straightforward it is easy to understand why Ben Lemon is the most important living philosopher. It hasn't been since A Modest Proposal that a pamphlet can our perceptions so dramatically.

Made in the USA
Middletown, DE
29 July 2020